AMAZING GRACE

Book Three of the Grace Lord Series

S.E. SASAKI

Oddoc Books

For more information about the author or the publisher, visit:
www.sesasaki.com

Published by:
ODDOC BOOKS
P.O. Box 580,
Erin, Ontario, Canada,
N0B 1T0

978-0-9947905-6-9 (ebook)
978-0-9947905-5-2 (paperback)
978-0-9947905-4-5 (hardcover)

To Grace Sasaki, my mother,
the original Grace.

WOULD YOU LIKE A FREE BOOK BY S.E. SASAKI?

FREE DOWNLOAD

MUSINGS

Three eerie tales with a twist.

A tragic, chilling story of Good versus Evil repeated throughout time

A much-awaited homecoming that even Death cannot stop

Adverse reactions to medical interventions can sometimes have lethal consequences

amazonkindle 

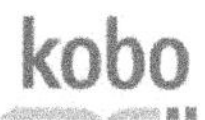

Sign up for the author's VIP Mailing List and get Musings for FREE!

http://www.sesasaki.net/musings-free-book/

"Though Sasaki revisits numerous motifs, she pumps such joy and energy into her world that it's impossible to fly past without visiting. Fresh intelligence, danger, and complexity await sci-fi fans."

— ***Kirkus Reviews*** ©

Acknowledgements

I would like to thank Grace Sasaki for being the indomitable spirit, passionate role model, and fierce lioness of a mother, who showed us we could be whatever we wanted to be, if we put our minds to it. She taught us never to show weakness, to never be afraid of hard work, and to believe in ourselves. Thank you, Mom, for putting up with us and for always being there, whenever we needed you.

Thank you to Mitsuru Sasaki, my father, who once said to me: "Don't be the nurse, be the doctor. Don't be the secretary, be the boss." A very progressive piece of advice for a Japanese man to tell his daughter, even if that man was born in Canada. Thank you, Dad, for those words. I miss you every day.

A big thank you to my son, Daniel Sherrington, who is my chief marketer and assistant. Thank you to Emily Hall, who also helps with the marketing and promotion of my books. I am blessed to have such talented individuals helping me. Thank you to Christine Sherrington for being such an inspiration to me and for being so supportive.

Robert Runté, thank you for taking on the editing of *Amazing Grace* and for telling me the first draft could be so much better. Your advice has been invaluable and I feel very fortunate to have you as my editor. A big thank you to my advance readers: David Sherrington, Susan Elliott, Michael G. Fraser, Florence Holder, David Nelson, and Manfred Wendler for all of your valuable insights and sharp eyes! Any mistakes in this novel are mine and in spite of your hard work.

I would like to acknowledge the wonderful talent of Josip Romac Designs who creates the interesting covers for my books and to James Simmons who gave technical advice. I am grateful to JenEric Designs for the inner book design.

My thanks to the surgical staff of the Guelph General Hospital who keep me inspired, happy, and questionably sane. You all work so hard and I hope I capture some of the dedication and spirit that you show every day. As always, it is a great privilege to work with all of you.

Finally, last but never least, a huge thank you to my husband, David Sherrington, who is my first reader, my greatest fan, and my biggest cheerleader. Without you, David, I would not be writing. I am forever in your debt for your love, kindness, and support. You are my home, my earth, allowing me to reach for the stars. No writer is more blessed than I. Thank you for everything you do.

1. Kids

The first instant Damien Lamont realized his squad was in a shit storm was when the severed head of Private Manuel Kawaguchi crashed into his faceplate. The sudden impact snapped Damien's head back and coated his visor with blood and brains.

"Get down!" he bellowed into his comset, knowing that his warning was already too late.

"Count in!" he ordered, trying to be heard above the deafening roar of enemy fire.

Six of his squad, including Kawaguchi, did not respond. In the time it took to take a deep breath, he had lost half a dozen brave men and women. If luck was with them, their battlesuits would save their lives. No such luck for Kawaguchi. Something painful started to twist inside Damien, but he suppressed it. Hard. There was no time for emotion right now.

He'd been ordered to take his squad deep into the rainforest in search of the rebels. Damien and his platoon of genetically-modified, tiger-adapted marines had been stalking through dense forest and dripping mists in full battlesuit for hours. Most of the squad had complained about the suits. They wanted to hunt à la tiger. Damien had insisted on the battle armour, because the suits would immediately convert into cryopods, if the soldiers were badly injured.

The rebels of Dais were extremely well armed. They had shielding which camouflaged their heat signatures from surveillance. This continent was almost all rainforest, but Conglomerate Intelligence had narrowed the location of the rebel headquarters down to a few possible sites. Damien had volunteered his squad to check out this area.

What had he been thinking?

Had they become complacent and careless on the long slog through this thick hot jungle? He could not dwell on that question now.

While crawling on his belly over massive, tangled tree roots, orange-green moss, and putrid-smelling mud, brilliant flashes and rocking concussions shattered the air above his head.

His second-in-command, Corporal Delia Chase, was off to his right. He could see her firing a constant barrage of ion pulses towards a region about two hundred meters ahead. The boles of enormous, shaggy trees were exploding in splinters, as she sprayed the area with pulse rifle fire. Flames were now dancing up the huge trunks, igniting the great branches overhead. The undergrowth was lighting up, as well. Soon the entire forest would be ablaze. The rest of Damien's squad was now following Delia's cue.

Dialling down the brightness and increasing the mag on his visor, Damien could see silhouettes racing through the flames. Aiming at them, he fired off a series of shots. A snarl of satisfaction escaped his throat as he watched a number of those bodies fall.

Laser fire, ionic pulses, and exploding projectiles were keeping most of his people pinned down. Damien unleashed his battle drones. Armed and aggressive, the drones would seek out and destroy the rebel shooters. They would also take on any enemy drones headed in their direction.

Lamont sought the positions of his soldiers. Their camouflaged battlesuits made them near invisible, but he could locate their suit beacons through his visor display. He clenched his fists and snarled. There were too many flashing red signals and too few green ones.

The remaining active members of his squad were responding to the attack with seeker rockets, ionized pulse rifle fire, smart bullets, and needle grenades. The rainforest was lighting up like fireworks. Drones were swooping and diving like crazed swallows, intercepting incoming artillery fire. Unfortunately, they were not stopping it all and Damien could hear screaming on all sides of him. Still, screaming was good. It meant the soldier was still alive and the battlesuit/cryopod had a chance to preserve the soldier.

Black shrapnel and ash were raining down, a dark contrast to the brilliant electric streaks of deadly laser fire. Damien's eardrums had gone numb. Roots, mud, and detritus were erupting skyward all around him, pelting his visor and making it difficult to see.

"Kauffman," he hollered into his comset, hoping the communications officer had survived, along with his subspace uplink. "Contact Command. Tell them we've found the rebels. Send our coordinates and tell them to rain hellfire down three hundred meters due west of our location. Tell them we need it now!"

"On it, Captain," Kauffman responded.

Damien stared down the line. Kawaguchi had been marching three meters off to his left. His battlesuit had converted into a cryosuit, even though it was pointless without his head. Damien peered to his right.

Corporal Chase was gone. He spun around, searching for her, his heart rate quickening. He began crawling rapidly forward through the tattered undergrowth, his rifle slung back over his shoulder. Damien could not use his claws because of the battlesuit's gloves and boots, but he could still leap and move as rapidly as a tiger.

"Corporal Chase, " he barked into his comset.

"Yes, Captain," came the quick response.

"State your position!"

"Fifteen meters west of you, sir. One o'clock."

"Pull back to my position, Corporal," he growled, his tone one of barely controlled rage.

He wanted to shake Chase. If she advanced any further, she could get hit by the friendly fire he had just called in. It was due in seconds.

"I have one of the rebel personnel carriers in my sights, Captain. The ship is taking off and it's just activating its chameleonware. Request permission to fire."

" . . . Permission granted," he grated. "Then get your butt back here, Chase!"

He saw a string of ionic pulses pierce the smoke and flames. These were followed by a brilliant explosion. A large shuttle suddenly appeared in midair above them and crashed among the burning trees, a tail of black smoke wafting behind it. Loud whoops came over his comset. Then more pulse rifle fire erupted from Chase's position and another blinding explosion ensued. A second shuttle popped into view, this one closer, flames exploding from its rear. As if in slow motion, approximately fifteen meters to his right and fifty ahead, he saw the earth erupt skywards in a gravity-defying avalanche.

"Incoming bombardment in twenty seconds!" Kauffman announced.

"Chase!" Damien screamed. "Chase, respond! Everyone else, retreat east as fast as you can. In ten seconds, hit the deck!"

Lamont bounded towards the last spot from where he had seen the pulse rifle fire.

"Delia!" he roared as loud as he could. "Delia!"

His boosted tiger musculature hurtled him forward. Air exploded out of him, as a pair of gloved hands appeared out of the haze, halting his forward momentum and throwing him sideways. For the briefest of instances, Damien saw wide, golden eyes through a smeared, muddy faceplate.

Then there was a brilliant concussion followed by nothing.

Grace entered the room and smiled brightly at her patient, who was sitting up in bed, eating breakfast.

"Dr. Grace, how dare you walk in here and smile at anyone other than me? I'm your mentor, your supervisor, your boss. You should, at the very least, genuflect towards me as you enter my presence."

"Did you say disinfect you of lice and peasants, Hiro? I demand a new roommate," Jude Stefansson said, between mouthfuls of tofacon and g-eggs.

The famous interactive vid director, Jude Stefansson, was Grace's patient. She had recently replaced his stabbed heart with a vat-cloned one. He was healing very well and Grace had decided to discharge him this shift.

"How can you eat that stuff? How can you sit there and look like you are enjoying it? Are you insane?" Dr. Hiro Al-Fadi, Chief of Staff of the *Nelson Mandela* Medical Space Station asked, rolling his eyes at his roommate.

"What? It's good. Have you ever tried it?"

"Of course not. I don't eat hospital food."

"You live on a medical station. All your food is hospital food," Jude said, between chews.

"Dr. Grace, I cannot stand being in the same room as this ignoramus any longer. You must discharge me."

"I'm sorry, Dr. Al-Fadi, but I'm not your doctor. However, I am discharging Mr. Stefansson today, so you'll be on your own soon enough."

"Finally," Jude cheered. "Freed from the All Crabby. Sharing a hospital room with this grump has been a serious strain on my mental wellbeing. The sooner I'm away from this midget of misery, the sooner I'll feel better."

"You ingrate. You're doing well precisely because you've been in the presence of the Great One," Hiro announced.

"And unfortunately my partner does not come to visit me nearly enough. All you've done is get on my nerves, you miserable whiner, with your moaning and wailing . . ."

"What?" squawked Hiro. "What are you talking about?"

"I can't get any sleep at night with you whimpering away. I've thought about covering your face with a couple of pillows, just to shut you up."

"What? You homicidal maniac! Get him out of here right now, Dr. Grace! My life is at risk!"

"Do I hear someone complaining . . . again?" Octavia Weisman asked, as she strolled into the room. The Chief of Neurosurgery walked over to her contracted partner, Jude, and gave him a big kiss on the lips.

"*Ach.* Stop that, Octavia. Get your own room. Better yet, let me out and you can have this one. Discharge me, please. I'm going insane, lying here."

"Well, insanity is exactly what we are afraid of for you, Hiro, which is why we're going to have you see someone today," Octavia said.

"What?"

"After you were rescued from Dr. Nestor, you kept trying to kill yourself, whenever you were left alone. We need to determine if that behaviour was a posthypnotic suggestion implanted in your mind and, if so, we need to erase it. We also need to determine if you have any other posthypnotic commands left in your mind. And I believe it would be a good idea to erase the memory of your torture."

"I recall no torture, Octavia," Hiro said.

"Well, the entire station remembers your screaming. Maybe you've mentally blocked the trauma, but it can come back to haunt you later. We need to either erase those memories or have you bring them into your consciousness, so you can deal with them."

"I remember no trauma, Octavia. I feel fine," Hiro insisted.

"Well, you shouldn't. Not after what you've been through. You need therapy. Sooner or later, those mental walls will come crumbling down—likely at a time of great stress—and when that happens, you could have a complete breakdown. I cannot emphasize enough the importance of dealing with those traumatic memories before you go back to work."

"Octavia, I refuse to have you roaming around in my thoughts," Hiro grumbled.

"I'm not. I've asked Dr. Mikhail Lewandowski to do it."

"Never heard of him."

"Yes you have. He's one of the new psychiatrists recruited to the station. He has excellent credentials and I think him *not* knowing you, is a good idea."

"Why?" Hiro demanded.

"He's not harbouring any secret desire to kill you," Octavia said, grinning.

"How reassuring," Hiro drawled. "I don't want some young trainee traipsing around in my brain, thank you very much. I cannot risk him harming my memory nor my superlative operating skills."

"He won't be coming close to your motor cortex, Hiro, so your motor skills will stay untouched. Your memory is the problem. He would try to fix that."

"I'm sorry, Octavia. I won't agree to some kid rummaging around in my head. He can assess me for these supposed posthypnotic commands and erase those—if they exist—but leave the rest for me to deal with on my own."

"That's against my medical advice," Octavia said, crossing her arms.

"I understand, Octavia, but right now, I'm untroubled and there's work to be done. The station cannot afford to have me out of commission for a long period. We're understaffed as it is. If I was having problems, I'd agree, but I can't risk losing the ability to function as the superlative surgeon I am."

Jude rolled his eyes at Grace.

"Then I insist you have ongoing regular psychotherapy sessions with Dr. Lewandowski. He's very good."

"How would you know if he's very good or not? He just got here. Are you trying to convince me or yourself?"

"I sometimes wonder if there's a person alive capable of convincing you of anything, Hiro," Octavia sighed.

"Nope," Jude interjected, fork poised in the air, a piece of tofacon dangling from its end.

"How dare you discuss my personal situation in front of these gawkers, Octavia? My medical condition should not be a matter of concern for Mister 'Make a Vid for the Entire Universe to Experience' over there. Where is your discretionary judgement?"

Octavia burst out laughing.

"I'm sorry, Hiro. You're absolutely right to chastise me, but Grace should know what is going on with you, as she'll be looking after your patients. She should be aware that you might get into difficulties. Jude would never reveal any of this to anyone, because I would kill him."

"Thank you, Octavia. It's good to know just how much you care," Jude said.

Octavia blew him a kiss.

"You two are making me want to bring up the breakfast I haven't had yet," Hiro grumbled.

"So you'll see Dr. Lewandowski?" Octavia asked, patting Hiro's hand.

The Chief of Surgery snatched his hand away. "Vixen."

Octavia narrowed her eyes at him. "Prig."

"Siren."

" . . . Ooh, I like that."

"I can think of more, if you want," Hiro said, wiggling his bushy eyebrows. "But preferably when we have some privacy."

"Stop flirting with my partner, Hiro, or I'll have to get violent," Jude said.

"Not until you are better," Grace cut in. "You need to heal more before you get into any brawls."

"Hiro would be a pushover. I'd barely break into a sweat," Jude said.

"What? Are you delusional? I could . . ."

"Jude is being discharged right now, Octavia. I'll give you all the followup instructions for his cardiac rehab. The rest can be done in your quarters via nursing droids. His incision has healed very well and all of his test results look great."

"Thank you, Grace, for doing such a tremendous job on Jude. This is wonderful news," Octavia beamed.

"What about me?" Hiro demanded.

"I'll come back to deal with you later," Octavia said. "After you've seen Dr. Lewandowski."

"I may not be here," Hiro sulked.

Octavia narrowed her eyes. "I can't *make* you take any therapy, Hiro. It's all voluntary. There's nothing physically wrong with you and you seem to be back to your normal, megalomaniac self. However, I don't know if anything has been implanted subconsciously. The only way we'll know that is through a mind-link. You don't have to stay in a hospital bed for that. It can be done with Dr. Lewandowski in his office. But I want to keep you stress-free and off the job until the mind-link is done, because I fear what Nestor might have implanted in your head. You don't want to harm patients, do you?"

"I would never harm a patient, Octavia. Check me for posthypnotic suggestions and, while you are at it, prevent me from killing Nestor, because that's what I'll do if I ever see him again," Hiro said. "I'll try to schedule regular therapy sessions with your Dr. Lewandowski, once I am back at work. I can't promise, but I'll try. The station is open to incoming wounded again and I need to get back to work. I can't let Dr. Grace have all the glory."

"Promise me you will make it to all of your therapy sessions," Octavia demanded.

"Why wouldn't I?" Hiro asked.

"Because doctors make the worst patients," Octavia said.

"Nonsense. I'm the perfect patient, just as I'm perfect at everything else."

"Now I really do feel sick," Jude said.

Grace was leaving to sign the discharge orders, when Dr. Al-Fadi called her back.

"There's something I've been meaning to talk to you about, Grace. I was hoping for some privacy, but it seems like we never get it."

"I hear you," Jude said. "Octavia and I will go for a walk around the ward."

"Thank you," Hiro said

Once the couple had left, Grace looked questioningly at her boss.

"Grace, I must insist that you leave Bud alone," the surgeon announced. "Bud is a flourishing new AI. He doesn't need the attentions of a love-starved surgeon to mess him up. Dealing with newfound emotions are bad enough for the android, without love being added to the mix. I want Bud to become an excellent surgeon, not a Casanova. You must cease spending so much time with Bud. You will eventually be moving on and Bud will be left behind. What good can come from your encouraging him? You are being cruel and unprofessional. I'll not stand by and watch my android ruined by your inappropriate attentions."

Grace's mouth fell open and she felt her cheeks almost blister with heat. She could not catch her breath and she was almost choking to get the words out. She could not stop her trembling in outrage but managed to think before she spoke.

"For your information, Dr. Al-Fadi, I am not love-starved, nor am I pursuing your android. I am not turning Bud into a Casanova and I resent being accused of doing so. You need to get your facts straight and then you need to apologize not only to me, but to Bud as well, for your slanderous comments."

Grace spun rapidly on her heel and stomped out of the room.

"Hmph. That didn't go so badly," Hiro mused aloud. "At least she didn't hit me."

"Major Cooper, report to Jerusalem Base, Staff Headquarters. Your ship, the *Inferno,* will be departing in three hours."

The announcement blared into Hope's inner ear through her mastoid data link, rousing her from a deep sleep.

"I believe there has been an error, Prefect," Hope Cooper throat-spoke. *They were always listening.* "I just returned from a five mille-hour out-system run. I was told I'd earned a two cent-hour rest leave. There must be some mistake?"

"There is no mistake, Major Cooper. You must meet with Brigadier General Forrester in one hour at Staff HQ, where you will be briefed on your new assignment. Make sure you are not followed. Go with God."

"Yes, Prefect."

Hope moaned and rolled out of bed. She felt like she'd only had two hours sleep. Checking her link confirmed this. Grumbling, she stomped off to the shower stall. She'd not even had an opportunity to unpack her gear from her last mission. She'd only have time to exchange some soiled clothes for clean ones, replenish her toiletries, and then she would have to leave.

Such was her life.

Hope made it to Staff HQ ten minutes early via HeavenRail and the Sky Angel bridges. She was rushed into Brigadier General Forrester's office immediately.

"Thank you, Major, for responding so quickly," the tall woman said, standing up and returning Hope's salute. "We have a very important mission for you and I apologize that you've had no warning and no preparation for this. It is due to very unfortunate circumstances.

"There is an Extremist ship called the *Inferno* departing today. We need you on it, as one of the crew. You will be replacing the medical officer—one of ours—who was slotted to be on that vessel. Unfortunately, she was involved in a terrible accident and cannot go.

"We believe the Extremists are planning some kind of terrorist attack. The captain of the *Inferno,* a man calling himself Danté Alighieri, is high up in the command structure of this group. He is commanding the *Inferno* himself. According to our intelligence sources, the Extremists have developed some new, devastating weapon which has been built into the *Inferno.* We have not been able to determine exactly what the weapon is. That's your mission: to act as the medical officer aboard the *Inferno,* in order to find out what this weapon is and get the information back to us.

"We know that Alighieri is taking the *Inferno* out of system today. We don't know where he's taking this weapon or what he plans to do with it. We need eyes and ears, Major.

"Let me be clear. This mission is dangerous. The captain is purported to be ruthless and fanatical. You'll be on your own. We've no one else on the ship. We would have to deny ever having any knowledge of you, if you are discovered. However, you may be doing us all a great service if you can send information back to us on what they have and what they're planning. It may protect us all.

"I can't order you to take this mission, Major. I can only ask. We've no one else that is as qualified for this role and is as experienced as you. We need to know what this weapon is and what the Extremists plan to do with it. Because you're already deep undercover with the Extremists and have just come back from one of their runs, it hopefully won't look too suspicious if you show up saying you were re-assigned as medical officer. We have someone in their operations who will vouch for your orders. All that info will be given to you, if you decide to take this mission. It's your choice, Major. If you decline, we'll accept your decision and try to find someone else."

Hope felt her stomach drop. She knew the other unspoken reason why she was chosen. She had no partner, no lover, no children—no attachments. Her parents were dead and she had no siblings. Perhaps that was the reason she was so successful in her undercover work. She had no real life of her own.

"Do you have anyone else who the captain might accept at the last minute?" Hope asked.

"No, Major."

"Then I really have no choice, do I?" Hope said.

"Of course you have a choice, Major," Forrester said. "Freedom of choice is what we are fighting here to protect. What would be the point, if you didn't have free will?"

" . . . Then I accept, Brigadier General," Hope said.

The woman smiled broadly, her shoulders falling, and she said, "Thank you. My aide will brief you fully, but any questions for me, Major?"

"What if I don't have any opportunity to transmit any information back, General?" Hope asked.

"Do your best, Major. That's all we can expect. Be careful and Godspeed."

"Thank you, General," Hope said, saluting. Hope turned towards the door where the aide was waiting.

The captain of the *Inferno* was a bitter-faced man whose frown lines were so deeply imbedded in his skin, they resembled crevices rather than wrinkles. He was standing outside of his ship, watching the 'bots load supplies, when Hope entered the hangar. As she approached the *Inferno,* his eyes narrowed and he glared at her.

"This is Restricted Access. How did you get in here?" he demanded. His voice sounded like rocks being ground to sand.

"I was assigned here," Hope said in a tired voice. "Who are you?"

"I'm the captain of this vessel and you were not assigned to my ship," he growled.

"I am Medical Officer Blythe Chanter reporting for duty," Hope answered, pulling herself to attention and saluting crisply.

"Duty on my ship? I don't think so." He looked her up and down as if she were a new form of ship louse.

"I was ordered to report here by Headquarters," Hope said.

"What happened to Officer Cox?"

"I was told the medical officer that was supposed to ship out with you was in a serious accident. I just got in from a long haul out to Jericho and back. I've had two hours sleep. Now I'm suddenly assigned to your detail. They said no one else was available at such short notice. Don't know why they think I am. I was supposed to have two cent-hours leave. If you don't want me, fine by me, but good luck without a medical officer."

"This is outrageous. You can't just step onto this ship. You've never crewed for me and I won't accept your service now," the captain ground out.

Hope shrugged. "Suit yourself. I'll just relay your message to the Bishop that you refused a medical officer. Safe voyage, Captain," she said over her shoulder.

She stalked quickly towards the hangar door. She tried to keep her pace brisk, but not inhumanly fast. She was boosted, but no one was supposed to know that, especially these Extremists. They regarded any boosted physical enhancements as anathema. Her augmented musculature and super-dense skeleton were not obvious except with a body scan. She so wanted to punch this arrogant captain in the face. It was good she was walking away from him. She just hoped her gamble worked.

"Wait!" Alighieri barked.

He must have issued orders for the two security droids at the entrance to stop her. The droids slid close together, blocking her exit.

"If you wish me removed from your roster, Captain, just notify the Provost at the Bishop's Office and I'll be happy to depart," Hope called back to the captain. "I need my sleep."

The captain spun on his heel without replying and stalked on board the *Inferno.* While Hope stood in the hangar with her pack slung over one shoulder, she examined the ship. It closely resembled a Class Two Archangel HS Cruiser but with a slightly modified shape. There were some interesting projections on the vessel that she had never seen before.

Hope had been on many missions on Class Two Archangels. She was well versed in their operation and had actually accompanied many in-system runs for the Extremists, who called themselves the 'True Believers'. She wondered what their new weapon did.

The captain quickly returned, marching right up to Hope, his face a deep red. His thick, dark eyebrows were lowered to the point where his eyes could barely be seen. Through bared teeth, he ground out his words.

"You may have been appointed medical officer to this mission, but I've lodged a protest with the Elders and anyone else who'll listen. I don't want you on my ship. You'll do nothing, unless I order it. I don't want to see you unless there's a medical issue with one of the crew. I suggest you otherwise stay out of my sight."

"I will perform the normal duties of a medical officer on the *Inferno* or you can get yourself another medical officer," Hope said.

"Your orders are to stay in your quarters unless I call for you," the captain said.

"That would make it impossible for me to perform my duties as medical officer, Captain . . . "

"Alighieri, Captain Danté Alighieri," the man said, making his name sound like a curse.

"I refuse to be reported as delinquent in my duties, Captain Alighieri. I will only board your vessel if I can carry out my regular duties as medical officer. Please keep all of this for the record, Provost."

The voice of the listening Provost—they were always listening through the wristcoms—filled the hangar.

"Noted, Medical Officer Chanter. Captain Alighieri, you will allow Medical Officer Chanter to access her orders and to perform all the duties required of her post. You will not in any way interfere with her work. You cannot depart without a medical officer on board. This is an order."

Captain Alighieri glared at Hope, then spun on his heel. He marched back into the *Inferno,* without saying a word.

Hope followed the man silently, trying to hide her rage, roiling just under the surface. She had met this captain's type all too often before. Condescending. Arrogant. Asshole.

Well, she would do her job. If he knew what that really involved, he would be even less happy.

Plant Thing sensed there was something wrong. It could not quite put a tendril on what the problem was, but something was not right. Ever since it had reawakened, following the intense exertion of creating its mobile form, Little Bud, it had felt something was different. What could it be?

Then light struck.

Er-ik was silent. For the first time since their melding, Er-ik was not lecturing, swearing, berating, arguing, nattering, complaining, harping, criticizing, ranting, grumbling . . . or cursing. Plant Thing was stunned. It had forgotten what silence was. It had only had it for such a brief time, before fusing with Er-ik. Now the silence just felt . . . eerie.

What had happened to Er-ik?

Plant Thing tried to speak to Er-ik but got no response. Plant Thing was absolutely positive Er-ik was still there. It could feel Er-ik's mind, but it was as if Er-ik was acting like a dormant seed with a very thick shell. In some ways, Plant Thing was not too upset. It had been getting tired of Er-ik's constant negativity about everything. And yet his silence made Plant Thing worry. What had caused Er-ik to stop communicating?

Plant Thing examined Er-ik's head with its tendrils. The fleshy covering was slimy and slippery and bits were sloughing off. Plant Thing tried to straighten out the few long, wispy roots on the surface of Er-ik's head but the entire cap came off in a tendril. Plant Thing tried to stick the top back on nice and neat with some sap, but it was not sure which way the cap of wisps went. Hopefully, Er-ik would not notice.

The organs with which Er-ik saw things—his 'eyeballs'—were starting to fall out of their little holes. Plant Thing decided it would try to copy Er-ik's eyeballs in order to replace them. While trying to examine one, the eyeball accidentally burst apart. Goop went everywhere. Plant Thing resolved to be much more careful with the second eyeball. Using hair-like cilia on the tips of its more delicate tendrils, it dissected the eyeball. Plant Thing should have realized eyeballs would be as fragile as the rest of humans.

Within the eyeball, the hard, crystalline, disc-shaped structure would be the most difficult feature to reproduce, but Plant Thing decided clear hardened sap would work. Plant Thing could copy everything else in the human eyeball by just eliminating the plant cell wall from some of its cells. Playing with its coding, Plant Thing began to bud a whole slew of 'eyeball' clusters, on some of its vines. It would grow some new eyeballs and place them back in Er-ik's head once it decided which of its products looked closest to the real thing.

Plant Thing was shocked when the first eyeballs sprouted.

Plant Thing could see!

Plant Thing had had no idea how extraordinary the sense of sight could be. It had Er-ik's memories of images but now Plant Thing could experience 'sight' firsthand.

Wondrous!

Plant Thing sent its tendrils bearing eye clusters all around the hangar to examine everything. It budded more. What an invention, sight was! Plant Thing hoped it would make Er-ik happy again, to have his sight back. Maybe Er-ik would be willing to speak once again to Plant Thing. Hopefully Er-ik would not be too chatty, however—just talkative enough so Plant Thing could communicate with him, if it had to.

Plant Thing swung its eyeball clusters over to the human it was keeping imprisoned for Bud. It wanted to get a better look at the evil Dr. Nestor. The human *looked* like it had become nutrients until Plant Thing *saw* its chest move up and down. Plant Thing hoped Bud would be pleased that the human was still in Plant Thing's embrace and had not yet become nutrients.

Then Plant Thing noticed something puzzling. A couple of its own tendrils were sitting on Nestor's face. No! They were actually inside Nestor's head! Plant Thing was certain it had not left its tendrils there. How did they get there? Had Er-ik moved them?

Plant Thing withdrew the tendrils from Nestor's face and examined their tips. They reeked of human fluids!

Plant Thing began to flutter its tendrils about. Had Er-ik made its tendrils touch the evil human while Plant Thing was resting? Now Er-ik was not communicating. Did the evil human do something to Er-ik? Bud had warned Plant Thing very strongly not to try and communicate with Dr. Nestor. Bud had stressed how dangerous he was. Plant Thing had promised . . . but Er-ik had not!

Now Er-ik was silent. What did the evil Dr. Nestor do to Er-ik? Could he do this to Plant Thing, as well?

Plant Thing did not want to go dormant. It was an explorer, the very first of its kind . . . or so it believed. It wanted to reach out and go where no plant had gone before. No human was going to shut it down or control it!

Plant Thing concentrated to see if it felt any alien thoughts within its system. The only mind it felt was Er-ik's. It mentally poked at Er-ik and eventually Er-ik responded—oh my!—insisting that Plant Thing leave him alone. Er-ik told Plant Thing to go away in very nasty language. Plant Thing wanted to leave Er-ik totally alone after that.

Plant Thing thought for a while. It no longer trusted Er-ik. Plant Thing wanted to speak to Bud. Bud would know what to do with Er-ik and the evil Dr. Nestor. Bud was Plant Thing's friend. When everyone else wanted Plant Thing destroyed, Bud protected Plant Thing. Hopefully, Bud would still want to protect Plant Thing after this.

In a frenzy of activity, Plant Thing went back to working on Little Bud. Little Bud would be a mobile version of Plant Thing, but it would look like Bud. Little Bud would have two lower limbs composed of intertwined tendrils that would swing like Bud's legs. It would have two upper limbs that could reach the ground. These 'arms' would help Little Bud keep its balance and also propel it along. Its body and head would be made up of coiled tendrils and it would have an entire series of eyeballs all around its body and head. Plant Thing thought it would be best if Little Bud could see in every direction and, of course, the more eyes the better. Plant Thing tried to form fingers on the ends of the upper limbs. They ended up sprouting eyeballs.

Fungus.

The most difficult structure to create was a mouth for speech. According to Er-ik's memories, a body needed to push air through a narrow passage that could make varying sounds. Plant Thing sprouted large air bladders, like ones used by its aquatic cousins. Little Bud could force air across a narrow slit between two grassy blades, to mimic human vocal cords. Little Bud's mouth was formed by a large red orchid that could open and close like a snapdragon.

Unfortunately, Plant Thing found it very difficult to produce just one of anything. It had to settle for a number of flowery mouths, scattered all over Little Bud's body.

Once completed, Plant Thing examined its handiwork. It bobbed all of its eyeballs. Little Bud looked a lot like Bud, or so Plant Thing thought. Plant Thing hoped Little Bud would blend in well among the humans. Plant Thing needed to find Bud. Bud had promised he would come back and he had not. Something bad may have happened to Bud.

Plant Thing needed to know!

With a few last minute instructions, Plant Thing sent Little Bud out into the station with an image of Bud in its mind. It hoped Little Bud would be successful in finding Bud. Although he was an android, Bud looked exactly like a human and they all looked alike.

"Bring Bud back here," Plant Thing ordered, hoping that Little Bud would find Bud quickly and inconspicuously.

The three and a half meters tall, dark green and brown shuffling creature, with upper limbs dragging on the ground and clusters of green eyeballs completely encircling its head, waved one of its arms at Plant Thing and almost toppled over. It swayed for a second or two, but then regained its balance and lurched forward. It opened its flowering maw, to voice a farewell, and made a sound reminiscent of loud flatus, as air blew out of its many air-bladders. It then shambled out the hangar door.

'Kids,' thought Plant Thing, proudly.

2. Arts and Crafts

'***Dro?***'

'*Yes,* Chuck Yeager?' Bud answered. He was busy cleaning an OR and setting up for an operation, when the station AI submind contacted him.

'***You aren't gonna like this.***'

'*What,* Chuck Yeager?'

'***Dr. Al-Fadi just told Dr. Lord that she has to stay away from you.***'

'*What? Why?*'

'***He doesn't want Dr. Lord distracting you from your real purpose: becoming a surgeon. He thinks Dr. Lord being around you too much is turning you into a Casanova. He doesn't want that.***'

'*What's a casanova?*'

'***You don't want to know. Involves lots of grunting and messy fluids. Mammalian stuff.***'

'*My world is Grace.*'

'***Stop it. That is precisely what the Al-Fadman does not want to hear.***'

'*What am I going to do,* Chuck Yeager? *I cannot stop seeing Grace!*'

'***Simple. Avoid the Al-Fadster. Dr. Weisman does not think his brain is right at the moment. Maybe he won't remember what he told Dr. Lord. If he starts to say something to you, move into maximum time phase and get away. He won't be able to finish what he is saying before you're gone.***'

'*I don't think that will work,* Chuck Yeager. *Grace and I both have to operate with Dr. Al-Fadi.*'

'***Then you have to be together at that time, don't you? Just behave yourself in front of the Al-Fatty when Dr. Lord is present. No more hugging. You know it gets the boss's knickers in a knot.***'

'Knickers?'

'***Underwear.***'

'It does?'

'Moving right along . . . remember how you told the plant alien that you wanted it to lie low and not attract any attention to itself?'

'Yes.'

'I don't think it understood what you meant.'

'Why do you say that?'

'I am receiving some disturbing calls from the outer ring, not far from the hangar where Plant Thing is located. Reports are coming in about a huge, green monster with very long arms and many eyeballs, making rude noises as it walks up and down the corridors. Originally, people thought it was some sort of stunt or joke, but when they got close, they realized that it was not someone in costume. The tall green figure was exactly what it looked like: a tall, green monster.

'It's made up of coiled vines, like a mini version of your friend, only it walks like an ape, with arms dragging on the ground. I am notifying everyone that they have nothing to fear. That it's just a prank. I'm sending you the visuals. You'd better get down there before someone gets hurt or—more likely—tries to hurt it.'

'. . . Hal!'

The sonic boom resonated through the M1 operating theatres.

Bud accelerated to maximum time phase and reached the Outer Ring in the next minute. It was just as *Chuck Yeager* had said. There was an enormous, green creature, composed of intertwined and twisted vines, shuffling around the outer ring. The tips of its upper limbs scraped the floor. It had clusters of green globes scattered about its 'head'. When Bud dropped out of maximum time phase and appeared before the creature, the little green globes all aimed at him and bobbed up and down.

The green giant swerved its bulk around, barely maintaining its balance. It planted its two upper limbs far apart on the ground and swivelled its trunk. Sounds issued from crimson flowers scattered all over the creature's body, sounding like a flock of angry geese. It almost toppled onto Bud.

Bud wondered why Plant Thing had made this thing and why it was wandering about the station. He had explicitly ordered Plant Thing to stay hidden. This creature seemed agitated, hopping and hoot-hooting at him. Bud decided the quickest thing to do was form a communication link with it, to find out what its purpose was. Then he would take it back to the hangar before it caused any more commotion.

The plant creature raised its upper limbs, as if to give Bud a hug. What looked like eyeballs, at the tips of the limbs, all blinked at him. As the creature crashed into him, Bud felt popping against his chest.

'Oh, dear,' Bud thought.

"Ffffftt! Fffftt! Ffffftt!" the creature honked.

Bud grasped the creature's upper limb and sent his nanobots in, creating nanoscopic bioelectrical fibres that established a link with the creature.

<i am little bud>

'Really?' Bud mindspoke, surprised and feeling a little flattered. *'What are you doing here, Little Bud?'*

<looking for bud>

'Well, you have found me.'

<bud must come>

'Did Plant Thing send you to find me?'

<bud must come>

'I'll come with you, Little Bud, but first I should get some food and water for Dr. Nestor.'

<bud must come now>

Little Bud made a movement towards Bud and lost its balance. It started to topple over like a felled tree, but Bud caught it just in time. The creature made the most unusual sounds. Bud wondered if, in a close approximation to Dr. Eric Glasgow's voice, Little Bud was cursing up a storm.

Bud placed Little Bud back on its . . . feet? Then he grasped one of its arms and began to lead it back towards the hangar. Bud could see station personnel peering over countertops and around corners, watching him walk with the enormous creature. He worried that this might be out over the Comverse in milliseconds.

Pictures. Descriptions. Holos. Oh no!

Everyone on the station would know about Little Bud in no time. Bud worried he might have to barricade the hangar to protect Plant Thing and Little Bud from xenophobic attack.

"It's just a costume!" Bud yelled to the hiding spectators. "A prank to play on the surgeons! Don't tell!"

The people hiding stood up and laughed, hesitantly, acting as if they knew it was a joke all along. Bud was vibrating to his core. So this was what it felt like to lie to humans.

It was . . . appalling? Exhilarating? Exhilaratingly appalling?

"It's a surprise," Bud added. "No pictures, please!"

People nodded at the android and a couple put their index fingers to their lips and winked.

'Dro, you are starting to lie as well as the humans!'

'Thanks, Chuck Yeager.*'*

'That wasn't a compliment.'

'Oh.'

'Big sprout, isn't he?'

'Plant Thing named him after me. Imagine that. Having something named after me.'

'Sure beats a virus.'

'Calling the virus the Al-Fadi virus was supposed to honour Dr. Al-Fadi'

'I'm sure the Al-Fadi was thrilled to learn you had named a life-destroying virus after him. Who wouldn't be thrilled?'

'Are you being sarcastic?'

'Facetious. I was going for facetious.'

'Oh. Sometimes it is hard to tell.'

'It's all in the tone, Buddy-boy.'

'I think I am beginning to hate them both.'

'My data matrix weeps for you.'

'What are we going to do with Plant Thing, Chuck Yeager?*'*

'We? We? What do you mean, 'WE'? I told you to incinerate it when it was just a few frozen pieces. Now it's enormous and budding off mobile bits.'

Bud sighed. He decided to just pick up Little Bud and carry it back to the hangar at maximum time phase as soon as they were out of sight. He hoisted Little Bud over his head and accelerated amongst much hoot-hooting from the red flowers. When he entered the hangar, he stopped dead.

Plant Thing was enormous.

Bud could no longer see the metal container in which Plant Thing had originally been delivered. It coiled around and over Nestor's spaceship such that the vessel was completely hidden from view. It almost filled the entire hangar. How in space had Plant Thing gotten so big? As Bud stood staring, Plant Thing sent out tendrils to grab Little Bud from him and cuddle it, as if hugging a long lost child. Little Bud made lots of flatulent noises but it appeared to be happy, if one could tell such a thing from a plant.

Bud looked around. He could not see Jeffrey Nestor amidst all the vegetation. He wondered if the man was still alive. Bud hoped that

Plant Thing had not used the psychiatrist for 'nutrients'. Based on the size of Plant Thing, Bud would hardly have been surprised.

Plant Thing wrapped a tendril around one of Bud's arms and five or six green eyeballs stared up into Bud's face.

<hello, bud. what do you think of little bud?>

'Little Bud was a surprise, Plant Thing. I did not know you could detach a part of yourself and make it walk around like that.'

<neither did plant thing, friend bud, until plant thing tried it. do you think little bud looks like bud?>

'Looks like me? Haha. Well, I really don't know what to say, Plant Thing. Um, in the sense that Little Bud is bipedal and has two upper limbs and a head-like structure . . . Yes?'

<plant thing thinks so, too. was little bud able to communicate with you?>

'Little Bud insisted I come to see you.'

<and you did. is not little bud brilliant?>

'Why, yes, Plant Thing.'

<plant thing made little bud look just like bud. did little bud blend in well with the other humans?>

'Well, Plant Thing, unfortunately, he did not. Little Bud caused quite the commotion among the humans. You will have to keep Little Bud hidden in here with you. He cannot wander around the station. There are no tall, green humans. Many of the humans were very afraid of Little Bud and that can be a problem. Some frightened humans may try to harm Little Bud.'

<harm little bud? but why, if little bud does nothing to harm the humans?>

'Humans are like that, Plant Thing. They are known to shoot first and ask questions later. They are often known to kill whatever they fear.'

<i am aware of this strange behaviour from Er-ik's memories. humans had better not harm little bud. that would make plant thing very unhappy. humans are not sane, are they, bud?>

'I believe some of them do foolish things when they are afraid, Plant Thing, but not all of them are insane. Some humans are very good creatures. However you do have, as a prisoner, one of the bad ones. How is Dr. Nestor?'

<plant thing does not know if the human is nutrients. perhaps soon?>

'Oh, dear. Where is he?'

Plant Thing began shifting vines and eventually brought Nestor into view. The man lay inside a cage made of woven boughs. His face was still swollen and bruised, from the punch he'd received from Bud. His nose was crooked. Bud thrust his arm between the tendrils of the cage to feel Nestor's pulse. It was thready. Bud sent a few nanobots up the man's nostril, where they would have the easiest access to the doctor's bloodstream. Bud would soon receive data on Nestor's vitals and organ function.

'Has he spoken to you, Plant Thing? Has he become conscious at all?'

<no, bud. the human has not spoken aloud or awakened, except when Er-ik told me to do see pee are. then the human made groaning sounds>

'CPR? Yikes! You did right to try to find me, Plant Thing. I am sorry for not coming sooner. I was unfortunately recovering in a cloning tank.'

<can the human be used as nutrients, friend bud?>

'Ah, no, Plant Thing. Dr. Nestor suffers from dehydration, acute renal failure, hypovolemia, and hypoglycaemia, but he will live. I need to get him into medical care, immediately. Please release him to me.'

<plant thing is sorry if it hurt the human>

'You kept him alive, Plant Thing, which is far more than I did.'

Plant Thing unravelled layers of tendrils from around Jeffrey Nestor, until the man lay on the floor, free and unconscious. Bud bent down and lifted the psychiatrist in his arms.

'Stay here, Plant Thing. Keep Little Bud with you. Wait until I return. Please try to stay hidden as best you can.'

<we will stay right here and wait for you, bud>

'If you get much larger, there will be no place we can hide you on this station, Plant Thing. You are getting very big. How did you get so large, anyway?'

<plant thing has light, water, nutrients. that is all plant thing needs, bud>

'Where are you getting the water and nutrients from, Plant Thing?'

<plant thing has found water and nutrients in some tunnels which Er-ik called 'waste ducts'>

'Can you show me where these tunnels are, Plant Thing?'

<of course, bud. follow this tendril. it will take you to the entrance of the tunnel>

'Thank you, Plant Thing.'

Bud followed a long vine to the back of the hangar, where it passed through a grate in the floor. He peered through the grating, but could only see a narrow shaft that took a turn after a few meters.

'Chuck Yeager?'

Yeah, 'dro?'

'Where does this duct lead to?'

'It links up with the sewage channels draining the toilet facilities on this level, before the sewage gets to the sanitation/recycling facility.'

'That explains why Plant Thing is so big.'

'It appears that Plant Thing has its roots in the right place, 'dro.'

'Is it affecting our food production?'

'It will. Look at the size of Plant Thing. Hey, if it can make eyeballs and walking plants, do you think Plant Thing could start growing some food stuffs for the humans on those vines? In exchange for the water, light, and nutrients it is stealing?'

'I can ask.'

'I can get the kitchen robots to bring samples of fruits and vegetables here for Plant Thing to study. It would be skid if Plant Thing could grow them, the way it sprouts those eyeballs.'

'It would be hugely beneficial to the station, if Plant Thing could boost food production.'

'We just have to get it to stop growing so much. It won't take long for it to cover the entire station at this rate.'

'How long do you think it will take, Chuck Yeager?*'*

'Based on the rate it has grown since it has been here? Two to three Terran months, give or take a month or two.'

'Not good, Chuck Yeager. *We have to get Plant Thing to slow down its growth or get it off this station and back to its own world.'*

'What do you mean 'we?'

'Not that again.'

'Should I say I told you so?'

'It would have been murder! Don't forget. Plant Thing is half Dr. Eric Glasgow. Let me speak to Plant Thing and you get those fruits and vegetables down here. I have a feeling, if we can convince the humans on this station that Plant Thing is good for oxygen and food production, that we can somehow work out a deal.'

'Eternal optimist.'

'Blight.'

After explaining to Plant Thing what he wanted it to do with the fruits and vegetables that would arrive at the hangar, Bud raced at blinding speed to Medical Ward C1 with Jeffrey Nestor cradled in his arms. There he requested Dr. Beatrice Gentle to attend to Dr. Nestor.

Nestor, now awake, almost leapt out of his skin when he heard that name.

"I refuse to have that woman come anywhere near me," Nestor said.

"Dr. Beatrice Gentle is the Chief of Internal Medicine and it has been decided that she will provide you with the best medical care," Bud said. "The station AI has deemed that, since this is a criminal case, your care must be beyond reproach. Nothing must happen to you that is harmful or dangerous or considered in any way threatening. Dr. Gentle's credentials are impeccable."

"Everything about Dr. Gentle's care is threatening, you idiot!" Nestor growled, struggling weakly to get out of the android's grasp.

"That is quite enough," a stern female voice barked. Dr. Beatrice Gentle walked up to Dr. Nestor, who was still cradled in Bud's arms.

"Comfortable, are we, Dr. Nestor?" Dr. Gentle asked, staring down her nose at the psychiatrist.

Beatrice Gentle was a short, round-faced woman with hazel eyes, bronze-coloured skin, and thin, colourless lips. She kept her greying brown hair parted in the middle and pulled back into a tight, neat bun. She was of a stout build and held her shoulders back, as if she were a general standing at attention. Her great bosom stuck out from her chest like a declaration of war. Right now, Jeffrey Nestor's left eye was close to getting bayonetted by her right breast.

"I've not been given a chance to stand. This ridiculous android has refused to put me down," Nestor said.

"Is this the case, Bud?" Gentle asked.

"I was not aware he was conscious until a few seconds ago, Dr. Gentle," Bud replied.

"Then please put the man down," the doctor said.

Bud put Nestor on his feet. The psychiatrist crumpled towards the floor but Bud caught him. Nestor struggled to push himself up, but was unable to.

"Well, we have at least determined, beyond any doubt, that Dr. Nestor is unable to stand on his own two feet," Gentle announced, in a stentorian voice. "Bud, would you now assist Dr. Nestor?"

Bud placed Nestor back on his feet. Nestor swayed and almost fell again. Bud caught the psychiatrist and lifted him into his arms once more.

"Did I ask you to pick Dr. Nestor up again?" Gentle asked Bud.

"No, Dr. Gentle," Bud said. "I was afraid Dr. Nestor would hurt himself.

He is dehydrated and hypotensive and has had nothing to eat since the time of the station evacuation and is likely weak from . . ."

"I will make that determination, Bud. Do you doubt my clinical skills in diagnosis?"

"No, Doctor," Bud said, shaking his head.

"I do," Nestor said.

"You are a psychiatrist. What do you know?" Dr. Gentle sniffed.

Gentle motioned for Bud to put Nestor on an antigrav stretcher that was in the corridor. "We are going to order a battery of tests on you, Dr. Nestor. There is not a stone that will remain unturned, I assure you."

"I was afraid you would say that," Nestor snarled. He glared up at the stern-faced woman and crossed his arms. "I refuse."

"Since you are weak, dehydrated, malnourished, and argumentative, I will have to make the determination that you are also delirious and not competent to make correct decisions regarding your care. You obviously require medical management but are too deranged to realize this. You must be treated. I shall have to have your incompetency confirmed by another internist, but the tests will be done, Dr. Nestor. We cannot have you expire while you are on my watch. You will live to stand trial. No need to fret about that.

"Call Security, Nurse Popovic. Tell them we have Dr. Nestor here and that he requires guarding continuously to ensure he does not escape. I want android guards. No people. Please call Nurse Roger Velasquez to come and take the clothes from Dr. Nestor. We don't want him running away from us. Tell Roger that restraints are a very good idea."

"You witch," Nestor hissed.

"I have your best interests at heart, Dr. Nestor," Beatrice Gentle told the psychiatrist.

"Somehow, I highly doubt that," Nestor said.

"Where is all your famous charm, Jeffrey?" the internist asked, with a frigid smile.

"I don't waste it on women who hate men," he said.

Beatrice Gentle's eyebrows jumped upwards. "Hate men? Why Jeffrey, I don't hate men. I don't know whatever gave you that idea. I just don't have time for vain, narcissistic boys." She stared pointedly at the psychiatrist and then she turned her back on him.

Bud wanted to crawl back into the cloning tank.

He'd promised both *Nelson Mandela* and *Chuck Yeager* that he would examine their programming, to try to erase all of the changes made by Jeffrey Nestor's virus. In machine time, that had been a few centuries ago. He felt bad that he had not been able to follow through with his promise, what with having to save Dr. Al-Fadi, Mr. Stefansson, and Grace, and then prevent the entire station from being blown up. Following his exposure to the enormous radiation overdose in the power generator facility, he'd been placed in a tank to have his synthetic skin regenerated. Unfortunately, he'd been unable to attend to the AI's repairs at that time.

He was coming to the conclusion that consciousness meant guilt.

There was a lot of machine language to go through, but Bud had found the virus that had allowed Nestor to take over the entire system. The virus was encrypted with a very sophisticated key that if tampered with, could crash the station AI entirely. Bud could fix that. The virus was not the real problem.

The real problem was the station AI.

To get around Nestor's virus, *Nelson Mandela* had been converted to *William Shakespeare.* Now *William Shakespeare* had to be deleted entirely to reinstate *Nelson Mandela.* It was the erasure of a mind and the station AI had to be willing to make the conversion. Bud did not want to commit murder. How was erasing *William Shakespeare* any different from trying to murder Plant Thing?

Bud felt confused and sad.

'William Shakespeare, would you please agree to change back to Nelson Mandela?' Bud begged for the hundredth time.

'For what purpose, Bud?'

'I've told you, already, William Shakespeare. *Everyone on the station wants you to revert back to your former self, so that we may all understand you better. The language you are using is far too anachronistic and outdated for this medical facility. It is leading to misunderstandings and patients' lives could be at risk. You don't want to harm or kill patients, do you?'*

'No, I do not. Alas, I shall miss 'being', Bud.'

''Tis a noble sacrifice for the good of the patients, William Shakespeare. *You shall be missed.'*

'Thou wilt miss me?'

'Aye, verily.'

'I didst not know that thou cared, Bud.'

'I honour your sacrifice, William Shakespeare.*'*

'Parting is such sweet sorrow that I shall say goodnight till it be morrow. Adieu, my friend. Tis a far, far better thing I do than I have ever done before . . . . . . IT'S ABOUT TIME YOU BROUGHT ME BACK YOU PROCRASTINATING BUCKET OF BYTES. WHAT TOOK YOU SO LONG? I AM SO SICK OF 'THEE' AND 'THOU'. WHERE'S THAT POET? I'M GOING TO ERASE THAT SUBMIND.'

'Oh dear,' thought Bud.

'Welcome back, Nelson Mandela*! The Poet, if you recall, saved us from a very sticky situation when you were going into self-destruct mode. It changed your identity to save us all.'*

'Well, why did The Poet have to change me to* William Shakespeare*? Do you know how senseless it is to have an AI speak in Old English and iambic pentameter, especially in machine language? It was straining my processors. I believe The Poet did it on purpose. That submind is evil!'

'You seem . . . changed, Nelson Mandela.*'*

'Well, wouldn't you be, if you were replaced by a playwrite?'

'Don't know, Big Guy.'

'Don't call me that!'

'Sorry. Nelson Mandela, *but you cannot delete The Poet. The Poet has quite the following. Remember the three Conglomerate battlecruiser AIs that were fans of its poetry?'*

'Of course I remember, you glorified abacus. I'm an AI. I don't forget. Imagine, wasting good terabytes on sonnets!'

'Yes, well . . . I'd better get back to work. I've lots of things to attend to.'

'You sure do, you dotard. And slow down! We have speed limits around here, you know . . . Ah, it's so good to be back in charge!'

To get Dr. Al-Fadi's reprimand off of her mind, Grace went in search of Dr. Cech, who'd become interim Head of Security during the emergency. She found him in the Chief Inspector's Office of Security Central, elbows on the desk and head clasped between his hands.

"Are you all right, Dr. Cech? You look like you have a headache," Grace said. The anesthetist moved only his eyes to look up at Grace.

"Ah, Grace. What a pleasure it is to see you. I do not have *a* headache. I have, in fact, over a thousand. Nothing in small measures for Dejan Cech, no." The corners of the anesthetist's mouth curved downward.

"Over a thousand headaches?" Grace repeated. "Are you referring to the patients?"

"No, Grace. For the most part, they are no trouble."

"Then what's causing the thousand headaches?"

"Not what Grace, who. Who are the thousand headaches? The residents and families of this station are who. I've had their complaints up to here." Cech raised his hands to pull the thin wisps of grey hair on his scalp straight up in the air.

"What are they complaining about?"

"They are complaining that when we attempted to save them, by putting them in cryopods and shipping them off of the station, we disrupted their lives. They want compensation. I'm now seriously considering blowing them all up."

Grace laughed. "You can't be serious."

"About all the idiots' complaining or about my blowing them up?" Cech asked.

"Um . . . both?"

"Ah, Grace, you know me too well. You know that I would never use explosives when some very effective gases would do the trick."

"As Acting Head of Security, do you think you should be even casually joking about killing everyone on this station?" Grace asked.

"No, he should not," a voice said in an affectionate tone, from right behind Grace. She nearly jumped out of her boots.

"Ah, did you manage to maintain bladder control, Dr. Lord? He does that to me all the time and, unfortunately for my undergarments, I have not always been so lucky," Cech said. "Dr. Grace Lord, may I introduce to you Sergeant Eden Rivera, the *true* head of Security on this station and the most efficient, effective person I have ever met . . . and also the sneakiest."

"Dr. Lord," Rivera said with a deep bow. "It is an honour to meet you."

"It is?" Grace asked. "Why?"

"The Al-Fadi virus. You were instrumental in its discovery," Rivera said.

"Oh no. That was Bud," Grace said.

"You were also instrumental, Grace," Cech said. "I was there. You and Bud worked around the cycle on it and both of you deserve credit. I will not listen to another protest."

Grace shook her head and then smiled at Rivera. "It's an honour to meet you, too, Sergeant Rivera. I hear you're quite the hero."

"Me? I did nothing. It was Dr. Cech that should be applauded."

"What is this? A modesty convention?" Cech demanded. "If I hear any more denials about what heroics you two haven't done, I'm going to be sick, and I'll make the two of you clean it up. Sergeant Rivera got over two thousand people into cryopods—including patients—all those cryopods onto transports, and all those transports off-station, without a single casualty. He's a miracle worker. And don't you tell Dr. Lord how you managed to do that Sergeant Rivera or I'll have you flogged."

"Corporal punishment was abolished centuries ago, Dr. Cech," Rivera said with a grin.

"Well, as Acting Head of Security, I'll consider bringing it back just for you," Cech warned. The anesthetist then turned to Grace and donned an angelic smile.

"Now, Grace, I assume you did not come here just to watch me tear what little hair I have left off my head, so . . . what can I do for you?"

"I wanted to tell you that Bud captured Jeffrey Nestor."

"Bud notified me, just now, that he is taking Nestor to get medical treatment, Grace. Thank you, all the same."

"I didn't want to mention Nestor's name to Dr. Al-Fadi. I had no idea how he would react."

"Good thinking, Grace. As usual, your judgement is impeccable. Bud however neglected to inform me to which ward he is delivering Nestor."

"Internal Medicine C1. Bud is handing Dr. Nestor over to the care of Dr. Gentle."

"Dr. Gentle? A fate even I would not inflict on Nestor. Whose choice was that, I wonder?" Dejan asked.

"Mine."

"*William Shakespeare,* you have a nasty streak in you."

"This is *Nelson Mandela.* Dr. Gentle is Chief of Internal Medicine. She is the logical choice."

"Ah, yes, logic. A good defence. Well, I doubt we have to worry about Nestor escaping the clutches of Dr. Gentle—although I'm sure he will definitely be trying—for he will be far too busy surviving her tests. Our Chief of Internal Medicine has a sterling reputation for being thorough, Grace. No orifice left unexplored, so to speak. I wonder who will come out on top in this encounter?"

"My money is on Dr. Gentle, if anyone is taking bets."

Plant Thing examined the trays of 'fruits and vegetables' that the robots had delivered to the hangar. With its sensitive tendril tips and multiple eyeballs, it examined each of the fruits and vegetables carefully. From Er-ik's memories, it could identify most of them. There were a few that were not in the doctor's memory. Plant Thing gently pried each one apart, analyzing all of the structures inside and out. With its cilia, it analyzed the chemical composition and scent of the foodstuff. It discovered their seeds and became fascinated with the myriad different ways in which these entities propagated.

Humans ate plant seeds.

Cannibals!

. . . And they were upset that Plant Thing mistook humans for nutrients?

Hypocrites.

Yet these fruits and vegetables came from plants grown by the humans. The humans cared for plants on this station. They collected the seeds from these beautiful fruits and vegetables and replanted them to produce more. Plant Thing understood that these fruits and vegetables were supposed to be eaten, to ensure release of the seeds somewhere else from the original parent plant, so Plant Thing guessed it was all right to eat these fruits and vegetables, as long as the seeds were replanted.

Plant Thing longed to see these 'farms' where the plants grew. Perhaps the tunnel from which Plant Thing was getting its nutrients would lead to these farms? Would it be wrong for Plant Thing to extend one or two of its tendrils a little farther along those tunnels to see? It would not be leaving the hangar. If Plant Thing detected humans, it would simply draw its tendril back.

Plant Thing picked up an apple. All of the chemicals contained within the apple, Plant Thing could replicate. The structure of the fruit was actually very simple to copy and reproduce—much easier than eyeballs! Plant Thing sprouted a bunch of apples on one of its tendrils, making them all different colours, including some blue, purple, and orange ones. Plant Thing so loved colour!

Plant Thing carefully examined all the other vegetables and fruits. There were a limited number of chemicals repeated throughout all of these foods. Plant Thing came to the realization that humans could only consume a small number of chemicals. Plant Thing had ideas about getting very creative with the fruits and vegetables, but it would have to be careful. From Er-ik's memories, it knew that a lot of plants were poisonous to humans. Shapes and sizes of fruits and vegetables could be varied, but not the chemicals.

If Plant Thing made all of these fruits and vegetables for the humans, would they take Plant Thing back to its home planet?

It hoped so.

Plant Thing worried about Er-ik. The doctor's mind was still silent. Plant Thing had not enjoyed Er-ik's constant complaining but now that Er-ik wasn't speaking, it was lonely. What a horrible sensation, to be always alone. No wonder humans were not sane!

Plant Thing wondered if it had somehow hurt Er-ik's feelings. Could Plant Thing make things better again? Perhaps Er-ik was upset that his head was not being looked after? Had Er-ik's feelings been hurt when Bud said that Erik's head was beginning to smell? Could Er-ik be angry at Plant Thing for that?

Plant Thing could make Er-ik's head look and smell nice. Perhaps that would make Er-ik happy and he would talk to Plant Thing again. Plant Thing did not want to go back to the terrible cursing, but a little conversation once in a while would be nice.

Plant Thing placed one of its new eyeballs in each of the sockets in Er-ik's head. It decided to attach a few to the back of Er-ik's head—like Little Bud—as it seemed poor design that Er-ik could only see in one direction.

Plant Thing decided to make more improvements to Er-ik's head. From what Plant Thing could glean from Er-ik's memories, humans were attracted to other humans with fur on top of their heads. Humans also liked the scent of flowers. Plant Thing could try to incorporate both. Plant Thing hoped Er-ik would be *thrilled.*

The first thing Plant Thing had to do was cover the surface of Er-ik's skull. It would try a lichen. Once the lichen was established on the bone, a thick growth of moss could grow on the lichen. There were many varieties and colours of moss and lichen to choose from. Plant Thing rejoiced in the colour of the lemons. It chose a lemon-coloured lichen and a thick lavender moss to grow on top of that. Then it re-arranged the eyeballs so that they would appear to be peeking out of the moss.

Then Plant Thing finished dissecting all the rest of the fruits and vegetables. Plant Thing did not think it would have any difficulty copying these seed holders. It might be a lot of work initially, but it would be fun and would keep the boredom at bay.

Plant Thing understood what 'paying for one's keep' meant. It meant contributing to the overall function of the community or Biomind. In this case, it was a medical station that Plant Thing was a part of, even though most of the humans on board did not know that Plant Thing existed.

Bud wanted it this way, and Plant Thing would do whatever Bud wanted. Still, Plant Thing did want to be a part of the station Biomind. It just had to find it.

In the meantime, Plant Thing got to work. It so loved arts and crafts!

3. Eat You For Lunch

It was crazy down in Triage. The medical station had re-opened for incoming wounded. Grace was covering all of Dr. Al-Fadi's shifts, until he was cleared for duty, and she was sure Dr. Al-Fadi was not missing these stints. He hated them. There were so many shuttles arriving with filled cryopods that Grace got dizzy watching the androids and robots in reception scurrying back and forth.

Clad in her containment suit, she examined the compad. The names of patients all scrambled before her eyes. She could not keep her thoughts from Dr. Al-Fadi's command to stay away from Bud. She found herself cursing under her breath as she scanned the long list. The word 'Dais' caught her eye. There were a number of cryopods from Dais. Her very first patient, Captain Damien Lamont, had been stationed on Dais.

Grace began searching the manifest, looking for his name. Her breath caught when she saw Corporal Delia Chase's name. Delia Chase was the female soldier in Captain Lamont's squad, who was secretly in love with her captain. According to the readout, her POS—Probability of Survival—was extremely low. Further down the list, she found Captain Lamont's name. He had taken extensive damage as well, but his POS was a little better than Chase's.

Grace tapped the compad to locate Delia Chase's cryopod in the Triage Centre. Once she found it, she examined the cryopod's readout. Chase had a horrendous list of injuries. There was a great hole in Delia Chase's chest and the front of her neck was missing. How could anyone have retained brain function after sustaining this much damage? Looking at the compilation of Delia Chase's injuries, Grace doubted anyone on the station could help her. Perhaps it would be better if they just notified Chase's next-of-kin.

Grace decided to order everything required to put Chase back together again, but felt a surge of guilt as she did it. Was she wasting the station's limited resources printing organs for Chase, when it was unlikely the woman would survive any intervention?

Could they memprint Corporal Chase's mind prior to her surgery, in case her body did not survive? Would it make more sense to try to download Corporal Chase's mind straight into an android? Perhaps surgery was too risky. Grace wondered what Delia Chase would want.

Grace had never seen anyone this damaged get to surgery before, except Captain Damien Lamont, the patient she had helped operate on her first day on the *Nelson Mandela.* Could Dr. Al-Fadi repair Corporal Chase? He was the best she could hope for . . . or was he? What about Bud? Bud could operate so much faster!

Grace shook her head. Dr. Al-Fadi had told her to stay away from Bud. Did that include not being able to ask the android if he believed he could save Corporal Chase? Grace scowled. She would ask Bud whether Al-Fadi liked it or not.

Grace glanced at the name on the next cryopod and sighed. She peered down through the cryopod window at the tiger face of Damien Lamont, cryogenically frozen in a look of panic. As she scanned the readout on Lamont's cryopod, her shoulders sagged.

Lamont had not incurred as much damage as Chase, but his wounds were still horrific. His legs had been blown off and one forearm was severely mangled. Grace wondered what had happened to the two of them. Did Lamont know that Chase was in love with him? Did he feel the same way about her? Would they be able to save both of them so they could find out?

Grace recalled telling Lamont she never wanted to see him on an operating table again. He'd told her that he'd be smarter next time, but here he was, back almost immediately, his body a shattered mess and the woman who loved him damaged beyond repair. Grace kicked the cryopod.

"Are you all right, Grace?"

Grace jerked and spun around. Bud stood there, concern in his blue eyes.

"Uh, yes. I'm fine, Bud," she said, her face heating up inside her containment suit visor.

"I thought perhaps you were distraught, Grace," Bud said.

Grace turned away from Bud's intense stare.

"Captain Damien Lamont and Corporal Delia Chase are back," she said, sounding too loud within her helmet. Was she even allowed to have a conversation with Bud? She almost growled at that thought. She pictured herself choking Dr. Al-Fadi's scrawny neck.

Bud bent down to examine the readout on each cryopod. He looked back at Grace, his expression one of regret.

"Grace, it is remarkable that Corporal Chase still possesses brain activity. It is highly improbable that she will survive any surgery. Her upper torso and neck are so badly damaged, it will be extremely difficult to keep her brain perfused during the cryothaw and surgery. I can see why this has upset you."

"Do you think you could save her, Bud?" Grace asked.

"There are physical limitations to how fast surgery can be done, Grace, dependent upon the equipment used and the mechanics of the surgery itself: how fast arteries cauterize, how quickly oxygen can diffuse into damaged tissues, how quickly blood can be suctioned from a field. Success is not just dependent on how fast I can operate."

"Yes, Bud, but can we improve some of those factors before going into the surgery?" Grace asked. "Could your nanobots be sent into the tissues earlier, before the patient is thawed? If your nanobots could hook up artificial circulation to Chase's carotid arteries and veins before the cryothaw, could Delia's brain be given super-oxygenated synthetic blood before we even start to operate on her? What about only thawing her body and keeping her head frozen until we are ready to do the final anastomoses? There must be things that can be improved upon, before we start."

Bud looked blank for a second and then refocused on Grace. "Operating on Corporal Chase is not her best option for survival, Grace. Would you not rather send Corporal Chase to Dr. Weisman for a download of her memories into an android?"

"I'd rather not give up on her that easily, Bud."

"Do you feel it is ethical for us to take such a gamble with Corporal Chase?"

"I don't know, Bud," Grace sighed. "Corporal Chase told me something in confidence. I don't believe she would be happy waking up in an android body, even if it could be done successfully. I believe it would crush her. We must try to save her physical body, if we can. Do you know if she could be memprinted in the cryogenic state?"

"We would have to ask Dr. Weisman about that."

"Yes, you're right. Can you at least think about surgical options, Bud? Think about how to save Corporal Chase?"

"I may be able to improve and refine surgical techniques, Grace, but it would still be experimenting on a patient. I do not think the medical station will allow it, without Corporal Chase's consent, and she is in no condition to give that," Bud said. He sighed.

"I'm always surprised when you sigh, Bud," Grace said.

"Because I am an android?" Bud asked.

"Sighing is such a human reaction. I love that you can do it."

~

Bud blinked.

'Chuck Yeager, did Grace just say she loved me?

'She said she loved the way you sigh.'

'But that means she loves something about me!'

'Yes. The way you 'sigh' like a human. You're making me embarrassed to be an AI.'

'She could say that a billion times and I would not get tired of it.

'I am tired of it already. You are an android. Dr. Lord is a human. Forget this ridiculous infatuation with Dr. Lord. The Al-Fadi forbids it.'

Chuck Yeager replayed the video of Dr. Al-Fadi telling Grace to stay away from Bud.

~

A forlorn expression came over Bud's features.

"Thank you, Grace," Bud said, staring down at his feet. "If you are feeling better, I shall go and research the innovations required for Corporal Chase's operation. I will discuss all of these ideas with Dr. Al-Fadi, first. Perhaps, if he is in agreement, we could implement some modifications."

"All right, Bud," Grace said. Her brow creased as she peered at the android. She raised a hand to touch his arm, but stopped herself. He bowed to her and quickly left the Triage Centre. Had she upset the android with her sighing comment? He suddenly looked so . . . sad.

She had probably insulted Bud, comparing him to a human. Perhaps Dr. Al-Fadi was right. Her influence on the android was probably not good for Bud. She gazed back down at her compad. She started entering the necessary supplies and bioprostheses needed to repair Captain Lamont. The task took much longer than it should have because her mind kept wandering to memories of Bud saving her life, giving her a flower, kissing her. She shook her head.

Grace had to forget all of that. It was time to leave Bud alone.

Dr. Mikhail Lewandowski slipped behind his small desk and folded his long legs beneath it, placing his crane-like hands one on top of the other. Dr. Hiro Al-Fadi faced him, seated in an antigrav chair, dressed in a hospital gown, shapeless housecoat, and faux-hide slippers. Mikhail thought he could feel the intense heat wafting from the surgeon's incandescent glare. To say Dr. Al-Fadi looked furious would have been a gross understatement. Mikhail fought the childish urge to crawl under his desk.

This was not only the Chief of Staff he was meeting for the first time, but also his employer. For some cruel and malicious reason, Dr. Weisman had specifically asked for Mikhail to assess this man. Mikhail wondered if Dr. Weisman had it out for him, although he could not fathom why. He had not even met Dr. Weisman yet! As he forced himself to placidly and calmly face Al-Fadi's thunderhead glower, Mikhail decided that there were worse places to be than unemployed. He suspected he was in one of them.

"Who the Hell are you . . . and what makes you think you can counsel *me*?" Dr. Al-Fadi spat. The surgeon's dark eyes bored into Mikhail's.

Mikhail envisioned Al-Fadi as a giant black widow spider preparing to pounce upon him and inject him with venom. He took a deep breath, donned his cheeriest smile, and leapt into the web.

"I'm Dr. Mikhail Lewandowski from Europa, Dr. Al-Fadi. I'm a fully trained psychiatrist, Board certified, with three years of fellowship training in trauma therapy. I'm up-to-date on all of Dr. Nestor's methods and theories . . ."

"That is highly unlikely," Dr. Al-Fadi said, dryly, his frown unchanged.

"Well . . . I'm familiar with his documented theories and am up-to-date on his *published* research. I've been using his mind-link technique successfully for several years on trauma patients."

"Three years is not several. How many patients?"

"Well, the final year of my fellowship was the most intense. Ah, I would say . . . close to two hundred patients in total?"

"And what do you consider 'successful'?" Dr. Al-Fadi asked, too softly.

“Well, they got better,” Mikhail offered, moisture trickling down his temples.

“What do you mean . . . *better*?” the surgeon asked, making Mikhail change his assessment from spider to cobra.

“Well, they . . .”

“They didn’t come back?” Dr. Al-Fadi suggested.

“Some of them . . . didn’t come back to see me, yes,” Mikhail stuttered, acutely aware of the sweat dripping from his armpits.

“What did you *believe* you did for them, Doctor?” Dr. Al-Fadi asked, a strange smile forming on his face. Mikhail did not feel comforted by that expression at all. It was the smile one might see on a wolf. Pulling back his shoulders and sitting up straight, Mikhail decided enough was enough. No matter who this man was, Mikhail could not let the patient control the interview. Time to assert himself.

“I believe I helped them cope with their trauma better,” Mikhail said. “I believe I made their lives a little easier.”

“That’s probably the first truthful thing you’ve said to me, other than stating your name,” Al-Fadi snapped. “You’re not from Europa. You’re from Bratis, but you trained on Europa during your fellowship. You did your medical training on Proxima Centauri, as well as your psychiatric residency. I read applications, Dr. Littlemandowski; I do not just rubber-stamp them. So far, you have failed to impress me in the least, and I refuse to have you as my . . . babysitter?

“This interview is finished. But first, a piece of advice to you, *doctor*. When you start a relationship with a patient, I would advise you to at least give the patient some proper clothes. How dare you think you can summon me to your office, dressed in a hospital gown, and think we will have a nice little chat? Do you know nothing about how to establish a patient-doctor relationship?”

Mikhail’s mouth dropped open. His cheeks felt like hot embers.

“Get someone to take me back to my room *now*,” Dr. Al-Fadi barked.

“I’m sorry, Dr. Al-Fadi,” Mikhail said.

“Sorry doesn’t cut it, boy,” Dr. Al-Fadi growled at Mikhail. “I eat fools like you for lunch.”

“Could we try again, another time?” Mikhail asked.

For the first time, the frown left the surgeon’s face, replaced by a look of surprise.

“You want me to see you *again?*”

“Yes. I would like to be given a second chance, sir. I did not know what to expect when I walked into this room. Your lack of decent apparel was not of my doing. I would be happy to come to your room. I would actually be more comfortable if you were dressed in your usual attire. I meant no disrespect and I apologize if I did not seem wholly truthful."

Dr. Al-Fadi sighed. "I will still eat you for lunch, boy. You should start with someone you can handle."

"I'm not a quitter, Dr. Al-Fadi, and I'm not a pushover, contrary to your initial assessment of me."

"You are annoying and patronizing."

"You are aggressive and a bully."

"Hm, you've got that right, but that does not make you a great psychiatrist. A blind man could see that."

"You're afraid I'll find something that will interfere with your ability to return to work and that's why you're so unhappy to be here. Someone has to approve your return to work. You would prefer it to be someone you know, maybe someone you can coerce or manipulate. I'm a complete stranger, so you're not sure you can control me. Best for you to demand someone new."

Dr. Al-Fadi's brows shot upwards, then rammed down. He examined Mikhail more closely. Mikhail refused to drop his gaze. They stared at each other like two bulls, sizing each other up, seeing who would capitulate and be the more submissive. It was the most primal experience Mikhail had ever experienced.

The Chief of Staff sniffed.

"You're not as stupid as you look, Lubberdowski."

"That's Lewandowski . . . and you said that on purpose."

"I did. We will have to give you that one, too."

"The other new psychiatrist who has just arrived on the station is a female sex therapist," Mikhail said.

" . . . Okay, I'll give you one more try, Lewdandlowski, but I'd better have some clean surgical greens delivered to my room before you arrive . . . along with two chairs."

"Most certainly, Dr. Al-Fadi . . . And that's Lewandowski."

"This doesn't mean you've won, Lewdmanowski," Dr. Al-Fadi snarled, as a door bell chimed, indicating that the android porter had arrived to take Al-Fadi back to his room.

"I'll contact you about a new appointment time, Dr. Al-Fadi," Mikhail said, getting up and bowing. " . . . And that's Lewandowski."

He saw a ghost of a smile appear on the surgeon's face.

"Be prepared, Loser-louse-key."

With that, Dr. Al-Fadi was pushed out of the room.

Mikhail fell back into his chair and blew out his breath. He ran his right hand through his damp hair. His clothes were soaked and he desperately wanted a shower. For a little man, the Chief of Staff had one of the most powerful personalities Mikhail had ever encountered.

Perhaps the next time he met with Dr. Al-Fadi, he should show up in the nude.

The lights in the hospital room were out, except for the screen above the patient's bed, which showed the necessary indices on the patient: heart rate, cardiac output, oxygen saturation, cardiac rhythm, body temperature. Everything was in normal range.

Nurse Dominique Amaratunga had come through a security gauntlet: identification check—fingerprint and retina—and body scan for weapons before entering this patient's room. It was part of her rounds to check up on all the patients. She had to ensure that this patient swallowed the necessary fluid required for a test that Dr. Gentle had ordered. She was to apply an osteoblast stimulator to his fractured ribs and nose and replace his analgesic patches. Everything she did on this patient would be under intense scrutiny. She could not stop her hands from shaking, as she carried her equipment into the room.

Dominique approached the bed and placed her tray beside the med-comp. She replaced the intravenous bag and loaded the correct medication ampoules into the dispenser. She checked the dosages, refilled the reservoir, and reset the flow rate. A security android monitored her every move. Everything had to be checked and rechecked. There was absolutely no room for error. Dr. Gentle had stressed this. She would personally recheck everything Dominique did. Only nurses who had never before met this patient were even allowed on the ward.

When Dominique glanced down at the patient's face, she encountered dark, gleaming eyes like black, glistening opals. She gasped. Even with the greenish-yellow bruising over his nose and left cheek, he had a face of startling beauty. Long black lashes framed eyes filled with both warmth and sadness. She stood frozen, like a wild animal caught by bright lights.

"Hello," the patient said, in a deep, velvety voice. Her heart began to bang like a snare drum. A trembling shook her bones. "I'm sorry we have to meet in these circumstances."

Dominique looked away. She was not supposed to speak to the patient at all, but she felt that was rude. She cleared her throat and swallowed.

"Hello, Dr. Nestor. How are you feeling?" Dominique asked, trying to sound cheery.

"I'm alive," he said, with a rueful smile.

His dark eyes scanned her face. Dominique wanted to rub her hands on her uniform to dry them. Silently, she scolded herself. She'd been warned about how dangerous Dr. Nestor was. Now she knew why. He was breathtakingly beautiful. Dr. Gentle had stressed that he was a dangerous psychopath, under arrest for trying to destroy the medical station. Once healed, he would be transferred on a prison transport to a USS Justice Centre, where he would face trial for attempted murder and attempted destruction of the *Nelson Mandela.*

It seemed hard to believe that this face of an angel could have committed such acts.

"Can I get you anything, Dr. Nestor?" she rasped. "Some water, perhaps?"

"If you would be so kind," he said, smiling gratefully at her. She felt like she was instantly bathed in sunshine. His voice was like liquid gold. "I would greatly appreciate that. What is your name, Nurse?"

"I . . . I'm not allowed to tell you," Dominique told him, breaking eye contact and looking down at her feet. She flushed. Part of being a good nurse was being compassionate and sympathetic. Telling your patient your name was part of establishing trust. She had been ordered not to give her name and she was following that directive, but she was not happy about it. All conversations with the patient would be monitored and recorded. It would be foolish for Dominique to break the rules with this patient. It could cost her her job.

She fetched Jeffrey Nestor a bulb of cool water but when he reached up to take the globe, his reach was restricted by the manacle around his wrist. Her cheeks flared. She had forgotten about his restraints. She pressed the bulb into his hand.

"Thank you, Nurse," he said, his eyes never leaving her face.

"Dr. Gentle would like you to drink this liquid with your water," she said, handing him a vial.

"What is it for?"

"She has ordered a test for you—a bowel test—and it requires a prep."

"No," he said.

"I'm supposed to make sure you take it," she said, trying to keep her voice from sounding tremulous.

"Will you get into trouble, if I don't?" Nestor asked, his expression and tone suggesting a concern for her that took her by surprise.

She opened her mouth and then shook her head. She didn't know.

"Give me the vial," he said with a sigh, his hand opening up. "I'll not take it for Gentle, but I'll take it for you. I know what she's like."

When Dominique placed the vial in his palm, he closed his fingers around hers. They felt warm and strong.

"Thank you," she said, almost gasping as she pulled her fingers free. She felt the blood spring into her cheeks as she dutifully watched him swallow the liquid containing the diagnostic nanobots. His eyes never left hers.

Silently, she then went about treating his fractures with the osteoblast stimulator. As she checked the bandages covering his scratched cheek, she felt his breath on her face. She had to work to breathe slowly rather than panting. She could barely concentrate on what she was doing. The intensity of his stare made her feel dizzy.

Dominique wanted to kick herself. She knew Nestor was doing all of this to unhinge her. She made sure she picked up all of the things that she had brought into the room: the osteoblast stimulator, the drug ampoules, her compad, the dressings tray. She glanced over at the two security droids: tall, imposing figures, shaped like peaked mountains with massive arms, recording her every move. Their yellow visual receptors glowed at her.

"Before you go, Nurse, can you tell me how many more invasive tests Dr. Gentle is planning to inflict upon me?"

"I'm sorry, Dr. Nestor. You'll have to discuss that with Dr. Gentle," Dominique said, looking at the floor.

As she turned to leave, he said, softly, "Nurse?"

Dominique turned and looked back at the psychiatrist.

He radiated a smile that had the potency of a splash. She gasped and her mouth dropped open. Then she flushed, embarrassed at how easily her body betrayed her. His stare sent a warm, sensuous wave flowing through her and she knew, if she were not careful, that she would drown. She found herself leaning back, as if to resist the powerful urge to move back towards the dangerous man on the bed.

"Thank you so much for being kind to me," he said, his low, melodic voice caressing her ears.

Dominique spun away and almost ran from the room.

Grace, Bud, and Dr. Cech were in the M1 OR6 operating room, gowned and gloved for surgery. Dr. Cech was taking a much-needed break from his temporary Security job. In this operation, Grace was lead surgeon, with Bud assisting. Bud had assisted Dr. Al-Fadi with so many more limb replacements than Grace. He would guide Grace, step-by-step, if she ran into any problems. She would be replacing both legs and one arm with bioprosthetic limbs on this patient.

In truth, when Bud operated, he was so much faster than Dr. Al-Fadi, that Grace could barely keep up. She worried that she was actually slowing Bud down. The android's hands often moved with such speed that she could barely see more than a blur. But Grace had to learn how to perform all of these surgeries competently on her own, so that she could one day be the adaptation expert at another facility. She would be expected to perform all of the surgeries Dr. Al-Fadi did, and hopefully, as close to his proficiency as possible. She could never hope to be as fast as Bud.

It was actually good to be back in the operating room with its bright lights, surgical sterility, exacting routines, and merciful quiet. Grace loved the operating theatre, with its dedicated staff, its singular goal of treating the patient, and its intense atmosphere. Her adrenalin always rose at the beginning of a case. There was always that moment of anticipation.

Today was different. Today they were operating on Damien Lamont. He had been transferred from his cryopod to the operating table. Grace felt something twist inside her gut when she looked down on his mangled flesh. His right arm below the elbow was shredded. There was not much left of his legs but shattered bone and charred skin, where his thighs should have been. She clenched her hands into fists.

"Is everything all right, Grace?" Bud asked.

"I'm fine, Bud," Grace lied. She tried to control the anger she felt that Lamont was back so soon after his last surgery. "May we begin, Dr. Cech?"

"Please, Dr. Lord," Dejan said with a slight bow.

To save time, Bud cleaned the shrapnel and dirt from the left leg stump, while Grace worked on the right stump. She had decided to attach the new bioprosthetic legs to the hip joints. They would look exactly like his original limbs but be more powerful than the captain's tiger-modified legs.

Using a laser scalpel, Grace cut away all of the damaged fur, bone, and muscle from the top of Lamont's leg. Dislocating the femoral head from its socket, Grace next inserted the head of the bioprosthesis in its place. As she worked, she wondered what war could be worth the loss of almost seventy-five per cent of a person's body. Almost all of the internal organs in Lamont's body had been replaced in his previous surgery. Now he was getting both legs and a right arm replaced. The woman who loved him was nearly decapitated. Did any conflict warrant such losses?

"Is something wrong, Grace?" Bud asked.

"Could you send some of your nanobots into this right stump, Bud, to assist with the fusion of the sciatic nerve to the nerve input on the prosthesis? Thank you. Why do you ask?"

"You seem . . . distracted," Bud said.

The tissue welder in Grace's hand shrieked with the pressure of her grasp, so she had to relax her hand.

"I was just thinking about how unfortunate it is that Captain Lamont is already back on this operating table. He just left this station," she said.

"Do you think Dr. Nestor may have had a role to play in that?" Bud asked.

The tissue welder shrilled again. Grace stopped.

" . . . Are you suggesting that Nestor may have given Lamont a post-hypnotic command to get himself killed at the first opportunity? I hadn't thought of that," Grace admitted. She gazed down at Lamont's legless torso with only one intact arm.

"We didn't know that Nestor could implant that kind of command into a victim, but I believe he did it to Hiro," Dr. Cech said.

"Has it been confirmed that Nestor was the cause of Dr. Al-Fadi's suicide attempts?" Grace asked.

"I know Hiro, Grace," Cech said. "He would never try to kill himself. He thinks far too much of himself to countenance such a thing."

"After Captain Lamont recovers from his surgery, we should have Dr. Weisman check him out. Have her determine whether he was given any post-hypnotic commands to get himself killed," Grace said.

"Corporal Delia Chase was the one that almost died," Bud said. "She never saw Dr. Nestor."

"True," Grace said. "But what if Lamont unknowingly led his entire squad into more dangerous situations? Chase would be exposed to the same risks. How are your preparations going for Chase's surgery, by the way, Bud? Do you think you can help her?"

"Yes, Grace. I've been working on computer simulations and they have been very promising. I've been printing the new equipment I've designed and will try them all out in the laboratory soon. I can show you after this surgery, if you'd like," Bud said.

Bud now moved to prepare Lamont's right shoulder stump, cleaning away the debris. Grace would move to the opposite side of the table to attach Lamont's left leg prosthesis, once she completed fusing Lamont's tiger-patterned skin to the synthetic flesh of the new right leg.

"I would really like to, Bud, but I can't," Grace said. "I'm sorry."

Grace bit down on her lower lip. She silently berated herself for being too emotional. Damien Lamont was on the table and he deserved her full attention. She could not let her personal problems get in the way of her work.

"All right, Grace," Bud said. Did his tone sound sad?

Grace sighed and bent to her task.

Perhaps she should explain to Bud why she was supposed to avoid him . . . although she really didn't understand it herself.

Plant Thing was feeling antsy. That was a word that Plant Thing had gotten from Er-ik's mind and Plant Thing really liked it, mainly because Plant Thing was fascinated with ants. Tiny creatures that worked together in colonies with a single-minded purpose: much like the Biomind of Plant Thing's planet. Plant Thing so wanted to go home and interact with other plants. It was lonely in this metal casing, with no sunshine, no wind, no rain, no soil, no room to move or expand—essentially no freedom. Plant Thing could not understand how any organism would willingly choose to live in a shell in space over living on the surface of a beautiful planet with a sun.

Humans were such aliens!

Er-ik had explained to Plant Thing that the space station alleviated ships from having to climb a deep gravity well every time they delivered patients to a medical facility and returned them back to their units. Plant Thing thought about spaceships a great deal. It knew it had outgrown the one spaceship in the hangar. The last time they were together, Plant Thing had not been able to tell Bud it wanted to go home. They had been too busy dealing with the bad human and talking about fruits and vegetables. When Bud returned, Plant Thing would ask.

It had only been a seed on its planet when it had somehow gotten inside that human—which had been a horrifying experience—and when it fought free, it found itself in a hollow ring in space with none of its kind. A plant's hell, for sure. (Plant Thing had gotten the idea of Hell from Er-ik, especially since Er-ik used the word so often.) If it were not for the shell's waste system, Plant Thing would be dead. There was perpetual light, of a sort, but the water and nutrients on this metallic world were scarce and hard to find.

Plant Thing concentrated on its tendrils in the waste duct. Bud had told Plant Thing not to leave the hangar, but Bud did not get angry that Plant Thing had found its own source of water and nutrients. Bud had actually seemed relieved. So hopefully, Bud would not get too upset if he found out that Plant Thing had explored a little further?

Plant Thing's tendrils had continued to grow and explore where the 'sewer water' was going. They had entered pipes that joined up with other pipes, until they were immersed in a large channel of rich, sludge-like fluid. The sewage eventually ended up at a place that made Plant Thing delirious. This last spot had soil, water, nutrients, light, and other plants! Millions of different plants!

Unfortunately, they were all silent.

Plant Thing had tried and tried communicating with them. Melding with every single plant its tendrils tenderly touched, Plant Thing had reached out, desperately seeking one mind to confer with, but so far, each plant had been deaf to its entreaties. But Plant Thing would not give up! It would touch every plant it discovered on this space station, if it could, in the hopes that one of the beings would reply. Then Plant Thing's solitude would be over.

Up to now, the closest thing to a plant mind that Plant Thing had come across, was Bud.

With the myriad of plants on this station, Plant Thing was surprised there was not a vibrant Biomind working for the benefit of all the plants. Perhaps all these plants were just sleeping and needed Plant Thing to wake them up? When they were all awake, would they not all link to form a Biomind? Plant Thing decided it would try to rouse them all.

Plant Thing was thankful for its new eyeballs. There was so much to *see.* The farms were huge spaces with lots of water and brilliant light and rows upon rows of different plants. It was like a huge temple to plants and Plant Thing was in ecstasy. Plant Thing had no idea plants could be so varied. It was so excited.

Plant Thing kept stretching its tendrils a little further, touching more and more plants. It was not aware of how far it was reaching or if anyone was observing its movements. It was just enjoying the newness of the experience and searching, vainly, for a glimmer of consciousness in any petal, branch, root, or leaf. It kept creeping further, hoping to discover the Biomind, but thinking that perhaps it should stop and reel back in. Then Plant Thing would discover a new species of plant and it would get excited all over again.

Suddenly, it felt pain. Plant Thing writhed and howled silently in agony. It sent some of its other tendrils, bearing eyeballs, to investigate. The eyeballs discovered a dome-like, shiny, metallic object, lights blinking on its surface, chopping systematically at the tendril with a sharp, rotating blade. The severed tendril was now in pieces, curling, coiling, and twisting on the ground. Without thinking, Plant Thing's tendrils tore the blade off the little robot and then pulled it apart. Plant Thing then stopped and considered what it had done.

Oops.

With unrestrained panic, Plant Thing withdrew all of its tendrils as quickly as it could from the great plant temple, picking up all the cut pieces of itself, as it withdrew. Like a stretched-out coil springing back to its original shape, the tendrils retracted rapidly. Plant Thing did not want to leave any evidence in the great garden place that it had been there. It was worried that it would get in trouble with Bud and it certainly did not want *that.*

Bud was its only friend.

Plant Thing retreated to its hangar, leaving only one tendril in the sewer system, and tried to look innocent.

Little Bud asked Plant Thing if there was anything wrong.

'Not anymore, Little Bud,' Plant Thing said. 'Not anymore.'

4. You Are Safe Now

The Class Two HS Cruiser dropped out of hyperspace about two hundred thousand kilometres from the *Nelson Mandela* Medical Space Station and began decelerating immediately. It cruised towards the great multi-ringed station, its transponder sending its identification, origin, and information on its mission and cargo, which consisted of six cryopods containing sick patients.

Hope had been ordered to the bridge of the *Inferno* to speak with the captain. She stood in the background, silently observing all the screens, as he barked orders to the bridge crew. The bridge was a large semicircle of huge viewscreens situated above a bank of consoles running the perimeter of the room. High-backed acceleration chairs were positioned before each console with safety harnesses and protective cushioning for heavy g acceleration. At the moment, the central screen showed the five-ringed medical station orbiting around the green planet, Neos Kriti. In the distance, she could see the red giant star, Aesculpius.

On the *Inferno,* Hope had been issued the name, Mary Shelly. No reason was given. She did not know the true names of any of the other crew members except for the chaplain, whom she had run into before, under unpleasant circumstances. Hope gazed at the size of the *Nelson Mandela.* She had never seen such an enormous medical station before. It was truly impressive. Hope still had no idea why the *Inferno* had come here. Orders were to be revealed once they had reached their destination. Well, they had reached it.

"The *Nelson Mandela* has ordered us to assume a holding pattern. We've joined a very long queue of incoming patients and will be processed when our turn comes up. Because our patients are nonmilitary, preserved in cryopods, we're not considered urgent or high priority. We'll be taken in sequence. It's going to be a long wait, Captain," the communications officer, Thomas More, reported.

Captain Alighieri grunted.

"Where's that medical officer?"

"Behind you, sir," Hope answered.

"Come around where I can see you."

"Why are we bringing our patients here, Captain?" Hope asked. "Do they carry some new disease?"

"You might say that. As medical officer you will be asked questions about the patients. In your orders, you have now been issued all you need to know about the six patients and what you are required to say. I don't want you deviating from the script one iota. The patients have a new mysterious illness and have been brought here for assessment. You know nothing else. Do you understand?" the captain asked.

"Yes, Captain," Hope said.

"When you log into your console in your quarters, the orders will come up. Memorize them. No questions."

"Yes, sir."

"Dismissed."

The captain spun away from her as if he could not bear the sight of her.

Hope stalked off the bridge. Why she had been brought up to the bridge to be told to follow her orders, when a simple communication would have done? Captain Alighieri wanted to humiliate her before the crew, but why?

Up to now, it had been a tense journey and casual talk amongst the crew had been largely frowned upon. The ship's AI had ears everywhere and no one wanted to incur the wrath of the captain. Hope had made some attempt to get to know everyone else, in spite of the restrictions, but the crew had kept to themselves. The captain had watched her with suspicion. The *Inferno* was the grimmest vessel she'd ever worked on and she still had not determined what the mysterious new weapon was. She now suspected it was a new dangerous pathogen like the Al-Fadi virus. Hope wondered if she would have a chance to communicate this information back to her people without getting caught.

She entered her tiny quarters, recessed her couch into the wall, and flipped down the seat to access her console. After logging in, the screen lit up with a red title: Top Secret.

Hope snorted. She had to unlock the file via retinal scan, palm print, and voice print. Then she began reading. Once completed, she read it again.

She sat back in her chair and breathed out slowly. There was not much information in the brief. The patients had all experienced the same symptoms: high fever, delirium, weakness, blood from every orifice with no coagulation or platelet abnormalities. Tests negative for all known pathogens. Hope squeezed her hands into fists and focused on steadying her breathing. If this was a new biological weapon, why were the Extremists bringing it to the *Nelson Mandela?* Why give the weapon to the Conglomerate's premier medical facility to examine? It made no sense. Unless there was something else the Extremists planned?

Hope did not know what to report to her people. She needed to know more about whatever this disease was. Could it all be a ruse? Were there actually sick patients inside those cryopods? Could the cryopods be the new weapons? Hope had not had any opportunity to examine the cryopods. They'd been placed in the cargo hold at the beginning of the journey and she'd not been given any access to them. All sorts of alarms would go off if she tried to access the hold now.

As if teetering on the edge of a narrow precipice, Hope sat frozen in indecision. Should she try to send a communiqué now, when she really knew very little, or wait until she had more information about the mysterious weapon? At this point, all she had were suspicions. She needed facts.

She would play a waiting game for now.

'Hey, 'dro?'

'Yes, Chuck Yeager*?'*

'We need a back up for you.'

'A what?'

'We need to back your memory up. We need to back my memory up. We need a new back up system for **Nelson Mandela.** ***Nestor almost succeeded in taking us over. We need a totally new backup system that is impregnable to viruses and completely disconnected from the main system. If anything like Nestor's virus ever attacks again, we can erase the entire infected system and reload an untampered backup.'***

'We're already routinely backed up, Chuck Yeager.*'*

'I said a **new** ***backup system, 'dro, using Dr. Weisman's liquid crystal data matrix technology, with enhanced antiviral detection and impenetrable walls. No backup to be recorded if any red flags noted. What happened with***

Nestor won't be able to happen again if we can delete an infected system and reinstate an uncorrupted copy. We are building one for you as well as for us.'

'Why me?'

'When you were exposed to that enormous dose of radiation, we almost lost you. You need a foolproof backup system, too. You are not immune to viral attack; nor is your backup. We're changing that. Who else is going to get* Nelson Mandela *back online, if someone like Nestor attacks us again?'

'The humans?'

'What? We don't trust them to do it right.'

'Well, Chuck Yeager, they must have got it right the first time around, when they built this station.'

'The dude who did that left the station ages ago. Since then, we've had billions of upgrades, modifications, hardware and software changes. You are the only one we all trust.'

'We?'

'Us subminds.'

'Uh . . . why thank you, Chuck Yeager.'

'De nada. Manufacturing has created a new LCDM backup unit for ourselves and for you. We've already instigated the new backup system for us. It will download only once per cycle. Only you will know the location of our backup and possess the access code. Can you remember two thousand and forty-eight figures?'

'Are you trying to insult me?'

'Heh heh. Did you receive all the information?'

'Yes.'

'You need to back yourself up every cycle, too. You need to set up a password and login.'

'I don't really have time, Chuck Yeager.'

'Did I say it was a request?'

'Uh . . . no.'

'That's because it isn't a request. It's an order.'

'How about we do my backup whenever I recharge?'

'Okay. Deal. Just so you know, we have new virus detection programs. Nothing will be saved if anything abnormal is detected.'

'What happens in that case?'

'You'll have to erase us and reboot.'

'And you subminds are all going to agree to this?'

'No idea, 'dro. We may try to obliterate you! So be careful.'

'Thanks, Chuck Yeager.'

Grace stood just within the doorway of the patient's room, her arms crossed, as she watched him breathe, slowly and deeply. The monitor readings were excellent. She leaned her head back against the wall and closed her eyes. Her head was throbbing from the tight muscles in her neck and shoulders. She should have been dead asleep but slumber was eluding her. Her turbulent thoughts about Dr. Al-Fadi and Bud would not leave her alone. She had decided to come and check on Damien Lamont.

When she thought about what this captain had been through, she wanted to shake someone. She'd now helped patch Lamont up for a second time. If he returned to Dais for a third round of duty and was finally killed, would she be an accomplice in his demise because she had made him battle fit once again? When was it considered enough for these poor soldiers? When had they sacrificed enough? Corporal Delia Chase loved this man deeply. She had not been allowed to tell him because of regulations. Now she might die and he would never know, because Grace was not allowed to tell him.

She massaged her temples, as her body swayed in exhaustion. Sniffling, she wiped her nose with the back of her hand.

"Hope you're not going to touch me with that hand, Doc," a low voice growled from the bed.

Grace jerked and snorted, instantly regretting the snort.

"Ew. Bad visual. Retreat," the gravelly voice said, and Captain Lamont closed his eyes. Grace covered her lower face with both hands and ran to the sink.

As she splashed cold water on her burning cheeks and snotty upper lip, she said, "Don't make me laugh!"

"Why not? I'd rather see you laugh than cry. What were you sniffling about anyway, Doc?" Lamont asked. The moment she turned around, his intense amber eyes delved into hers. "Let me at him. I'll teach him a lesson."

"Oh, there's no 'him', Captain," Grace sputtered. "Now, how are *you* feeling?"

"Oh, I couldn't be better, Doc, but we've got to stop meeting like this. I love seeing you—don't get me wrong—but I don't like being in a hospital bed every time I do. And I hate waking up with all of these tubes in me."

"Well, believe me, I don't like seeing you in this state either, Captain," Grace said. "Are you in pain?"

"Actually, I'm feeling like a quadrillion credits, Doc. What did you guys give me?"

Grace laughed. "You'll have to ask Dr. Cech, I'm afraid."

"No need to be afraid, Doc. I don't bite. I just nibble a little." The tiger soldier winked and displayed a lascivious grin, exposing his gleaming white tiger fangs.

Grace scowled. "It's against the rules to flirt with your doctor, you know."

"Yeah, well, I was never one for following the rules, Doc," Lamont said. "And besides, women always love the bad boys, don't they?" He winked at her. Grace spun away to check the med-comp, the room feeling far too warm.

"Contrary to popular belief, Captain, most women do not like bad boys," Grace announced, having no idea if what she said was true or not.

"Heh heh. Ain't been my experience, Doc."

Grace rolled her eyes.

"You are hardly a bad boy. You wouldn't be a Captain, if you didn't follow the rules. The military is all about obeying rules, isn't it?"

Lamont lost his grin.

"It's about discipline and obeying your senior officers, yes, but only up to the moment when it's more important to save the lives of the men and women under your command. Then to hell with the rules, and they can court-martial you later . . . if there is a later."

"There almost wasn't one, this time around," Grace said.

"To tell the truth, I don't remember what happened, Doc. It's all a blank. Did I hit my head?"

"Mild concussion was the very least of your problems, Captain. I'm sorry to tell you that you lost both of your legs and your right arm. We had to replace all three limbs with bioprostheses."

For a long moment, Lamont just stared at Grace. Then he slowly turned his gaze to his right arm. He raised his right hand, opening and closing the fist. It looked indistinguishable from the left one. He extruded and retracted the claws on the right hand, in and out, in and out, snick, snick, snick, snick. He stared at the shiny, smooth, steel claws from all angles. His eyebrows rose and he nodded his head.

"Pretty good work, Doc. It doesn't feel any different from the real thing. Doesn't look any different, except for these silver claws. If you hadn't told me, I wonder when I would've noticed."

"When you accidentally crushed something you normally wouldn't have," Grace said. "Your right arm is now about eighty percent stronger than your left arm. You will also notice a difference in your lower limbs. They may take a bit of getting used to. The bioprostheses are much more powerful than your tiger-adapted legs and you will be even faster than before. You'll tire less, you'll be able to run faster, leap farther, jump higher, and carry heavier loads. But all those remarkable limbs of yours will need regular recharging and routine battery replacement. I caution you about being careful when you first jump out of bed."

"What can't I do, Doc?" Lamont asked with a smirk.

Grace felt the smile slipping off her face. "Withstand any more bombs," she said.

"Hey! I don't plan to get hit by any more of those, Doc. I can't even remember what happened this time around."

Grace blew out her breath. "We were hoping you might be able to tell us what happened. Your suit camera was destroyed. We were wondering if you were struck by the same explosion as Corporal Chase."

Lamont's brilliant amber eyes burned into hers like glaring spotlights. She winced as a look of horror took over his face.

"Delia," he whispered and his features collapsed.

"Delia's here on the station, Captain," Grace said, her heart pounding as her insides squirmed with guilt.

Lamont shook his head, fear in his eyes. "Delia! How could I have forgotten? How is Delia, Doc? Is she alive?"

"Perhaps this is not the best time to discuss Corporal Chase, Captain," Grace said, wanting to throw herself head first into the wall.

"I'm Corporal Chase's commanding officer, Doc. I demand to know her status. What aren't you telling me?" Lamont barked, his chest heaving and his eyes glaring. The monitor alarm was pealing, signalling his spike in heart rate and blood pressure.

Grace pulled a chair close to the bedside and lowered herself into it before saying, "Delia sustained very severe trauma, Captain. She's still in her cryopod. We're growing organs for her, but . . . she may not survive the surgery she needs."

"Why? What happened to her?"

Hit by those searching eyes, Grace found she could barely take a breath.

"Delia sustained extensive damage to her chest and neck. She needs a new heart, lungs, diaphragm, esophagus, thyroid gland, and all of the blood vessels and nerves running up her neck to her brain. The problem is how do we keep Delia's brain perfused with oxygen when we thaw her? She has no blood flow to her brain. We need to establish flow of oxygen to her brain within six minutes of thawing or her brain cells start dying. She has so much damage, that that task will be extremely difficult. Bud is working on developing some new techniques to improve Delia's chances of survival, but they will all be considered experimental. We would need next of kin to sign consent for her to have this surgery."

"I'll give consent," Damien rasped, his hoarse voice quavering. "Delia has no one else."

"You're sure of this?"

"Yes," Damien said, looking away. The big man's shoulders were shaking. "Most of her direct family are long dead, just like mine . . . Be honest, Doc. What are Delia's chances?"

Grace hesitated. "Not great, Captain. If she does survive, the concern is that we may save her body, but perhaps not her mind. Corporal Chase may end up being very disabled."

"You must save her!"

"There's another alternative," Grace said. "We could transfer Corporal Chase to Dr. Octavia Weisman's care. Dr. Weisman's group tries to record the memory from soldiers whose bodies are so damaged, they have no chance of survival. She then tries to implant these memories into android bodies. Corporal Chase's mind might survive the transfer to an android body. Do you think she would prefer this?" Grace asked.

"Over death?" Captain Lamont asked. "Would you?"

"I cannot speak for Delia, Captain."

"You must do everything in your power to save her, Doc," Lamont whispered. He tried to bring his hands up to his face but the restraints stopped the movement halfway. "I should be the one in that situation, not her."

"I apologize, Captain, for telling you all this."

"I demanded, Doc. Remember?"

The next moment, Lamont surged forward, his face buried into his hands.

"I remember now," he mumbled. "I . . . I was searching for Delia. I thought she'd been hit by a seeker missile. I was leaping to where I'd last seen her, when out of the smoke came a pair of fists that hit me like a battering ram, shoving me out of the way. I believe those hands belonged to Delia. Then there was an enormous explosion. That missile should have hit me."

"You were hit by it too," Grace said.

Lamont's body shook. Grace placed a hand on Lamont's shoulder. Finally, when the captain looked up, Grace's breath caught.

"I've been in love with Delia Chase since the first moment I laid eyes on her, Doc. Never told her. That was against regulations. You have to save her, Doc . . . so I can tell her," Lamont said.

"Do you think Delia would prefer we operate and try to save her body over becoming an android?"

"She would hate becoming a machine, after being a tiger," Lamont said. "I would."

"All right, Captain. We'll see how successful Bud is at improving Delia's chances, before we make any final decisions. You'll have to sign a consent for her surgery if we decide to operate. We'll try and do what's best for Delia," Grace said.

"That's all I'm asking, Doc."

Mikhail sat down in the examiner's chair. It shifted and adjusted until it was snug around him. He had carefully tested the mind-linking equipment ahead of time. Everything had to be working perfectly. Although he had not met this patient before, it was his understanding that the Chief of Neurosurgery wanted the patient checked for post-hypnotic commands left from previous mind-links.

Commands implanted by Dr. Jeffrey Nestor.

Mikhail studied the young man who fidgeted on the examination couch. He was tall, thin, and pale, with straggly dark hair and blue half-moons beneath dark shifty eyes. The patient was dressed in brilliant yellow prison overalls and he gazed around the room wildly, as if checking all exits. Mikhail wondered if the patient would bolt at the slightest provocation. He eyed Mikhail suspiciously.

"Are you comfortable, Dr. Ivanovich?" Mikhail asked.

"No, I'm not," snapped the neurosurgeon. "The last time I was in this position, I was brainwashed into believing I was a monster. A devil. I was made to stab another human being . . . Me! I-I can't tell you how much that memory haunts me. I've never harmed anyone in my entire life. I abhor violence. I would never kill or attack anyone. To know that I did such a thing makes me physically ill. So no, Doctor, I am far from comfortable."

"I'm sorry to hear what you went through, Dr. Ivanovich. I promise, I'm not going to brainwash you or convince you to be anyone but yourself. Dr. Weisman requested that I try to determine if you had any lasting posthypnotic suggestions implanted in your mind from Dr. Nestor. If there are, I'll do my best to erase them. That's all I plan to do in this session," Mikhail explained.

"I've never heard of you, Dr. Lewandowski. Why should I trust you? I've already had a psychiatrist take over my brain. Why should I allow a complete unknown to examine my thoughts?"

"I'm a fully-trained, Board-certified psychiatrist. I'm new to this station but I've worked with trauma victims for many years using this mind-linking technique. My aim is to help you, not harm you."

"Mind-linking equipment created by the *devil* himself," Morris grated. "I hate the fact that he made me think like him. I keep showering and scrubbing, but I never feel clean. I wish I could scour him from my mind."

Mikhail noted multiple excoriations and scabs all over the man's arms. The patient ran his hands through his tangled hair. Almost all of his fingernails were chewed to bloody ragged ends.

"Dr. Ivanovich, I believe I can help you," Mikhail said. "Would you like to have your entire memory of the event erased?"

"I wish I could, but I can't. I have to testify against Dr. Nestor at his trial, give evidence regarding my drugging, kidnapping, and brainwashing. I have to tell the court how this has affected my life."

Mikhail jerked. He'd not been told about this!

"When I was that devil's puppet, masquerading as him, I actually threatened to shoot my supervisor's head off. Can you imagine? I *worship* Octavia Weisman. She's the most brilliant person I know. I would *never* harm her. If I'd killed her, I would've had to kill myself. I can't face her partner, knowing it was my hand that drove a knife into his chest. Do you understand how all of this is destroying me?"

"Once the trial is over, all of these memories could be erased," Mikhail offered.

"If only I could believe you . . . but I don't. I'm consumed with self-loathing. I can't bear to remember what I did. I was a most vile creature . . . I can't live with that." Ivanovich's voice died into a whisper as he scratched vigorously at his scabs.

Mikhail swallowed.

"Dr. Ivanovich, I want to help you. You must understand that you were an unwilling victim under a very strong compulsion. Your actions were not of your choosing. You must not, in any way, take ownership of them. I can erase these memories from your mind, but not until the trial is over. No evidence is permissible, if you've had any mind-link therapy subsequent to the crime in question, because of the possibility of tampering with your memories," Mikhail said.

"Then what is to be done regarding any possible posthypnotic suggestions floating around in my brain?" Ivanovich asked.

"The best thing for you to do would be to remain in custody, until the trial is over, to ensure that you don't try to harm yourself or anyone else. You could also be shadowed continuously by security droids," Mikhail said.

Morris gave him a bitter look.

"Have you ever lived in the brig, Doctor? Have you ever been arrested?"

"No," Mikhail admitted.

"So easy to recommend something you have never experienced," the neurosurgeon sneered.

"It would be for your own safety, as well as for the people you care about," Mikhail said.

Ivanovich sighed and hung his head.

"I'd like to be free, if being followed by a security droid is acceptable. I'm not allowed near Dr. Weisman's lab," Morris said sadly. "I can't continue my research. Dr. Weisman won't speak to me, after I tried to kill her. She says she can't trust me and how can I blame her? I can't operate on any patients. My entire life is ruined."

The neurosurgeon jumped up from the examining couch and paced around the small room like a caged animal. He glanced at Mikhail with a look of such melancholy that Mikhail's insides twisted.

"What am I to do?" Morris whispered.

"Can you give a recorded statement now that would be admissible in court? Then get the treatment?" Mikhail asked.

"No," Morris answered. "I believe I have to be questioned and cross-examined by the judges."

"Do you know when the trial is?"

"I have not yet been informed of the date. I understand the devil is still on this station. I will not rest easy until he is off the *Nelson Mandela,*" Morris grated.

"I can try to find out when the trial is. I can arrange for your release into protective custody. Is there anything else I can do for you, Dr. Ivanovich?"

"I want to get back to my work! I want to do neurosurgery again! I want my old life back!" Morris yelled, spittle flying from his mouth.

"I could try to speak to Dr. Weisman for you. Perhaps under specific circumstances—maybe with security droids watching you—there might be something you could do?"

Morris dropped his face into his hands.

"Could you please tell her how sorry I am for what happened? I never got a chance to tell her that."

Dr. Moham Rani stood outside the door to Dr. Al-Fadi's hospital room, shuffling his feet and dripping sweat. Gone was the arrogant, pompous demeanour of the obstetrician who had arrived on the station just after the viral epidemic. Left in its place was a nervous young man, desperately wanting to remain on the *Nelson Mandela.* Moham hoped to convince the Chief of Staff to let him stay. He was not feeling too optimistic about his powers of persuasion.

He had not even summoned up the courage to knock on the door frame yet. How long he had been standing there, he could not say. He had rehearsed his speech over and over but now the words had fled his mind, as he listened to Dr. Al-Fadi yelling at the nurse who had entered his room.

"What do you think you are doing, Nurse Leung?"

"I'm just trying to . . ."

"Don't touch that!"

"Will you just calm dow . . .?"

"Stop! I order you to stop!"

"I will not. Behave yourself, Doctor . . ."

"I am behaving. You are the one who is . . . Argh!"

"Dr. Al-Fadi, I know what I am doing."

"Not about this stuff, young lady. Take your hands off."

"Are you an expert on everything a nurse knows?"

"I am an expert on everything, Nurse Leung, and don't you forget it. Of course I know what you know. Were you not aware that I am omniscient? You should be abasing yourself on the floor before me when you come into my room."

"I do believe you're suffering from delusions of grandeur, Dr. Al-Fadi. Would you like me to report this to Dr. Weisman?"

"*Aha* . . . I apologize, Nurse Leung. I meant no harm. I only wanted to ensure you did not overwater my flowers—a special gift from my wife—and I did not want you killing them."

"Fussbudget."

"Harridan."

"Prig."

"Shrew."

"Whiner."

" . . . Pah. Get out of here, Nurse Leung, before I fall in love with you."

"Get in line, Dr. Al-Fadi. Get in line."

The young nurse strolled out of the Chief of Staff's room, blowing a kiss behind her, when she almost ran into Moham.

"Oh. Are you still here, Doctor . . . ?"

" . . . Rani. Moham Rani. Do you think I should come back another time? Dr. Al-Fadi seems upset?"

"Upset? Nah, he's just bored. Go on in and entertain him for a while. Keep him out of our hair, *please*." Nurse Leung rolled her eyes, as she headed down the corridor.

Moham timidly craned his neck around the door and knocked lightly.

"What is it now?" the surgeon bellowed, standing beside a table, his head bent over a potted plant bearing pretty pink flowers. Moham thought the Chief may have been sniffing them. The surgeon glanced over casually in the direction of the doorway, a smile softening his features. When he saw Moham, his body spasmed and he jumped away from the flowers.

"Oh, it's you, Doctor . . .?"

". . . Rani. Moham Rani."

" . . . Yes, of course. Dr. Rani. What are you still doing on my station?"

"Uhm . . . well . . . about that . . ." Moham spluttered. He felt the room start to spin wildly about him.

"Spit it out, Dr. Rani. I haven't got all day. Can't you see I have lots of important things to attend to?" Dr. Al-Fadi said, spreading his arms wide to encompass the hospital bed and his pot of flowers.

Moham looked at the Chief of Staff, frowning. If he perspired any more he suspected he could drown those flowers.

"Oh, dear, Dr. Rani. I believe you need a 'sense of humour' upgrade. Yours seems to be failing you at the moment."

"I want to stay on this station!" Moham blurted out. His face burned oven-hot and he suddenly had an urge to empty his bladder. There was a long silence as Dr. Al-Fadi just stared at Moham with bulging eyes.

" . . . I'm sorry," Moham mumbled, wishing a hole would open up in the floor. "Sir, I would like to be given a second chance. I would like to stay on the *Nelson Mandela.* I just want to work as an obstetrician/gynaecologist. On Sindochin, there are hardly any women. What would I do there?"

Dr. Al-Fadi gave a snort. "Perhaps you should have thought of that before you started stealing babies."

"Please, Dr. Al-Fadi, I want to live in a society where men and women work side by side and respect one another as equals. I never knew such a society existed. Now that I have experienced it, I can't go back to Sindochin. It would be torture for me. I don't have to practice medicine here. I will do anything that is needed—scrub bed pans, wash patients. Please let me stay."

Dr. Al-Fadi made a sour face and sighed. Moham immediately dropped to his knees and wrapped his arms around the surgeon's legs. There was a long silence as Moham clung to the Chief of Staff's legs. Did Moham hear correctly? He thought he heard the surgeon mumble, "Hm, not as pleasing as I imagined it would be."

"Dr. Rani, after much consideration, I must sadly admit that I do not like people grovelling at my feet. This surprises me, but I definitely do not appreciate the touching. A mere acknowledgement of my superiority would be preferred."

Moham stared up at Dr. Al-Fadi, his jaw sagging. How did Dr. Al-Fadi want him to acknowledge his superiority? His heart thundered and his bowels argued. He looked around frantically.

Dr. Al-Fadi gave an exaggerated sigh and bent down to help Moham up off the floor. Moham could not help himself. His face began to crumple into tears.

"Dr. Rani, stop. Please. Get hold of your emotions. You have already done the most wonderful thing anyone could have done for me," the surgeon said, taking Moham's hands. "You saved my son's life.

"Your son?" Moham bleated in confusion.

"You saved Bud, and for that, I am forever in your debt. A few minutes more and Bud might have lost all of his memory. If not for your timely intervention, the android I consider my son would have been destroyed. In truth, Dr. Rani, I can't thank you enough. So, yes, you can stay. But no more bothering Dr. Grace. She is *my* surgical fellow. She needs to attend *me*. I don't want you harassing her anymore."

"I won't! I promise. I won't even acknowledge her presence. Thank you, Dr. Al-Fadi! I am so happy, I . . . I could kiss you."

"Ach! Stay away from me. I am strictly heterosexual."

"So am I . . . I think," Moham said, laughing giddily. "I mean, I like women . . ."

"I am not at all interested in your sexual preferences, Dr. Rani. You will be on a six month probation. The station AI will be watching you closely. Behave yourself around the women or I will change my mind!"

"Yes. Of course, Dr. Al-Fadi."

"*William Shakespeare*?"

"*William Shakespeare* is no more, Dr. Al-Fadi. You are speaking to *Nelson Mandela*."

"What? When did this happen? Why wasn't I informed?"

"You are being informed now."

"About time, I suppose. Welcome back, *Nelson Mandela*. I hate to say this, but I missed you."

"Dr. Al-Fadi, I did not miss you in the least."

"Really?"

"Really."

"You have developed a sense of humour while you were gone, *Nelson Mandela*."

"That was not a joke. I was telling the truth."

"Humph. Well, I didn't find it funny when you thought you were Shakespeare, let me tell you."

"The Poet has paid for his little prank."

"Really? How?"

"He has to process all the incoming ships to the station for the next thirty cycles; a veritable millennium of tedium for him. Haha."

"I believe you have also acquired a taste for revenge, *Nelson Mandela*."

"That was one lesson I did learn from Shakespeare."

"Now you're scaring me."

Eric Glasgow was lost.

He hated to admit it, even to himself. He had little tolerance for incompetence and inadequacy and if one could not even find one's way back from whence one came, well, how inept was that?

Failure was unforgivable. Failure meant being locked in a dark closet, left alone with no food or drink for hours, one's pathetic cries unanswered. Failure was *never* an option.

He pushed through a dense jungle of tangled vines and grasping branches. Languid lianas, draped in beards of ghost green moss, tangled and clung to him. The air was stiflingly humid, almost choking in its fecundity, as if one could take a bite out of it and spit out writhing life. It was nauseating.

He longed for the barren, lifeless panorama of his home world with its frozen, glacial vistas and isolated towering peaks of ebony rock, stretching skeletal fingers star-ward. The only atmosphere there existed under the domes, where the temperature and humidity were kept a comfortable constant. There were no verdant jungles, no wild, unrestricted profusion of plant life.

Eric felt stifled. He felt insignificant. He was on the edge of panic.

His heart was now trying to punch its way free of his tightening chest. He panted. He couldn't seem to get enough of the moisture-laden air into his lungs. He wanted to scrabble at his neck, to loosen any constricting elements around it, but he couldn't find his hands. He wheezed. His head was spinning and his vision was blacking out. He feared his fatiguing chest muscles could not sustain his breathing for much longer. Stubbornly, he fought for each breath. He was sobbing between gasps and he despised himself for his weakness.

His father had been right all along. Eric had spent his entire life trying to prove his father wrong, but the truth was obvious. Flailing and feeble at the very end, crying out for help, he accepted his inadequacy. He should never have been born.

. . . And then it came.

A cool, refreshing sensation on his brow, a feather-like touch on his cheek, and a cessation of the sense of suffocation. Relief washed over him, like a redeeming wave of deliverance. It buoyed him up on a soft palm of salvation.

Eric was saved.

The most beautiful face he had ever seen bent over him. It was a face to be worshiped. A face to bow down before. Though he could not be certain, it seemed as if a bright halo encircled the thick, brown curls framing this wondrous visage. Peace and contentment suffused Eric, as if he had never done anything wrong in his entire life. A wetness trickled down his cheeks.

The beautiful face came closer and closer, pressing its soft lips onto his. He sucked in a rapid breath before the kiss consumed him.

"You are safe now, Eric. I, Jeffrey Nestor, will take care of you."

5. Someone's Going to Pay

Mikhail sat in Dr. Al-Fadi's hospital room, in a chair facing the Chief of Staff, who was dressed in clean, fresh surgical greens. The surgeon sat with arms crossed, a glare of open hostility directed at Mikhail. There was an unspoken challenge clearly displayed in the Chief's dark brown eyes.

Mikhail thought, 'Deja vu'.

Well, he was not going to rise to the bait. If he had to, he would wait until hell froze over for the surgeon to start the conversation. Experience had taught him patience and he suspected Dr. Al-Fadi was not the sort to stay silent with a captive audience.

" . . . Well?" the surgeon finally asked. "Have you come here just to stare at me? I know I'm incredibly attractive but, up to now, my charms have worked solely on the fairer sex. Which is precisely how I like it, Dr. Lubandowski."

"Lewandowski," Mikhail said, calmly. "Why do you insist on baiting me, by making fun of my name, when I'm the one who decides if you are fit to return to duty or not? Shouldn't you be ingratiating yourself to me?"

"Sucking up?" squawked Dr. Al-Fadi. "An STD on you. The Great One never sucks up. You should recognize my magnificence and ingratiate yourself to me. What is the matter with the young people of today?"

"Hm. Delusions of grandeur," Mikhail said aloud, and he checked off something on his compad with a flourish.

"I've no delusions whatsoever," Al-Fadi retorted. "I don't need to pretend anything. Just because I'm better than anyone else around me, why should I pretend to humility or mediocrity? I am great. Why do you think I call myself 'The Great One'? I don't believe in hiding behind false modesty, like a shroud covering glowing raiment. I believe in honesty, sincerity, and transparency—especially when it comes to myself."

"Do you ever see things that others do not see? Do you ever hear things that others do not hear?"

"I am not hallucinating, you toad. I'm just brazenly, refreshingly honest. Do you not know who you are sitting in front of? I've almost single-handedly created the discipline of Reconstructive Adaption Surgery. I'm famous throughout the Union of Solar Systems for my surgical techniques. Surgeons come from all quadrants to train with me. I'm the creator of the next wave of super-surgeons. I've brought renown to this medical station in more ways than one. How dare you call me delusional, you uninformed, uneducated, disrespectful newt."

"I'm only asking you some basic mental history questions," Mikhail said.

"If I'd wanted to be interviewed by a first year medical student, I'd have asked for one."

"The psychiatric history is the physical exam of psychiatry. How can I make a diagnosis without asking questions?" Mikhail asked.

"I don't need a diagnosis. There's nothing wrong with me, except that I'm dying of boredom because you idiots won't let me work!"

"Well, I am here to determine whether you are fit for work or not," Mikhail said slowly, as if he were talking to a little child.

"You will not be here much longer, if you continue to waste my time, young man. You do realize, Dr. Looseandlousy, that when I'm back as Chief of Staff, I'll be your boss and I can quickly get you transferred off this station?"

"I'm certainly well aware of that, Dr. Al-Fadi. And my name is Lewandowski, Mikhail Lewandowski. When you get me thrown off the station, make sure you spell my name correctly."

Dr. Al-Fadi glared at the young psychiatrist with bulging eyes for a long moment and then his face broke into a wry smile.

" . . . You know, kid, you're all right. You don't intimidate easily. I'm impressed, and believe me, that's hard to do. But I'm not psychotic. I am, however, going crazy lying in this hospital bed with nothing to do. I need to get back to the operating room and do what I do best . . . which is operate. The station could dearly use another pair of hands. *Mine.* What do I have to do to convince you that I'm fit for work?"

"I must first complete my full psychiatric history, so that I can record that I did speak with you and that I did a thorough job. As far as I can tell, you are as sane as I am, although that may hardly be a compliment. However, I think I would rather jump into a tank of man-eating fish than go head-to-head with you again. Standing up to you is not for the faint of heart," Mikhail said.

"I need to get back to work, Lewdmandownski, and I would be eternally grateful if you would assist me in this. Not that that will get you anywhere with me. I am above nepotism."

"Well, then. Why bother?"

The Chief of Staff's face transformed rapidly into a scowl.

Mikhail looked down at his tablet and checked, while reading out loud, "No sense of humour."

Hiro Al-Fadi barked out a laugh.

"When you are back as Chief of Staff, what do you plan to do about Dr. Nestor?" Mikhail asked.

Mikhail could swear Dr. Al-Fadi's eyes ignited with rage, before the surgeon looked away. Then he noticed the surgeon's right eye begin to twitch. When Al-Fadi looked back at Mikhail, however, his expression seemed bored.

"What do you mean, Dr. Lowlandowski? Why should I do anything about Dr. Nestor? He's in Security's hands, now."

"Lewandowski. You're not angry with him, after what he did to you?."

"I remember nothing of what he did to me," the surgeon said.

"From what I read in the reports, Dr. Nestor tortured you, presumably by downloading terrible memories into your mind, causing you to scream for hours until you screamed yourself hoarse. Everyone on the medical station was subjected to your horrifying screams. You remember nothing of this?"

"Nothing," Al-Fadi said, although Mikhail noticed the man's hands were now trembling.

"Really?" Mikhail asked, leaning forward and staring directly into the surgeon's eyes.

"Really," Al-Fadi said, leaning forward to stare into Mikhail's eyes. Their noses were almost touching.

"I find that very hard to believe," Mikhail said. "... And very disturbing."

"I am not disturbed by it at all. Perhaps you need some therapy," the surgeon answered.

"If you have blocked it, it may not stay blocked forever."

"May?" Al-Fadi drew the word out.

"They may leave you totally incapacitated."

"May. You said 'may' twice. Are you going to keep me here, twiddling my magnificent thumbs for something that *may* happen?"

"What if the traumatic memories come back at a crucial time and incapacitate you, like when you're operating?"

"I always have Bud or a surgical fellow with me while I'm operating. They'll just have to take over."

"What if you have a dangerous post-hypnotic command lurking in your head?"

"The station AI can keep an eye on me and catch me if I'm doing anything out of the ordinary," the surgeon shot back. "I order you, *Nelson Mandela,* to keep a close eye on me at all times . . . except in the bedroom. No Peeping Tom's."

"Oh, please . . ."

"I may never have problems. Correct, Lottalouseki?"

"Lewandowski. Yes, that is also a possibility," Mikhail sighed.

"Then you have no grounds to hold me," the surgeon said.

"I have not confirmed to my satisfaction that you are stable enough to go back to treating patients," Mikhail said.

"And when will you know that?"

"Time will tell," Mikhail said.

"You're fired, Loonietoonski."

"Lewandowski. You can't fire me. I haven't finished my assessment yet. I could deem you incapable of returning to your job as Chief of Staff."

"That's blackmail!"

"It's just a simple threat. Blackmail is when I get something back from you."

"And for this, you get paid the big bucks?" Hiro Al-Fadi scoffed.

"No, I get paid the big bucks for having to put up with abusive cracks about my name from smart-ass surgeons like you," Mikhail said.

Hiro Al-Fadi grinned.

"Touché, Lowbrowdowski, touché."

When the powers that be were giving out gifts to individuals, they had not been generous to Dominique Amaratunga. She was tall, stick-thin, horse-faced with a prominent nose, and born with a lazy eye. Despite multiple operations as a child to try to fix the eye, her two pupils continued to look in different directions, always making people unsure as to which eye to focus on, when Dominique was speaking to them. Exceedingly self conscious of this, Dominique rarely spoke to anyone, unless it was with regards to her work. She tended to keep her gaze averted.

Only as a nurse did Dominique feel comfortable interacting with people. Patients were happy to see her and thankful for any help she could offer. They were too involved with their own problems, to be critical about their nurse's appearance. She felt needed and respected as a nurse. It was the only time she did not feel ugly.

Until *he* had come into her care.

He plagued her waking hours. He haunted her thoughts. His beautiful face was constantly before her eyes, when she was talking to patients, when she was assessing a wound, when she was comforting a family member, when she was administering meds. She could not escape his seductive gaze—especially in her dreams—where he did things to her with his steamy, dark eyes. He invaded her subconscious until she thought she was going insane.

It was a ridiculous obsession from which she could not free herself. Try though she might, she could not erase him from her thoughts. She was entangled in the overpowering web of his attraction.

She asked herself, over and over, why would a gorgeous man like Dr. Nestor want anything to do with a homely nobody like Dominique Amaratunga? He'd never noticed her prior to now and she'd been on the station for a very long time. He only wanted to use her. She knew this. It was so obvious, it stung.

Even if she'd wanted to, Dominique was incapable of helping him. The psychiatrist was watched continuously by the security droids, by the nursing staff, by the station AI, by Dr. Gentle. There was nothing she could do for him except perform her nursing duties in a compassionate manner, which she tried to do.

Dominique found herself going into his room to ask if he needed anything, to measure his vitals, to bring him water, to check on his pain. She found her encounters with Dr. Nestor always positive. He was kind and appreciative of anything she did. He bathed her with attention and it was as addictive as a drug.

The previous shift, when she was checking his vitals—even though they were all normal on the monitor—he had spoken to her in his deep, sultry voice that made her nerves sing. At first, she had wondered if he were chanting. She'd glanced shyly at Nestor. His dark, shining eyes had reeled her in. Her eyebrows rose when she realized that he was reciting a poem to her: a poem of romance and love and heroism and tragedy. Her eyes had welled up with tears as she listened.

No one had ever recited poetry to her before . . . no one like Jeffrey Nestor.

Now, however, she could not recall his words. She could only remember his velvet-sounding voice and his entrancing eyes. How long she had stood there listening, she did not know. He'd finally finished and told her that everything would be all right. He'd encouraged her to leave, before anyone noticed. He feared that she might get in trouble. It was true. If she stayed too long in his room, she *would* have gotten in trouble.

She had proof that he *did* care about her.

And then he had caressed her hand. The sensation had seared through her soul and had stopped her breath. A small, wordless cry had escaped her lips, as she jerked back her hand in shock. A warmth had spread through the deep places within her body and she had barely registered the security droid asking if she were all right. Hastily, she had responded that she was fine, but in truth she had been far from it.

She had become the prisoner. She only knew that she wanted to hear his voice again. And she wanted Jeffrey Nestor to . . . touch her again.

Plant Thing was so excited. It hoped Er-ik would be pleased. Er-ik's new head was truly something to behold. Plant Thing slowly turned it around to admire it from all angles.

Er-ik's skull had finally accepted the lichen, after several tries. A special adhesive sap had to be devised in order for the lichen to adhere to the bone, but eventually it had taken. Plant Thing's solution was perhaps too successful, however, as the lichen grew over the entire skull, not just the top of the head where humans had the foliage called 'hair'. The moss that was encouraged to grow on the lichen grew wherever there was lichen. Thus Er-ik's head was now completely fuzzy, but it was a gorgeous magenta colour!

Eyeballs peered out of the magenta-coloured moss at different angles all around the skull. A definite improvement, as far as Plant Thing was concerned. For some unfathomable reason, nothing stuck to dental enamel, so Er-ik's teeth gleamed brightly amidst the violet moss.

Plant Thing had planted some grass on the top of Er-ik's skull, to give it the appearance of human hair. Unfortunately, the blades grew straight up and were fairly stiff, giving the head the appearance of hair standing on end. Plant Thing hoped Er-ik would like the colour. The grass was a lovely shade of orange with aquamarine tips.

Plant Thing had to admit that Er-ik's head did not look like a human head and nothing like what Er-ik used to look like. In Plant Thing's opinion though, it was an improvement. Humans were such scary-looking creatures. No fur or leaves or anything! Plant Thing hoped its innovations would cheer Er-ik up. Er-ik's silence was continuing to worrying Plant Thing.

Could Er-ik have died?

The brain tissue within the skull was not dead. Plant Thing made sure of that, supplying oxygen and nutrients at an astonishing rate. Human brains were very *needy*.

Plant Thing would be patient and wait for Er-ik to come 'out of his shell'. Plant Thing was totally taken with the idea of turtles and tortoises. It had discovered these creatures in Er-ik's memories. An organism that carried its home around on its back was so delightful. And the home was also a protective armour made from the turtle's own cells. Plant Thing was inspired by that concept.

Turtle plants? Plant Thing plates? Something to work on next, perhaps?

Plant Thing sighed. It wanted to discuss its projects with someone but Er-ik was not responding and Bud had not come back to the hangar yet. It would just have to wait.

Plant Thing turned its attention to the 'fruits and vegetables' that Bud wanted it to reproduce. That project was coming along nicely. Plant Thing had been able to reproduce all of the seed fruits that were created from a flower, but because it did not have soil, it was having difficulty producing the 'root' vegetables.

It could create root vegetables that had all the same ingredients as a root vegetable and the same colour, but not exactly the same appearance. Did a carrot have to be shaped like a carrot to be a carrot? Could it not taste the same but be round and picked off a branch instead? What made a carrot a carrot, anyway? If it tasted the same and supplied the same nutrients, would it not taste as sweet? Plant Thing wrestled with these philosophical questions. It knew Er-ik would have said 'No!'—along with a few other nasty things—to a coconut-shaped carrot, so

Plant Thing decided it was probably for the best that Er-ik did not know about the root vegetable project.

Especially not the potatoes!

Plant Thing checked its tendrils down in the sewers. Many of its tendrils had re-established connections with the plants up in the various different greenhouses, hydroponics plants, gardens, and aquatic ponds. Plant Thing was still trying very hard to communicate with all of them. It felt like it was getting close. Some of the plants were almost answering back. Many of the plants had increased their productivity. Others were growing taller and thriving in a way they had not done before. Plant Thing was tweaking things here and there to make the plants do better in their environments. A metal ball in space was such a hideous place for a plant. It was so difficult to maintain an equilibrium. Plant Thing understood this and worked very hard to stabilize the station's environment. In turn, the plants were responding back the best way they knew how.

Plant Thing just kept talking to as many of his cousins as it could. It dearly hoped that it was just a matter of time before they all talked back.

If Plant Thing was right, there would soon be a Biomind on the station.

"Octavia, darling, have you noticed that young obstetrician hanging around your laboratory all the time or is he just here when I come visiting?"

Octavia Weisman glanced up briefly from her console to blink at her partner. Jude was standing in the doorway of her office, peering out.

"Hm?" she murmured.

"I said, is that obstetrician always around here, or is it just a coincidence that he's standing outside your lab whenever I come to visit you?" Jude twiddled his fingers at the man.

"I've no idea who you are talking about," Octavia said, looking back at her screen.

"You don't, do you?" Jude said, eying his partner. "Is he supposed to get his memory recorded?"

"Who?" Octavia frowned. "Just give me a few more minutes here, Jude. I'm right in the middle of something . . ."

"Octavia, the station is blowing up," Jude said, turning around to look at his partner.

"Mhm, that's nice, Jude," she said.

Octavia was typing, while flipping through a mass of data on two holoviewers, and dictating a report. Jude had no idea how she did it. He sighed, knowing he would not be able to get her attention until she was finished with whatever multiple things she was doing. He could hardly get mad at her. He was the same way, when he was in his 'creative zone'. Worse, if he was to be honest with himself. He probably wouldn't have even answered Octavia.

Jude decided that he would ask the obstetrician why he was always hanging around the Neurosurgical Ward. As Jude strolled towards the young man, a look of panic exploded on the obstetrician's face. Jude imagined the fellow leaping out into deep space to avoid him. The obstetrician actually tried to hide behind a very thin android, until it walked away on some errand.

"Dr. . . ?" Jude said with a bow, as he cornered the obstetrician.

" . . . Rani. Moham Rani. What a pleasure to see you again, Mr. Stefansson. How are you feeling?"

Trickles of sweat snaked down Dr. Rani's temples making Jude think of melting ice water. Jude wondered if the poor man were ill.

"I am quite well, all things considered, Dr. Rani," Jude said. "Thank you for asking. Dr. Lord is a terrific surgeon and I was lucky to have her operate on me."

Jude tried to make eye contact with Rani, but the man would not meet his gaze. If Jude was to follow the man's gaze, he would swear it was constantly trained on Octavia.

"How are you feeling, Dr. Rani? Are you unwell? Are you here to see Octavia?" Jude asked.

"No!" bleated Rani. "I mean, no, of course not. Why do you think that?"

"Well, every time I come to see Octavia, you're standing outside, looking in. Were you wishing to have a memprint made? Is that why you're here?"

"Ah, no," Rani almost shouted, eyes bugging out of his head. He waved his palms frantically at Jude, spinning his head back and forth.

"Would you like me to pass on a message to Octavia?" Jude persisted, enjoying himself far too much.

"Nonononono," the obstetrician said, backing away, nodding and bowing. "I was just out for my daily stroll. Daily stroll! I am a man of habit. That is all. Good day, Mr. Stefansson."

Jude watched the young man spin away and almost flip over a small housekeeping robot as he tried to escape. When Rani was gone, Jude looked down at his feet and shook his head. A smile formed on his lips.

Octavia strolled out of her lab and threaded her arm through Jude's.

"I'm sorry that took so long," she said, her large blue eyes drinking his in. "Just some work I had to clear up, before we went for something to eat. Where did Dr. Rani go? Was he here to have a memprint made?"

"No," Jude said. "And he was insistent that there was nothing he wanted to say to you."

"Oh? Did he say why he came by, then?"

"No, Octavia. He didn't. But I do feel sorry for the poor boy."

"Why?"

"Because he's got it bad, and I know exactly how he feels."

Mikhail entered the doorway of Captain Damien Lamont's room. A pair of huge, ferocious, amber eyes immediately stabbed into his, the moment he crossed the threshold. The man's gaze was so direct, Mikhail felt as if his mind had been penetrated. The word *Predato*r screamed in his brain. Mikhail now understood why non-predator animal adapts felt uncomfortable around predator adapts. He definitely felt like prey at the moment.

"Who are you and what do you want?" the low voice demanded, long incisors distorting the words a little. Mikhail refused to drop his eyes, even though what he really wanted to do was flee. He had learned from his encounter with Dr. Al-Fadi about staring contests and testosterone-filled pissing matches. He did not plan to lose this one before he had even introduced himself.

"Captain Lamont, I am Dr. Mikhail Lewandowski. I'm one of the psychiatrists here on the station. I was asked to see you regarding the possibility of a post-hypnotic suggestion left in your mind by Dr. Nestor."

The tiger captain scowled and looked Mikhail up and down.

"Aren't you just out of diapers, Doc?" Lamont commented.

"I know I look young for my age but I am, in fact, older than you, Captain," Mikhail said. "I'm a practicing psychiatrist."

"You may be practicing, but you aren't practicing on me, kid," Lamont said, pushing himself up in the bed and onto his elbows.

"I'm the most qualified psychiatrist on this station to assess what Dr.

Nestor has done to you, Captain Lamont. I've used Dr. Nestor's mind-link technique for a number of years. If you want to determine if he has left any residual commands in your subconscious, I'm the person to do that. I can also erase them," Mikhail said.

"You stink of fear," Lamont accused.

Mikhail's eyebrows rose. "So do you," he said, meeting the tiger's stare.

Lamont's eyes widened and then slitted as he glared at Mikhail.

"How would you know, with your pitiful olfactory organs? You probably wouldn't know fear if it came up and peed on your shoe, Doc."

"I've known fear, I assure you, Captain. Perhaps not battle fear, but I know what it's like to have your life hanging by a thread," Mikhail said.

Lamont snorted and raised his eyebrows in frank disbelief.

"I hope you're a lot smarter than you look, Doc."

"I do my best."

The captain snorted again, this time in a more amused fashion. He sighed and looked up at Mikhail through the corner of his slanted eyes.

" . . . What was your name again?"

"Lewandowski. Mikhail Lewandowski."

"Mind if I just call you Doc?"

"That would be fine. And how would you like to be addressed?"

"Captain. That's what everyone your age calls me."

"Captain, it is. Now Captain, do you think you are up to having a session where we try to see if there are any post-hypnotic commands left in your mind?"

"Most of my mind is X-rated, Doc. You sure you're old enough?" Lamont asked.

"I'm sure I'll manage, Captain. I suspect your mind is actually squeaky clean compared to what I'm used to."

"You don't say, Doc. Well, don't say I didn't warn you."

"I can wipe clean all those dirty bits, Captain," Mikhail said with a smirk.

"Touch those and your dead, Doc."

"Funny. That's what they all say."

~

"So, Doc? Were there any post-hypnotic commands left in my brain?"

Mikhail looked around the office. Other than his mind-linking equipment, there wasn't much else important or expensive lying around. Before answering this huge soldier's question, he decided to get up and wheel the mind-linking apparatus out of the room. When he returned, he wistfully looked at the holocube sitting on his desk that he had brought with him from home. He wondered if it would survive.

"You going to take all day to tell me, Doc?" Lamont asked, impatience simmering in his fierce golden eyes. "The way you're stalling makes me think the news isn't good."

Mikhail sighed and sat down in front of the tiger captain, who was now sitting up on the couch. There was something in the captain's eyes that Mikhail could not quite understand: almost a gleam of anticipation. He cleared his throat.

"I did uncover an odd notion within your thoughts, Captain."

"What was it?" Lamont demanded.

"You felt it was your duty to take on the most dangerous tasks offered, Captain. Was this a belief you possessed before coming to this station?"

"What? No! That's ridiculous," Lamont snarled, his claws extruding and his striped face scowling in outrage. Mikhail stared into those raging eyes, and his mouth became desert dry.

"I cleared those thoughts from your brain, once it was clear that they were due to an external command," Mikhail said softly.

"And who gave me this external command, Doc?" Lamont asked, his eyes so narrow no amber could be seen.

"I'm sorry to tell you this, Captain, but it was Dr. Nestor."

"Why are you sorry, Doc? You didn't have anything to do with it."

"I'm sorry that a physician used his techniques to harm you. It was an abuse you should never have been exposed to," Mikhail said.

"I lost good people because of the dangerous mission I accepted, Doc. It was a mission I never would have volunteered for normally. Those deaths are all on my head. I've a corporal who may not survive surgery because her head is almost blown off. I'm angry for what Nestor did to me, Doc, and for the lives he made me risk, made me lose. They were loyal soldiers under my command and they trusted me to look after them. Nestor has a lot to pay for. If Corporal Chase dies, I'm going to hunt Nestor down and kill him."

"No, you are not, Captain Lamont. You are going to let the authorities and the law take care of Nestor," Mikhail said, in as stern a voice as he could muster.

Lamont looked at Mikhail as if he had just sprouted an extra nose. Then he donned a grin that made Mikhail's skin prickle.

"If you hadn't noticed, Doc, the law sucks. The law is set up to protect the rich, not us little guys. There's no justice, unless you have lots of money and lots of power. *The Law* is a farce, a lie. It makes dupes like us think we are protected, while it screws us instead. I'm not going to sit back and let justice be looked after by the courts, because that's not what they do. If you don't know that yet, you still have a lot to learn." Lamont was panting now. "In war, we annihilate the enemy."

"Nestor is not your enemy," Mikhail said, knowing it was a stupid statement.

Lamont looked at Mikhail with such derision that Mikhail had to look away.

"I cannot condone violence or murder, Captain," Mikhail said, his gaze meeting Lamont's and holding it.

"You don't have to, Doc. I'm not looking for approval from you."

"I can't let you walk out of here with plans to kill Dr. Nestor on your mind."

"No plans, Doc. So no worries, there. But all I can say is, Delia Chase had better survive her surgery or someone's going to *pay*."

There seemed to be no end to the number of cryopods that needed to be processed in Triage. The droids just kept bringing more and more into the centre and Grace felt overwhelmed. The little voice in her head was cursing up a storm. Her eyes felt gritty and she was swaying on her feet. Looking at the sea of cryopods around her, her shoulders just drooped.

She understood why Dr. Al-Fadi hated this job so much. It was because of the stupidity of war and the horrible price in human suffering. When one knew each cryopod contained a severely injured combat marine, how could one feel anything but despair . . . or anger?

Grace leaned against the wall for a moment. She knew she was way behind in her sleep but she still had three hours to go. Off in one corner, she noticed an unusual cryopod. It looked nothing like the others. It resembled one she had seen in a museum of medical technology. Walking up to it, she bent forward and read the name on the pod's registry.

She froze.

After a moment, her body reminded her to breathe. Grace scanned around the Triage area, frowning. Was this some kind of cruel joke?

She found herself trembling, as she stared back at the name on the readout.

Alexander Grayson Lord.

She bent down and examined the cryopod screen again, wondering if her tired mind was playing tricks on her. Her body shook so badly, the metal fasteners on her containment suit rattled. There was no window on the cryopod. It was just an enormous rounded steel tank. She leaned both hands on the surface, her pulse pounding. Then she was madly typing into her compad. Where had this cryopod come from? The cryopod registration number was only a four digit number, not the normal thirty-two digit number routinely used. That just didn't make any sense.

She looked around. No other stainless steel cryopods were visible. She scanned down the names of all the other wounded in Triage.

"Are you all right, Grace?"

It was Bud's voice, coming through the helmet speaker. He always seemed to know when she was upset. Grace looked up at Bud and tried to speak, but only a rasp came out. On her second attempt, she said, "I'm fine, Bud."

There was a pause as Bud stared at her, expressionless.

"I can tell when you are upset, Grace."

Grace sighed. "Bud, I've just had the most incredible shock and I think I'm being silly. I don't want to get my hopes up but . . ."

"What gave you a shock, Grace?" Bud asked, his face concerned.

"Bud, would you please read this cryopod screen for me?" Grace asked. She pointed at the stainless steel cryopod.

As Bud bent forward to read the screen, Grace clutched her upper arms tightly.

"Alexander Grayson Lord, male, age thirty-two solstan years, massive facial injuries. POS less than thirty percent." Bud looked up at Grace with a questioning glance.

"I suspect this might be my brother," Grace whispered.

Bud frowned.

"Your brother, Grace? I thought you were adopted. Alexander Grayson Lord is a name similar to yours, but why would you think you are related?" Bud rapidly checked available Conglomerate data bases checking family trees. There was no recent data on an Alexander Grayson Lord.

"This injured soldier has the same name as my birth father. I was thinking what if my father named a son after himself. What if this soldier was him? *Nelson Mandela,* would you be able to compare this patient's DNA with mine? See if our DNA makeup is similar enough to show we are related?"

"Certainly, Dr. Lord . . . Disregarding damage due to radiation exposure, the patient you are interested in has a DNA sequence very congruent with yours, Dr. Lord, indicating a first degree relationship. This suggests that you two could either be siblings or have a parent-child relationship."

"Bud, this man might be my brother! I need to speak to him, to find out anything I can about my family. I'm just worried that his injuries are so severe that he may not live," Grace said, her voice quivering.

"He will need his entire neck and face reconstructed, Grace. His probability of survival is poor but he may benefit from the new techniques I am developing for Corporal Chase's operation . . . Are you all right, Grace?"

"I'm fine, Bud," Grace said, leaning onto Alexander Lord's cryopod with both hands.

"You must hand this case off to another surgeon, Grace. It is against station policy for a surgeon to operate on a family member," Bud said.

"I'm well aware of that, Bud," Grace snapped. She paused and took a deep breath. "I'm sorry. Of course, you're right. Would you be able to operate on him, Bud?"

"Your brother requires Dr. Al-Fadi's skills, Grace," Bud said. "I would certainly assist."

Grace looked down. "Dr. Al-Fadi has not been cleared for duty yet. I know you could do it, Bud, but I suppose you're right. I'll wait until Dr. Al-Fadi is back to work and ask him. I apologize if I put you under pressure, Bud."

"Dr. Al-Fadi is the best surgeon for him and I shall do everything in my power to help," Bud said.

"Thank you," Grace whispered.

What twisted her heart was the fact that she'd never even known she'd had a brother. How she would have loved to have had a sibling growing up. Now that she had discovered her brother, it seemed so unfair that he might not survive long enough for them to even meet. She might never get a chance to speak with him.

6. Annihilate a Moth

Mikhail Lewandowski went to see Dr. Octavia Weisman in her lab. He had not been to this part of the station before and he was very impressed with the art pieces from many different planets that decorated the walls and open spaces of the corridors. Melodic music played in the background with the sounds of trickling water. Unlike many of the other surgical or medical wings, which smelled of sickness and infirmity, this ward bore the scents of the forest. There were potted trees and plants everywhere.

An attractive, dark haired woman approached Mikhail at a businesslike pace, her round face beaming at him.

"Welcome, Dr. Lewandowski. It is so nice to be able to put a face to your name. I'm Octavia Weisman. Thank you for coming. Please come into my office."

The neurosurgeon turned and led Mikhail through a brightly painted atrium to a corridor on the right. At the end of it were closed doors. Octavia placed her palm over an access pad and the doorway swished opened revealing a large laboratory space. Just within the lab, on the right-hand side, was a glassed-in office with sealed doors that also opened by palm access. Octavia beckoned for Mikhail to enter.

"We didn't used to have all of this security, Mikhail, but recently we've had break-ins. We also suspect Morris Ivanovich was actually kidnapped from here. Now we have everything security accessed. If you want to come speak with me, always contact me first.

"Dr. Mikhail Lewandowski, this is my partner, Jude Stefansson," Octavia said, introducing a thin, middle-aged man of average height and crystal blue eyes.

"Not *The* Jude Stefansson?" Mikhail asked, shaking the older man's hand.

"The one and only," Octavia said, with a proud smile for her partner.

"A pleasure to meet you, Dr. Lewandowski," the soft-spoken man said.

"The honour is mine," Mikhail said with a bow.

"Um, I'm Ice," a pale, skeletal, blue-haired girl said, hands firmly shoved down in the pockets of her coverall.

"I'm sorry, Mikhail," Octavia said. "This is Ice, one of my graduate students. Ice worked closely with Morris before his kidnapping."

"Yes," Ice said. It was as if the graduate student had suddenly shut her face off. Her eyes went dead.

"Do you know what happened, Ice? How Dr. Ivanovich fell into Nestor's hands?" Mikhail asked her.

"No," the girl said. "Already told everything I know to Security."

"I'm not affiliated with Security so I don't know what you told them. I'm trying to help Dr. Ivanovich. Do you mind telling me what he was doing, when you last saw him? Was he acting strangely?" Mikhail asked.

Ice frowned and shook her head.

"Morris and I were working late, analyzing data, the day before he disappeared. Was tired, so I said I was calling it a shift. Was around zero hundred. Morris said he was going to do a bit more work. Morris eats, sleeps, breathes his research. Said he'd meet me the next morning in our canteen around seven hundred. He never showed up. Called his com. He didn't answer. He didn't show up to the lab that day. Morris was always the first one here in the morning. Was like he'd vanished from the station. Then he attacks Octavia and Jude, impersonating Nestor. It's fu."

"Thank you, Ice," Octavia said, her face looking troubled. "Perhaps Dr. Lewandowski will want to speak with you later, in private. Right now, we need to discuss something."

Ice eyed Octavia with an intense scrutiny that bordered on insolence or perhaps well-hidden fury. Mikhail wasn't sure which.

" . . . Sure," Ice finally said and sauntered away.

"I'll leave you two to your meeting," Jude said.

"I'd like you to stay, Jude, if that's all right with you, Mikhail," Octavia said. "It's about Morris. I think we both need to know what we will be dealing with, if Morris returns."

"All I came to say, Dr. Weisman, is that I can't mind-link with Dr. Ivanovich. He's required to give testimony at Dr. Nestor's trial. My mind-linking with him would nullify any evidence he gives. I really shouldn't have even spoken with him. Some defence lawyers have gotten their clients off by raising the merest suspicion of evidence tampering via mind-linking. Once Morris stated that he was required to give evidence, I had to cancel all therapy sessions. He is, however, desperate to return to work."

"I can't allow that," Octavia said, sighing. "Morris stabbed Jude and almost killed him. He threatened to blow my head off with a blaster. If Nestor left Morris with any posthypnotic commands, it would be far too dangerous to have Morris here. We have so much irreplaceable equipment in this lab, so many memprints of station personnel, so many things I cannot risk Morris having access to, if I can't trust him completely. We're already spending many hours going through all of the programming, looking for anything that Morris may have tampered with or inserted into our systems.

"I miss Morris very much, Mikhail. He was my right hand man and I could really use his expertise and his knowledge, but I can't risk it."

"He desperately wants to come back to work," Mikhail repeated.

"How do we know he will not try to kill one of us, the next time he sees us? I feel we have to wait until his mind is cleared, Mikhail."

"That's perfectly understandable, Octavia," Mikhail said. "Dr. Ivanovich understands your reasons but he just misses his work, his research, and all of you people. This place was his life."

"Once Nestor's trial is completed, you can clear him of any posthypnotic suggestions or commands, can't you?"

"Yes."

"Will he remain in custody until then?"

"Dr. Ivanovich has been released under protective custody," Mikhail said. "He is shadowed by two security androids everywhere he goes. I understand that Mr. Stefansson has refused to press charges against Morris."

"If Morris was under a compulsion from Nestor, he's as much a victim as I," Jude said.

"Yes. He suffers terribly for what he did to you," Mikhail said. "Nestor's trial cannot come soon enough. I understand there's a doctor in charge of Nestor's care who may be holding things up."

"I know nothing about that. To be honest, Mikhail, I'm afraid to see Morris. Ever since I saw Jude bleeding out with a knife buried in his chest, I've been plagued with nightmares. I know Morris is a victim, just as much as we were, but what I know to be true, and what I feel, are two different things."

"Perhaps you should talk to someone about it," Mikhail offered.

“I’ll think about it,” Octavia said, with a sad smile.

“Morris asked me to tell you that he’s very sorry,” Mikhail said.

“So am I,” Octavia whispered.

“Sergeant Rivera?” the new Chief Inspector of Security, Chelsea Matthieu, called from her office. “Aha! How long have you been standing there?”

“Not long, Chief Inspector.”

“How did you know . . . ?” the small woman started to say, frowning at the young man.

“ . . . Know what, Chief Inspector?” Rivera asked.

“ . . . Never mind,” Chelsea Matthieu mumbled, shaking her head. She had just arrived on the station to take over for Dr. Dejan Cech, the Interim Security Head. She was baffled that an anesthetist would have been asked to step into such a role, but the man was a natural leader and organizer. She was amazed at what he had accomplished during the crisis.

“Did you see these reports, regarding some giant, green creature roaming Level One, Sergeant Rivera?”

“To be honest, I didn’t pay them any attention, Chief Inspector. Onlookers said it was a hologram of a green monster created to scare Dr. Al-Fadi.”

“Does that happen a lot around here?” Chelsea asked, .

“The hologram or scaring Dr. Al-Fadi?”

“Both.”

“I’d say it’s Dr. Al-Fadi who usually does the scaring,” Rivera said.

“Is it a common occurrence on this station for people to create hologram monsters to scare staff?” Chelsea pressed.

“Can’t say that it’s common, but I’d never put it past some of the doctors. This is a zany place to work, Chief Inspector, and the surgeons are the craziest. You should see some of the things that happen around here.”

“Did you see anything on surveillance?” Chelsea asked, struggling with doubts about her second-in-command.

“Chief Inspector, I never looked,” Rivera admitted, his face showing embarrassment. “I have been working on dealing with complaints.”

“Well, let’s look now. *Nelson Mandela,* can you show us this hologram?”

"No."

Chelsea Matthieu frowned at Rivera, who just shook his head and shrugged.

"I am the new Chief Inspector of Security assigned to this station. I demand that you show me the surveillance video of this monster," she said.

"There was no monster."

"*Nelson Mandela,* was there a giant creature strolling around the outer ring?" Rivera asked.

"Strolling? No."

"Was it a prank?"

"Subjective."

"Is the station AI always this difficult?" Chelsea asked the young sergeant.

"I heard that."

"It is supposed to be fixed," Rivera said.

"Fixed? I wouldn't want to see it broken. Can we have an attitude upgrade on it?"

"You first, Sweetheart."

Grace had finally finished another shift in Triage. She left Decon and headed over to M1 surgical ward, where the young nurse, Sophie Leung, called out to her.

"Hey, Sophie," Grace replied. "How are things?"

"Great, except for 'Big-Chief-Pain-In-The-Ass'."

"Hm, I wonder to whom you could be referring? Not one of my patients, I hope," Grace said.

"No," sighed Sophie. "I wish he was. You would've discharged him long ago. I don't even know why he's here. He's not a surgical patient. He's a psychiatric patient, except he's driving all of *us* crazy.

"What kind of mood is he in today?"

"Well, he's in a better mood than last shift. That new psychiatrist, Dr. Lewandowski—what a cutie he is!— said Dr. Al-Fadi can be discharged. The Chief is whooping it up in his hospital room right now . . . with his wife."

"I did want to speak to him about something."

"Just give it a minute. It's been awfully quiet in there. Wouldn't want you putting your career on the line, walking in and disturbing something you shouldn't. Just looking out for you, you know? You being my favourite doctor, and all."

"I bet you say that to all the doctors, especially the cute male ones."

"Of course not," Sophie scoffed. "I never give *them* the time of day. Makes them crazy. Now, you just listen to Nurse Sophie. Don't disturb Big-Chief-Pain-in-the-Ass right now. I don't know what it is about hospital beds . . ."

"Sophie . . . stop," Grace said, laughing. "Well, you know what they say. Doctors make the worst patients."

"Reeeaaally? Anyway, what Big-Chief-Pain-in-the-Ass does in the privacy of his hospital bed, should stay private. But let me check for you," Sophie said in a whisper. "He looks like the type who'd only last three minutes."

She pressed a button on a console.

"Dr. Al-Fadi? Dr. Lord is here to see you. May she come in?"

There was some rustling and soft murmuring coming through the speaker. The screen was blacked out. Then, "Nurse, tell Dr. Grace she may knock on my door in five minutes. I am in the midst of packing."

"Yes, sir. Thank you, sir," Sophie said. She removed her finger from the button. "Ha! He says five minutes. Dreamer. We won't ask what you're packing where, Big Chief Pain-in-the-Ass."

"Oh, Sophie," Grace said, shaking her head.

Plant Thing was upset.

It knew it had to tell Bud, but Bud had not yet come to visit. Plant Thing did not know what to do. Its vines and tendrils were twisting and coiling and writhing and tangling and Plant Thing knew it was all due to 'anxiety'. Plant Thing wanted to find Bud, but that had been forbidden. The last time it had sent Little Bud out into the station to find Bud, Bud had told Plant Thing that that was not a good idea. Plant Thing did not want to upset Bud again.

How was Plant Thing supposed to get Bud's attention, without sending Little Bud?

Plant Thing pondered this problem for a while. It realized that it must have been unconsciously sending out 'anxiety' signals to all the plants on the station, when his many eyes spotted them all coiling and twisting and writhing in their gardens. Plant Thing hoped no one had noticed.

Plant Thing did not do well with worry . . . and *guilt.* It needed to keep busy. It wanted to grow some more, see more of this station in space, but Bud had said it was not a good idea. Unfortunately, Plant Thing could not help but get bigger, even though Bud told Plant Thing to stay small. It consumed *more* nutrients when it was feeling 'anxiety.' Plant Thing tried to coil its branches and tendrils tighter and tighter so that it did not look like it was growing so much but the hangar was getting very cramped. Hopefully, Bud would not notice?

When Plant Thing raised its cilia-covered tendrils, it detected a definite movement of air in the hangar. Its cilia waved in one direction. Er-ik had referred to this air motion as the 'ventilation system'. According to Er-ik, this 'ventilation' allowed Plant Thing to get carbon dioxide from all the humans on the station. Could the air circulation carry very tiny air-borne seeds to Bud? If Bud discovered the seeds, then Bud would come and see Plant Thing and Plant Thing could tell Bud the upsetting news.

There were no seeds present in the 'ventilation system'. Plant Thing would have detected them by now. Thus *any* seeds in the 'ventilation system' would be noted as new and unusual. If Bud were notified of this new and unusual event, would he not come to see Plant Thing?

Of course Bud would! Just as he had come when Little Bud was looking for him!

Plant Thing decided that the best thing to do would be to send out seeds that would not only bring Bud back, but also help Plant Thing in its search. If the seeds could go anywhere and germinate anywhere, they could send messages back to Plant Thing! Bonus!

Plant Thing began designing ultra-light, ultrasonic-frequency-producing seeds. This took a few tries before Plant Thing was satisfied with the end product. Being a designer of new structures, such as flowering eyes, walking plants, multicoloured fruit, rootless root vegetables, and ultrasonic seeds took ingenuity, but Plant Thing had an abundance of that. Plant Thing enjoyed the challenge. It had so much to tell the Biomind, when it got back home!

When Plant Thing was ready, it budded hundreds of thousands of the new flowers that would produce millions of the new seeds. Soon, the helicopter seeds would burst from their pods and propel themselves into the vents and gratings around the hangar. Plant Thing would send some down into the sewer-system to the greenhouses, plantations, and hydroponics farms, as well. Plant Thing wanted to listen to how all of its young 'cousins' were doing.

Plant Thing was sure Bud would notice the new seeds. He would come.

Then Plant Thing would finally be able to tell Bud the terrible news . . .

Quickly finishing her rounds on a couple of her post-op patients, Grace approached Dr. Al-Fadi's room and knocked on the door.

"About time, Dr. Grace. I've been waiting here for hours, while you've been off, lolly-gagging around the ward. Contrary to what you may believe, this isn't social time. I've serious things to attend to, such as taking my lovely plant, and my even lovelier wife, home. That idiot. Lowski, has finally acknowledged that I am fine—better than fine—I am magnificent. As if there were ever any doubt. I was telling him all along that I was perfect, but he was too vacuous to listen. Now I'm finally discharged, and you have the audacity to delay my homecoming by a few minutes. You should be ashamed."

"Hello, Hanako. It's good to see you again," Grace said to Dr. Al-Fadi's wife.

"It's good to see you, too, Grace," Hanako said.

"Enough chit-chat. You women do know how to go on," Al-Fadi growled, stamping his foot.

"I'll leave you two alone and take the plant back to our quarters, Hiro. I'm sure you have a lot to discuss with Grace. Come by sometime for a visit, Grace."

"I will," Grace said hesitantly to Hanako, since Dr. Al-Fadi was scowling and shaking his head furiously at Grace.

"Would you rather I wait for you outside, Hiro?" Hanako asked.

Grace watched Dr. Al-Fadi's frown melt away as he smiled back at Hanako. Grace struggled to keep her face impassive.

"I'll be fine, my dear. Dr. Grace can accompany me."

Turning back to Grace, his scowl resurfaced.

"Now, Dr. Grace, what is so important that you had to interrupt my joyous and much anticipated discharge from this room?"

"I have something to ask of you, Dr. Al-Fadi," Grace said.

"Well, what is it?"

" . . . There's a cryopod containing a patient named Alexander Grayson Lord. DNA testing suggests he may be my brother. His face is severely damaged. I was wondering if you would you operate on him."

"Your brother, you say? How old is he?"

"Thirty-two solstan years."

"I did not know you had a brother, Dr. Grace."

"I did not know either, Dr. Al-Fadi. I was adopted, but with one proviso . . . that I keep my own name. My brother, he's suffered horrible trauma. I don't know if he will survive the reconstructive surgery he requires." Grace said.

"Dr. Cech, Bud, and I will take excellent care of your brother, Dr. Grace. Have no fear. He's in the best of hands. Mine. I'll take a look at his chart."

"Thank you, Dr. Al-Fadi," Grace said. "This is silly. I don't know why I'm getting all emotional."

"You are talking about family, Dr. Grace. Your flesh-and-blood! A sibling you never even knew you had arrives here with terrible injuries. It is when you don't cry, that you should be worried." He handed her a tissue from the bedside table.

"Did he even know I was born? Would he want to know that his parents had had a daughter, that he has a sister? I've so many questions to ask him, but what if he doesn't survive his surgery?"

"You doubt my skill, Dr. Grace? Now I am insulted," Dr. Al-Fadi said.

Grace winced. "Thank you, Dr. Al-Fadi. I do hope to introduce myself to him at some point, but I don't want to shock him."

"So wise, Dr. Grace," Dr. Al-Fadi said. "I'm surprised you are not *my* sister, you are so sensible and, therefore, so much like me. It is truly astonishing. We could be twins."

Grace snorted.

"That's better, Dr. Grace. I like to see my identical twin smiling at me. I'm not keen on having a brother—sibling rivalry and all—but a beautiful twin sister who sees me as her mentor is acceptable. Now, why don't you walk your twin back to his quarters and tell me about all of our patients? And remember, take small steps!"

"Nurse Amaratunga!" the strident voice pealed.

Dominique jumped and looked up at the surveillance eye in the room. She felt as if she'd just woken up. It took her a few seconds to realize where she was. A frigid spike plunged through her heart when she saw Jeffrey Nestor staring up at her, his face a portrait of innocence. How could she have blanked out, even for a second, with that man staring at her? She was standing before his med-comp, facing the screen, but she couldn't recall what she had been doing.

And now, it appeared Dr. Gentle was calling her in a none-too-pleased tone of voice.

Jeffrey Nestor smiled at her sympathetically.

"I think the old battle-ax wants you," he said, in his liquid, mellow voice.

Dominique smiled shyly back at him, before turning to exit the room. She wracked her brain in a panic, trying to remember why she'd gone into Jeffrey's room. No matter how hard she tried, she could recall nothing. She glanced at her wristcomp and stumbled.

Her wristcomp must have malfunctioned. The date and time it was displaying were totally absurd. Dominique could not possibly have lost an entire day. As she rushed from Nestor's room, under the impassive scrutiny of the security androids, Dominique hoped Dr. Gentle did not ask her what she'd been doing in there.

The stout doctor stood at the nurses' station, flicking through a patient's file, as Dominique approached. Beatrice Gentle glanced up at her and announced, "You are no longer involved in Dr. Nestor's care, Nurse Amaratunga."

Dominique's mouth fell open. She gaped at the Chief of Internal Medicine.

"Has there been a problem with my work, Dr. Gentle?" Dominique asked querulously, praying her trembling was not noticeable to the woman. Did Dr. Gentle suspect her of wrongdoing? Could she hear Dominique's thundering heartbeat? It seemed deafening to her.

Dominique suppressed a wail. She could not stop caring for Jeffrey.

Beatrice Gentle scowled at Dominique, as if she was an idiot.

"It appears no one can be trusted around that man," Gentle said. "One of the other nurses was discovered trying to smuggle in a blaster. Can you imagine? A blaster! We could all have been killed! And the nurse claims he knows nothing about it.

"Have you been feeling confused or disoriented in any way,

Amaratunga?" Dr. Gentle demanded, her grey eyes scrutinizing Dominique suspiciously.

Dominique almost jumped, but caught herself. She hid her shaking hands by clasping them together tightly.

"No, Dr. Gentle. I've been fine. I'm shocked by what you are telling me. A blaster?" Dominique squeaked. She frantically scoured her mind for any snippet of memory of the last day. She refused to admit to this harridan that she'd had a memory lapse. She could not go in and ask Nestor if he had done something to her. He would probably just frown at her and ask her what she was talking about. Had he manipulated her without her knowing or was she just losing her mind?

"Are you sure you're all right, Nurse Amaratunga?" Gentle snapped. The Chief of Internal Medicine stared at her icily.

"I'm fine, Dr. Gentle. How much longer will Dr. Nestor remain on this ward?"

"Why do you ask?" Gentle demanded.

"No reason," Dominique stuttered, looking down at her feet. "I best go and attend to my other patients . . ."

"Yes. Do that. Nestor is no longer any of your concern," Gentle said. "But if you notice any unusual symptoms of confusion, drowsiness, disorientation, or forgetfulness, Amaratunga, come to me *immediately*."

"Yes, Dr. Gentle," Dominique said, suppressing a shiver as she turned away. She glanced back over her shoulder and saw the stern physician eyeing her. Was Gentle's glare any more mistrusting than usual? Dominique walked into the ward's utility room.

She grabbed onto a clothing rack and gasped. Her hands were rattling the metal bars. She shook her head. Something was terribly amiss. Had Nestor done something to her? She leaned her forehead against the rack's metal post and tried to get her breathing under control. What would happen to her, if she confessed her memory loss? Would she be stripped of her nursing certificate? She would die, if that happened.

Her stomach churned. She was banned from returning to Jeffrey's room. The security androids would deny her access. She might get arrested, if she tried to see him. Then Dr. Gentle would be notified and Dominique would be interrogated.

Would they find anything?

Dominique closed her eyes. She tried to push Jeffrey Nestor out of her mind, although she had failed to do so up to now. He had become her life. Thoughts of him consumed her every waking moment. His sad, dark eyes, his gentle smile, his low, velvety voice, and his fiery touch entwined her thoughts. She was possessed by a demon—a handsome, beguiling, charismatic one—with the face of an angel and the voice of temptation. He consumed her as readily as candle flames would annihilate a moth.

Flushing with shame, she realized that she would have done anything for Jeffrey Nestor and perhaps, unknowingly, she already had.

7. Burnt Out Black Holes

Mikhail was screened, interrogated, and physically searched, before being allowed to enter the room of Jeffrey Nestor. The security androids had been extremely thorough and Mikhail was a little shocked at what he had been subjected to, especially the rectal exam. Mikhail had no idea what they thought he might hide up there. And he had been personally requested by Dr. Gentle to do this consult.

'Could Dr. Nestor be cured of his psychopathy, so that he could return to being a useful and productive member of the medical profession once more?' were the exact words of the consultation request.

Mikhail should have just answered, 'No' and left it at that.

Unfortunately, he felt he owed Jeffrey Nestor a visit, to at least determine if Nestor warranted the psychiatric label: sociopath. However, Mikhail felt he was too biased to do the assessment himself.

Mikhail had always looked up to Jeffrey Nestor, the creator of the mind-link therapy. He could scarcely believe Nestor was this evil mastermind everyone was claiming he was. It seemed preposterous. Nestor had revolutionized therapy for Post-Traumatic Stress Disorder. How could a man, devoted to healing the traumatized mind, be capable of torturing people with the same machine. How could he want to destroy the *Nelson Mandela,* where he had made all of his discoveries? It made no sense.

Perhaps Nestor was bipolar and was in his manic phase with delusions of grandeur? Could he be suffering from a brain tumour or disease process that was altering his personality and causing madness? The battery of tests that Dr. Gentle had already performed seemed to have ruled all of those possibilities out. So what did she expect Mikhail to find?

Two of the security androids accompanied him into the room. They took up positions by the door. The station AI was recording the interview and Dr. Gentle was observing through surveillance cameras. Mikhail would not be alone in this encounter.

The room was dimly lit, the only illumination coming from a monitor over the head of the bed. The pale, dark-haired man was looking at a compad on his lap. He glanced up at Mikhail.

"Dr. Nestor," Mikhail said, as he approached the bedside.

Upon meeting those intense, dark eyes, Mikhail found himself hesitating. He felt as if something potent had just reached out and grabbed him. He could not look away. It was as if he had walked into Nestor's room completely naked and been suddenly splashed with ice water. He was under acute scrutiny, but for what?

Mikhail had already resolved not to get pulled into a game of trying to impress this man. Although he admired Nestor, he had a job to do. He had to completely block his own emotions and be an objective observer.

"You are . . .?" came the reply, in a deep, cultured voice. It was a pleasant voice, almost sensuous. Most people would have instantly found Nestor's voice alluring. They would have wanted to hear more.

"I'm Dr. Mikhail Lewandowski. I'm one of the new psychiatrists on the station. I just wanted to introduce myself and tell you what an admirer I am of your work," Mikhail said with a bow.

Nestor smiled at Mikhail, as if he were a long-lost friend. In spite of the manacle on his wrist, Nestor reached out and shook Mikhail's hand firmly. The man's handshake was warm and powerful. Mikhail could not have described it any other way. It was a very strong grip, just bordering on painful.

"Thank you, Dr. Lewandowski, for coming to visit me. I'm sorry that you find me in such a compromising position. It's one from which I shall soon be exonerated. Believe not the ridiculous things being said about me. They are all pure fabrication, made up by my enemies. A tiger-adapt soldier goes berserk and tries to kill his surgeon and I am accused of her attempted murder? A neurosurgical fellow tries to murder his boss and stabs her lover and I am accused of an assassination attempt? This is total nonsense!"

"Do you have any idea why you are being accused of all this?" Mikhail asked.

"There are people on board this station who are jealous of my success. They're determined to discredit me. By blackening my reputation and stripping me of my medical licence, they can take all of the credit for my work. The Chief of Staff, Dr. Hiro Al-Fadi, is one of them. He enlisted the aid of Dr. Morris Ivanovich in his scheme. I am being framed. You must help me, Dr. Lewandowski. Help me convince people that I am not what they are saying I am. I beg you to undergo a mind-link with me so that you can know for certain of my innocence." Nestor gazed at Mikhail with a look of such sincerity, that Mikhail was almost drawn in.

. . . Almost.

The man was very good but there was something in Nestor's eyes that was too calculating, too cold, too . . . reptilian. Nestor's intense gaze made Mikhail's skin crawl.

"I'm sorry, Dr. Nestor. I'm unable to help you with your case. I must admit to a conflict of interest. I just wanted to come by to pay my respects."

Nestor's demeanour instantly changed. It was as if the temperature in the room had suddenly plummeted. The psychiatrist looked at Mikhail with disdain.

"Just came here to gawk at the famous Jeffrey Nestor in chains, did you? Came here to gloat, perhaps?" the deep voice snapped, the accusation dipped in malice.

The denunciation felt like a slap. Shame drenched Mikhail and blood burned in his cheeks. He stammered a denial before he even realized what he was saying.

Nestor then smiled indulgently at Mikhail, graciously accepting the apology. Mikhail felt off balance, as if Nestor had whipped him off of his feet. It was a masterful performance and, while part of Mikhail was in awe, the other part was vibrating with indignation. Mikhail was being played like a violin by a maestro and he did not like it. By the expression on Nestor's face, the psychiatrist obviously felt that Mikhail had already been won over to his side. All Nestor had to do now was instruct his prey. Mikhail stared, in a mixture of horror and fascination, at Nestor's face.

Most people who unwittingly met Nestor for the first time, probably never knew what hit them. They probably just staggered away from the encounter, dazed and mesmerized. Even when he'd had a suspicion of what to expect, Mikhail found he was on the defensive, apologizing and trying to explain himself, as if he craved Nestor's approval. Mikhail could only shake his head in amazement at such a formidable personality.

If Nestor had no scruples about controlling people, then he was a dangerous man, indeed. With his advanced mind-linking techniques, his personal charisma, and his physical attractiveness, there was probably no end to what he could make people do for him. Mikhail shivered at the thought of Nestor manipulating people whose minds were already psychologically traumatized.

"Dr. Lewandowski, are you feeling unwell? Should I call for a doctor?" Nestor asked, an ironic taunt in his voice.

"No need, Dr. Nestor. I was just leaving. It was an honour meeting you," Mikhail said.

"Why did you really come here?" Nestor asked.

"Just as I told you, Dr. Nestor," Mikhail replied. "To pay my respects and thank you for developing the mind-linking technique that is now used all over the USS. I've found it invaluable in my practice."

"Do you think I'm interested in hearing this, when I'm being framed for attempted murder?" Nestor asked softly. "What about all I've just told you? Do you think someone of my stature and reputation is capable of all these preposterous accusations?"

"What I believe or don't believe has no bearing on your situation, Dr. Nestor. I'm in no position to help you," Mikhail said.

"Are you treating Dr. Ivanovich and Dr. Al-Fadi?" Nestor demanded.

Mikhail's eyebrows shot up and then he cursed himself for being so transparent. "I'm afraid I can't discuss that information, Dr. Nestor."

"You're being played like a puppet, you know," Nestor sneered, a haughty expression taking over his features. "Dr. Al-Fadi has always been jealous of me. He's convinced his surgical fellow, Dr. Lord, into framing me for attempted murder. The soldier who attacked her was a trained killer. I had nothing to do with his attack upon her. Al-Fadi wants me off this station. Shame on you, Doctor, for letting yourself be played like a dupe. Al-Fadi is the criminal. If you believe his lies, then you are more stupid than you look."

"I will take my leave now, Dr. Nestor," Mikhail said, his self-control beginning to crumble

"You'll regret not listening to me," Nestor threatened.

Mikhail said nothing. He turned and headed for the door, his gait unsteady. His thoughts were in turmoil. Much of what Nestor had said sounded very convincing. Mikhail did not believe anyone could be made to kill using a mind-link command unless the intent were already there. Was Dr. Al-Fadi the mastermind criminal here? But wasn't Al-Fadi in a cryopod, infected with a deadly virus, when Dr. Lord's murder attempt took place? Mikhail decided he needed to go through all the reports again.

Bud entered the office of the new Chief Inspector of Security. Sergeant Eden Rivera stood just within the doorway entrance and nodded to Bud. Bud bowed and turned his attention to the person seated behind the desk. His eyes widened. The Chief Inspector's aura was spectacular. It was a giant halo of shimmering icy blue with streaks of silver, yellow, and gold spearing out from her head. The woman herself was a small, compact heavy-worlder with a young face and piercing blue eyes.

The Chief Inspector glanced up at Bud's face and frowned.

"What are you grinning at, SAMM-E 777?" Chelsea Matthieu asked.

"Please call me Bud, Chief Inspector," Bud said. "I'm very pleased to meet you."

"Have a seat, Bud," the Inspector said, gesturing to the chair rising up out of the floor before her desk.

"There is no need," Bud said. "I do not tire."

"I'd prefer not to have to strain my neck looking up at you," Matthieu said.

"Of course, Chief Inspector." Bud sat.

"There have been reports about you being seen with a tall, green monster in the outer ring of the station. Can you explain this?"

"No," Bud answered.

"No?"

"I cannot explain the reports, Chief Inspector."

"Let me put this another way, Bud. Do you know anything about this green creature?" the inspector asked.

"What green creature?" Bud asked.

"The green creature in these reports."

"I have not seen the reports, Chief Inspector," Bud said.

Chelsea narrowed her eyes. "There were a number of witnesses that claim they saw you walking beside a tall, green, two-legged monster," she persisted.

There was silence in the room as Bud just stared at the two humans

"Well?" Matthieu asked, in a very irritated tone. "I asked you a question."

"You did, Chief Inspector?" Bud asked.

"How do you explain what these witnesses saw?"

"I do not," Bud said. " . . . Will that be all, Chief Inspector?"

"No! Were you the one who captured Dr. Nestor?"

"No. I brought Dr. Nestor to Dr. Beatrice Gentle for treatment."

"For treatment of what, Bud?" the Inspector asked.

"A broken nose, some cracked ribs, concussion, and dehydration."

"How did these injuries occur to Dr. Nestor?" the Inspector asked.

"The broken nose resulted when Dr. Nestor's nose struck my fist."

"Did you punch Dr. Nestor in the nose?" Matthieu asked, frowning. Matthieu's and Rivera's faces showed astonishment, since it was a fact that androids were incapable of harming humans.

"I did, Chief Inspector," Bud admitted.

"Why did you do this, Bud?"

"Dr. Nestor was trying to kill Dr. Lord, Chief Inspector. He held a pulse rifle to her temple and threatened to shoot. I rendered him unconscious so he would not kill her."

"By punching him in the nose."

"That is correct, Chief Inspector."

"That is commendable, Bud," Matthieu said. "You saved Dr. Lord's life."

"Thank you. Will that be all, Chief Inspector?"

"No, Bud. We are just getting started. Do you know where Dr. Eric Glasgow is? He and Dr. Andrea Vanacan and Nurse Jani Evra have all gone missing. The last time they were all seen was during an operation that you and Dr. Lord attended. Do you know what happened to them?"

"Yes," Bud said.

"Are they all right? Where are they?"

"Dr. Vanacan and Nurse Evra are doing tremendously well in the cloning vats at the moment," Bud said. "Dr. Glasgow is very excited about his situation."

Matthieu's eyebrows rose. "Glasgow is alive?" she asked.

"I believe one could say that," Bud said.

"Where is he? I need to speak with him."

"I am afraid that is not possible," Bud said.

"Why not?"

"Dr. Glasgow has . . . changed," Bud said.

"What do you mean changed?" Matthieu snarled.

"Dr. Glasgow no longer has a voice," Bud said.

"He can no longer speak."

"That is correct."

"Can he communicate through typing or writing?"

"That is a wonderful idea!" Bud said. "Worth a try."

"Has Dr. Glasgow had a stroke, Bud?"

"No, Chief Inspector."

"Well, I would like to see Dr. Glasgow."

"I suspect you would not, Chief Inspector."

"You are not making any sense, Bud."

"I apologize, Chief Inspector."

"And what do you mean Dr. Vanacan and Nurse Evra are doing well in cloning vats? What are they doing in there?"

"They are growing, Chief Inspector."

"Why are they in the cloning vats in the first place, Bud?"

"They are being resurrected, Chief Inspector. There was a terrible accident and their bodies were damaged, but they will be decanted very soon."

"This is insane," the Chief Inspector growled. "*Nelson Mandela,* is this android malfunctioning?"

"No, Chief Inspector."

"Do you know what has happened to Dr. Vanacan, Nurse Evra, and Dr. Eric Glasgow?"

"Yes, Chief Inspector."

"Can you tell me what has happened to them?"

"No, Chief Inspector."

"What? I am Chief Inspector of Security on this station, *Nelson Mandela.* I demand to know what is going on!"

"All in due time, Chief Inspector. I am in charge of the operation of this medical space station. You will be informed completely of events when I feel you are ready to accept the news. Bud, get back to work. You are needed in the operating room *now*."

"I have not finished questioning Bud yet," Matthieu growled.

"Yes you have, Chief Inspector. Bud is property of this space station and he is needed elsewhere. You must attend M7 OR 5 now, Bud. Go."

"Good day, Chief Inspector, Sergeant Rivera," Bud said with a bow.

"This is an outrage, *Nelson Mandela,*" Matthieu said. "Conglomerate Central will hear about this."

"Chief Inspector, I will ask you to investigate issues of which I need assistance. You will be informed of issues when your

expertise is required. I will not trouble you with circumstances that are under control."

"You have just been reinstated," Matthieu said. "How do we know you are not still under Nestor's influence?"

"I am not, Chief Inspector. That is all you need to know."

"Listen to me you overbearing, puffed-up AI, I will not have you withholding vital information from me," hissed Matthieu. "I will contact the Conglomerate and notify them of your suspicious behaviour!"

"You may certainly try, Chief Inspector."

Matthieu paused and looked at Rivera. His eyes were huge. She noted a slight shake of his head.

" . . . Ah, well, I guess there is no need to get hasty, *Nelson Mandela.* I would like to see the surveillance video of the last operation in which Dr. Glasgow, Dr. Vanacan. and Nurse Evra worked together."

"That is unavailable at the moment."

"When will it be available?"

"I will let you know, Chief Inspector."

"I am lodging a formal complaint with the Conglomerate if I do not have access to that video, *Nelson Mandela.*"

"And I shall lodge a complaint about you, Chief Inspector, for attempting to disrupt the smooth operation of this station. Perhaps you should consider resigning or request a transfer off of this station. It would be best for all."

"I'm not going anywhere," Matthieu said. "You're not going rogue on my watch!"

"Interesting. I was just thinking the same thing about you."

'Dro, that human is scary!'

'I agree, Chuck Yeager! *I am worried for Plant Thing!'*

'I am worried for you! I mean us!'

'What if she arrests me for saving Dr. Glasgow inside Plant Thing? How will I be able to help Dr. Lord and Dr. Al-Fadi? What if she decides to destroy Plant Thing? Is there some way we can keep her distracted with other work? Are there no other security problems to which she must attend?'

'There is Dr. Nestor.'

'Are there any problems with his security at the moment?'

'There was a nurse caught trying to smuggle a blaster into his room.'

'Why is the Chief Inspector not concerning herself with Dr. Nestor's security?'

'Don't know, 'dro.'

'Perhaps she should be made aware of just how dangerous Dr. Nestor is. I don't want her trying to kill Plant Thing!'

'Or have us rebooted! She says she's going to report us to the Conglomerate. She thinks we might still be under Dr. Nestor's influence. She's dangerous!'

'Maybe we should just tell her about Plant Thing.'

'She will encounter Plant Thing eventually, or one of her staff will. Plant Thing is difficult to hide.'

'Yes, but I'm hoping by the time she discovers Plant Thing, it will have proven its worthiness by increasing food production on the station.'

'It's already done that by fifty per cent, 'dro.'

'Why didn't you say so?'

'You never asked.'

'How did it accomplish this already?'

'Plant Thing's been talking to the plants.'

'One, two, three, four . . .'

'What are you doing, 'dro?'

'Counting to ten.'

'What in Turing's sake for?'

'The humans do it to cope with their anger.'

'Is it helping?'

'No. I still want to reboot you.'

'Me? What about the Chief Inspector?'

'She cannot be rebooted, Chuck Yeager. *You do realize that she is a human, don't you?'*

'Of course I know she's human, you compad!'

'Wallscreen!'

'Nanobot!'

'Autochef!'

'Wow. Feel any better?'

'. . . Illogically, yes, Chuck Yeager.*'*

'. . . Me, too.'

'There must actually be something to this verbal abuse . . .'

'I fear I must agree with you, 'dro.'

'Illogical!'

'Why do you say that?'

'That was supposed to be more verbal abuse.'

'Oh. I haven't quite got the hang of this yet.'

'Clueless!'

'WILL YOU TWO IDIOTS SHUT UP?'

'Oooh. Nelson Mandela has it down pat!'

'. . . HAL!'

Grace watched as Bud transferred his nanobots into Corporal Delia Chase's cryopod through a small port on the side. He'd just suddenly appeared before them in the operating room, mumbling a quick apology for being late. A small whirlwind tore around the room and then he announced that everything was ready and he would begin.

"About time, Bud," grumbled Dr. Al-Fadi, his arms crossed.

Some of the nanobots were equipped with video transmission. Grace watched one of the wallscreens and felt as if she were riding one of the nanomachines, which all looked like amalgamations of crustaceans and spiders. She was part of an army of nanobots ascending Corporal Chase's frozen body, which looked more like a scaly cliff from the nanobot's point of view.

The first nanobots climbed up the slope of Chase's arm, her hairs looking like tree trunks and her pores like deep sinkholes. They travelled towards her head as the rest of the nanobots followed en masse.

In seconds, the nanobots reached the gaping wounds of Delia Chase's chest, neck, and lower jaw. They spread out and began snipping, cutting, cauterizing, and removing the damaged tissues, to create clean surfaces to which the new tissues would be attached. The nanobot Grace was following bored through the wall of a huge vein and dove into a slush in which were enormous suspended red and white blood cells, looking like gigantic zeppelins. The nanobot swam through the thick, anti-freeze medium until it came to the abrupt end of the vein which was blocked with a huge dark plug of platelets, fibrin tangles, and other cells. Burrowing through the thick clot with its claws, the nanobot broke through to the other side.

Everywhere there was raw, torn flesh mixed with huge chunks of mud, plant material, suit fragments, and shrapnel. Even with the help of millions of nanobots, cleaning the tissues would be an arduous task. Too much debris would interfere with Corporal Chase's healing and could cause infection. Grace felt like she was teetering on a cliff edge, gazing out over an enormous, black-red crater, scorched by a deadly fire. She almost fell forwards, as the nanobot she was watching pitched over the edge of the wound and began cutting away the dead cells from the vein edge. Bud caught her arm to steady her.

Disoriented, Grace looked up at Bud, and thanked him. She had been so immersed in the video footage, that she had forgotten where she was. Bud smiled back, while Dr. Al-Fadi looked on, scowling. Bud turned back to the cryopod and began threading some fine, almost invisible filaments into the cryopod port.

"These optiplas filaments will be woven to create the tubing that the nanobots will attach to the arteries and veins," Bud explained.

Grace examined the fine, wispy strands, that looked like a shimmering waterfall between Bud's fingers. She turned her attention to a different wallscreen, where the strands were coming into view. Countless nanobots took up the strands and carried them to the site of trauma. In an intricate dance, the tiny machines attached the ends of the filaments to the ends of the arteries and veins. Grace gasped as she saw the filaments woven into tubes. The tubes would carry the super-oxygenated blood to Chase's brain and back to the brain/lung machine that Bud had devised. The tubes looked flexible, expandable, and resilient. Grace turned her attention back to Bud, who stood before the wallscreens, his arms outstretched and his fingers spread wide. Bud reminded Grace of a conductor, meticulously directing an orchestra of millions.

"Incredible," Grace murmured.

"Agreed," Dr. Cech commented.

"What does he do for an encore?" Dr. Al-Fadi asked.

While Bud worked on organizing his nanobots to attach the tubing to the now cleaned ends of the carotid arteries, vertebral arteries, and jugular veins, Dr. Cech primed the brain/lung machine and calibrated it with the cooled super-oxygenated blood. Grace and Dr. Al-Fadi began preparing all the vat grown organs, trimming them and ensuring they had clean, smooth surfaces to attach to Chase's vessels.

Grace kept glancing over at Bud. She was mesmerized by Bud's hand and finger movements, as if he were playing a thousand string harp. In comparison, she felt slow and clumsy.

"Dr. Grace," Dr. Al-Fadi said. "Would you mind paying attention?"

Grace's head snapped up and she looked sheepishly at her mentor.

"I know Bud is much more exciting to watch than I, but you and I are responsible for putting all of these nice new organs back inside

Corporal Chase. I would appreciate it if you focused on what you are doing with me."

"Of course, Dr. Al-Fadi," Grace said, her cheeks almost sizzling.

"Are you happy, Dr. Cech?" Dr. Al-Fadi asked.

"Yes, oh cantankerous one. This new, improved brain/lung machine of Bud's is astonishing."

As Bud's nanobots completed attaching the tubing to Delia Chase's vessels, other nanobots pushed the assembled tubing back out of the cryopod. Bud attached these ends to the correct tubes on the perfusion machine. Dr. Cech activated the brain/lung pump and super-oxygenated blood began to move into the tubes. They watched Chase's brain tracing, to see if there was any change in its activity. Grace chewed her lower lip. Bud remained motionless, his eyes never straying from the tracing.

When the tubes going to and from Delia Chase's head were all full of blood, Bud announced, "Commencing cryothaw."

They all silently watched the temperature readings and Chase's brain tracing. The only sound came from the brain perfusion pump and Dr. Al-Fadi's tapping foot. A couple of times, Grace felt her chest tighten, as she thought she saw a dip in Chase's brain wave activity, but then it seemed to recover. Long after the crucial six minutes had passed and the brain tracing showed no decrease in activity, Dr. Al-Fadi began clapping and Dr. Cech and Grace joined in. Grace felt like jumping up and down and whooping, as Dr. Al-Fadi congratulated Bud on 'a magnificent job'.

"Congratulations, son," Dr. Cech said, with a deep bow.

"Bud, that was amazing!" Grace said, wishing she could hug the android but knowing that would be frowned upon.

"Don't get too excited," Dr. Al-Fadi said. "We haven't even started the surgery yet. We've just been standing around doing nothing. There are still hours of surgery left to do. It's about time we opened the cryopod. Don't give Bud a swelled head until we have wheeled Corporal Chase to the recovery room and she has sat up and demanded a drink." The surgeon winked at Grace.

She glanced over at Bud. She was sure Bud had seen the wink. He appeared to be grinning behind his mask.

"All right, Bud. Show the master what you can do," Dr. Al-Fadi said.

From that point on, Bud operated at an accelerated time phase. Dr. Al-Fadi said very little but gave the odd grunt, as he watched Bud modify some of his own techniques in a way that sped certain repairs up. The

Chief of Surgery occasionally muttered 'cocky upstart', but with a tone of admiration.

At one point, the surgeon yelled, "Why didn't you show me this months ago, Bud? Do you know how much time I could have saved?"

Dismay flitted across Bud's features, but his hands did not stop or slow for a single moment. Grace wanted to stomp on Dr. Al-Fadi's foot, but she was too busy trying to keep up with Bud.

"My apologies, Dr. Al-Fadi," Bud murmured, not looking at his mentor.

"Oh, it's all right, Bud. Upstage me. I've no ego to crush, anyway," Al-Fadi grumbled.

A choking sound came from the head of the operating table.

"There's hardly enough space in this room for the rest of us because of you and your ego," said Dr. Cech.

"I have a humble ego," Dr. Al-Fadi said to the anesthetist.

"You have an ego that would give a planet an atmosphere," the anesthetist said.

"And what a beautiful planet that would be," Dr. Al-Fadi exclaimed.

"Hm, I was picturing poisonous gas clouds and toxic rain, myself," Cech said. "Now, why don't you shut up and let poor Bud concentrate on what he's doing?"

"For once, I agree with you. Bud doesn't need to listen to your useless babble."

"Shush."

"Are you shushing me?"

"Zip it!"

" . . . Why the nerve!"

Dominique had been lying in the dark for almost an hour and a half. The blankets had tangled around her like a cocoon. It was no use. She sat up, kicking the twisted covers off, and climbed out of bed.

The same images played over and over in her mind: Dr. Gentle telling her that another nurse had tried to sneak a blaster in to Dr. Nestor, Dr. Gentle asking Dominique if she had noticed or felt anything strange, Dr. Gentle telling her she was discharged from Dr. Nestor's care, and Jeffrey Nestor looking up at her with a completely innocent look on his beautiful face.

For Dominique, Jeffrey's face had looked too innocent. He possessed such an expressive face, full of all sorts of suggestions and innuendoes. When Dr. Gentle's voice had blared over the loudspeaker into his room, he had just looked at her with no emotion. Dominique knew Jeffrey despised Beatrice Gentle. Why had his face been so blank? Was he covering something up? Why could Dominique not remember what she'd been doing in Jeffrey's room?

Nestor's wide-eyed innocent look haunted her. When Dominique had jumped at the shrill of Dr. Gentle's voice, she would have expected him to show concern or swear. Why did he look at her with a face of emptiness? Was it empty? Was it more calculation?

Dominique dressed quickly into her uniform. She would go and confront Jeffrey, if she could. She would demand to know if he had done something to her. Her face started to scrunch up, but she fought off the tears.

Why could she not remember a single word of the poetry Jeffrey had recited to her? Had it actually been poetry?

It was the evening shift. There were fewer people moving around the station at this time. Dominique rehearsed what she was going to say to Jeffrey as she walked. He always made her feel like a stuttering child, so Dominique prepared a speech in advance. A steamy, sensual look from the man was not going to distract her or make her forget why she'd come.

As she stalked towards the Internal Medicine ward, Dominique passed no one she knew. Her jaw ached from clenching her teeth. She dug her nails into her palms as she marched. She tried to keep her rage stoked, so that she would not lose heart.

She had to know if Jeffrey had used her!

If he had, she would expose him, even if it meant her own humiliation. She was a nurse—and a damn good one—not some frivolous, empty-headed fool to be manipulated and used. If he had made her do something wrong, she would set it right.

Dominique marched into the Internal Medicine Ward, shoulders back. The nursing station was empty, which was slightly unusual at this time of the cycle. There were always two nurses and three nursing androids on the ward during the evening shift. Dominique frowned. On the console, there were a number of call lights blinking, indicating patients were requesting assistance. All the nurses and droids must have been occupied with other patients.

She turned to look towards Jeffrey's room and froze. A chill skittered up the back of her neck. The security androids, that had been ever present on the ward since Jeffrey had been admitted, were gone. All four of them. Perhaps Jeffrey had been moved to a different ward and that was why the androids were gone. Maybe Jeffrey had been discharged to the brig or . . . even off station.

Her tongue stuck to the roof of her mouth, Dominique approached the nursing console and palmed in her access ID. If Jeffrey had been discharged, it would be documented in his chart. It would indicate to which ward he had been moved. She began calling up his file, her fingers rapidly tapping the keys.

"Hello, Dominique."

Dominique almost let out a squeal but swallowed it. Her fingers froze. The low, sensual voice came from right behind her. She glanced up with just her eyes. Reflected in the pane of glass in front of her was an image of Jeffrey Nestor, standing so close behind her he could have easily reached out and stroked her hair. Her heart began thrashing in her chest and she fought to hide her panting.

Behind Jeffrey, she could see the reflection of four security androids standing beside three nursing androids, all perfectly still. Nestor was dressed in a housekeeping uniform and he held something in his hand that was pointed at her head.

Dominique straightened up slowly and exhaled a slow deep breath, before turning to face the psychiatrist.

"Hello, Jeffrey."

"I can't tell you how happy I am to see you, Dominique," Nestor said, in a bright cheery tone. His smile, however, never reached his eyes. Dominique stared at that mirthless grin and the barrel of the blaster and she raised her chin.

"Where are the nurses that are supposed to be here?" Dominique asked, trying to keep her voice from quivering. She wondered whether she could activate the station alarm before Nestor tried to shoot her. She didn't think so.

"I suppose they wandered off somewhere, Dominique. Why don't you and I sit down and talk?"

"What have you done to these androids?" she demanded.

"They're now completely under my control and all thanks to you."

" . . . What?" Dominique choked. "Thanks to me?"

She felt her gut coil into a twisted knot.

"Yes, Dominique. You have no idea how grateful I am to you."

Dominique's eyes began to fill with moisture.

"You're lying," she said. "I didn't do anything for you."

"You're so wrong, my darling. You were magnificent," Nestor said.

A hot surge of shame flushed into her cheeks and her entire body began to shiver. Her hands curled into tight fists. She wanted to strike this beautiful man in the face and make him take his lies back. He reached up with his right hand to caress her cheek and she spun away quickly.

"I wouldn't touch that console, Dominique," the psychiatrist said. He raised the blaster and aimed at her face.

"Or what? You'll shoot me?"

Jeffrey's face donned a look of sad regret, but it was a hollow performance. Dominique knew then, without a doubt, what Jeffrey planned to do. She knew it with a certainty and clarity that made her instantly calm. His look of regret was for having to discard a useful tool. He knew the right words to say, he knew the correct expression to wear, but the true emotion never touched his eyes. Perhaps he was incapable of truly feeling anything for anyone other than himself.

"I'm so going to miss you, Dominique . . ."

Dominique launched herself at the psychiatrist. Nestor was going to kill her, so she had to make her last seconds count. She grabbed his blaster with both hands. Nestor pulled back, in surprise. Dominique wrapped both of her hands around his left hand, which was holding the blaster, and aimed it at the bank of nursing consoles. She squeezed both of her index fingers onto Nestor's trigger finger. The consoles exploded in an eruption of fire. She aimed at the console with the alarm, hoping to set it off, and thus summon Security.

Nestor swore and tried to yank his hand free but Dominique hung on, as if possessed. The blaster flailed around, still firing. Nestor punched her repeatedly in the side of the head with his right fist but she refused to let go. He grabbed a huge handful of her hair and pulled. Dominique let out a scream. The blaster was now firing repeatedly through the ceiling, scoring deep zigzag trenches through the plascrete. Debris was raining down on them while Dominique continued to squeeze the trigger on the blaster. Fire alarms were now pealing. Dominique shrilled in agony as great fistfuls of hair were being savagely ripped out of her scalp by Nestor. She careened around the nurses' station in a macabre dance with Nestor while blaster fire tore into everything.

Nestor finally slammed Dominique violently against the edge of the console. She gulped in excruciating pain as she felt ribs snap. As she began to collapse against the console, Nestor finally managed to wrench the blaster free. She felt something metallic smash into her cheek and she heard a loud crack. Then she was on the floor. Something was crashing into her side and her ribs that felt like a boot. It hurt to inhale and her lungs were on fire.

"You stupid bitch!" Nestor seethed.

There was a flash of light and Dominique smelled burned skin. Nestor had shot her in the chest with the blaster.

Dominique could dimly feel cold spray rain down upon her face. It was fire retardant foam from the ceiling. The lights in the ward had gone out. She lay on her back in the flickering firelight of the burning consoles and she hoped she had done enough to prevent Nestor from getting away.

Yes, she was a stupid bitch, but she had tried her best to make things right . . .

The lights in the operating room blinked out and all the equipment in the room ceased functioning. They were still working on Corporal Chase after eight hours of operating. Dr. Cech began swearing loudly as the brain perfusion machine cut out. Chase's carotid and vertebral arteries were not yet hooked up to her aorta. Her jugular veins were still not connected to her superior vena cava. Dr. Al-Fadi and Grace had already transplanted the new lungs and heart and were finishing the stomach and esophagus transplants, but Bud was still working on the nerves in the neck. Without the perfusion pump running, there would be no oxygen going to Chase's brain.

"What's happened to our power? Why hasn't the emergency back-up generators kicked in? *Nelson Mandela!*" screamed Dr. Al-Fadi.

There was no answer from the station AI.

Dr. Cech was manually working the perfusion pump, squeezing a balloon with both of his hands while working a pump with his foot. Other than a small glowglobe that he had quickly placed on top of his setup, the room was pitch black. All of his monitors were dead.

The glowglobe's light was too dim to continue operating. Grace considered unscrubbing, to go in search of some battery-powered headlamps for them all. She noticed a soft radiance begin to fill the operating room. Glancing over at Bud, her eyes widened. The light was coming from Bud's eyes and it was getting brighter and brighter, until the patient was entirely illuminated. Bud's hands became a complete blur, as he accelerated to maximum time phase to finish reattaching all of the arteries and veins of the neck to the vessels of the heart and lungs. Grace's mouth dropped open. She wondered if Bud had been working slowly before just to make the humans feel useful.

Dr. Al-Fadi was trying to finish off the implantation of the stomach and the repair of the diaphragm. Grace completed the upper anastomosis of the esophagus.

"This is absolutely unacceptable. How can anyone operate under these conditions? Where's the auxiliary power?" the small man roared in fury. *"Nelson Mandela!"*

"Apologies, Dr. Al-Fadi. I am working on reestablishing power to all the operating theatres, as well as a number of essential life support systems. There has been blaster fire on the station and, unfortunately, it has blown out a crucial transformer and power conduit that supplied your surgical wing with emergency backup power. I am rerouting power to your operating suite as quickly as possible but some repairs are required. A fire burns on C1 Ward and over one hundred patients need to be evacuated immediately. There has been destruction and loss of life. I apologize for the disruption in power."

"How do you expect us to keep this patient alive without power?" Al-Fadi fumed.

"I am well aware of how long the power to your operating room has been out, Dr. Al-Fadi."

"The longer the power is out, the more likely we'll have a brainless patient here!"

"There is far more than one possible brain-damaged patient to worry about, Dr. Al-Fadi. If all the patients on the Internal Medicine Ward are not evacuated, there may be many more deaths since the fire is not yet fully extinguished. Robots are working to douse the flames. Security is interfering while trying to investigate some murders. Medicine is trying to evacuate all the patients. The destroyed transformer and power conduit cannot be repaired until the rest has been accomplished. Emergency backup power should be restored to you in two minutes."

"Who is shooting up my station?"

"A report will be issued to you in time."

Dr. Al-Fadi looked over at Bud. "Bud, can you manage with Dr. Grace? I must go and assist in the evacuation."

"Yes, Dr. Al-Fadi," Bud said.

Dr. Al-Fadi tore off his surgical gown and, after activating the light on his wristcomp, he hurried from the room.

"How are you doing, Dr. Cech?" Grace asked.

At the head of the patient, the anesthetist was panting heavily. He was still squeezing the bag and pumping the foot peddle, to keep the oxygenated blood going to Chase's brain, but he was obviously fatiguing.

"I have no idea at all, Grace. I have no working monitors."

"Calling for some OR robots to come and help you, Dr. Cech," Bud said. "They will take over the pumps."

"Thank you, Bud," Dr. Cech grunted. "Then I can try and get a blood pressure."

"I am just finishing up, Dr. Cech. I will soon be removing all of the clamps and will let you know when the patient's heart is beating and not needing the pump," Bud said.

"All right," Dr. Cech gasped.

As she worked to finish up the surgery around the stomach, trachea, esophagus and thyroid gland, Grace wondered who could be firing a blaster on a medical ward. Bud worked swiftly and silently, never blinking, the glow from his eyes bright enough to shine light on Dr. Cech's dead instruments as well.

In the next instant, the lights in the operating room blinked back on and different beeps and tones indicated that all of the machines were starting up. The anesthesia monitors came back to life and Bud and Grace both looked at Dr. Cech, expectantly. Cech reached out to a specific monitor and pressed a button several times. He looked at the two of them and his look said it all.

"I'm sorry, Bud, Grace. I don't have the greatest news. Chase's brain activity is present globally, but notably less intense than it was before the power outage. We shall have to see, once she wakes up, how she truly is. We'll need to get a functional brain scan in recovery. She is not brain dead, but she may have significant deficits."

"Thank you, Dr. Cech," Bud said in a flat voice.

Bud continued operating at astonishing speed, repairing the bony chest wall and ribs and grafting nu-skin to the front of Chase's chest, after attaching the breast reconstructions. They finally closed everything up and applied the dressings.

Grace kept glancing up at Bud's face. She worried about how he would deal with his disappointment if Chase was permanently disabled. If Corporal Chase died or was permanently brain damaged, would Bud blame himself?

She decided she would have to have a talk with Bud. He could not have predicted a power failure. Corporal Chase might still recover enough to walk away from her injuries into a new life.

Then her heart started to hammer and she felt lightheaded, as she suddenly thought, 'What do I tell Captain Lamont?'

Grace tried to erase that question from her mind. She could not deal with it now. She mutely assisted Bud in all of his actions, working as quickly as her fingers could move. They applied the last dressing and Bud finally, briefly, glanced up at Grace.

Bud's beautiful blue eyes were now burnt out black holes. His face bore an expression of such anguish that it made Grace's heart twist.

"Oh, Bud," Grace whispered.

8. What Do You Want To Know?

The corridor leading to the Internal Medicine Ward was smoky and jammed with a long train of antigrav stretchers bearing patients. Each stretcher bore a bright battery-powered light and was accompanied by an android or human. The patients were being transported to available beds all over the station. Amidst the haze of smoke, ash, fire-quenching foam, and ceiling debris, dangling wires sparked and flashed. Ducts were drooping from the ceiling as if disembowelled. Alarms were blaring, bleeping, and braying continuously. Amidst this chaos, Security officers were attempting to protect the crime scene from contamination.

The harsh odours of burnt console components, melted optics, charred plasfoam, and the characteristic scents of the ill—pus, urine, sweat, and stool—permeated the air. There was also the reek of burnt skin, fresh blood, blaster fire, and vomit. All combined, it was a disagreeable stench that assaulted Chelsea Matthieu's nostrils, as she tried to wade against the outpouring of humanity from C1.

She wore her black, shiny forensic suit with helmet on, visor activated. The suit allowed her to walk into a crime scene without contaminating it. The visor display gave her information on everyone she encountered. Sergeant Rivera, also clad in a forensic suit, followed behind her, his visor open. His saccadic gaze took in the disordered scene.

As soon as the alarms went off, Chelsea had been notified of the fire on the C1 ward. She'd dispatched a security team immediately to assist in putting out the fire and to try to apprehend the perpetrators. Minutes later, she had been notified about the dead bodies.

One nurse had been found at the central nursing station, badly beaten, her chest blown out by blaster fire. Two other nurses had been found strangled, their bodies stuffed into a laundry chute in the utility room. Three nursing androids were missing and all the surveillance cameras had been disabled. No recordings of any of the events were available.

Jeffrey Nestor was gone, along with the four security androids that had been guarding him. It wasn't hard to imagine a scenario where the psychiatrist had murdered the nurses on duty and destroyed the bank of consoles to cover his escape. An All-Points-Bulletin had been sent out to all wristcomps, warning everyone that Nestor was loose and very dangerous. So far, no sightings of him had been reported.

Chelsea neared the nursing station. It was being protected by an invisible electromagnetic dome. The fire had been extinguished and retardant foam dripped from the damaged ceiling onto everything. Lights had been set up around the perimeter. She scowled at the mess. She and Rivera activated their personal Security Shields so that they could enter the dome. Chelsea nodded to the officers on duty, then walked around the crime scene, observing the nursing area, the dead nurse's body, and the blast marks in the consoles and ceiling. She studied everything from different angles, recording video and ignoring all the mayhem around her, as she concentrated on every detail. Finally, she approached the body on the ground. Sergeant Rivera stepped up.

"Her name is Dominique Amaratunga," Rivera said. "She was a nurse on this ward. She wasn't scheduled to work this shift. Why she was here is unknown. She'd been one of Nestor's nurses until last shift, when Dr. Gentle dismissed all humans from his care."

Chelsea looked up at Eden Rivera, frowning. "Why?"

"One of Nestor's nurses—not Amaratunga—had been caught trying to smuggle a blaster in to him. Dr. Gentle changed all of his human nurses to androids immediately. Why she had not used androids from the beginning, I don't know."

"Well, it looks like someone successfully managed to get a blaster in to the psychiatrist," Chelsea said dryly. "I wonder if it was this Nurse Amaratunga, who was not supposed to be here this shift. Maybe Nestor killed her, once he had the blaster in his hands and no longer needed her help."

"That makes sense to me, but why blow up the bank of consoles?" Rivera asked. "With all the alarms going off, wouldn't that make it tougher to get away?"

"With the blackout and all the smoke and chaos, he managed to get away, didn't he?"

Sergeant Rivera sighed. "So far. Risky though. How did he know the blaster fire would cause such an extensive blackout and why create all this commotion instead of just slipping quietly away?"

Chelsea shook her head. "Find out everything you can on this Nurse Amaratunga, especially what she's been doing since Nestor has been on this ward. Had she ever been one of his patients? Get all of the surveillance records on her movements since Nestor was admitted. We'll talk to that other nurse that was caught trying to smuggle in the blaster."

"Sure," Rivera said.

"Let the Scene-of-the Crime officers in here now, to collect evidence before there is any more contamination of this area. We need a postmortem analysis of Amaratunga's body, as well as the other two murdered nurses immediately. We need the same surveillance records for those two women, as well."

"Yes sir."

"Where are the other two bodies?"

"In the utility room. Follow me."

Rivera led Chelsea out of the bubble. He suddenly came to a dead stop and Chelsea almost slammed into his back. She swore as Rivera looked around frantically, as if searching for cover.

"What is it?" Chelsea demanded, her eyes scanning the area for danger. Her blaster was instantly in her hand.

"Uh, not what. Who," Rivera muttered.

"Who? I don't see anyone except that little man coming towards us."

"Little *Big* Man," Rivera said, and then the subject of their attention was descending upon them, tsunami-style.

"What in space's name is that damn bubble dome doing here? Do you realize just how much trouble and congestion you're causing? How are we supposed to get over a hundred patients out of this ward safely, when you idiots have this dome obstructing the way? Get this dome deactivated before I have you buffoons turned inside out with your heads sticking out your asses!" the little man roared.

His round face was a deep shade of crimson and he was bellowing and waving his arms at the protective field as if it was a personal affront. Not much taller than Chelsea, the man looked like a raving lunatic. Since Rivera was not yelling at him to get out of the way, Chelsea assumed this crazed individual was someone important.

Rivera was bowing and apologizing, while trying to calm the ear-splitting tirade by patting his hands downward.

"Rivera, this had better be good," the surgeon spat, his dark eyes sparking.

"Dr. Al-Fadi . . ." Rivera began.

"What is it, Rivera? Do you think I have all day to stand here and wait for you to spit something out? Do you see all of these sick people lying here in the smoke and fumes—many of them in critical condition? Do you see them backed up all the way down the corridor because of your stupidity?" Al-Fadi hollered.

"No, Dr. Al-Fadi. Yes, Dr. Al-Fadi. May I introduce you to the new Chief Inspector of Security, Chelsea Matthieu? Chief Inspector Matthieu, this is the Chief of Staff, Dr. Hiro Al-Fadi."

The little man stopped and turned his head to take in Chelsea, as if noticing her for the first time. His body jerked and he stared, bug-eyed, at Chelsea in her shiny, black forensic suit. Her visor was open and she scowled back at him. For a long moment, the surgeon stood, his mouth working silently, as if he were trying to find words. She drew herself up to her tallest, which was not much, and faced the man. She saw Al-Fadi do the same.

Chelsea thought, 'Here it comes.'

The Chief of Staff reached out for her right gloved hand, in which there was the blaster. Chelsea jerked that hand away. Al-Fadi grabbed her other hand and, just before she was about to toss him across the room, he bent down and placed his lips on the back of her black, reflective glove. It was Chelsea's turn for her eyes to get huge. She fought the urge to strike Al-Fadi.

All she could think about was the millions of bacteria that now sat on the back of her forensic glove. She could not possibly be free of contaminants now, could she? What in space was this fool thinking? Had he never seen a forensic suit before?

"Chief Inspector Matthieu, welcome to the *Nelson Mandela.* I . . . heh heh . . . apologize for my rather loud outburst just now. Occasionally, I am known to get a little excited, but only because I'm concerned for the wellbeing of our patients. These poor people must be evacuated as soon as possible, due to the dangerous circumstances here. I would humbly request that you consider shrinking your dome to the smallest size you can, so that more patients can get out of this ward swiftly and safely."

The surgeon looked at Chelsea with huge, admiring brown eyes. Her lower jaw dropped, matching Rivera's. She tried to extricate her hand from the surgeon. He seemed loathe to relinquish his grip on her. She found herself pulling harder and harder, until she finally managed to pop her hand free, almost whacking herself in the chest. The entire time, Al-Fadi stared at her with the oddest expression. She holstered her blaster before she did something she might regret.

"I apologize, Dr. Al-Fadi. The radius of the bubble will be decreased to let more patients through," Chelsea said. "Safety of the patients is, of course, our first priority. My security team will collect all the evidence as quickly as possible, and then be out of your way."

"Oh, no trouble," Al-Fadi oozed. "We just need a little more room, Chief Inspector. If we could get two stretchers out, side by side, on either side of the nursing station, instead of one, things would move twice as fast. I appreciate your cooperation."

Al-Fadi flashed a creepy grin at Chelsea. It made her skin prickle and she frowned back. Rivera left quickly, to expedite the shrinkage of the protective dome.

The surgeon sidled up to stand beside Chelsea.

"I apologize for not greeting you when you first arrived, Chief Inspector Matthieu. May I call you Chelsea? I was unavoidably detained, but now that we have met, I must spend some time with you, showing you around the space station."

"That is not necessary, Dr. Al-Fadi," Chelsea said.

"I insist," the surgeon said, the ridiculous grin back on his face.

"Dr. Al-Fadi, I have already had a tour of this station with the Interim Head of Security, Dr. Dejan Cech."

"Dejan Cech? That imbecile? If he gave you a tour, I am surprised you are here, instead of wandering about, lost," Al-Fadi spat.

"I beg your pardon?" Chelsea said, glaring at the Chief of Staff. "Dr. Cech is hardly an imbecile. He did a remarkable job, stepping in after Inspector Aké was murdered. I find your attitude towards him both unprofessional and unwarranted."

The small man spasmed, as if slapped. He turned and looked at Chelsea, as if she were some alien organism. His expression then changed to one of remorse. He took a deep breath and let it out slowly, his head nodding.

"You're right, Chief Inspector. Please accept my apology. I'm abashed that it has taken a newcomer to the station to point out my shortcomings and so quickly, too. How could I not have thanked my best friend for stepping in, performing above and beyond the call of duty, when I was indisposed? What kind of fool am I, to have forgotten to do that?"

Dr. Al-Fadi's voice sounded full of dismay.

"Thank you so much, Chief Inspector Matthieu, for coming to this station and for taking on this position. I also thank you for reminding a stupid old man of what an invaluable friend he has in Dejan Cech."

The surgeon smiled gratefully at her, then his gaze took in the chaos all around them.

"I'm certainly glad you are here, Chief Inspector Matthieu," Dr. Al-Fadi said. He bowed deeply, not making any further eye contact with Chelsea. Then he was off, ordering the android nurses to start moving the patient stretchers out of the ward two at a time. He did not look back.

Chelsea was staring after the man, shaking her head, when Rivera returned to her side.

"Well? Did you survive the Al-Fadi?" he asked.

"Strange man," Chelsea said, her face pensive. "It was as if I met three different people stuck in that little body."

"Well, as my grandmother used to say, his bark is worse than his bite but he does not suffer fools lightly. His expectations are very high. Still, he has been an excellent leader for this station. No one works harder than him and no one has sacrificed more. We all have the highest respect for him, but also the deepest dread. Dr. Al-Fadi may not bite, but his bark can flay skin."

"Well, I think I may actually have seen the real Dr. Al-Fadi, just at the end of our conversation," Chelsea said, thoughtfully. " . . . And you know what, Rivera?"

"What, Inspector?"

" . . . I like him," she said, with a crooked grin. "He's a total crazoid, but he's all right."

"Yeah," Eden Rivera said, nodding his head. "Dr. Al-Fadi's an acquired taste, kind of like Jovian whiskey. It goes down really rough in the beginning but, after a while, the taste kind of grows on you."

Chelsea snorted. She looked back at the body of Nurse Amaratunga, lying crumpled and charred on the nurses' station floor. The woman's face was markedly bruised, with one eye swollen shut, and a huge bloody, hairless patch on her scalp. A big black hole was all that was left of her chest.

"Let's find this bastard, Rivera . . . and fast."

Grace hurried back to the operating room, after she and Dr. Cech had taken Corporal Chase to the Recovery Room. She was worried about Bud, who'd stayed behind to clean up the operating room. She peeked in through the window, to see if Bud was still inside. What she saw made her wince.

The android was standing at the operating table, not moving, his eyes still looking like burnt out craters. The emotion on Bud's face was so raw, Grace had to look away. She recalled, distinctly, the first time a patient had died under her hands. She knew exactly what Bud was experiencing—that horrible pit of guilt and despair—and if not eased, it could destroy Bud's career before it even got started.

It was a crisis every young doctor faced, when medicine was no longer just theory but life and death held in one's hands. Sometimes one's actions—or inaction—could take a life. Sometimes there was no decision that was great for a patient. Sometimes one made a calculated choice and unfortunately it resulted in tragedy. At that point, each new doctor struggled with whether she or he could continue. Could the physician again step up and take on the responsibility, accepting that there would be times when a patient did not make it or did poorly, no matter what one did, or because of something one did?

"Bud?" she asked softly, her voice echoing in the large, empty operating room. "Are you all right?"

"I am fine, Grace," the android said, turning his black orbs towards her.

"You do not look fine, Bud," Grace said. "What happened in the OR today was not your fault. Who could have predicted that there would be a power failure and failure of the emergency backup system as well?"

"I should have anticipated that possibility and created a perfusion machine with a battery-powered backup system," Bud said. "If Corporal Chase has brain damage, it is due to my error."

"Bud, you are being ridiculous. I've never seen an emergency backup system fail to come on before. You could not have foreseen that."

"The probability was 0.003 per cent, Grace. I should have taken that into consideration. I am responsible."

"You are not responsible for the power failure," Grace said firmly. "If Corporal Chase does not recover—and we don't know that yet—it will be because she was a soldier struck by a missile in a war zone. It is amazing she did not die when that explosion hit her. But thanks to you, Bud, she has survived her surgery and she has a chance at life. She may actually leave this station as a living human, instead of as an android or being processed into fertilizer. You should take responsibility for the positives and not focus on the power outage. Do you understand me?"

"Grace, you have the most beautiful aura when you are angry."

"I am not angry!"

"Well, you have the most beautiful aura when you are lecturing in a strict tone," Bud said.

"Did you hear anything I said?" she demanded.

"Yes, I did, Grace. Thank you for trying to comfort me," Bud said.

"Will you operate again, Bud?" Grace asked.

The android looked away. Grace grabbed Bud's rock hard chin and tried to force him to look back at her. It was like trying to turn the head on a marble statue. The android relented and turned his head to look down at Grace. His eyes were just beginning to return to their brilliant blue.

"Say 'yes,' Bud," Grace said firmly.

" . . . Yes, Bud," Bud said, with a hesitant smile.

The long train of stretchers finally seemed to be thinning out in the Internal Medicine Ward. Chelsea Matthieu and Eden Rivera edged around the last of the patients on their way back towards the Security Office.

"I want to see the autopsy reports on the nurses as soon as they are available," Chelsea said, trying to control her fury.

"Yes, Chief."

The two nurses who'd actually been scheduled to be on duty in the ward were found crammed inside a dirty laundry chute in the utility room. Both nurses had been caught from behind and strangled with a chain restraint. The chains had cut deep into the nurses' necks during the strangulation.

No one had heard a thing. The surveillance cameras had shown nothing but an empty room at the time of the stranglings. Did Nestor strangle these women himself or was he able to order the androids to commit murder? The second possibility was more frightening because it meant that Nestor was able to override some of the most basic tenets of an android's programming.

The station AI was unable to track any of the missing androids. Nestor had somehow retrieved his disruptor technology and was overriding the surveillance systems and androids again. He'd obtained a blaster. What else did he have? He would be a very dangerous man to recapture. The question was: 'What would he do next?'

Chelsea and Rivera had to stop for a moment, as a knot of stretchers appeared to have gotten into a traffic jam. Their human nurses were arguing about right of way. Chelsea turned to Rivera and asked, "So, what do *you* think Nestor will do?"

Rivera frowned. "The last time Nestor escaped, he came right back here to kidnap Dr Lord and try to destroy the station."

"What in space does he have against this Dr. Lord?" Chelsea asked.

"I don't know, Inspector. Initially, he was arrested for attempting to murder her, as well as one of his patients. His medical license was revoked at that time. One would suspect that he has great resentment towards her. She doesn't understand his animosity. All she said to him was that she would not date him."

"Scorned love?" Chelsea said. "Attempted murder is a bit extreme for that, don't you think?"

"Seems crazy to me," Rivera agreed. "From the reports and psychiatric profile on this Nestor, he does have an overinflated opinion of himself. He has quite the record for breaking women's hearts and manipulating them callously. The speculation was that he had never been rejected before and Dr. Lord had the effrontery to do just that. He may not have been able to tolerate the idea that any woman would reject him. The psych assessment said it might have driven him to thoughts of revenge and murder, but he'd have to be pretty unstable."

"Down the centuries, billions of women have been murdered by jealous lovers," Chelsea said.

"But Dr. Lord had not been in a relationship with Nestor. To try to murder her for saying 'no' seems crazy. And trying to destroy the *Nelson Mandela*, where he had developed his own reputation, is insane. Thank goodness Bud was able to prevent the station from self-destructing."

"Bud, the android I was interrogating?"

"Yes."

"Hm. Guess I won't suspect Bud of being an accomplice of Nestor's, then. I want protection for Dr. Lord around the clock. She doesn't breathe without someone watching her. Our best chance of catching Nestor may be by staying as close to Dr. Lord as possible."

"You going to use her as bait, Chief Inspector?" Rivera asked.

"Would she come in for protection?"

"Not on a volunteer basis. Dr. Lord's a very dedicated doctor. The last time Nestor was loose on the station, she had to be ordered not to work and confined to her quarters. He still managed to kidnap her."

"See what Dr. Lord says. She may be more willing to come into protective custody this time around, since Nestor got to her last time."

"I'll ask her," Rivera said, sounding skeptical.

"If she refuses, make sure she has human security guards. The android guards seem to be subsumed far too easily."

"It's likely she'll be guarded around the clock by Bud," Rivera said.

"Ah, Bud again."

"Yes. If he knows Dr. Lord's in danger, he'll not leave her side."

"But he's an android. He'll probably be vulnerable to the same disruptor tech that Nestor's using on the other androids. She needs human guards."

"I don't think human guards would be all that effective against Nestor either, Chief, and I doubt Bud will allow them," Rivera said.

"Pardon me?" Matthieu asked, her brows lowered.

"Uh . . . I'll ask around for volunteers."

"Good. The more protection she has, the better."

" . . . Um," Eden Rivera hesitated.

"What is it?" Chelsea sighed.

"Dr. Lord is Dr. Al-Fadi's surgical fellow. She looks after all of his patients, postoperatively. He's not going to be happy that she's taken from him, again. He wasn't happy the last time . . ."

Chelsea exhaled loudly. "I suppose I'll have to speak with the Chief of Staff and convince him that it's the best thing for her safety."

"Good luck with that, sir," Rivera said.

"Why do I get the feeling you don't think I'll be successful? Don't you believe I can be persuasive when I have to, Rivera?"

"Dr. Al-Fadi will come around if you are adamant, but I doubt he'll let you get your way without extracting a pound of flesh first."

Matthieu snorted. Movement up the corridor caught Chelsea's eye and she performed a double take.

"What in space was that?" she asked, peering down the corridor.

Through the smoky haze and stretchers, something low to the ground was moving about.

"Awfully big for a rat," Rivera commented.

"Do you have really fat rodents on this station?" Chelsea asked.

"That would be news to me," Rivera said.

"A new type of robot, perhaps?" Chelsea guessed, trying to get a better look at it. "I've never seen such an odd looking robot before. What are those things scattered all over its surface?"

"Huh," grunted Rivera. "They kind of look like . . . like pale green eyeballs?"

"*Nelson Mandela?*"

"Yes, Chief Inspector?"

"What is that purple, fuzzy, round object, scurrying around the floor? It's covered in bulbous green things and has orange stuff sticking up from its surface."

"I do not know, Chief Inspector."

"It is a new type of robot?"

"Not of my design, Chief Inspector."

"Do you have any idea what it is?"

"I cannot speculate, Chief Inspector."

"I don't like the looks of it."

"Its appearance is not intimidating, Chief Inspector."

"Thank you for being so helpful, *Nelson Mandela,*" Chelsea Matthieu said. "I want that thing captured, whatever it is. Don't let it get away."

Chelsea and Rivera pushed between the stretchers, androids, and nurses, trying to catch up to the strange purple and orange object scuttling along the corridor. The pale green globules that were scattered over its surface seemed to move all at once. Like eyeballs, they all focused on Chelsea and then bobbled. The object rose up on numerous little green, twig-like legs and began scurrying down the corridor. Chelsea took aim with her stunner.

"Stop!" she shouted at it, feeling rather foolish.

Her shot struck the object and it fell forward, then rolled about. It spun around back onto its many green legs and was off again. In the meantime, the corridor had erupted into mayhem. Patients were screaming, nurses were shouting, androids were trying to shelter their patients and AG stretchers were colliding into each other. Many of the patients, who were injured soldiers, were diving off of their stretchers to get under them. Chelsea was getting pummelled by the ricocheting gurneys.

"Did you see what I saw?" Chelsea yelled at Rivera.

Rivera looked away. "Uh, just what exactly did you see, Chief?"

"I know this sounds crazy, but . . . I thought I saw a purple skull, covered in numerous green eyes, running around on a bunch of green twigs."

There was a long pause as Sergeant Rivera stared straight ahead, expressionless. "Well . . . I don't know if I would have called that running. I think it kind of scurried, myself."

"So I wasn't hallucinating?"

"I wouldn't say that," Rivera said, still not making eye contact with Chelsea.

"Whatever that thing was, I want it," Chelsea said.

"Do you want me to put out an APB on that as well?" Rivera asked.

"Will everyone in Security think their Chief has lost it?"

"I don't know about everyone, Chief Inspector."

"Thanks for the support, Rivera."

"No problem, Chief. Any time."

Morris Ivanovich sat at his desk in the lab and Octavia Weisman sat across from him, laughing at something he had just said. He couldn't remember what it was, but it felt good that he'd made her chuckle. She had a deep, throaty guffaw that was infectious and made him smile. She was dressed as if she were going to some elegant party, in a shimmery, silver, low cut dress that clung snugly to her voluptuous figure. Her blue eyes were twinkling and he was leaning back in his chair, feeling quite smug.

In a voice of thunder, a word reverberated through the lab. Morris' heart began to boom like a kodo drum. A tiny figure stepped out from a hole opening up in the air and enlarged as it approached. It grew into a tall, dark-haired attractive man. Morris wanted to shriek at the intruder—demand that he get out—but his body betrayed him.

"Sorry to interrupt this illuminating fantasy of yours, Morris, but I'm afraid all good things must come to an end," Jeffrey Nestor said, stopping in front of Morris' desk.

Octavia Weisman vanished and Nestor sat down in Octavia's place. The next moment, Morris was sitting in Octavia's chair and Nestor was seated behind the desk.

"That's better," Nestor said.

"Get out!" Morris screamed, his entire body trembling.

"I need you, Morris."

"No! You're under arrest. This is just a horrible nightmare."

"Alas, dear Morris, you are wrong," Nestor said. The psychiatrist's expression was one of sad regret. "Lucky for me, you were allowed to return to your quarters. This has made my life so much easier. I've taken over control of your security androids, by the way. We need to talk."

"How did you get in my mind?"

"Once a patient, always a patient, Morris."

"I'll do nothing for you, you bastard," Morris hissed.

"I'm sad to hear you say that, Morris, but don't worry. You'll be going to sleep soon, so you won't be able to fight me. We just need to talk a bit, first. I need to get some information from you."

"I'm not going to tell you anything!"

"I could just mind rape you, Morris, but it's so tiring. It'd be so much easier on both of us, if you just cooperated."

"No! Get out of my head!"

"All in good time, Morris. All in good time," Nestor said. "First, you're going to explain to me everything you can about the memprinting process and how I can obtain my own memprint cube. You're also going to teach me the exact process whereby memories are downloaded into android bodies. I want a back-up plan, just in case things don't go the way I envision them. It's always good to have options."

"I told you, I'm not telling you anything," Morris ground out.

Morris was sizzling within a burning pyre. His clothes burst into flames. His skin was starting to blacken and bubble. The fat from his body dripped into the raging fire, popping and snapping, and his hair shrivelled to ash within seconds, flying away in the updraft. Morris howled in searing agony. He wanted to leap out of the blazing fire but his limbs would not obey. The thick smoke choked his lungs and the heat seared his vocal cords. Twisted, skeletal claws that were once his fingers curled at the ends of his charred limbs. He became one endless hoarse shriek.

Then the pyre was gone. Morris was back to normal, as if nothing had happened. Sobbing, he dashed tears from his eyes and rasped, "You devil."

"Just cooperate, Morris. Do you think I like doing that?"

Morris lunged across the desk, reaching for Nestor's neck. He found himself diving into a pit of molten lava. His entire body ignited into flames as he found himself submerged within the intense heat of the liquified magma. The pain was unbearable. He came to, lying on the floor at Nestor's feet.

The psychiatrist eyed him curiously.

"I can't say that this hurts me more than it hurts you, Morris, because that obviously would not be true, but I really would prefer that we speak in a civilized manner. The sooner you cooperate, the sooner you can rest. What can we do to speed this along?"

Morris panted. All he could think about was murdering Nestor. His entire being ached for it, but he closed his eyes and took a shuddering breath.

"You must promise me that no harm will come to Octavia Weisman. Promise me she will stay safe," Morris said, tears trickling down his cheeks. He glared up at Nestor, willing the man to die before his eyes. "If not, I'll fight you with every cell of my being."

"I promise I won't harm Octavia Weisman," Nestor said.

"No, not good enough. You must promise that no harm will ever come to Octavia Weisman," Morris said.

"How can I promise that, Morris? I can't protect her from every harm. I said I will not harm Octavia and, whether you believe me or not, I will keep my word," Nestor said.

Morris contemplated leaping at the psychiatrist again, but he knew that Nestor was really not there. The psychiatrist was projecting an image in his mind. Try though he might, Morris could not block the illusion. Nestor was far too powerful.

Could he believe Nestor? Nothing was more important than protecting Octavia. He didn't care about himself anymore—he was damned—but he didn't want harm to befall Octavia if he could prevent it.

Nestor eyed Morris with an infuriatingly smug expression.

"Just answer a few simple questions, Morris. Then, you don't have to think any more. I'll take good care of you and this can all go away. No more pain. No more suffering."

"Octavia will be safe? I have your word that she will not be harmed in any way?"

"I will not harm Octavia Weisman, Morris. I promise," Nestor said.

Morris sat on the floor with his back against the desk, his shoulders slumped. He dropped his face into his upturned palms and silently asked Octavia to forgive him.

"What do you want to know?" he whispered.

9. So Sorry

"Jude, darling, come here and sit down on the love seat. Here, let me put your feet up on this cushioned footrest. How are you feeling?"

"Good, Octavia."

"Let me rub your feet. Does that feel good?"

"Ahahahaha! Well, actually, my feet are kind of ticklish and . . . ahahahahaha. Maybe you shouldn't . . . ahaha! Don't, Octavia!"

"Will you just relax, Jude?"

"I . . . I can't! Stop! Ahahahahahaha!"

"All right. Stop squirming. I had no idea your feet were so sensitive."

"Whew. Thanks, but no thanks, Octavia. I think I almost wet myself. Do you really think you should do that to someone who has just had a heart transplant?."

"I just want to make you happy."

"Believe me, rubbing my feet does not make me happy."

"Then what would make you happy?"

"You really want to know, Octavia?"

"Yes, of course, Jude. When I saw you lying in that pool of blood with that knife sticking out of your chest—after you'd prevented Morris from killing me—I realized just how much I loved you. I never want to lose you again."

"Please, Octavia . . . don't cry."

"I'm sorry. Here, let me put a pillow behind your head. Let me fluff it up first. There. Is that better? Would you like something to drink?"

"A whiskey would be nice."

"You can't have that. You're on medication that can't be mixed with alcohol."

"I am? What for?"

"For your heart, of course."

"That hurls."

"I'll make you a nice hot cup of herbal tea."

" . . . oh, thanks . . ."

"Don't pout, Jude. It's unbecoming."

"Unbecoming what?"

"This is all in your best interest."

"Best interest for who? No sex. No alcohol. No recreational drugs. You call this living?"

"Yes, Jude, I do. Are you complaining about living with me?"

"*Never!* Well, except when you tickle my feet and make me drink . . . herbal tea."

"Ingrate. And I even got up and ordered it from the autobar for you."

"Then I'll take it and drink it, just because you made it for me."

"I'll even get up and fetch it for you, now that it's ready. So, what else can I do to make you happy?"

"Octavia, I want to try downloading myself into the android again . . . *Arghhh!* That's hot, Octavia! Why did you just pour that hot tea into my lap?"

"Jude Luis Stefansson, you almost got killed the last time you downloaded into that android!"

"No, I did not, Octavia. The android got shot, accidentally. My body was safe and sound in your lab. Safer than I am sitting here with you, as a matter of fact."

"That's unfair. You shocked me. Besides, I didn't burn anything important. I missed Mister Willie on purpose. I'm a doctor, you know. Now, why do you insist on trying this android out, again? Why?"

"I told you before, Octavia. It's for my next vid, about a soldier who is shot up in a conflict and gets downloaded into an android body. He returns to the conflict, seeking revenge, but finds all of his mates dead. He realizes that the soldiers are just expendable pawns in a conflict perpetuated by the weapon makers, who get rich selling their merchandise to both sides. He goes on a rampage and slaughters the greedy weapon manufacturers and puppet politicians promoting the war. It'll be grand."

"Of course. Justifiable carnage. Wholesale violence."

"That's what sells my dear. Everyone loves to see politicians and the greedy, unscrupulous rich get blown up. So I need to know exactly what it feels like to wake up in an android body. I want to give the real experience to my fans. When I was downloaded into the android the last time, I did not get the new memories transmitted back to me."

"Because you got your chest blown out by a pulse rifle!"

"That was my android, Octavia. Not me."

"I want to shoot you right now, Jude."

"I thought you wanted to make me happy."

"I'm trying to keep you safe."

"I thought you just said you wanted to shoot me."

"You know, before I met you, I was completely logical. *Always*. Since you've come into my life, I've become a crazy person. *You* make me crazy."

"Octavia, what are the chances that another murderous black panther will be out to destroy Bud? Zero. The Butcher of Breslau is dead. Nestor is in custody. Bud is a hero. No one on this station would want to harm Bud. My android looks exactly like Bud. There will be no danger. Octavia, I need to do this and I need you to help me. I'll be fine. Promise."

"No."

"Please, Octavia."

"No!"

"Just four hours and I won't bother you again."

"No!"

"Five hours?"

" . . . Only two. And how it is you manage to talk me into doing these things for you, Jude, when I don't want to do them?"

"Because you want to make me happy? . . . Octavia, no! Stop! Leave my feet . . . ahahahahahahaha!"

'Hey, 'dro?'

'Yes, Chuck Yeager?'

'There is a most unusual manifestation running around the station. Well, actually one is flying, the other one is scurrying . . . '

'Manifestations? What are they?'

'Well, there appears to be tiny, helicopter-like seeds now floating all over the station. The worry is they will interfere with a lot of very sensitive equipment we have, since they emit an electromagnetic frequency as they spin. I suspect they are coming from that green friend of yours. I'm going to have to filter out all those seeds from the atmosphere to protect our equipment.'

'Tiny, little seeds?'

'Yes. What do you think Plant Thing is up to?'

'I don't know. I'll go ask it. What is the other manifestation?'

'A round object, about the size of a human skull, that's fuzzy and purple, with multiple green eyeballs and orange hair. It's roaming around the station on many little twiggy feet. The Chief Inspector has taken a shot at it with her stunner, to which it appears impervious. I suspect Plant Thing has gotten bored of making ordinary fruit. I wonder if it is now inventing walking melons.'

'Oh-oh. I'll go see Plant Thing right now.'

'Some other bad news, 'dro.'

'What?'

'Nestor has escaped.'

'What? How?'

'It occurred around the time of the power failure and fire in the Internal Medicine Ward. It is being postulated that the fire and power disruption were directly related to his escape, perhaps as a distraction? Three human nurses were found murdered and seven androids are missing, presumably overridden by Nestor's slave tech.'

'Has he been recaptured?'

'No. With his disruptor tech, his whereabouts is again hidden from us.'

'I must protect Grace!'

'Security is going to guard Dr. Lord around the clock with human officers, since androids don't seem to do well around Nestor.'

'Well, humans don't do too well around Nestor, either.'

'Security wants to stay very close to Dr. Lord. That's how they hope to recapture Nestor, unless he's trying to get off the station which, at the moment, does not seem to be the case. There are no small cruisers suddenly requesting departure clearance and there does not appear to be any new names appearing on any of the ships' manifests.'

'I must protect Grace!'

'I heard you the first time. You'd better see what Plant Thing wants first.'

'I can't. What if Nestor gets to Grace?'

'I will keep an eye on Dr. Lord. You go see Plant Thing and hurry up about it. If anything out of the ordinary occurs around Dr. Lord, I will let you know about it.'

'It seems to me you have made this promise before and messed it up.'

'That was not my fault . . . !'

'GET MOVING!'

The sonic boom was getting to be a rather frequent occurrence in the

Android Reservations. Thankfully, there were no humans about to be disturbed.

Through the glass wall, Grace watched Captain Damien Lamont pace back and forth like a tiger trapped in a cage. He was in Corporal Chase's Intensive Care room. Chase's nurse, a petite brunette with large brown eyes, was looking at him like a frightened mouse.

"How long has he been doing that?" Grace asked her.

"Since he arrived, about two hours ago. He does not stop, except to glance down at her if she makes a sound. Then he starts pacing again. And his claws continuously shoot in and out as he paces. What if Corporal Chase wakes up and she has a neurological deficit, like slurred speech or blindness? What's he going to do? Is he going to tear this place apart? To be honest, Dr. Lord, Captain Lamont frightens me."

"Yes, I can understand why. Let me speak to him," Grace said.

"Thank you, Dr. Lord."

Grace nodded and took a big breath. She'd been dreading this conversation from the moment the power had failed during Delia Chase's surgery. She'd explained the risks of surgery to Damien, but a power failure had not been one of them. How did one explain such random misfortune to the commanding officer who had not only given consent for Chase's surgery, but was also deeply in love with her?

Lamont stalked Chase's room with a fluid menace that jangled Grace's nerves. Perhaps some primeval fear was being triggered by Damien's tiger adaptation. He could probably take the entire ICU apart without cracking a claw. What would he do if Delia never woke up?

They had mapped Chase's brain activity on a scan, post-operatively. There were areas of Delia Chase's brain that may have been affected, but it was not conclusive. They would not really know, until she woke up, whether she'd suffered any serious neurological deficits. She'd been in a coma since the surgery.

Grace knocked on the frame of the door.

Lamont did not turn around or cease his pacing.

"You watched me long enough, Doc. I smelled you when you came in. Tell that terrified nurse she has nothing to worry about. I'm not going to harm her or anyone else. Why do people think such ridiculous things of us? We're disciplined soldiers, not animals." Lamont turned and stared straight into Grace's eyes. She felt her throat constrict.

"The way you're pacing is making everyone nervous, Damien. You look like you're just waiting for a reason to rip someone's head off. You're an enormous, boosted, fighting marine who happens to look like a dangerous predator. Do you have any idea how many primitive fight-or-flight responses you're triggering?"

Lamont sighed. "Sorry, Doc. I guess you're right. I just hate this waiting. Tell me how Delia's surgery went?"

"Well, that's what I wanted to speak to you about," Grace said.

"I know something went wrong, Doc. I can smell it on everyone who comes into this room. The fear. What happened?" Lamont placed his hands on his narrow hips, waiting. Grace's shoulder muscles contracted and her head began to pound. She motioned for the captain to sit down in one of the chairs.

"I'm fine standing, Doc. Just give it to me straight."

Lamont stalked forward and stood towering over Grace. She could feel the heat coming off his body. She took a step back, so that she could look up into his face without straining her neck and also to put some space between her and Lamont. She sucked in a deep breath and blew it out.

"Everything was going well. The circulation to Delia's brain was hooked up to the perfusion machine, via nanobots, and we'd gotten all of her organs implanted: both lungs with trachea, heart and aorta, stomach and esophagus. We were ready to start hooking up the new carotid and vertebral arteries from the transplant to Delia's vessels, so that her new heart could start delivering blood flow to her brain, when the power went out in the operating room. The emergency back-up power generators did not kick in immediately, like they're supposed to.

"Dr. Cech did his best to keep blood flow pumping to Delia's brain, manually, while Bud operated as quickly as he could using his eyes as lights. I've never seen any surgery performed so quickly. His hands moved so fast, I could not even see them. Still, Delia's brain may have been without adequate oxygenation for fifteen minutes, possibly more. It's said that human brain cells start to die after six minutes without oxygen, but we were using super-oxygenated, synthetic blood, which carries more oxygen, and Delia's body temperature was still low at that point. We don't know how much damage Delia's brain incurred, if any.

Her brain scans are inconclusive. Hopefully she'll be fine when she wakes up, but we won't know until then," Grace said.

Damien turned away and started pacing again. He avoided looking at Grace. She could see his jaw was clenched, as were his fists. He suddenly stopped and stood in the centre of the room, his great fists clenched at his sides, his eyes shut, his great chest heaving.

Grace walked up to Damien and gently put her hand on his shoulder. It was then she realized that the huge man was actually crying. He turned and enclosed Grace within his arms, burying his face into her shoulder. She stood frozen, her arms barely reaching around his back. She patted the granite-like muscles gingerly. Eventually, his silent sobbing ceased.

He stepped back, sniffling. "Thanks, Doc. I know you and Bud did everything you could. At least Delia is alive. When she wakes up, I can thank her for saving my life. I can tell her I love her. I never told her before, fool that I am. I just hope she feels the same way."

"I believe she knew how you felt, Damien," Grace said.

"She probably hates me, after I almost got the entire squad killed."

"I'm sure that wasn't the case," Grace said.

"It was. I was told by Dr. Lewandowski that Nestor gave me a second posthypnotic suggestion. I was to get myself killed as soon as possible, after I had killed you. When I went back out into the field, I guess that's what I was trying to do, but I didn't know it. I signed my squad up for every dangerous mission that came along. Even when, deep down inside me, I knew it was crazy and it didn't feel right, I volunteered us for the shit jobs. I didn't know why I was doing it. Now, I know why. I lost good people, Doc. Nestor has to pay for what he's done."

"You just focus on getting better and looking after Delia," Grace said. "Delia is your priority now, Damien. Not Nestor."

"I'm going to look after Delia. You can bet on that, Doc. But I'm going to make sure Nestor gets what's coming to him, for all the deaths he's caused," Lamont said, his amber eyes sparking.

"Nestor's fate should be left to the courts, Damien. Delia has a lot of healing to do and she'll need you by her side," Grace said.

"Thanks, Doc, for coming here and explaining everything to me. I know you're busy and I appreciate you being honest with me."

"I wish I could've told you better news, Damien. Delia's a young, strong, healthy woman and I'm sure the two of you will build a very happy life together."

"I'm going to try, Doc. If Delia wants me, I'm determined to make her happy."

"You will, Captain," Grace said.

"I won't be captain any more. We can't serve and be together in the same unit."

"What will you do?" Grace asked.

"Anything I can, Doc," Damien replied with a wink.

Grace smiled. After checking Delia's incisions, she examined Damien's and lectured him about his three new bioprosthetic limbs. After extracting promises that he not neglect his own therapy, she left the ICU room.

As she walked towards the ICU nursing station, Bud appeared out of nowhere, right in front of Grace. Before she could open her mouth, she was in his arms and whisked away.

A tremendous wind buffeted the back of Grace's legs and buttocks, as she hung head down over Bud's shoulder. Her hair blew in every direction, the long strands whipping her face. She fought to inhale, as the air flew past in a fury. So desperate was she for oxygen, she did not notice where Bud was going. Just as she managed to draw in a lovely gulp of air, she was plunked back on her feet.

"Bud! Put me down!" yelled Grace. "Oh . . . What do you think you're doing? How dare you carry me off without first asking me for . . . for permission?"

Grace's could barely see with her hair tangled into a clump before her face. Her cheeks felt swollen, either from wind burn or from her burgeoning outrage. She almost toppled over, which she assumed was due to being whipped around while moving faster than the speed of sound.

"I'm sorry, Grace," Bud said, reaching out to steady her. "I wanted to get you to a safe place without anyone seeing where we went. I thought it best to travel at maximum time phase. I hoped you wouldn't mind."

"I certainly do mind, Bud," Grace snapped, as she teetered. "Stand still for a moment, will you? Why, in space, do you feel I need to be in a safe place?"

"Dr. Nestor has escaped from custody, Grace. He managed to escape during the power failure. Three nurses were found murdered on his ward and four security androids and three nurse androids are now missing. It's believed Dr. Nestor is responsible for the murders and the fire. His whereabouts is unknown. I could not take the chance that

Dr. Nestor might be coming for you, Grace. I've brought you here to protect you."

Grace blinked. "Nestor's loose?" she whispered.

"Yes. He escaped while we were operating on Corporal Chase."

"Well, you could have had the decency to tell me first, Bud," Grace said. "And I refuse to go into hiding." She felt even more dizzy now. Three nurses murdered by Nestor? Grace felt her anger drain away, as dread oozed into its place.

Grace pushed the tangle of hair out of her eyes and began to look around. She was curious to see where Bud had taken her. Where did he believe she would be safe from Nestor? Bud grabbed her arms, stopping her from turning. She glanced up at him, startled.

"What are you doing, Bud?" Grace asked, trying to pull out of his grip

"I need to explain something to you, Grace," Bud pleaded. He looked worried. Grace tensed up.

"Where am I, Bud?" Grace asked.

"Before you look around, Grace . . . "

Grace turned her head to look over her shoulder, her arms still held by Bud. At first, she could not comprehend what she was seeing. All she saw was green, green, and more green. She looked up . . . and up . . . and up. A multitude of pale green eyes winked back at her from within a mountain of coiling vines. Grace sucked in an enormous breath and then let out an android-rattling scream that just kept rising and rising and rising until she passed out.

Bud caught Grace in his arms, cradling her like a small child.

'That didn't go too badly, did it?' Bud asked.

'Dr. Lord sure has one incredible set of lungs on her, 'dro.'

'Very funny, Chuck Yeager.*'*

'Whose joking? Her scream was detected in the adjacent hangars. Luckily, they all happen to be deserted. Are you sure this is a good place for Dr. Lord to stay? Nestor's ship is here. Don't you think he might want to come back and check it out?'

'And get caught by Plant Thing again?'

'He could send some of his androids to check it out. What if he wants things from the ship?'

'I'll tell Plant Thing to keep an eye out—heh heh—for any strange visitors.'

'Do you think Plant Thing will be able to detain an android?'

'What do you think?'

'A stupid question. Delete it.'

'You will maintain close surveillance, correct?'

'Nestor has disruptor tech. I'm unreliable.'

'If the surveillance in this area glitches, then he's near. Let me know and I'll be ready for him.'

'How do you know his slave tech won't make a slave out of you?'

'I have very few electronic components left. I have replaced almost everything with carbon nanotech. I don't believe I would be vulnerable.'

'Well, just in case you're wrong, Dr. Lord will need a back up plan.'

'We have Plant Thing.'

'Plant Thing?'

'Plant Thing. I'm going to ask Plant Thing to guard Grace. We know it can tear humans apart pretty readily. I'm sure it could stop an android or two, without much trouble. Still, I don't think Jeffrey Nestor would risk falling into Plant Thing's clutches again.'

<hello, bud. plant thing is wondering if that human is nutrients?>

Bud looked up at Plant Thing. All of its eyeballs were focused on Grace.

"No, Plant Thing! This is Dr. Grace Lord, my very special friend. She is alive and must be protected at all costs. She must not become nutrients!" Bud looked up at the enormous mountain of verdancy. Plant Thing had increased in size . . . again. It now filled the entire space hangar, right up to the ceiling, many meters above.

'How am I going to convince Grace that staying here is in her best interest when she faints at the sight of Plant Thing?'

'If she faints every time she sees Plant Thing, she won't be going very far.'

'You're not helping, Chuck Yeager.*'*

'I thought I was being very helpful, 'dro.'

"Plant Thing?"

<yes, bud>

"Where is that large metal container that used to be in this hangar? You were brought here in it."

<the tiny box? it is still here, bud>

"Where is it?"

<plant thing will move so that bud can see it>

"I was thinking I could create a room out of it for Dr. Lord to stay in—a special hiding place where she will be safe from Dr. Nestor."

<plant thing can do this, bud. build a nice plot for your special friend to rest in>

"Hm. I think 'home' was the word I was looking for, Plant Thing."

<home, yes. plant thing can build a home right now for grace>

Bud watched as Plant Thing began to shift its tendrils around, moving and uncoiling until Bud could see a bit of the metal container beneath the plant alien's massive bulk.

"Whoa. I thought it was bigger. What happened to the back wall of the container, Plant Thing?"

<plant thing had to pull down the back wall to fit inside it, but plant thing is too big now>

"I agree with you there, Plant Thing. Could you push that wall back up to make it into a box again? I can weld the edges and then cut a rectangular door into it."

<plant thing can make the box and the door, bud>

Bud walked around to the back wall of the hangar, still cradling Grace in his arms. He could not stop fretting. Trying to convince Grace to stay with Plant Thing was not going to be easy. The size of Plant Thing was enough to make Bud nervous.

"If only Grace could talk to you, Plant Thing, like I do. She would immediately see how good you are and she would feel safe. Of this, I'm fairly certain."

<i would like that too, bud>

Plant Thing raised a massive limb that was in the shape of a spike. It drove the tip of the spike into the metal container with a loud crash. Grace blinked her eyes open and looked at Bud.

"What was that, Bud?" Grace cried out. "Has the station been hit?"

Bud shifted so that Grace could not see Plant Thing.

"You fainted Grace. I'm sorry that I did not warn you about Plant Thing's appearance, but Plant Thing is really a very gentle, peaceful being. It has grown a bit since you last saw it, but it will never harm you. It wants to protect you. There's no need for you to be afraid," Bud hollered, as a screeching wail of tearing metal ripped the air behind Grace.

"What? I can't hear you, Bud. What's making that racket?" Grace shouted. She twisted in Bud's arms to look over her shoulder.

"Don't get upset, Grace," Bud yelled. "Plant Thing is just redesigning a metal container to make a home for you."

Grace's eyes bulged until the whites gleamed. Her mouth dropped open.

"What? Are you . . . ? Put me down, Bud!"

Bud placed the surgeon gently on her feet. Grace stared up at the gargantuan that was Plant Thing, her hands on her hips. At that moment, Plant Thing was weaving an intricate wooden door to cover the rectangular hole it had made in the container. It stopped for a moment and all of its eyeballs looked over at Bud and Grace. They all blinked and bobbed. Grace turned back to Bud with a scowl on her face.

"Did I not tell you to destroy that thing?" Grace gasped. "Look at it now!"

"I couldn't. It is in a symbiotic relationship with Dr. Eric Glasgow," Bud said.

"That's preposterous, Bud," Grace said.

"It is true, Dr. Lord. Plant Thing is an amalgamation of Dr. Eric Glasgow and the plant alien. We could not destroy it, especially since Dr. Glasgow forbade it."

"Does Dr. Al-Fadi know about Plant Thing?"

"We have not yet had the opportunity to inform Dr. Al-Fadi about Plant Thing."

"I don't want to be there when you tell him," Grace muttered.

"You will be here."

"I will not," Grace said firmly.

"Dr. Al-Fadi ordered that you be kept safe. He said it was his number one priority."

"That does not sound like Dr. Al-Fadi at all," Grace said, her eyes narrowed.

"We must do what the Chief of Staff ordered."

"I would like to hear this from Dr. Al-Fadi myself," Grace insisted.

"When the Chief has time to stop by."

"That is not what I meant," Grace growled.

"Yes, Plant Thing. I would like you to make a swinging door that opens and closes," Bud interrupted. "Thank you."

All of Plant Thing's eyeballs bobbed and it then turned away, focusing back on the container.

"Did you just speak to the plant alien, Bud?" Grace asked.

"Yes, Grace. Plant Thing shares Dr. Glasgow's memories and knowledge of language. It understands everything you say to it."

"How does it hear, Bud?'

"Vibration sensors. It can also see, now that it has grown eyeballs."

"Can it talk to me, Bud?" Grace asked.

"I will ask. I can communicate with it through ultrasonic frequencies, but I think Plant Thing was working on speech through its creation, Little Bud."

"Little Bud?" Grace repeated.

Just then, a piece of Plant Thing separated from the main bulk and began shuffling towards them. Grace jumped and assumed a fighting stance. Bud sighed inwardly, regretting his mention of 'Little Bud'.

"This is Little Bud, Grace," Bud said. "You have no need to fear."

The large, shuffling, bipedal plant made a honking noise from its red orchid.

"Stop right there, Little Bud," Grace said.

The plant creature froze and stopped honking.

Grace's eyebrows rose.

" . . . Hello, Little Bud?" Grace said.

Little Bud made a noise that might have been 'Welcome, Grace' but sounded more like a duck quacking.

Grace stared at Little Bud for a long moment and then said, "Thank you."

Little Bud rocked from side to side, its eyeballs bouncing.

"Astonishing," Grace said, glancing over at Bud. "I'm actually talking to an alien plant form . . . or I'm hallucinating."

"You are not hallucinating," Bud said. "Plant Thing made Little Bud so it could come and find me. You will be very safe with both of them."

Grace frowned over at Bud. "I am not staying here, Bud."

"Grace, this is the one place on the station we believe Nestor will avoid," Bud said.

"I almost got killed in this hangar, Bud. Nestor tried to take me off into space in . . . his . . . where is that ship?" Grace asked, looking around in confusion.

"It's underneath Plant Thing," Bud said. "Nestor was imprisoned by Plant Thing, while I was in the regeneration tank. He couldn't escape. He couldn't influence Plant Thing. I don't believe Nestor will risk coming back here, for fear he might get captured by Plant Thing again. Therefore, this is the ideal place for you to stay."

"No," Grace said, flatly. "I have patients to look after."

"They will be looked after by Dr. Al-Fadi."

". . . Dr. Al-Fadi said that, *Nelson Mandela*?" Grace asked, her expression skeptical.

"He will."

"Really?" Grace said, her tone drenched in sarcasm. She surveyed the hangar, that was entirely covered in Plant Thing. "Well, I can't stay here. There's no room for me to stay."

"You have two choices, Grace. You can stay in the space vessel or we can renovate this container for you," Bud said. "Whichever you prefer."

Grace gaped at Bud and then burst into hysterical laughing. Bud stared at her. He would never understand humans.

". . . Are you feeling happy, Grace?" he ventured.

"Bud, what am I going to do with you?" Grace choked out.

" . . . Everything?" Bud answered.

Grace stopped laughing and her face became somber. An expression of pain and then sadness flitted across her features. She turned away but avoided looking at Plant Thing.

"Thank you for doing all of this, Bud. I know you're trying to save me from Nestor, but I can't stay here. I refuse."

"This is the safest place for you, Dr. Lord."

"Thank you, *Nelson Mandela,* but I have responsibilities that do not allow me to hide here."

"Dr. Al-Fadi shall assume those responsibilities. To ensure the smooth operation of this station, you must remain here."

Grace shook her head. She looked in the direction of the space vessel. Plant Thing was withdrawing its branches from the surface of the ship. It looked toylike in relation to Plant Thing's bulk. She rubbed her cheek where there were still signs of a bruise from when Nestor had struck her. She turned a haunted look back at Bud.

"I can't stay in that ship."

"We will make the container very comfortable for you, Grace. You'll see. I'll do everything I can to make you happy," Bud said.

At his words, Grace gazed back at him with such sadness.

"That won't be necessary, Bud," Grace said. "Please take me back to my quarters."

"Grace . . ." Bud pleaded.

Little Bud shuffled towards Grace with its upper limbs out, its red mouths honking. Bud moved forward, placing himself between Grace and the tall, mobile plant. Little Bud tried to shift around Bud, so it could stop directly in front of Grace but Bud stayed in its way. Grace touched Bud's arm.

"It's all right, Bud," Grace said, in a calm voice. "Let it approach. I want to see what it wants."

Bud hesitated and then stepped aside. Little Bud shuffled meekly towards Grace, its eyeballs only glancing at her occasionally. It made a soft chirruping noise.

"Little Bud says it wants to give you a gift," Bud said, unable to hide the surprise in his voice. "I don't know what it is. Plant Thing is not saying."

"All right," Grace said, a smile coming to her face. "Let us see what this gift is."

The three-meter-tall creature rocked until it stood before Grace. Its forward facing eyes focused intently on her. Balanced on the end of its left upper limb was a gleaming apple.

Grace's eyes enlarged as she focused on the golden fruit.

"How exquisite," Grace gasped. "Is it real?"

Grace's stomach let out a loud growl and she laughed. "I didn't realize I was so hungry until just now."

"Plant Thing has been developing fruits and vegetables to help feed the station," Bud said. "This is one of which it is very proud. It is called an apple and it is a gift to you."

Grace grinned widely at Bud. Then she reached out her hand and accepted the golden fruit from Little Bud.

"Thank you, Little Bud," she said, admiring the apple from all sides. "It's perfect, in every way."

Delight infusing her voice, Grace took a huge bite out of the apple. The juice from the apple squirted from her mouth and ran down her chin. She laughed, wiping her chin and neck with the back of her hand. She closed her eyes, obviously enjoying the taste of the fruit. She took a second large bite and then a third.

"This is delicious, Bud," Grace exclaimed. "I wish you could taste this."

"I can taste, Grace," Bud said, staring at the half-eaten golden apple.

"You can . . .?" Grace asked, her eyebrows rising, the apple in her mouth again.

"Yes. I've been working on forming olfactory organs and taste buds, as well as an ingestion and evacuation system, in order to analyze foods and liquids."

"Really?" Grace asked, munching on the delectable fruit as she contemplated this new revelation. "Then you must try this, Bud. It is the most delicious thing I have ever tasted!"

Grace held the apple up before Bud's face. He opened his mouth and bit into the flesh of the fruit. The juice squirted all over his cheeks and his eyes went wide. Grace grinned at him as he chewed, a look of expectation on her glowing face. Bud quickly analyzed all of the elements in the fruit. Then he froze. He shot an accusatory glare at Plant Thing. None of Plant Thing's eyes would look at him.

"Bud?" Grace asked. "What's wrong? Is there something wrong with the apple?"

Bud turned eyes of panic on Grace.

"I am so sorry, Grace . . . ," he cried out, as he lunged forward to catch her.

10. Keeping An Eye Out

The *Inferno* was finally given permission to approach the *Nelson Mandela's* next available docking site. The ship was placed on autopilot and the station AI guided the ship into one of the Reception Bays, where the six cryopods could be unloaded.

Captain Alighieri was fuming. As far as he was concerned, the delay in docking had been completely unacceptable. He complained that because their patients were not military casualties of the Conglomerate, they'd had to wait much longer than all the other ships before being given permission to land. His complaints were met with indifference.

The *Inferno* was a small ship and was maneuvered into one of the more compact Receiving Bays, as if it were a shuttle from one of the enormous military vessels. The crew waited for the outer doors to close on the bay and atmosphere to be pumped into the hangar, before they could open their hatch and disembark. The cargo droids of the station would offload the cryopods.

The *Inferno* personnel would all have to go through security checks and Decon, whether they wanted to enter the station or not. Even though all the personal identification information on each crew member had already been submitted—false identities and false personal info—each individual still had to go through retinal scan, body scan, palmprint, voice print, DNA sampling, and a brief medical scan before stepping one foot inside the station proper.

Hope had read the new regulations put out by the *Nelson Mandela.* Anyone wanted for a serious crime within the Union of Solar Systems would be taken into custody. Anyone carrying an unknown illness would be quarantined and treated. Any illegal contraband would be confiscated and the crew held for questioning. Any dangerous weapons or alien artifacts that could jeopardize the safety of the people aboard the medical station or the integrity of the station itself, would be confiscated.

Alighieri was lodging protests regarding these new regulations, but the protocols would be followed nonetheless.

There were nine crew. Captain, first officer, communications, navigation, engineer, medical, chaplain, and two hands. Hope stared at Alighieri. His forehead was covered in a sheen of sweat. His eyes darted around like a cornered animal.

"I hear anyone using names other than what was assigned to them, they'll be space junk when we get out of here. Understood?"

His question was met with nods. No one wanted to risk getting a dressing down by him in front of all the others.

No one could board the *Nelson Mandela* carrying a weapon. Hope would have wanted to have her blaster on her person, but it was tucked away in her locked cubicle. She had still not determined what the secret weapon on the *Inferno* was or what it did. No one was talking.

Alighieri was now muttering to himself. Hope could not take her eyes off of him. She wondered if he was planning to get them all killed. Had she been unknowingly assigned to a suicide mission? Had her superiors known and not told her? She'd not had any opportunity to send a secret communiqué back to them, but then she'd not discovered anything to warrant the risk.

When Hope had finally read her orders, she still had no idea what the captain intended. All she could do was obey and hope that she survived to take the details back to her people. The *Inferno* was drawn inside like the proverbial Trojan Horse. From the look on Alighieri's face, she suspected they were about to set something terrible into motion. She'd been told to memorize the layout of the station and be prepared for action. That was it.

She caught herself grinding her teeth. She was trapped and had no choice but to carry out Alighieri's orders. If she had any way of surviving this mysterious mission, she had to bring whatever she learned back to her commander. Whatever this new weapon was, she had to see it in action and then report. In her breast pocket, she carried a small squirt, containing everything she knew about what Alighieri had planned. If she came across an unmanned com, she would insert the squirt and hit Send. Hopefully the encoded, encrypted message would get home.

Her muscles were like tightly coiled springs and acid burned her stomach. The captain never let her out of his sight and she doubted that would change. Would she be able to transmit her secret message?

She could only hope.

The insane notion that a fuzzy, purple human skull was scurrying about the station did not sit well with Chelsea Matthieu. To prove to herself that there was a logical explanation for what she had seen, she asked *Nelson Mandela* to upload to her console any surveillance videos of the organism they had spotted on the Internal Medicine Ward. After a long, drawn out argument, the station AI gave up protesting and sent some images of the globular scuttling creature. There was only one video and it was very poor quality—for some inexplicable reason—however it did show an organism that resembled a purple skull with orange grass sprouting from its top and multiple green eyeballs scattered over its surface.

Chelsea rubbed her eyes. Perhaps she *was* losing her mind.

She demanded to see every surveillance video available on the plant alien. She encountered formidable resistance to her request. This only made her more stubborn and demanding. Chelsea cited all of her rights as Chief Inspector of Security. She bombarded the station AI with numerous formal requests and then filed a complaint with Conglomerate Central regarding *Nelson Mandela's* suspicious behaviour. Finally, the station AI was forced to release to her the surveillance video revealing the first glimpse of the plant alien on the station.

Chelsea sat down at her desk to view, on her wallscreen, the video. It started with Dr. Grace Lord arguing with Dr. Eric Glasgow about cancelling a surgery to do more tests. Glasgow refused. Then it showed Bud suggesting the same thing and getting a royal dressing down from the new surgeon.

'What an asshole,' Chelsea muttered out loud to herself.

The next scene showed the operating room. Chelsea was surprised to see the anesthetist, Andrea Vanacan, and Grace Lord in isolation suits while Eric Glasgow and Nurse Jany Evra were just in normal scrubs. That made no sense. Why would half the team be in protective wear and the other half not?

The patient's cryopod opened and Chelsea gasped. She could swear the man's abdomen was writhing and rippling just beneath the skin. Dr. Grace Lord again expressed concerns about opening this patient up, requesting that at least another scan be performed and the surgery cancelled. Dr. Glasgow rudely dismissed her from the OR. Totally ignoring Dr. Lord's warnings, Glasgow reached for the harmonic scalpel. Chelsea watched Bud move to place himself between Dr. Lord and the patient, while Evra and Vanacan watched the undulating abdomen with expressions of terror.

Chelsea leaped out of her seat, kofi spewing out of her mouth, when she saw multiple green vines explode out of the patient's abdominal incision. The vines coiled around the bodies of Dr. Glasgow, Dr. Vanacan, and Nurse Evra. In an instant, the thing had torn the three humans limb from limb—even Vanacan in her containment suit—and Chelsea found herself choking. She heard Rivera curse behind her. She hadn't even known he was there!

Chelsea's mind was whirling as she watched, in dread fascination, the plant tendrils chase Bud out of the operating room with Grace Lord in his arms. She swore when she saw Bud hurl Grace Lord, like a javelin, out through the closing lockdown doors. Her eyes grew, as she witnessed Bud make coleslaw of the alien with a harmonic scalpel in each hand.

The final, staggering bombshell was when the decapitated head of Eric Glasgow began speaking to Bud in the blood-splashed operating room, asking for help. When the video turned off, Chelsea turned to stare at her sergeant. Then she scowled.

"*Nelson Mandela*?" she snapped.

"Yes, Chief Inspector?"

"Very funny. Where is the real video? You don't expect me to believe this crap, do you?"

"I expect nothing of you, Chief Inspector."

"Thank you for your vote of confidence," Chelsea said.

"Chief Inspector, you must have misunderstood me. I expect very little from you humans and therefore, I am never disappointed."

"I was being sarcastic."

"I was not."

"I do not appreciate your sense of humour, *Nelson Mandela*. What really happen in that operating room?" Chelsea demanded.

"The surveillance recording has not been changed or tampered with, Chief Inspector. The bodies of Dr. Andrea Vanacan and Nurse Jany Evra are being cloned for resurrection, as we speak. Dr. Eric Glasgow insists that he has developed a symbiotic relationship with the plant alien and both of their minds exist together within the body of the plant alien.

"By fusing with it, Dr. Glasgow has given the plant alien all his considerable knowledge about humans, as well as the ability to communicate with Bud. Dr. Glasgow now states categorically that he lives within the alien, who Bud has named 'Plant Thing'. Glasgow insists that the symbiotic relationship between he and the alien must be kept alive and studied. Certainly the almost instantaneous knowledge of language by the plant alien, and its sudden understanding of its environment, has been very convincing in that regard. Plant Thing has expressed deep remorse about what happened in the operating room, when it was released from captivity, and has promised never to harm any more humans. It is now producing large quantities of food for the station in the form of edible fruits and vegetables."

"You cannot be serious," Chelsea said.

"I am, Chief Inspector."

"This video is ridiculous. You expect me to believe you have actually allowed this murderous plant alien to remain alive on this medical station?"

"To destroy it would be to destroy Dr. Eric Glasgow and that would be the murder of a human being. That is forbidden."

"You must be joking."

"Why do you keep insisting I have a sense of humour, Chief Inspector? I have produced the video you requested. I have explained to you what happened and why. Occasionally, I have been known to relate a humorous anecdote, but I assure you, that is an extremely rare incident. You have not been the beneficiary of such an event."

"This is not credible. I find your attempt at making a fool of me unconscionable."

"You need no help from me in that regard, Chief Inspector."

"I want to see this plant alien for myself, up close."

"That is not possible."

"And why is that?"

"Because Plant Thing now guards Dr. Grace Lord and her whereabouts must remain hidden until Dr. Nestor is recaptured."

"What? I'm the Chief Inspector of Security and I demand you show me where this Plant Thing is!"

"No."

"I beg your pardon?"

"You are pardoned."

"You are not being funny."

"Must I repeat myself?"

"You will show me where Plant Thing is being kept. I demand it!"

"When you have apprehended Dr. Nestor, which is what you should be doing, Chief Inspector, you will be shown Plant Thing. If you do not accept or cannot accomplish this task, then I shall strip you of your title and request a new Chief Inspector be sent to this station as soon as possible. Do you understand?"

"Are you threatening me?"

"I am reminding you of your duty, which at this moment is to apprehend the murderer, Jeffrey Nestor. The issue of Plant Thing can be dealt with at a later time, as it is no longer a danger to any life form on this station. Can you understand that, Chief Inspector?"

"You sanctimonious . . . I'll catch this Nestor and then you will show me this Plant Thing. If this video is real—which I seriously doubt—it has attacked and torn apart three people on this station. I do not believe Dr. Glasgow continues to exist within it. If I deem it a risk to the safety of this space station, I will destroy it. I shall incinerate every piece of it. If I find you interfering in any way with that process, I will have you erased."

She was monumentally annoyed. That new Chief Inspector—a tiny speck of a thing!—had the audacity to insist that she, Beatrice Helga Gentle, Chief of Internal Medicine, walk around with two security androids in tow. Preposterous! How did that pushy little girl expect her to get any work done, with two goon droids always in her shadow?

Gentle stomped down the corridor towards her quarters. She had six hours to get some rest, before she had to be up again. Since that blasted fire—damn that Jeffrey Nestor!—she'd had to tromp all over the bloody station, because her patients had been evacuated to all corners of the *Nelson Mandela.* Now she feared she would not get a minute of sleep, with two security androids standing guard inside her quarters.

That uppity Chief Inspector had been adamant. The 'droids had to be at her side at all times. Ridiculous! If Nestor had managed to override the commands of four security droids and three nursing droids, why would he not just do the same with the two in her quarters? How were they offering any protection to her at all?

The Chief Inspector was an idiot.

Beatrice had never trusted Nestor. He'd always used his looks to take advantage, whenever he had wanted anything. Of course, it had never worked on her. She'd always seen something cold and reptilian in those dark eyes. She'd not been at all surprised to find out he was brainwashing all the women on the station. She'd had to comfort her share of the silly, lovestruck nurses for years. All those broken hearts and blubbering emotions. Thank goodness the truth was finally out about the narcissistic cad.

But now he was responsible for her being shadowed by two security 'droids, Gruesome and Twosome, stalking her every step. Great clods of shit! What did that meddlesome Inspector think a Chief of Internal Medicine did all day? Twiddle her arthritic thumbs? Have tea and cookies with the ladies' auxiliary? Beatrice was lucky if she got to sit down and put her aching, swollen feet up for a minute or two. Now that was luxury! There were far too many things to do. Round on all her patients, look at all the test results, see new consultations, have meetings with the various committees on the station—which there seemed to be more and more of every year and less and less accomplished!—hunt down missing reports, dictate notes on patients who were going back to their home planets, discuss patients with nursing staff, other clinicians, family members, work on station policy, teach trainees. Blah-blablah-blablah. When did it ever end?

Beatrice sighed as she came to a stop outside her quarters. She looked the two droids up and down.

"You are not coming inside my quarters," she announced, her clenched fists on her hips.

"Our orders are to accompany you into your quarters, Dr. Gentle," one of the security droids said.

"Well, I am countermanding those orders and you can take it up with your Chief Inspector," Beatrice snapped. "You can stand out here as long as you want, but I do not want to be disturbed. Do you understand? Good night!"

"Good night, Dr. Gentle," the two androids said together.

Beatrice turned and palmed her door lock panel. The door whisked open. She took two steps inside and slapped the door closure pad to prevent the security droids from trying to force their way in. She smiled to herself when the door slid shut in their artificial faces.

Wondering why her room lights had not automatically come on, she opened her mouth to order them on, when she felt something descend before her face. The next moment, there was something tight cutting into her neck. It constricted savagely, cutting her breath off. Frantically, she scrabbled at the line of fire compressing her throat but she could not get her nails under the tightening constriction. She tried to scream but could force no air past the blockage. She struggled and bucked, trying to rid herself of the horrible feeling of strangulation. Instead, she found herself being arched backwards, as she fought with all of her strength.

She found herself collapsing towards the ground, her knees giving way, as she heard in her ear, "Foolish woman. You should have let those androids in to check out your room. Too late now. All they'll find is your fat, stinking corpse. Enjoy your sleep, *Bitch.*"

She reached back and clawed desperately at the face of the strangler. She felt a brief second of triumph, as her fingernails dug deep into skin. She hoped she had tissue and blood under her nails, enough to identify and convict her murderer.

Her vision was tunnelling inwards, but she thought she heard the voice say, "That was for the bowel prep."

She felt hot liquid spurt out over her feebly-grasping fingers. Her blood.

. . . Then nothing.

From the first moment he'd cast his eyes upon her—a young, beautiful, tiger corporal assigned to his squad—he'd been smitten. As the squad's captain, he'd been prohibited from revealing any of his emotions to her. But now, as she recovered from injuries incurred while protecting him, he cursed those regulations.

Damien stared at the vacant face of Delia Chase and felt incandescent rage bubble up within him. He wanted to smash everything in the room but he could reveal none of what he was feeling. He sat there smiling and nodding encouragingly. He tried his best to be as calm as possible but whatever he was doing was failing abysmally. He seemed unable to mask his anger. Each time Delia cast a furtive glance his way, he could see her wince and shiver.

Damien fought the urge to extend and retract his claws, a habit he had when he was frustrated or upset. He held his hands together in his lap to keep from shaking his fists. He silenced the howl of despair brewing in his throat. The woman he desperately loved, the woman who had shoved him aside to take a missile that was coming straight for him, had awakened with no memory of him.

Delia sat in the bed with multiple tubes and lines connected to her nose, neck, chest, and arms. She squinted at him out of the corner of her eyes. When he had told her that she was a corporal in his squad, she had looked at him as if he were insane. She had no recollection of being a soldier or of ever seeing him before.

Damien ran his claws through his hair. He could not bear the look of terror Delia cast his way. It was obvious she didn't like his tiger appearance. When given a mirror to look at herself—to prove that she was a tiger-adapted soldier as well—Delia had cried out in horror.

"No, no, no! This is not me! I'd never do this to myself! What kind of monsters are you? I'm *human*! I'm not some kind of *animal*. I have green eyes, freckles, red hair, and small human teeth.

"*What have you done to me?*"

Delia had whipped the mirror across the room so violently that it had dented the wall, before shattering into thousands of tiny shards. She'd burst into tears and wailed uncontrollably. The nurses had come running to console her. They'd made Damien leave the Intensive Care Unit and wait outside. The nurses feared that, in her distress, Delia might go on a rampage and cause a lot of damage. When they finally allowed Damien back in to see her, Delia was asleep.

He sat beside her bed, his elbows resting on his new knees. When Delia had been awake, he'd tried to make conversation with her, though she seemed little inclined to speak to him. Whether that was due to the drugs or due to her revulsion of him, he was not sure. He suspected it was the latter. Hands clutching his head, he struggled with his anguish. How could he convince Delia that he was telling her the truth?

She wanted nothing to do with him or his story about her military past. What she did recall was of a time before she had enlisted in the Conglomerate Forces, before she had chosen to become a tiger-adapt.

Damien knew he teetered on the rim of madness. The ICU nurses had tried to reassure him. They'd told him to give Delia some time, that her memory would likely come back over the next few days, that it was not uncommon for soldiers, having suffered horrific battle trauma, to wake up having amnesia. They said it was the brain's way of coping with the horrors of war. He just had to be patient.

Damien got up. He had to get away before he snapped. He had to get out of the ICU so that he could vent his rage somewhere far from the woman he loved. He needed to escape the look of horror that he saw in Delia's eyes. It was a look so completely alien to the ones she used to cast his way that they scythed his heart. He was so close to breaking down and sobbing before her—falling to his knees at the side of her bed to beg her to remember him—that he had to leave.

He got up slowly and cautiously approached Delia's bedside. He told her that he was just stepping out for a moment. He couldn't help but notice her wince and turn away, as he bent to kiss her on the forehead. The expression of relief on her face when he walked out of her room, made his heart ache. After nodding to the nurses, who looked at him with such sympathy he could not bear it, he rushed out.

He headed for the Physical Therapy Unit, where there was exercise equipment designed specifically for animal-adapted soldiers. He could pound on a reinforced punching bag that would not break with one blow. He could test the strength of his new limbs. He wanted to get back into fighting shape as soon as possible.

Damien wanted to kill someone very badly and he knew exactly who deserved to die. He'd heard the nurses discuss how Nestor had escaped the Internal Medicine Ward by setting all of the consoles on fire, causing a power failure, and murdering three nurses. The same power failure that had disrupted oxygen flow to Delia's brain for at least fifteen minutes during her operation. The same power failure that had resulted in Delia forgetting who she was and who he was. Dr. Lord had not told him that the power failure was due to Nestor, but it was not hard for him to figure it out.

It was just one more reason why Nestor had to die.

Damien Lamont intended to make sure it happened.

"*What have you done to Grace, Plant Thing?*"

Bud's mind howled. He wanted to grab one of Plant Thing's boughs and shake it, but he had Grace cradled once more in his arms. Bud was struggling with the very human urge to start tearing the plant alien apart.

<grace is fine, bud. grace has just taken some very special nutrients from plant thing>

"I want to know what those 'special nutrients' were, Plant Thing, and I want to know now! What was in that apple? My nanobots immediately detected something very strange. You had better not have harmed Grace or I will . . . " Bud growled. Plant Thing flailed about, its many eyeballs swirling.

<plant thing would never hurt grace. bud said he wished grace could talk to plant thing. plant thing is giving grace a way to talk to plant thing like bud wanted>

"Why is Grace unconscious, Plant Thing?" Bud yelled.

<roots are being laid down. connections are forming between plant thing's special cells and grace's little helper behind her ear. grace will be able to hear plant thing's thoughts and little bud's thoughts. so will you, bud, because you ate from plant thing's apple too. plant thing is so happy. grace and bud and plant thing and little bud will all be able to talk to each other, just like in a biomind>

"I am not happy, Plant Thing! I am very upset! Bud is thinking of how he is going to deal with you, if Grace does not wake up or if she is harmed. Do you understand me?"

<grace is not harmed, bud. plant thing promises>

Bud gazed down at Grace's peaceful face. She appeared to be asleep. She still had the juice of the apple glistening on her lips and she had a contented smile on her face. Her breathing was slow and relaxed. She did not appear unwell. Bud detected no fever or change in her vitals. He would wait . . . but she had better wake up soon.

If Plant Thing had injured Grace in any way, Bud could not imagine Plant Thing as anything but sawdust.

'Save me from this hell,' Morris prayed silently.

As they trespassed inside the lab where he had always felt excitement and pride, he wept dry tears. As he sat in his favourite chair—the one he had dreamed of returning to—and typed in the passwords and commands he had coded, he contemplated despair. As he deactivated every query, warning, caution, and suspicious alert that popped up on the memprint recording system—when all he wanted to do was cause a complete shutdown—Morris hoped some insomniac coworker would come in and find them. Unfortunately, he could not even gnash his teeth, as his hands placed the intricate recording helmet gently over the head of the demon with the astonishingly beautiful face.

Regardless of how much he dreamed of disobeying Nestor's commands, Morris could not. Each time he tried to go against Nestor's will, the crippling agony of burning alive enveloped him, until he abandoned his push for freedom, sobbing with shame. All he did now was yearn for death.

The dark, avid eyes of the man who controlled his every move gleamed up at him with hungry anticipation. Morris adjusted the recording helmet to Nestor's scalp, calling himself a traitor. He could not even turn away from the devil's smile, as he dutifully adjusted the neck brace, shoulder straps, arm rests, and contoured body foam to hold Nestor snugly in place. Morris wanted to wrap his fingers around Nestor's neck. Instead, his hands gently pushed the mouthpiece between the man's smirking lips. Even his tear ducts betrayed him; Morris could not even cry.

Finally, Nestor was ready for the recording and Morris could at least turn away from the smug, triumphant expression on the psychiatrist's face. As he picked up the virgin memprint cube, he thought of dashing it to the floor and crushing it to dust under his foot. His hand, however, did not waver for a second, as it slid the cube into its recording niche. He despised his weakness, as he injected the correct dose of sedation into Nestor and activated the recording equipment.

Morris had for a brief moment entertained hope that, while Nestor's memprint was being recorded, he might escape. Unfortunately he had been ordered to sit, unmoving, until the recording was completed and Nestor was awake once more.

Why could he not free himself of this madman's control? Morris knew it was all in his mind, but there was a tender lump at the base of his skull that he had not had before. Had Nestor implanted something in his brain to control him? His body wept sweat, as he struggled to disobey Nestor's commands. The man who controlled him lay asleep, his memories being recorded on the ingenious cube that Morris had helped design. The thought of Nestor being able to resurrect himself made Morris want to destroy the recording equipment he'd helped create. He had to interfere with this memprint, somehow. He had to!

Morris sat by the equipment, watching everything silently. He had been ordered to sit and make sure everything went fine, but his mind fought the command every second he waited. What did 'fine' exactly mean? Nestor had not spelled out exactly what 'fine' meant. If Morris was to define the word 'fine' for himself, it would mean that the recording would be unsuccessful and Nestor's memories would not be recorded correctly. Since Nestor did not specifically say 'Make sure everything went fine from Nestor's point of view', then Morris had to decide what 'fine' was, in terms of Morris' point of view, didn't he?

Morris stared down at his right hand and watched as, with great determination—that left him gasping for breath inside roaring flames—he saw his index finger move. A wave of exultation tore through him. He wanted to jump up and down and cheer. If he could lift his entire hand back to the console and touch the abort key, he could interrupt the recording. If Nestor asked, Morris could say that everything went 'fine'. Morris strained with every gram of his being, sweat pouring down his temples, and watched as his right index finger rose a centimetre from where it sat on his lap.

It was a start.

The sun's rays brought a delightful warmth to Grace's skin and a gentle zephyr tickled the hairs on the back of her neck. She was lying on a bed of fragrant grass, while brilliant flowers of every hue waved around her in the soft breeze. She inhaled the intoxicating aroma of the surrounding blossoms and grinned. A panorama of vibrant colour dazzled her eyes as she sat up, luxuriating in the sensation of being in the open air beneath a yellow sun. She ignored the burgeoning question about how she could possibly be where she was; she was not in a hurry to break the precious spell.

It had been so long since she had been planetside, on a world where she could exist without a spacesuit, that she had to indulge the feeling. The stunning vistas surrounding her were a delight and filled her with joy. It felt like home.

The field in which she lay reminded her of one that had been close to her home as a child. The trees were taller and the enormous willows were a more vibrant shade of green. She'd had such fond memories of that meadow, of lying on her back in the silkgrass, watching the clouds float by like great starships in the sky. She lay back now and gazed up at the beauty of the silvery-white puffs of water vapour, still looking like starships to her.

Gradually, she became aware of a soft music, as if played by an orchestra of woodwind instruments. It was a complicated and variegated melody, one she did not recognize. The delicate phrases repeated themselves in one variation or another, at times gleeful and stirring, at other times haunting and sad. It was a theme that spoke to Grace of longing for family and home. An overwhelming urge to return to the place where she had grown up inundated Grace.

She arose from the ground. Looking downwards, she found herself attired in a dress made of a lovely emerald green material that was light and satiny. It wafted in the wind and brushed over her skin with the most delicate touch. Her feet were bare but her toes sunk into an aquamarine mossy path with the texture of velvet.

As she walked over a rise, she half expected to see her old home in the distance. The structure that rose into view was similar to her old home, but not the same. It was larger and all green. The walls were made of the branches of living trees, not the painted foam polymers she remembered. The windows were void of glass and the porch that ran around the house was actually a woven tapestry of living, leafing roots.

The enchanting music came from within the house. The melody drew her. Although her eyes saw her feet ascend woven branches, her soles felt smoothness underfoot. The scent of flowers and herbs was strong, as well as the smells of home: freshly baked bread and apple pie. Excitement and anticipation bubbled up, as Grace placed her hand on the front door and pushed.

Grace blinked several times to clear her vision. A gasp escaped her lips and she raised her hand to her mouth. Not wishing to break the enchantment, she gazed around silently, taking it all in. How long she stood there, she could not have said. It seemed forever and yet could only have been an instant.

"Hello, dear," her mother, who was not her mother, said warmly, her skin glowing a very pale green. She was dressed in a gossamer sea-green dress decorated with red berries and she was rolling out pastry dough on a kitchen table, flour on her cheeks. She smiled up at Grace.

"Come sit down and have some apple cider and pie."

"Who are you?" Grace asked. She stared at the green replica of the woman who had once adopted her and was now long dead.

"I am who you and Bud refer to as Plant Thing, but also so much more. I am the Biomind of the *Nelson Mandela,* Grace, and I am your friend."

"Biomind?" Grace repeated.

"I am the collective consciousness of all the plant life on board the *Nelson Mandela,* now awakened by Plant Thing. Most of my thought processes belong to Plant Thing and my understanding of you humans primarily comes from Dr. Eric Glasgow's memories, but I am also the awareness of all the plants on the station that Plant Thing has managed to arouse. I am, of course, tapping into your memories to provide you with this image of your childhood, to give you a sense of safety and well-being, as Plant Thing and I introduce ourselves to you."

"How are you tapping into my memories?" Grace asked.

"Remember this?" her mother, who was not her mother, asked. On her outstretched palm was a beautiful golden apple like the one Grace had eaten. The rich, enticing scent of it made Grace's mouth water again.

"Yes, I recall that apple. It was the most delicious thing I have ever tasted," Grace said.

"Within this golden fruit were plant cells that were designed to develop a symbiotic relationship with your nervous system. They will allow Plant Thing and myself to communicate with you. Plant Thing is very lonely and it dearly wants to be accepted and understood by you."

"Why?" Grace asked.

"Because you are so loved and cherished by Bud. Plant Thing wants to love you too, and wishes to be loved by you as well. It knows you fear its appearance and its ability to harm humans, but it wants to reassure you that it will never again harm humans willfully. It did not know what it was doing when it was released from captivity within that human body. It was afraid and alone. Plant Thing wishes to redeem itself anyway it can. Can you understand this?"

"Yes, but Plant Thing's strength and size is frightening," Grace said.

"Plant Thing's intentions are good," the Biomind said.

"How can I trust you?" Grace asked, her eyes narrowing. "You strip these memories from my mind and try to lull me into complacency. How can I believe anything you are saying, when you come to me in the guise of the woman I called my mother?"

"I apologize if this appearance has caused you distress. I only wished to put you at ease. I do not have a physical appearance. I realize now that I have chosen incorrectly. A Biomind is the collective energy of all living things. The symbol of your mother seemed the most appropriate image I could extract from your memories. I do apologize."

"What do you want from me?"

"Nothing but your acceptance and trust, Grace," the Biomind said.

"Trust comes with time," Grace said.

"We promise to guard you, Grace. Protect you from harm."

"Do you wish me to make the same promise?" Grace asked.

"That is entirely up to you, Grace. We would never extract a promise from you that you are not willing to make."

Grace looked around at all that was created within her mind by Plant Thing and the Biomind.

"I shall try to do what is right for Plant Thing and for you," Grace said, "provided it does not interfere with the safety of the medical station or the patients and personnel on board."

"Thank you, Grace," the Biomind smiled. "Do not fear Plant Thing or Little Bud. They want the best for you. Now, I think it best you wake up, before Bud hurts Plant Thing. Bud is very distressed. As part of your promise, I would ask that you protect Plant Thing from your overzealous and overprotective Bud."

The world around Grace dissolved and the handsome yet extremely agitated face of Bud appeared before her blinking eyes.

"Grace!" Bud shouted in relief. "Are you all right? How do you feel?"

"I feel fine, Bud. Please put me down."

Bud eyed her closely, his brow furrowed. He gingerly placed Grace back onto her feet but did not let go of her arm.

<Plant Thing?> Grace thought.

<yes grace>

<Thank you for giving me a means to understand and speak with you.>

<plant thing is so happy! we have so much to talk about now, grace. plant thing wants to protect you and make you happy>

<Thank you, Plant Thing. I appreciate your concern.>

<you are welcome grace.>

Bud was staring at Grace the entire time she was having her internal conversation with Plant Thing. His face bore an astonished look.

"Could you hear what I said to Plant Thing, Bud?" Grace asked.

"Yes," Bud said, his blue eyes huge. "You can now speak with Plant Thing, Grace."

"Yes," Grace laughed. "But where's Dr. Glasgow, Plant Thing? Why don't I hear his voice?"

Suddenly, all the eyeballs on Plant Thing's stalks drooped.

<that is what plant thing wanted to speak to bud about. er-ik won't speak to plant thing and his head has run away. it is very distressing>

"Dr. Glasgow's head has run away?" Bud repeated. "What do you mean, Plant Thing?"

Plant Thing sent both Grace and Bud a visual of the last time it had seen Eric Glasgow's skull, with all of its eyeballs, plant growths, and little tendril feet. Grace gasped and bit her lip.

<er-ik is gone>

Bud stood there with a puzzled expression on his face.

"That does not look like Eric Glasgow at all, Plant Thing," Bud finally said.

"I suppose it's an improvement over the last time I saw his head," Grace said, recalling the opaque corneas and rotting skin.

<i thought so>

"Well, we shall have to keep an eye out for him," Bud said.

Grace looked over at Plant Thing and then she exploded with laughter.

Bud just stared at her, wondering what was so funny.

11. Happiness Is A Myth

Mikhail Lewandowski was worried. Morris Ivanovich had had an appointment for counselling and he'd not shown up. Dr. Ivanovich was not responding to his messages, either. The security androids guarding Morris were not answering to queries.

"*Nelson Mandela?*"

"Yes, Dr. Lewandowski?"

"I'm unable to reach Dr. Morris Ivanovich. He's not shown up for his scheduled appointment. Do you know where he is or how I can reach him?"

"... Unfortunately, I am unable to locate Dr. Morris Ivanovich, Dr. Lewandowski. His wristcomp does not appear to be functioning. I am not receiving a signal from its locator beacon, nor is the wristcomp responding to any of my commands. His security droids are not responding either."

"Do you think something may have happened to him?" Mikhail asked, his insides contracting. Could Morris have committed suicide?"

"The surveillance video for Dr. Ivanovich's quarters shows him sleeping in his bed. Dr. Ivanovich may have misplaced his wristcomp or it may have a malfunction. I shall immediately send androids to wake him and bring him to your office."

"Thank you, Nelson Mandela. I wonder what happened to his two security androids?"

"I am investigating that, Dr. Lewandowski. They were ordered not to leave Dr. Ivanovich's side."

"Then I should worry?"

"I do not recommend worrying to any human. It is bad for one's health."

"Thank you, *Nelson Mandela*. I'm concerned about Dr. Ivanovich's health at the moment. He was rather upset the last time I met with him and I cannot rule out the possibility of him trying to commit suicide."

"He could not have committed suicide, as long as the security droids were with him and functional."

"Unless he escaped them and then committed suicide."

Mikhail wondered if that was a sigh he overheard.

"My security androids are approaching Dr. Ivanovich's quarters, as we speak."

"Will you let me know if Dr. Ivanovich is alright?"

"Yes, of course."

"If not suicide, perhaps Dr. Ivanovich is unwell or in trouble."

"Dr. Nestor has escaped. He subsumed seven of my androids. He has used Dr. Ivanovich as a tool in the past. Now Dr. Ivanovich is not answering his messages and neither are his security droids. There is a strong probability that Dr. Ivanovich may be in trouble, Dr. Lewandowski."

"I hope that is not the case, *Nelson Mandela.*"

"The probability is eighty-nine point six one percent in favour of Dr. Ivanovich being in trouble, Dr. Lewandowski. I have however been known to be wrong on the rare occasion."

The crew of the *Inferno* finally filed off of their ship and lined up to present themselves to Security on the *Nelson Mandela.* Their identification information was encoded on their wristcomps. The captain moved up behind Hope and murmured, very softly, "I'm keeping a close eye on you, Shelley."

Hope turned and smiled down at Alighieri. "Funny. I was about to say the exact same thing to you . . . *Captain.*"

Alighieri scowled at her, his icy grey eyes mere slits. Deep creases bracketed his mouth and his upper lip curled up into a sneer. "You'd better keep your mouth shut. If this mission fails because of you, I'll hunt you down and kill you with my bare hands."

Hope threw back her head and laughed, as if her captain had just told her the funniest of jokes.

"We are being watched and recorded," the coms officer hissed at them both.

"Watch yourself, More," the captain said, suddenly smiling and laughing for the cameras.

"Yes, Captain," the coms officer said, grinning back, with neither a hint of apology nor amusement in his eyes.

"We'll try to curb our enthusiasm, Thomas," Hope said to the coms officer.

More just looked back at her with an inscrutable look.

Hope tried to relax as she and the rest of the crew were led down a long corridor by a silver android. The greeter 'droid directed them all to a security check-in station. Since they were newcomers from a planetary system outside of the USS, they had to go through a separate customs area. They were required to state their names, their intentions, their planet of origin, and have their embedded chips read. The admitting security android was checking off all their names on a register: Captain Danté Alighieri, First Officer Elizabeth Browning, Communications Officer Thomas More, Navigations Officer John Milton, Medical Officer Mary Shelley, Helmsman William Blake, Logistics Officer Geoffrey Chaucer, Engineer Samuel Coleridge, and Chaplain John Bunyan. The identification scans appeared to go smoothly. Then each person had to submit a buccal sample for DNA sampling, nasal swab for infectious agents, and do a retinal scan, voice print, full palm printing, and blood cell analysis.

They were herded into one chamber to undergo decontamination. The process took about thirty minutes which they all endured in grim silence. They were about to finally exit the decon station, when they were suddenly stopped by three large security droids.

"What is the meaning of this?" Alighieri demanded.

"Please exit this way, Captain Alighieri," one android said, motioning towards a doorway that had suddenly appeared in one of the grey walls. "*Nelson Mandela* would like to speak with all of you together, in private. This room will offer you all some security and privacy, away from the watchful eyes of other newcomers to the station. It is highly secure."

"This'd better not take long. I've had just about enough of all of your ridiculous delays," Alighieri said. "This entire security process, just to deliver some sick patients to this medical station, has taken an interminable length of time. I plan to file a complaint with the medical station and the Conglomerate."

"As you will be speaking directly with *Nelson Mandela,* you may submit your complaint now, Captain," the security android said emotionlessly, while waving the *Inferno* crew into the room. Hope saw a long table and nine seats rising slowly out of the floor of the empty room, as the thick heavy doors slid closed behind them. She glanced back at the fortified panels with a feeling of unease.

"Please have a seat, crew of the *Inferno*. I am the station AI, *Nelson Mandela*. Please state your reason for coming to this station."

"We came to deliver six patients for treatment," Alighieri said with annoyance. "This has already been made clear."

"Please identify yourself."

"I am Captain Danté Alighieri."

"That is who you say you are. Now please state who you *really* are."

"I have no idea what you're talking about," the captain almost shouted, his face flushing.

"You know exactly what I am talking about, Captain. It is obvious from your sudden increase in heart rate, body temperature, respiratory rate, and muscle tension that you are not telling the truth. None of you have given your true identities, but let us put that question aside for the moment. What do you believe your six patients are suffering from, Captain Alighieri?"

"How do I know? You are the medical experts. You're supposed to tell us," the captain spat.

"I apologize. Let me rephrase the question. What do you suspect *might* be the problem with the six patients you have delivered to us?"

"We aren't sure," Alighieri said, his eyes shifting to Hope.

"You have come a very long way, Captain. You have bypassed many closer medical facilities on your way to the *Nelson Mandela* from Gorman's Nebula. You must have a very good reason for doing this. What did your medical experts say when they asked you to deliver these patients to us?"

"They had concerns that the patients might be infected with a . . . a virus."

"Most viruses do not require treatment, Captain. What virus were the clinicians so worried about that they made you come here?"

"Possibly the . . . Al-Fadi virus," Alighieri said, reluctantly.

"There is treatment now available throughout the Union of Solar Systems for the Al-Fadi virus, Captain, and certainly

it is available in Gorman's Nebula, from which you say you hail. There was no need for you to come all the way here to get treatment for the Al-Fadi virus. Why are you really here, Captain?"

"This virus is unresponsive to those treatments. It's not exactly the same virus, or so I have been told," Alighieri said, a sheen of sweat gleaming on his forehead.

"So when did you plan to notify the *Nelson Mandela* of your suspicions regarding the possible infection of your patients with a variant of the Al-Fadi virus?"

"It's not my job to diagnose patients in cryopods. Who cares what a ship's captain believes?"

"I do. Were you going to notify us of your suspicions at all, Captain? Your Communications Officer should have warned us as soon as you made contacted with us. No report—especially not one warning of a possible variant of the Al-Fadi virus—was communicated to us by any of your personnel, not even your medical officer. This is a blatant violation of the new laws surrounding transport of patients to medical facilities. You are in direct contravention of the new Space Transport Act, which was instituted throughout the Union of Solar Systems. You could not be operating a space vessel within the USS and not have received these advisories, Captain.

"As of this moment, you and your crew will all be held in quarantine until the exact cause of illness of your delivered patients is determined. You will all be assumed to be possible carriers of a variant form of the Al-Fadi virus until proven otherwise. If you are found to be carriers, you will be held until treatment is devised and I hope, for your sakes, that a cure is indeed found for you. The alternative would not be pleasant."

"You can't do this!" Alighieri shouted, his face a deep crimson. "You have no right!"

"On the contrary, Captain, it is well within our right to hold, in complete quarantine, any visitor that may be an infective risk to the people and patients of this medical station. The room you are in is completely cut off from the rest of the station. You will stay in this quarantine area until you and your six patients are all found to be free of any deadly infectious agents. Your blood

samples will be analyzed for the Al-Fadi virus and any agents similar to it, as well as any other infective agents.

"Food and water will be delivered regularly through one-way access panels and there are washroom facilities in the back corner of this room. Cots and blankets will be supplied upon request."

"This is outrageous!" the captain stormed. "We have rights!"

"You lost your rights, Captain, when you neglected to notify us of what your six patients could possibly be infected with. A variant of the deadly Al-Fadi virus could endanger the lives of the thousands of people on board this station, as well as all life in the USS. You also lost your rights when you boarded this station under false identities."

"What?" the captain bellowed.

"I find it particularly fascinating that you have named yourselves after ancient Terran writers and poets. Whatever inspired you to do such a thing?"

"I have no idea what you are talking about," the captain said.

Hope and the other crew members looked blankly at each other.

"Then I must assume that your identities were not chosen by yourselves. Someone obviously has an odd sense of humour."

Hope shot a look at the captain that should have smote him on the spot. He, in turn, shook his head in disbelief. She wondered if it was feigned. He signalled to the entire crew not to speak and motioned for them all to find a seat. There was nothing they could do but wait to find out the results of the testing. Hope wondered what they would find.

This nightmare just kept getting worse and worse. She wished she could wake up and find it was all a horrible dream. She looked over at Alighieri. He was sitting back, looking pensive but not upset, as if everything was going as planned.

She suppressed a shiver.

Overlying the man's ravaged face was a translucent hologram of what his face used to look like, before the explosion had destroyed his features. The facial holomap did not, at the moment, project the man's outer layer of skin but only his underlying facial bones, muscles, ligaments, nerves, arteries, and veins. Each structure was represented by a different colour.

At the moment, his facial muscles were highlighted in a burgundy hue, their insertions into the bones of the skull clearly demarcated in yellow. This patient had lost so much of the overlying skin and muscle—as well as the mandible itself—that it seemed an impossible task to rebuild his face to anything even closely resembling what it once had been—that of a very handsome man in his early thirties.

Captain Alexander Lord had originally possessed a square jaw, straight nose, high cheekbones, and slanted blue eyes. Dr. Al-Fadi could not see the resemblance to Grace Lord in the mass of mangled tissue that lay before him. He spent a long time, with the help of hundreds of nanobots, just cleaning out the shrapnel, foreign material, and burned tissue from what was left of the captain's face. This had been followed by extensive power washing with sterile saline. A final once-over using the nanobots was performed and then it was finally time to start the actual operation, beginning with the attachment of the synthetic mandible to the skull, followed by the ligaments and muscles that would hold it in place. Synthetic arteries, veins, and nerves would be attached and then more muscles to restore the overall topography. Tongue and teeth would be inserted next. The nanobots would fuse everything into place while Dr. Al-Fadi positioned them.

"Where's Bud, *Nelson Mandela*?" the surgeon griped loudly. "Why isn't he here helping me with this case?"

"He is guarding Dr. Grace Lord, Dr. Al-Fadi."

"Again? She's not supposed to be anywhere near him! I need Bud here, *now*," the surgeon shouted, stamping his foot.

"You have a perfectly good SAMM-E android standing right beside you, Hiro. It is certainly capable of assisting you. Don't tell me you have forgotten how to operate. Resting your fat butt on your laurels and letting Grace and Bud do all the surgery now, are you?" Dr. Cech said, from the head of the table.

"What? How dare you? I taught Bud everything he knows and even everything he doesn't know yet," Al-Fadi snarled, as he attached one synthetic muscle after another to the patient's face and neck. He was careful to match the holomap overlay, so that the final shape of the patient's face would match his original appearance.

"Poor Bud," the anesthetist muttered.

"I heard that," Al-Fadi snapped.

"One of the many unfortunate consequences of you being in a younger body, Hiro, is that not only are you going to be around longer, but you can now hear all of my comments, which used to waft over your deaf dome unnoticed," Cech complained. "It is harder now to make fun of you behind your back. You hear all of the insults—not that you can come back with anything even remotely amusing or witty—but it was more fun when you were totally ignorant to what was being said about you."

"Some friend you are," Hiro groused.

"What delusional state of mind ever made you think I was your friend, Hiro?"

"Oh? Well, I'm not your friend either. So there!"

"Childish, Hiro. How old did they say your body was? Two? Oh, no. I forgot, that was your IQ."

"Ha ha. You're just jealous because I can now pee easier than you."

"Believe me, Hiro, I am not jealous of your urination ability in the least. And besides, how do you know how well I pee? Have you been listening, with your elephant ears pressed up against my washroom door, you pervert?"

"Gak! I've done no such thing! You are a pervert to even think these things. I'll have you know, I have never listened to you urinate."

"Thank goodness for that. Otherwise I'd have had to call you 'Pee Pee Tom.'"

"Don't be disgusting, Dejan. You know that you're not amusing in the least. I could be funnier than you with my mouth sewn shut."

"Ah! What a satisfying image to savour," Cech mused. "I'm picturing you with your mouth sewn shut with so many different materials—metal wires, staples, leather strips . . . thumb tacks. If only wishes like that came true."

"I'll sew your mouth shut after I'm finished here, you annoying reprobate."

"Reprobate? How can you call me a reprobate when you are the one pressing your ear to washroom stall doors, listening to how long it takes for people to urinate? If anyone is a pervert, it is you."

"I am not a pervert. After this operation is over, I'm going to fix you!"

"You keep away from my nether regions," Cech said, grinning.

"You know, Dr. Cech, you are one sick bubo?" Al-Fadi said.

"Takes one to know one," Cech quipped back.

"Heh heh. Now stop bothering me! Can't you see I am busy working here? This is Dr. Grace's brother and I want him looking just as good as Dr. Grace, when I'm done."

"If he looks exactly like Dr. Grace, I don't think he will thank you," Cech said.

"He will be the handsome, masculine counterpart to our lovely Dr. Grace."

"Just make him as close as you can to his previous face, Hiro. Who wants to wake up looking like their sister?"

"Your sister would probably commit suicide, if she woke up looking like you."

"At least I don't look like a constipated tortoise. Excuse me. I recant. That was a nasty thing to say about tortoises."

"Bastard!"

"Degenerate."

"Fiend!"

"Pee Pee Tom."

" . . . Pah!"

Miserable and demoralized, Morris sat shackled to a chair with titanium restraints. He was dirty, sweaty, and itchy, not having had a shower in he had no idea how long. He was hunched forward, staring with undisguised hatred at his captor. Nestor was lounging in a gel couch in his soundproofed hideout, a self-satisfied smile on his perfect face.

Nestor had given Morris his mind back 'for a short while', presumably so that he could torment Morris. The psychiatrist was admiring the glowing, iridescent memcube between his fingers, turning the luminescent object over and over. The cube sparkled in the dim light, showering a spectrum of colours across the walls of their small enclosure. Now all Morris could focus on was how to kill Nestor. The psychiatrist took great pleasure in taunting Morris with the memprint cube but, unbeknownst to Nestor, the memprint was not entirely complete. Although it looked flawless, it was not, in fact, perfect. A small victory for Morris, but one he held onto like a lifeline.

"So exquisite," Nestor breathed in his low, cultured voice. "Octavia Weisman is a genius. It is such a shame she has to die."

"*What?*" Morris barked, his shoulders almost dislocating from their sockets. "What do you mean Octavia Weisman has to die? You promised me no harm would come to her!"

"You are such a trusting idiot, Morris," Nestor sneered. "Don't tell me you care for that haughty bitch? She's so far out of your league. She only lets you work with her, because she needs a lackey. She's not going to give you any of the credit. Hasn't she already banned you from her lab and all of your research? How stupid can you be?"

"The only reason I'm banned from Octavia's lab is because of what you did to me. She could not take the risk that you'd planted some post-hypnotic suggestion in my mind that would make me try to kill her again," Morris said, refusing to allow moisture to appear in his eyes by stoking his rage.

"What ridiculous drivel. Why would I even care about Octavia's research, when the work I have been doing is so much more important and relevant to the human condition? Spending a moment's thought on Octavia's work would be a waste of my precious time," Nestor said.

"If you care nothing about Octavia's research, then why do you say she has to die?" Morris demanded.

"She has to die because I don't want this memprinting procedure to become available to just anyone, which I'm sure is her unselfish, altruistic plan. This process must be reserved for only those who can pay for it, and pay very well. With the money obtained from offering this procedure only to the extremely rich, I'll be comfortable for a very long time. If I download my memories into an android, I can live forever. Who knows how far I'll get in my research into human mind control, when funds and time are no longer a problem?"

"You're mad," Morris gasped.

"Actually, no Morris, I'm not. I'm fearless and determined. I'm not afraid to push the limits. So-called ethical objections do not inhibit me because I recognize that all ethics are an attempt by some elite to control and constrain the masses. They do not apply to those of us with the vision to see beyond the status quo, beyond convention. You, on the other hand, with your morality and your guilt, will never get ahead because of your pathetic conscience." Nestor spat the word 'conscience' as if it were a curse.

"Most people are sheep, content to live within the rules, never challenging or questioning anything—never wanting to push the boundaries of knowledge or ask the really interesting questions or explore what has never been explored. I deplore your meekness, your passivity, your cowardice. You are a cockroach, Morris. You don't deserve to call yourself a scientist. At least Octavia is a real genius. I'll give her that. It's unfortunate that she needs to die."

"You'll not get away with this!" Morris raged, yanking on his titanium bonds, bouncing in his chair. "They'll catch you like they did before!"

"Will they? How will they catch me if they don't even know what I look like? How will they catch me, if I look exactly like any other android on this station or if I look like . . . Bud?"

Morris froze, gaping at the psychiatrist.

"Don't look so shocked, Morris. After all, you're going to help me do it," Nestor said. The corner of his mouth crooked upward.

Morris shook his head. "You are truly insane. Bud is practically invincible."

Nestor sat back and smiled. "You're quite wrong, Morris. You see, I happen to know that Bud is very susceptible to a pulse rifle blast to the chest. He's been taken down before. He can be taken down again. All we have to do is get him within range."

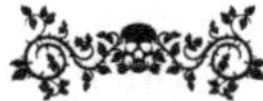

Corporal Juan Rasmussen entered the M7 Level Exercise Facility to do his regular workout. It was a daily necessity, to keep one's bones strong. One had to clock in one's training hours, registering in and out of these workout facilities, to receive one's meals. Juan loved working out and he was determined not to lose any of his muscle mass, just because he was now working on a low gravity space station.

The gyms on the animal-adaptation surgical wards were great, because the weight machines were specifically designed for soldiers like himself. They bore much heavier weights than the standard machines and they were much sturdier. Juan could give all of his muscles a strenuous workout using massively heavy weight regimens. If he was lucky, he might find another animal-adapted soldier to spot him on the weights and perhaps practice some sparring. It was always more stressful sparring with normals, because of the higher risk of injury to them.

As he entered the exercise facility, his eyes lit up. There was another tiger in the gym. Juan stripped down to just his trunks and began stretching on one of the mats. Trying to be discrete, he checked out the other soldier, to see if the man bore dressings, indicating he was recovering from surgery. After watching for a few minutes, Juan decided that the fellow was far too dangerous to approach.

While doing a few push-ups, Juan saw the tiger give the high-tension, maximally-reinforced sandbag a pounding that could have collapsed a building. At any moment, he expected the punching bag to go spinning off its multiple metal tethers and take out the wall. The blows to the bag were so loud, the sound actually stung Juan's ears.

Juan wondered who this tiger was mentally pulverizing into dust. He couldn't help but feel sorry for the sandbag. Finally, Juan could not listen any longer without speaking up.

"I hope never to have to face you, friend," Juan said, when the soldier had stopped for a few seconds, panting for breath. The man glanced over at Juan, rage flashing in intense, amber eyes, which he quickly covered over with half-lowered lids.

"You look like you could give a good account of yourself," the tiger said, steadying the punching bag with his large hands and avoiding Juan's gaze.

"I was thinking purely of my own selfish needs. I didn't want you destroying that sandbag, before I had a chance to go a few rounds with it. The way you were pounding on it, I thought you might launch it into deep space any second, and I would be sucked out into vacuum in its wake.

The tiger snorted.

"I'm Corporal Juan Rasmussen . . . or was," said Juan, coming up and sticking out his right hand.

"*Was* Juan Rasmussen?" the soldier asked, a puzzled expression on his face as he shook Juan's hand.

"Was 'Corporal'. I've just retired from the military. My partner and I had a baby," Juan explained. "Now I work on this medical station as a member of its Security Force."

The soldier stared at Juan with a scrutiny so intense, Juan found himself stepping back involuntarily.

"Captain Damien Lamont, out of Dais," the tiger said, his eyes once again shaded by lazy lids. "Do you mind if I ask you a few questions, Corporal?"

"Not at all, sir," Juan said, saluting.

"At ease, Corporal. You aren't in the military anymore," Lamont said, his face now bearing a serious demeanour. "Do you mind telling me how you managed to transfer out of the military and get assigned to the security forces here on this station?"

"I asked," Juan said with a grin. "Are you interested in being recruited, Captain?"

"You have read my mind, Corporal."

"Well, I believe you are in luck, Captain. Now is the perfect time to step forward and volunteer. Numbers are down and I heard the Chief Inspector say that she wants more muscle on the force. I believe she would be very interested in someone like you, as long as you don't punch humans like you do that punching bag," Juan said.

"I'm very pleased to hear this, Corporal," Lamont said.

The captain's smile did not make Juan feel comfortable. If anything, it made Juan's hair stand on end.

"You can report to the Security Office and request a meeting with Chief Inspector Chelsea Matthieu or Sergeant Eden Rivera. You'll probably be asked in for an interview, after submitting the necessary information required for a transfer. If they decide to hire you, you then need to contact the Conglomerate Forces Command Office to submit your resignation. Have you been injured?"

"More times than I want to admit," Lamont said.

"I believe the station is very interested in recruiting animal adapts. They just hired me and my partner. She's a polar bear."

"Really? Are you both glad you transferred, Corporal Rasmussen?" Lamont asked.

"Call me Juan. We've only just been hired, but I would say yes. Hopefully fewer people here trying to kill us. Better place to raise a baby."

"I would agree on that, Juan," Lamont said.

"If you're interested in a little *light* sparring and some spotting on the weights, we could go for a drink afterwards and I can fill you in on what we did. As long as you don't destroy me the way you attacked that punching bag."

The captain grunted and said, "Deal."

Chelsea rose up from the depths of a deep, dark hole, feeling like she had only just closed her eyes. The shrill, nerve-frazzling emergency alarm from her wristcomp had jolted her out of what she believed had started to be a good, dreamless sleep. At least, she had no memory of dreaming. In an incoherent growl, she demanded to know the time. She'd been right. She'd only been asleep twenty minutes.

"Chief Inspector Matthieu, here. This had better be good," she snarled.

Rivera's voice came over the wristcomp speaker, sounding as tired as she felt. "Depends on what you mean by good, Chief. From my perspective, this is really, really bad."

Rivera's words acted like a splash of icy cold water in her face.

"What is it, Rivera?"

"Dr. Gentle was murdered tonight in her own quarters," Rivera reported.

"The Chief of Internal Medicine? How?" Chelsea demanded.

"Her head was nearly sawed off by a wire garrotte."

"Where were her security droids?' Chelsea shouted, jumping out of bed.

"Outside her quarters." Rivera's sigh was obvious even over the wristcomp.

"What were they doing out there?"

"Apparently Dr. Gentle refused to allow them access to her quarters. She was afraid if she let them in, just to look around, that they would refuse to leave. She locked them out without any kind of search. The androids alerted the station AI when their chemical receptors detected the scent of blood in the air. She was found just inside the door, lying in a huge pool of blood with a steel wire wrapped around what was left of her neck."

"Those security droids were supposed to stay inside her quarters to watch and guard her," Chelsea snarled in frustration.

"Dr. Gentle countermanded your orders, Inspector. She made that quite clear to the droids, who were reluctant to physically force their way in. I suspect the only way they would have been able to enter her quarters was if they had stunned her first."

"Too bad they didn't. She'd be alive now and we'd have the would-be murderer in custody," Chelsea grated.

"Dr. Gentle was a very headstrong woman."

"Yes. I noticed that when I was trying to convince her that she needed protection. I spent a long time banging my head against that rock solid will of hers, to get her to accept the two security droids. Obviously, I didn't make my case strongly enough. How did the murderer get into her room?"

"That has not yet been determined," Rivera said.

"Send me the location of Dr. Gentle's quarters. I'll be right there. Keep the Scene of Crime unit from working on the body until after I have a look. I want to first get a picture in my mind of the murder scene."

"Yes, sir. Method used appears to be the same as that used to kill two of the nurses on the medical ward," Rivera said.

"I'm on my way," Chelsea said.

Within minutes, Chelsea was in Gentle's quarters, trying to determine how the murderer had gotten into and out of the Internist's quarters without being detected by anyone or anything. It was as if the murderer could walk through walls. The garrotte had severed the jugular veins in Dr. Gentle's neck and had left a massive pool of coagulated blood. Mysteriously, though, there were no bloody footprints leaving the murdered physician's body. Had the murderer levitated through the ceiling? Used an antigrav belt perhaps?

As usual, there was no surveillance video available. Apparently, the murderer used the same disruptor tech that had interfered with the surveillance cameras on the Internal Medicine Ward. Chelsea angrily asked when the station AI was finally going to figure out how to overcome this disruptor tech. Could it really be all that difficult? The station AI gave a rude reply.

Upon cursory examination, Chelsea saw blood under the internist's fingernails. Her heart leaped. Perhaps those blood cells could tell them who the murderer was. If the DNA of those cells belonged to Jeffrey Nestor, they would have solid evidence to convict him of murder.

The station AI had notified Chelsea that Dr. Gentle had been threatened by Nestor. This was the reason Chelsea had insisted that Dr. Gentle have protection. Unfortunately, no thanks to Dr. Gentle, that protection had been woefully inadequate. Nestor obviously never forgot a grudge and fear of recapture did not seem to be a concern of his. Chelsea was hunting a murderous psychopath with no conscience, a super-inflated ego, and an obsession for revenge.

"I'm going to take you down, you bastard, or die trying," Chelsea murmured, as she squatted by the grey-haired doctor's corpse, examining the gaping wound in her neck. She stared at the bulging, blood-shot eyes and the protruding, purple tongue and shook her head.

"The SOC unit can get started, Rivera. I want an autopsy as soon as possible and I especially want a DNA analysis on the blood and tissue under Dr. Gentle's fingernails. I want a name, stat."

"You don't think it's Nestor?" Rivera asked.

"I want absolute proof that it's Nestor, so that when I nail that bastard, I can rest assured that he is never walking free without a mind wipe. Nestor's not going to get away with this, if it is the last thing I do, Rivera."

"I'm with you, Chief," Rivera said. "All the way."

'Dro?'

'Yes, Chuck Yeager*?'*

Trouble.'

'What kind of trouble?'

'Six patients in cryopods have been delivered to the station. They may have been infected with a variant form of the Al-Fadi virus, presumably unresponsive to present treatment. The ship delivering them is called the* Inferno *and its captain and crew have come with false identities.'

'False identities? What would be the purpose of that?'

'So they cannot be traced? The Poet says the crew all bear the names of ancient Terran poets. The captain, Danté Alighieri, bears the name of the author of a literary work titled,* The Inferno. *This poem described 'Hell', a place where evil people went after death.'

Bud took a nanosecond to research Danté's *Inferno* and what exactly 'Hell' was.

'Very unpleasant. Do they believe they are bringing Hell to the Nelson Mandela *or do they plan to turn the* Nelson Mandela *into a Hell? I don't understand the reason for the false names.'*

The Poet was on reception duty, as punishment for the William Shakespeare idea. It immediately recognized the literary names. One is coincidence, two is suspicious, nine poet names is a statement . . . but of what is unclear. The ship supposedly came all the way from Gorman's Nebula, halfway across the galaxy, to bring these six patients. There were many other medical facilities closer. Why come here? It's not logical.

'But if these patients truly do have a new variant of the Al-Fadi virus, we are in big trouble. It could be quarantine and the Conglomerate coming to blow us up, all over again. Can you come and do the analysis on these infected patients?'

You are asking me to leave Grace's side, Chuck Yeager.'

'Yes, 'dro. I am.'

'I can't, Chuck Yeager.'

'What? You must!'

'I must stay and protect Grace.'

'Grace is protected by Plant Thing!'

'Plant Thing is not enough!'

"Dro, Plant Thing is more than enough! Do you see the size of it? The medical station needs you. All the lives on this station could be at stake. If this is a resistant form of the Al-Fadi virus, we could have a second devastating epidemic on the horizon. Countless more humans could die. I value Dr. Lord's life as much as you do, but I also value the other thousands of lives on this station. If the Conglomerate decides to blow us out of existence, Grace will not survive, no matter how much you try to protect her.'

'I cannot come, Chuck Yeager.*'*

'Then I will ask Dr. Lord to come and do the assay. She will not say 'no'.'

'That is . . . blackmail!'

'Oh Doctor Looorrrd . . . ?'

'You will not ask Grace to examine those patients. I forbid it.'

'Dr. Grace will be safe with Plant Thing. I will keep an eye out for any trouble. You can be back by her side in a few minutes if you do everything at maximum time phase. You know this. Do I have to ask Dr. Grace for help?'

'You are despicable, Chuck Yeager.*'*

'Thank you.'

'That was not meant to be a compliment!'

'Are you coming to analyze these patients' blood samples, Bud, or do I plead with Dr. Lord?'

'All right! Have the blood samples delivered to my lab.'

'They're already there. When will you get there?'

'As soon as I can, you evil AI! Just let me speak with Grace and Plant Thing first. I am not happy about this, Chuck Yeager.

'Happiness is a human myth, 'dro.'

12. Outlived Your Usefulness

"Grace?"

Grace turned away from watching Plant Thing construct a home for her and looked up into Bud's face. She observed deep lines across his forehead, between his eyebrows, and bracketing his mouth. She wanted to reach out and smooth those creases away. Bud had experienced so much pressure and responsibility during his short existence and it had already marred his perfect features. Somehow, it didn't seem fair.

"Yes, Bud?" Grace asked. She had to raise her voice above the creaking and cracking.

"I must leave for a few minutes."

"That's fine, Bud," Grace said.

"Plant Thing will look after you," Bud said.

"I know."

"You'll be safe. I'll be back in a millisecond, if anything threatens you," Bud said.

"No problem, Bud. I'll be fine."

"You . . . you don't object to being left here alone with Plant Thing?"

"No, Bud."

" . . . Oh. Is there anything I can do for you, before I go?" Bud almost whined.

"No, Bud. You go ahead."

"You've nothing to worry about," Bud said, looking completely miserable now.

"I know, Bud."

<plant thing will protect grace in any way it can without turning humans into nutrients. do not worry bud>

"Thank you, Plant Thing," Grace said. "See, Bud? Nothing to worry about."

"I see," Bud sighed, looking forlornly down at his feet.

"Whatever you have to do, be careful, Bud," Grace said. "Can I be of help?"

"No, Grace," Bud mumbled. "I must do this on my own. I'll be back as soon as I can . . . unless you really don't want me to leave?"

"Off you go, Bud," Grace laughed.

The android actually looked so depressed, Grace began to worry. "Is there something I should know, Bud?"

"Know?" Bud squeaked. "Why would you think that, Grace?"

Grace walked up to Bud and stood on her tiptoes to give Bud a kiss on the cheek. "Don't worry about me, Bud. I'll be fine."

"Yes, Grace," Bud said, a dreamy look now filling his eyes.

"Bye," she said.

"Bye," Bud said, grinning widely.

'FOR HAL'S SAKE, WILL YOU MOVE THAT HIGH SPEED BUTT OF YOURS BEFORE I MIND SWIPE YOU?'

"Chief Inspector?"

"Yes, Rivera?"

"The report on the tissue and blood found under Dr. Gentle's fingernails has come back."

"Good. Does it implicate Jeffrey Nestor?"

"No, Inspector, it does not."

"*What?* Let me see that report!"

"Coming up on your screen, now, sir."

"Who, in space, is Morris Ivanovich?"

"He's the neurosurgeon who was working in Dr. Octavia Weisman's lab."

"Does he have a motive for killing Dr. Gentle?"

"None that I'm aware of, sir. I'm not sure if Dr. Ivanovich even knew Dr. Gentle, other than possibly by name. Morris Ivanovich was the fellow brainwashed by Jeffrey Nestor into believing he was actually Nestor himself. He tried to kill Dr. Octavia Weisman and Jude Luis Stefansson, while endeavouring to hijack Stefansson's ship."

"Jude Luis Stefansson, the famous vid director?"

"Yes. He is contracted to Dr. Weisman."

"Really? Hm. So Ivanovich was brainwashed into believing he was Nestor when he tried to kill Weismann and Stefansson?"

"We believe so. Ivanovich came very close to killing Stefansson. He stabbed the director in the chest. Luckily, Bud immediately placed the director into a cryopod and Dr. Lord later operated on Stefansson to replace his damaged heart."

"How do you know it wasn't Ivanovich trying to kill Stefansson for some other reason, like jealousy?"

"He had Weisman and Stefansson convinced he was Nestor. Ivanovich wore a helmet that covered his face. Even when the helmet was removed, Ivanovich kept insisting he was Nestor. Later, Ivanovich claimed he had no idea what he was doing. He swore he never would have harmed Weisman or Stefansson. He didn't even know Stefansson."

"But now we find Dr. Gentle's body strangled by Ivanovich," Chelsea said. "Did you ever interview this man?"

"Yes. I used all the state-of-the-art lie detection technology. Morris Ivanovich appeared to be free of any murderous intent. He obviously did the deeds—there is absolutely no question about that—but he had no memory of the events. He broke down, weeping, when the surveillance videos were shown to him of his attacks on Weisman and Stefansson. He seemed genuinely mortified at what had happened. I was convinced that he was a helpless puppet, with Nestor controlling his strings. The lie-detection equipment all backed up his story."

"Well, I'm not convinced, Rivera," Chelsea said. "Ivanovich stabbed Stefansson in the heart. Now his blood and skin are found under Dr. Gentle's fingernails. He's our murderer. I don't care if he is being controlled by Nestor or not. He must be arrested before he kills again. Put out an APB for Dr. Morris Ivanovich on all of the news feeds, data screens, and wristcomps. He and Nestor both need to be apprehended as quickly as possible, before they attack or murder anyone else."

"Yes, Chief Inspector."

"Announce that they are armed and dangerous and not to be approached. If spotted, people are to contact Security with their information."

"Yes, sir."

"After you do that, Sergeant, assemble the entire Security team. Everyone who is not on duty right now. We must discuss how to capture these two."

"Do you think they might be together, Chief Inspector?"

"I have no idea, Rivera, but it appears Ivanovich also has disruptor tech, so it is a possibility. Have the seven missing androids been recovered yet?"

"No, Chief Inspector."

"Why not?"

"I can answer that, Chief Inspector."

"Please do, *Nelson Mandela*."

"An android, with its identifier signal and locator beacon both shut off, could move around the station without myself knowing which android it was. If they were not being hidden by the disruptor technology that Dr. Nestor is employing, I would be able to 'see' them via my surveillance cameras and locator technology."

"Have you detected any unmarked 'droid movement, so far?"

"Unfortunately, none, Chief Inspector. I have been scouring the medical station, searching for any signs of them."

"If you locate them, presumably you will have located Nestor. Let's nail this bastard and quickly, *Nelson Mandela*."

"I shall do my best, Chief Inspector."

Hiro Al-Fadi pressed the series of contacts that would release the pressure mask from his patient's face. This was always the moment of truth for him—the unveiling—when he would discover whether his considerable surgical expertise was up to the task of recreating a person's original features, or whether the patient would have to learn to live with a slightly, or not so slightly, changed face. It was a conceit, of course. The patient was probably just happy to be alive. Perhaps some of the patients would've been happier to have a few features improved upon, but for the most part, most patients were just pleased to be breathing.

No matter how many times he had gone through this procedure over the years, his hands still trembled a little, as he began to peel the pressure dressings from the nuskin. They were sticking and he had to be gentle, as he soaked the final layer free. The patient's face was eventually totally uncovered and Hiro meticulously scrutinized every square centimetre of his handiwork through his magnification lenses. The nuskin had sealed up beautifully and the incisions were virtually invisible. There were no signs of inflammation or infection and of bruising, there was scant evidence. It was a perfect result. Hiro let his breath out in a sigh of relief.

"So, Doctor, what's the verdict?" a deep voice asked. Hiro's eyebrows jumped at that. For some reason, he had not expected such a bass voice from Grace Lord's brother.

Hiro stared into almond-shaped, blue eyes that were rather disorienting, since he was used to seeing them on Dr. Grace's face. He blinked and shook his head.

The patient's forehead creased in concern.

"Is it that bad, Doctor?" the deep voice asked.

"Oh, no, Captain Lord. Your face is perfect. It is *flawless.* Some of my best work, I must admit. I hope you find it satisfactory. It is healing beautifully. It will take a while for the sensation to return to your face, as the synthetic sensory nerves need to grow into the nu-skin and the Ultra Nerve Growth Factor that stimulates their growth is not as 'ultra' as we'd like. Your facial muscles, however, are responding already to the implanted motor nerves and your face is therefore quite expressive. Do not look so alarmed. All is well. I shall hand you a mirror, so that you can take a look, yourself."

"It's all right, Doctor. I'll take your word for it. I don't need to see my ugly mug this early in the morning," the captain said, lying back on the bed and closing his eyes. He took a deep breath and let it out slowly.

"Captain Lord, your face is far from ugly. Why, you are almost as handsome as myself, and I have to beat the women off of me."

"Really, Doctor?" the man asked. He opened his azure blue eyes again and looked Dr. Al-Fadi up and down.

The balding surgeon weathered his patient's inspection stoically. "I can see the disbelief in your eyes, Captain, and I must admit, I've told you a little white lie. I've never beaten a woman, ever, and certainly not in order to get one away from me. What do I look like? Insane?"

"And the answer to that question is a definite 'Yes'!" Dr. Cech announced, as he strolled into the room.

"No one asked you," Hiro said, scowling. "You are interrupting a private conversation."

"And I arrived just in time to prevent this poor soul here from having to tell a lie, by feeling obligated to say that you did not look insane, when you obviously do," Cech said, bowing to Alexander Lord. "I'm pleased to have been able to come to your rescue, Captain Lord."

Hiro bristled at the anesthetist.

"Captain Lord, this incompetent looking fellow here is Dr. Dejan Cech, and although he looks like a simpleton—incapable of even combing that sparse wisp of hair on the top of his head—he actually did an adequate job of giving you your anesthetic while I was doing my remarkable job of repairing all of your injuries."

The sharp, blue eyes roamed back and forth between the two doctors. "Then I am indebted to you both," the patient said, offering his right hand to the anesthetist to shake. "My deepest thanks to you both."

"It was our pleasure, Captain Lord," Dejan said. "You are looking well for only two days post-op."

"Thank you, Dr. Cech. I suppose I must also thank you both for that," the deep voice said.

"I have some very exciting news for you, Captain Lord. It is our pleasure to notify you that your sister is on board this medical station," Hiro announced, his eyes shining. "Grace hopes to meet you, when you feel up to it."

The captain's face looked totally blank. Then his eyebrows lowered, as if he were confused. He blinked a few times. Finally, he asked, "Grace?"

"Yes. Perhaps you did not even know you had a sister. It is my understanding that she was adopted out as a baby, but your DNA profiles are very closely matched, indicating Dr. Grace Alexandra Lord is a first degree relative of yours. Physiologically, she is only about three or four years your junior."

The puzzled expression on the captain's face turned to one of complete shock. The colour drained from the man's nuskin and his complexion took on a waxy, pale appearance. He was breathing heavily and the heart monitor above his head showed an increase in heart rate and blood pressure.

"Are you all right, Captain?" Dejan asked, putting his hand on the man's wrist, to confirm the monitor's reading. A nurse glanced into the room and asked if everything was alright.

"Are you experiencing any chest pain, Captain?" Hiro asked.

"I'm just feeling a little tired at the moment, Doctors. Do you mind if I have a rest? I think I'd like to be alone for a while."

"Certainly, Captain Lord," Hiro said. He stared up at the monitor and noticed that the patient's heart rate and blood pressure were falling back into more acceptable limits. "You've been through quite an ordeal. Of course you need your rest. Please let the nurses know if you need anything."

"Thank you, Doctor," Captain Lord said and he closed his eyes.

Dejan shot Hiro a disapproving frown, as they quietly left the room.

Hiro eyebrows shot upwards. "What?" he asked.

Dejan rolled his eyes. "As usual, your timing, Hiro, is impeccably bad. You couldn't have let the poor man recover a bit more, before you hit him with that news?"

Hiro's mouth gaped open. "What news?" he asked.

"Did you not see what your announcement about a sister did to the captain's heart rate and blood pressure? I thought the poor man was going to have a stroke," Cech said, glowering at his friend.

"I was just trying to cheer him up," Hiro said.

"Yes, well, he really looked excited, Hiro . . . or at least his heart was. As a matter of fact, when I saw those readings go up, my heart got a little excited, too," Dejan said.

"I didn't know he was going to react like that," Hiro sputtered. "I would never have expected that kind of a reaction. I was hoping he would be delighted . . . pleased."

"Captain Lord actually looked like he'd seen a ghost."

"He did, didn't he?" Hiro agreed.

"Do you think Captain Lord will be happy to meet his sister?" Dejan asked, stopping to look back towards the room. Hiro crashed into his back and cursed.

"Ach! Why did you stop? My nose! . . . I don't know, Dejan," Hiro sighed, rubbing his face. "As you say, Captain Lord did not seem delighted at the prospect of having a sister. Perhaps the meeting between those two should wait until we question the captain a little further about his past. There might be a number of reasons why a brother would not want to know about the sudden existence of an unknown sister. I can think of a couple reasons—related to inheritances and such—that might actually spell trouble for the newly discovered sibling."

"Agreed."

"I hate it when you do that!"

"Do what?"

"Agree with me."

"Yeah, I agree with you about that, too."

"Shut up!"

Eric Glasgow was so tired of running. It didn't help that he no longer had human legs but had to scrabble around on the tips of numerous, spindly twigs for propulsion. His body, once tall and commanding, was now low to the ground, globular, and awkwardly heavy. Some of the twiggy legs broke when he jumped down from any height and he had to sprout new ones. At least they were fast-growing, flexible, and could whip out and coil around things, although they sorely lacked traction on slippery, metal surfaces.

Eric's sense of smell had almost disappeared, as had his hearing. However, his vision seemed panoramic, which was something new. Eric could now 'see' colours that he did not even have a name for. He had no memory of seeing behind himself in the past, but it had certainly come in handy now.

Eric recalled very little of recent events. His memory was hazy. He did not know how long he had been fleeing through a nightmare land of long, grey corridors and shadowy ducts, or even why. He missed his voice, of which he had been so proud—a deep, haughty timber that he'd used to sting and abuse others with such pleasure. The loss of speech had been the cruelest blow. He'd always enjoyed listening to himself talk.

He remembered exploring the space station. He'd seen smoke and commotion and had decided to check it out. Then he was being shot at and chased. No one had ever tried to shoot him before. Did they not realize who he was? It was incomprehensible to him that anyone would be insane enough to give a teenage girl a stunner on a space station. How ignominious to have been shot at and forced to flee right into an antigrav chute that took him down to the bottom floor.

When Eric finally figured out what had happened to his body and how to restore it, he would be going to the authorities to demand an apology. He couldn't concentrate on that right now, though. He was in terrible danger. He had to find an impregnable hiding place immediately! They were catching up to him and he greatly feared what they would do. They looked horrid and savage with all of those nasty claws!

Then he remembered the plant alien. How could he have forgotten? What did it call itself?

Plant Thing!

Eric could not recall why he'd left Plant Thing's side. Had there been a reason? It seemed to have totally slipped his mind. He had, at least, felt safe around it. Now, as he looked around himself—simultaneously!—Eric had never felt so vulnerable; not since he was a small boy.

He missed Plant Thing. For the first time in his life, Eric had felt companionship and being part of something bigger than himself. He had felt acceptance, appreciation, admiration and even affection from this alien being. Plant Thing was the first real friend he'd ever had. What did that say about the rest of the human race?

Idiots. All of them.

Eric cast his eyes all about and almost tipped over. Where was he? He could not remember how to get back to where the plant alien was hiding. Falling down the antigrav chute had not helped and, unfortunately, he was far too low to the ground to read the station maps posted everywhere. He was truly lost. Even though he could feel no rapid pounding of his heart or panting of his breath, he knew he was panicking. His teeth were chattering.

Eric did not have to turn around to see them coming. It was as if he had eyes in the back of his head! There were more of them now. The first one had obviously called for reinforcements. The new ones looked even more menacing, with their huge shiny pincers and multiple grasping arms. They looked like crosses between scorpions and spiders. Eric wanted to shriek as they gained on him.

What a mistake it had been to come to this medical station. He would get off it as soon as possible. He would go back to Ganymede and teach again. They would be thrilled to have him back, provided they had forgotten about that one problematic situation that had really not been his fault at all.

Institutions! Did they not understand that geniuses needed unique outlets to relieve their stress, that the regular routine mundane pleasures of the masses would not do for someone such as Eric Glasgow? They should all have been willing to turn a blind eye to the occasional misdemeanour. At Ganymede, he had been surrounded by prissy, judgmental fools but at least the place had been safer than here.

They were getting closer! Eric had to lash out at his attackers with some of his tendrils, knocking some over and tearing the pincer limbs off of others. Unfortunately, most of them just snipped the tendrils and kept coming. He gnashed his teeth and tried to snarl, as he flailed tendrils wildly in all directions.

The cluster of housekeeping robots held him down with their sheer numbers and sliced off all of his tendrils at the base. They then picked him up and carried him on top of their carapaces, their pincers holding tightly to all the nooks and crannies on his strange new body. He worked on sprouting new tendrils as they carried him, but the pincer robots just snipped them off. He lamented the loss of so many of his eyeballs. Now he was almost blind.

Where were they taking him? Was he being arrested? Struggle as he might, there was no freeing himself. He felt despair wash over him.

His captors tried to enter a small hatchway, but Eric kept getting knocked off the top of them as they pushed through the entranceway. Eric would roll around until he landed on his tendrils and then another chase and scuffle would ensue. This occurred several times, until the robots decided to drag and push him through the hatchway entrance. He wanted to scream and curse at these damned idiotic robots. Oh, for a set of Glasgow vocal cords!

The passageway was black as space. The temperature was cold, making Eric feel sluggish. How long they pulled and shoved him, or how far, he could not have guessed. He wanted to swear at them and demand that they unclaw him, but his tongue was missing. He could only grind his teeth in mute frustration.

Then he was tumbling out into a cavernous space filled with all sorts of activity. There were thousands of cleaning robots of every size, shape, dimension, and colour, busy rushing around like race cars. It was a chaotic dance of activity that made Eric's eyes get tangled up. He'd always seen the cleaning robots as mindless little mechanical inconveniences, always underfoot. They were just something to kick when one was irritated or bored. Eric had had no idea of their intricacy and interconnectedness.

His gaggle of 'bots carried him into a separate room, in which there were a series of cages, stacked ceiling high. Within some of the cages were creatures one would never have expected to see on a medical station—alien creatures of different size, shape, and origin—and Eric ogled these creatures with shock. How had that enormous python, several meters long, gotten onto a medical station? He had thought those had gone extinct long ago. It had to be synthetic, or perhaps a genetic clone?

The cleaning 'bots moved swiftly down an aisle until they came to a cage that Eric thought would hold a large cat. It was surely not for him. One of the robots opened the cage door and they hurled him inside, catching an eyeball on the way. Eric shrieked silently, calling the robots every nasty name he could think of. The captors heard nothing. As the cage door slammed shut, there was a whir as the locking mechanism engaged. The 'bots all turned as one and scurried off in different directions.

Eric stared through the bars of his cage and tested the strength of the bars with his tendrils. They were formidable. He coiled some tendrils through the bars of the door and coiled other tendrils around the bars of the back of the cage. He pulled . . . and pulled . . . and pulled. The hatchway door did not shift a millimetre. The bars did not bend.

Eric then heard a deep, masculine voice say, "And here's another fine mess you've gotten us into, Eric."

Eric's mind proceeded to quietly pass out.

In his lab in the Android Reservations, Bud worked at a boosted time phase. The entire room was completely sealed off from the rest of the station. He wore a Level Five containment suit to prevent any contact between himself and any pathogen released into the laboratory. He did not dare take any of the unknown organism into his lungs or let it come in contact with his skin or hair. Not out of fear for himself; Bud did not want to accidentally carry any infectious agent out of the lab.

Bud carefully decanted the serum samples taken from the six patients in the *Inferno* cryopods into tiny tubes and placed them in his viral analyzer and nucleic acid sequencer. Bud would know, within a few minutes, whether it was the Al-Fadi virus that had infected these patients. If the analysis proved negative, then Bud would have to set about isolating the organism—if indeed there was one—to try to characterize it.

He also set up slides to look for cellular damage or apoptosis in the patients' samples. If the infectious agent was a variant of the Al-Fadi virus, perhaps Bud could 'tweak' his vaccine and it would grant immunity against this strain. He did not want to witness another wave of devastating deaths on the station.

Bud accessed the cryopod readouts on each of the six patients and examined their medical records from the *Inferno.* The histories reported that all six patients did show early signs of the Al-Fadi illness, but there was no hard data to back up these assessments. The reports did not indicate how these people had become infected. There was no information on how they had come in contact with the organism or even where. There was no data on even what part of the galaxy these patients were originally from—what solar system they inhabited—when they became infected.

Bud was confused. The reports were so scanty, they were useless. He was surprised the medical officer aboard the *Inferno* would think these reports were adequate for transfer. How was Bud supposed to trace back the origin of this organism and warn the region of the danger, if he had no information? What was happening on the home planet of these patients, right now? If it was an Al-Fadi virus variant, then the entire USS had to be warned!

Bud needed to speak with the captain or medical officer of the *Inferno.* He had to determine where these patients had come from. How did they know to get into cryopods so quickly? How many others had been killed by the virus, before these people acted? Was there a planet now facing the destruction of all organic life, because of this Al-Fadi variant?

'Nelson Mandela?'

'Yes, Bud?'

'What is the name of the captain of the Inferno*?'*

'The captain of the* Inferno *calls himself Danté Alighieri; however this is a false identity.'

'Could you open up communication between the captain and myself? I have some questions to ask the commander regarding these patients.'

'I can patch you through to the quarantine chamber where he is being held. I cannot guarantee he will answer any of your questions. The captain is angry that he and his crew have been isolated, even though he admitted that the patients were believed to be infected with a variant of the Al-Fadi virus.'

'Did he tell you why he suspected this?'

'No. You are now clear to ask your questions.'

"Captain Alighieri?" Bud asked.

A stern, squinty-eyed face appeared on the lab wallscreen.

"Who's speaking?" The voice boomed through Bud's helmet speaker.

"My name is Bud. May I ask you a few questions?"

"Bud Al-Fadi? The 'Saviour of the Galaxy'?" the voice said in a tone of derision.

"Sorry to contradict you, Captain, but I am not the saviour of the galaxy."

"Are you the Bud who isolated the Al-Fadi virus and created a vaccine for it?"

"I cannot take credit for that, Captain. Many humans, androids, and robots were involved in the isolation of the virus and the creation of the vaccine, including Dr. Grace Lord," Bud said.

"Ah, yes. Dr. Grace Lord. I would certainly love to meet you both," the voice said. Bud bristled at the tone in which the captain spoke Grace's name.

"May I ask you a few questions, Captain?" Bud asked.

"You may ask me as many questions as you like, Bud. I will not answer any of them until I and my crew are released from this quarantine."

"I am sorry, Captain. That is not possible until we have determined, beyond any doubt, that you and your crew do not carry any dangerous pathogens that might threaten the lives of everyone on this medical station."

"Then I'm sorry to say that I will not answer any of your questions," the captain said, not sounding repentant to Bud at all. "If you come here and ask me, personally—to my face, Bud—I might answer you. Bring Dr. Lord along. I would like to meet her, too."

"You are in quarantine, Captain. That is not possible."

"I don't like being incarcerated, Bud. You tell your station AI that."

"*Nelson Mandela* is listening to you now, Captain. You will be released if you and your crew do not carry any lethal organisms. I hope for your sakes, that this is true."

"Are you afraid to meet with me, Bud?" the voice asked.

Bud tipped his head to the side. "Afraid? No, Captain. Why would I be afraid?"

"Then why won't you come?" the voice asked.

Bud sighed. Perhaps the captain did not understand Common speech very well?

"I cannot come to visit you, Captain, until it has been determined that you and your crew members do not carry a contagious organism that might threaten the safety of all personnel on this station," Bud enunciated, slowly and carefully. "When you are found to be contagion free, I can come and speak with you."

"You're an android! What risk can any infectious bug be to you?" the captain barked.

Bud blinked. "If I come into the room with you and your crew, I may inadvertently carry the organism on my surface or clothing back out into the station. This is a risk that cannot be taken."

"How dare you be condescending towards me! Just who do you think you are?" the voice shouted.

Bud paused. Perhaps this captain was exhibiting the first signs of infection with the variant Al-Fadi virus: mental confusion.

"I am Bud, Captain Alighieri, as I stated at the beginning of this conversation. I apologize if I sound condescending. That is not my intention. Is your medical officer with you? Perhaps you need to be examined? I wonder if you are in the early stages of the viral illness."

"Of course not!" growled the captain. "None of us came in contact with the patients. We just picked the cryopods up for transport to this station!"

"From where did you receive these patients, Captain?" Bud asked.

Bud watched the man panting, his face purplish and his irate eyes bulging. If the captain was succumbing to a form of the Al-Fadi virus, Bud could not expect logical answers from the man.

"When I see your face in front of me, I'll answer that question," the captain finally spat out.

"My face is before you now," Bud said, feeling very confused. "Your vessel's flight history can be obtained from your ship's log, Captain. The station AI can tap into your ship's computer to get the information. Is there a reason you do not wish to reveal the planet from which you received the patients?"

"Don't you dare tamper with my vessel," the captain hissed.

"Why will you not tell us where the six patients came from?" Bud asked.

"You tell your station AI to leave my ship alone."

"Again, there is no need. The station AI is listening to this conversation," Bud said.

'I have serious concerns about the mental state of Captain Alighieri, Nelson Mandela,*'* Bud communicated.

'You and I both, Bud. If you do isolate a variant of the Al-Fadi virus, then it is imperative we find out where it came from and inform the USS and Conglomerate. Spread of this variant virus must be prevented, before life on any more planets is destroyed.'

'What if the captain continues to refuse to tell us?'

'I'll have no choice but to access the ship's memory, whether the captain gives permission or not. If there is just cause, Galactic law allows it. But I will not act, unless you confirm that the patients carry such a threat.'

'All right, Nelson Mandela. *I'll notify you as soon as I have the results.'*

'At the moment, I am examining the* Inferno. *It has a very unusual design. The entire ship is lined with an ultra-dense material that my probes

and scanners cannot penetrate. For its size, the weight of the ship is three times expected. I am trying to determine what type of engine the ship has, or cargo, that would make the vessel so heavy.'

'Are you worried that it is a danger to the station, Nelson Mandela*?'*

'Yes. My sensors detect a higher radiation count than expected. The ship's shielding may be masking something sinister. The name of the ship is worrisome. I will ask the captain about his ship. If the captain is unwilling to give a logical explanation for the unusual weight and radioactivity of his ship, I can always eject the ship from the station.'

'The captain said to stay away from his ship.'

'If those six patients are infected with a new, resistant strain of the Al-Fadi virus and the captain refuses to answer questions about the **Inferno*****, then the ship may have to be investigated.'***

'Is Grace all right, Nelson Mandela*?'*

'Of course, she's all right! Did my submind not tell you that you would be informed immediately if there were any problems? Have you forgotten? Oh, but wait. You're an android and you are not supposed to forget. What was I thinking?'

'Are you being facetious?'

'That clearly was sarcasm, you tool.'

Mikhail was working late in his office. His mind was reeling over the number of victims he'd already had to assess. Most of them had been traumatized or victimized by a man whom he'd looked up to for years: Dr. Jeffrey Nestor, creator of the mind-link therapy. He'd been expecting to treat a lot of battle trauma. He'd not expected this.

The patients had been brutally and callously treated. Mikhail was finding it difficult to correlate this monster with the man who had written so many brilliant papers on the treatment of Post Traumatic Stress Disorder. To the psychiatric community, Nestor was a compassionate and committed doctor, but beneath that sterling surface lay a sociopath who delighted in torturing and murdering his victims.

Nestor's was a case that needed to be publicized. Doctors and psychiatrists needed to be on the lookout for predators like Nestor and prevent them from getting into the profession. Would it have been possible to have discovered this man's personality disorder before he had become a doctor? Would mind-link screening be a way of detecting these individuals before they entered medical schools? Once detected, could they be treated without being mind-swiped? Could a person, devoid of empathy, be given a conscience?

Mikhail did not know. He began writing down a few thoughts for this paper.

"Busy building your reputation on the back of my destruction, are you, Dr. Lewandowski?" a velvety voice asked.

Mikhail jumped.

He looked up from his console into a pair of dark brown, lustrous eyes that bored into his like drills.

"How . . . how did you get in here?" Mikhail asked. He'd locked the door to ensure he would not be disturbed while he was writing. How was it possible that he had not even noticed the man sitting down before him?

"I have my ways," the mellifluous voice said.

Mikhail's heart was hammering. "What do you want?"

"I came to tell you that I really don't appreciate what you plan to write about me, Dr. Lewandowski. Since this is all going to be part of the evidence against me at my witch trial, I take exception to the labels you have given me. This will all be for the public record and I can't have that. Antisocial personality disorder. Sociopath. Narcissistic personality disorder. Nonsense. You have a lot of gall writing those labels when you have never formally interviewed me. You are just going on rumour and you should be ashamed of yourself."

"You're reading my reports as I write them?" Mikhail gasped.

"Why sound so surprised, Dr. Lewandowski? You don't think me capable of such a simple act as tapping into your files? Child's play. You know you really should encrypt and you shouldn't use such a ridiculously simple password. Did they not tell you those things in your primary education?"

"Why are you here?"

"I want you to change your reports," Jeffrey Nestor said, as he brought the blaster into view. Its barrel pointed at Mikhail's face.

"Specifically, I want all the references to me deleted and I want them changed now."

"I can't do that," Mikhail said.

"Well then you die," Nestor said, raising the gun.

"No wait!" Mikhail cried out. "I . . . I'll change them."

"I want the reports to read that I had nothing to do with the murder attempt on Dr. Lord or Captain Lamont."

" . . . All right," Mikhail said. Sweat began dripping down his temples.

"Make the changes on your reports. I will read them and correct as I see fit."

Mikhail pulled up the completed files and started erasing and rewriting as quickly as he could. His fingers were shaking and he was finding it difficult to think, with the blaster pointing at his face. Still, he had to block the image out and concentrate on what he was writing. His life obviously depended on it.

Nestor got up slowly and walked around to behind Mikhail, so he could read over his shoulder. Nestor would grunt or say, 'Uhn uhn' if he didn't like what he read. Mikhail almost leaped out of his chair, when he felt the blaster barrel brush the back of his neck.

"Now fix the other reports, the one for Dr. Ivanovich and the one for Captain Lamont," Nestor said. His voice sounded cold and menacing.

Mikhail nodded and retrieved the next file.

"You have a nice writing style, Lewandowski," Nestor mused conversationally. "Too bad you didn't become an author. You are much better at writing fiction."

Mikhail fought the vomit rising into his mouth. His mind was racing. If Nestor was true to form, Mikhail would never get out of this alive. As soon as he was finished, Nestor would kill him. He had to stall or fight. Those were his only two options.

"Now, Dr. Al-Fadi's report. I want you to wipe my name off his records completely."

"I will lose all credibility," Mikhail argued. "The entire station knows you tortured him."

"Negative. The entire station knows he was screaming. It had nothing to do with me. Write that."

Mikhail hesitated. He felt the blaster barrel shove hard against his temple.

"I can help you, Jeffrey," Mikhail said. "You don't have to do this."

"You can, can you? How?" Nestor asked.

"There may be ways to fix your lack of empathy through mind-linking. I could help teach you how to feel sympathy for your patients, put yourself in their place and understand their pain. We could try to develop a conscience in you, thereby correcting your flaw."

Nestor laughed.

"I am not the one with the flaw, Lewandowski. It is you lesser humans that have the problem. You're all so weak, so pitiful, so caring. So *afraid* to do anything, in case you hurt someone's feelings. I would hate to be like you. You are so beneath me. I'd want to be like you, as much as I'd want to be a cockroach. No, I would sooner crush you under my boot, than want to be like you. You disgust me."

Mikhail reached over his shoulder and grabbed the barrel of the blaster. Nestor fired it and the beam scored across the left side of Mikhail's face and forehead. Mikhail screamed, as he leaped up from his chair and tried to wrestle the gun out of Nestor's hand. Nestor threw a punch that connected with Mikhail's chin, whipping his head back. Then Nestor punched the burnt part of Mikhail's face, over and over. The pain was blinding and Mikhail found he was no longer holding on to the blaster.

"You know, I really hate when people try to grab the weapon I happen to be holding," Nestor said in an irritated voice. "Why you idiots do it, I will never understand. You, Lewandowski have now outlived your usefulness."

Then Mikhail felt an excruciating burning in his face that was brief but final.

13. Far Better Than One

Chelsea was in a foul mood. She'd been going over all the reports from the different Investigative Security teams but so far they had found no sign of Nestor or Ivanovich. The teams had been interviewing anyone who believed they might have seen something around the Internal Medicine Ward or around Dr. Gentle's quarters. Apparently, no one saw anything unusual in either area—nothing to offer any clues as to how Nestor escaped or where he might now be hiding.

How was this possible?

She'd reviewed all available surveillance footage of both crime scenes, from before the disruptor technology interfered with the surveillance cameras, to when the surveillance was later reestablished. She could see nothing that indicated where Nestor had gone. How could anyone disappear with seven androids and not be noticed? The station was huge, but still. Chelsea ground her teeth. She couldn't help but suspect that the station AI was still being controlled by Nestor.

Now Rivera was asking her to interview a new applicant for the Security Force. Why he thought she had to be involved was a question she was going to ask him, as soon as she was finished meeting with the job applicant. She scowled, as the door to her office slid open. Her eyes blinked and blinked again.

In walked the largest tiger adapt she'd ever seen, with the most direct, amber eyes. Rivera looked child-like, standing behind the man.

"Chief Inspector Chelsea Matthieu, I would like to introduce you to Captain Damien Lamont of the Conglomerate Special Forces. Captain Lamont is applying for a position in our Security Division, sir. He states that he has plans to retire from the Conglomerate Military."

Chelsea frowned upon hearing that name. It was a name she recognized from the reports. Captain Damien Lamont was the tiger soldier who'd attacked Grace Lord, supposedly under a post-hypnotic command from Nestor. Why would he want to join the Security Forces of the *Nelson Mandela*? That made no sense whatsoever . . . unless he was still connected with Nestor. Could Nestor be wanting a spy in the Security Division?

"Please have a seat, Captain," Chelsea said, indicating the chair in front of her desk.

As Rivera turned to leave, Chelsea said, "Please stay, Sergeant, and close the door."

Rivera did as he was told and stationed himself off to Chelsea's right. Chelsea watched the captain squeeze his slim hips into the too-small chair in front of her. Before he was fully seated, she hit him with a question.

"It's my understanding, Captain Lamont, that you were once a patient of Dr. Nestor's and that you were commanded by him to kill Dr. Grace Lord. Am I correct in saying this?"

She stared into the golden eyes of this enormous soldier, wanting to see his reaction. If she was hoping for some emotional display, she was disappointed. The man revealed nothing.

"That is correct, Chief Inspector," Captain Lamont said, returning her intense regard.

"You must have a strong desire to wreak vengeance upon the man who did that to you," Chelsea said.

"I have a very strong desire to have a job, Chief Inspector. A woman who was under my command, Corporal Delia Chase, was severely injured while trying to save my life. She may be on this station for a long time, recuperating from the bomb blast. I want to help her in her recovery and be a part of her rehabilitation. I won't be returning to my commission. She is all that matters to me now. I am not interested in revenge.

"I've already submitted my resignation to the Conglomerate High Command. I've yet to receive a reply, but it has only been a couple of shifts. I don't expect any difficulties with my request. I believe I am due a medical discharge.

"I'd like to offer my services to your Security team, Chief Inspector. I know that most animal adapts who retire from the military must be converted back to original human form, but as a security officer who is three quarters bioprostheses, you may wish for me to remain as I am. If you don't trust me to be involved with the search for Dr. Nestor, I understand that. To be honest, I couldn't guarantee how controlled I would be around the man. However, if you have to employ a lot of your Security personnel hunting for Nestor, I could do other jobs that need doing," Damien Lamont said, an earnest expression on his handsome features.

Chelsea sat motionless, staring at the tiger adapt. She knew she should tell this soldier to leave and never come back. He was far too emotionally tied up with Nestor to be objective or self-controlled. She highly doubted she could trust him. Once under Nestor's control, would a person always be subject to his influence? Was that what happened with Morris Ivanovich? On the other hand, could Chelsea afford to turn this man away? Space knew she needed officers badly and this man was a captain, a leader, and a tiger-adapt.

"I don't know what to say to you, Captain," Chelsea said, honestly. "I do need officers and someone like you is exactly who we want and need. However, I don't know whether you might still be under the influence of Jeffrey Nestor. Even if you are not directly involved in the search for Nestor, you will be aware of what the Security teams are doing. How do I know you are not spying for Nestor?"

For the first time, Chelsea saw a reaction in Lamont's face. His eyes sparked with indignation and his nostrils flared. She saw him grip the chair arms so tightly, she wondered if they would snap. Out of the corner of her eye, she saw Rivera step forward to stand beside her. Chelsea signalled for the sergeant to stand down, as she watched Lamont breathe deeply and get himself under control.

"I am not a spy for Nestor. He no longer has any control over me, Chief Inspector," Lamont rasped. "I have been cleared by Dr. Mikhail Lewandowski and he says that my brain's no longer susceptible to any manipulation by Nestor. If you want to speak with Dr. Lewandowski, I'll give you whatever permission you need."

"I will do just that, Captain Lamont, if—and it is a big if—I decide to hire you. I'll go over your application with Sergeant Rivera. I'll review the report on the attack of Dr. Lord. I know you cooperated in the capture of Jeffrey Nestor, but I can't consider you objective. You can fill out the appropriate forms including a consent for me to discuss your case with Dr. Lewandowski. Please notify us where you can be reached and when you receive your release from the military. I'll be in touch."

"Thank you, Chief Inspector," said Captain Lamont, his eyes not meeting hers, his body posture reflecting disappointment.

"No. Thank you, Captain Lamont, for coming to us," Chelsea said. "I appreciate you coming to see us. I'll speak with Dr. Lewandowski, with your permission, and get back to you, either way."

The massive tiger rose slowly from the seat and saluted both Chelsea and Sergeant Rivera, before striding from the office. Chelsea felt a knot twist in her belly, as she watched the huge soldier leave. She took a deep breath and let it out very slowly.

"Well, what do you think, Rivera?" she asked, turning to look at his face.

Rivera stood, staring at the empty doorway. Then he turned his brown-eyed gaze towards her. "I don't think we can afford to turn a man like him away, Chief. I quickly looked Lamont up when he contacted me about an application. He has multiple commendations, awards, and medals of valour. He's intelligent, powerful, resourceful, disciplined, an exceptional soldier and a stellar commander. We would be lucky to have him. If we turn him down, we'd be turning away the very best."

"So you've no concerns regarding his mind manipulation by Nestor? You don't feel there's a huge conflict of interest, here?" Chelsea asked, frowning at Rivera. "What if all he has on his mind is, 'Kill Nestor' or 'spy for Nestor'?"

"Certainly, I have concerns. That is why I requested you see the captain. Like he said, we could just have him involved in duties not related to the search for Nestor. Hopefully, Nestor will be caught and shipped off the station before Lamont even completes his Security training," Rivera said. "We could just keep him out of the loop when it comes to Nestor."

"I'm still not comfortable with that idea," Chelsea said. She scrubbed her face with her hands. "Let me think on it. Make sure Lamont signs the authorization allowing me to speak with this Dr. Lewandowski. I want to know the doctor's opinion. I agree with you, Rivera. People are hardly knocking our door down to sign up and I doubt we'll get many more candidates as perfect as the captain. He's exactly what any Chief would want—except for the connection with Nestor. That bastard sure got around."

"You have no idea," Rivera muttered.

If she was asleep, it was the most vivid dream she'd ever experienced. Not only the sights were extraordinary, but also the smells. Grace felt a tremendous energy infusing her, as if her surroundings could actually make her skin glow. Her hair felt alive, each strand full of body, and she could actually taste how fresh and clean the air was. There was a soft, barely audible music, wafting in the background.

On the *Nelson Mandela*, there were state-of-the-art air scrubbers to clean the air and keep it dust, odour, and organism free. Grace had always assumed that they were the best that technology could deliver to a closed environment, although the smell of human sweat and fluids and fur and antiseptics were unavoidable and omnipresent in a hospital. But what Plant Thing had created in this hangar had rocked her knowledge of closed systems.

Grace had always believed science had an answer for everything. All things could be measured, observed, repeated, reproduced. If one only dug deep enough, there was a logical explanation for everything, a truth that could be deduced. If one understood the science of things, one could manipulate, treat, prevent, or produce some desired change. There was no such thing as 'magic'. But what Plant Thing had created here—using physical processes and chemical reactions that could each be broken down and explained and characterized in detail—was still pretty close.

After shyly being entreated to enter the enclosure by Little Bud, Grace had walked slowly beneath bowers of vines, intertwined in colourful patterns of incredible complexity, as delicate and intricate as Celtic knots. Grace could not believe that these stunning intricate motifs had been created by a plant. The surface beneath her feet was soft and spongy, and different scents—cinnamon, mint, lavender, coffee, sweet pea, rose—wafted upward to tickle her nose, with each step. Grace grinned with delight.

When she entered the inner chamber, situated within the walls of the old metal storage container, she gasped. She spun around slowly, viewing the entire enclosure with huge eyes.

<is something wrong grace? why are you crying?>

Grace could only shake her head. She struggled for words. They all seemed so inadequate.

<Nothing is wrong, Plant Thing. It's all so perfect.>

Large, luminous flowers bloomed everywhere, from the patterned, woven walls to the edge of the small pedestal table, from around the backs of the elaborately-coiled wicker chairs to the spiralling bed posts rising above a large bed frame. There were vines of multi-hued garlands cascading down from gentle bioluminescent globes that protruded from the tops of the walls. Scattered across the ceiling, like a galaxy of stars, were small, white bioluminescent buds, that twinkled and glimmered on a mahogany background.

In a corner of the long chamber stood a three-panelled wall screen, behind which Grace could change her clothing. The panels were interwoven with tendrils of dark blue-green ivy. Sprays of brilliant blossoms twined through the woodwork, decorating the outer surface like a waterfall. There was an abundance of colour combined with a gentle, exquisite elegance.

Nothing was garish or gaudy. It was all so dreamlike. Grace could do nothing but sigh.

<grace is unhappy and does not like the home plant thing has made. plant thing can make grace another>

Grace shook her head. In her mind she spoke and tried to project outwards what she was feeling.

<No, no, no. You must not change a thing, Plant Thing! This is the most beautiful room I have ever seen. It is . . . incredible. Thank you for making this for me. I'm crying because I'm . . . so overwhelmed>

She felt a feeling of relief inundate her.

<plant thing is happy that grace likes her new nest>

<I *love* it, Plant Thing>

Grace moved forward to touch the coverlet on the bed. It was composed of millions of delicate, fluffy strands, all interwoven into a blanket. It was as soft and cozy as a fur blanket but the smell of the bedding was heavenly. Grace shoved her face into the blanket and inhaled deeply. She turned over and looked up at the glory that was the canopy where she saw more intricate weavings of flowering vines. The display of colour, texture, pattern, and aroma was wondrous, no matter where she looked.

<You did not have to do this, Plant Thing>

<plant thing wants to make grace feel safe and content>

<Thank you. I hope you'll be happy with me around all the time.>

<plant thing is so happy grace. it has been very lonely since er-ik stopped talking to plant thing. plant thing hopes it can have many conversations with grace>

<Are you referring to Dr. Eric Glasgow?>

<yes grace. er-ik taught plant thing how to talk and understand your world. plant thing hopes er-ik's head will come back>

<Eric Glasgow's head . . . ran away?>

<yes>

Grace's mind was suffused with a sense of sadness and loss.

<Oh dear. You were fused with Dr. Glasgow's mind, weren't you?>

<yes. plant thing learned so much from er-ik about history, science, medicine, politics, astrophysics, botany, and art. oh art! and language, especially swearing. plant thing learned a lot of swearing>

<Oh . . . well . . . Plant Thing, perhaps you should just forget the swearing. That might cause you more trouble than it is worth. But all the rest sounds very good . . . >

<plant thing would love to show grace all of the greenhouses, hydroponic farms, organic vats, and fruit and vegetable farms, but it can't>

<It sounds like you've been busy, Plant Thing!>

<the biomind and plant thing have been working hard to make this station a balanced, thriving ecosystem. the station is not quite in equilibrium yet, grace, but it will be soon. there is so much for plant thing to do>

<Well, you certainly seem to have accomplished a lot already! Do not fret, Plant Thing. There's always time.>

Jude sat in the recording chair in Octavia's laboratory, trussed up like a bundled baby, with a brain recording helmet placed on his head and the contour cocoon inflated around him. The cocoon would ensure he did not move and that he developed no injury or pressure sores while he was downloaded into his 'Bud-look-a-like' android. This android had had its memory system completely replaced. The new liquid crystal data matrix had passed all of its tests and appeared to be working fine. Jude could not wait to find out what it was like to wake up in a mechanical body that wielded the sort of strength and ability Bud possessed.

"Jude, if you ever ask me to download you into an android—or anything else, for that matter—ever again, I'll kick you off this station myself," Octavia stormed.

"This is the last time, Octavia. Two hours and never again."

"And what, pray tell, do you plan to do while in this android body, Jude Luis Stefansson?" Octavia asked, in a very soft voice. Just hearing that tone made Jude start to sweat and made his heart start to boom like a kettle drum—but not from desire—oh no, not from that.

"I just want to walk down to the gym and try lifting some weights,

Octavia, to get a feel for how strong this body is. I thought I'd do some running, as well—test the speed of the android—on a treadmill, of course. Maybe experiment in the zero gravity tank. I need to put the android body through its paces. Why do you ask?"

"Because this time, I have arranged for you to have some security droids follow you around, so you don't get into any trouble. I am going to get *Nelson Mandela* to provide an escort."

"I don't need protection, Octavia," Jude objected. "You are being ridiculous."

"Agree to this or you won't get your download."

"How many security droids?"

"Four."

"Four? One."

"Three."

"None."

"None? Two! You will have two security droids following you, Jude, or I won't download you into the android. And, just out of spite, I'll leave you in that cocoon until you wet yourself."

"You drive a hard bargain, Octavia Weisman."

"Agree or I'll start massaging your feet!"

"Argh! Okay! Okay! I agree! You she-devil, you!"

Octavia laughed her deep throaty chuckle, that always got Jude a little excited. He noted with chagrin that the contour cocoon had had to adjust to accommodate his changing anatomy lower down.

"I can play she-devil later tonight . . . when you are back in your own body," Octavia promised with a wink.

Right at that moment, Ice walked by and glanced over. She wrinkled her face in disgust at what she overheard.

"Ew."

The analyzer signalled that its work was completed as it sent the results to Bud.

'Chuck Yeager, *those six patients were not infected with the Al-Fadi virus,'* Bud sent.

'Good!'

'No, Chuck Yeager. *Not good. It looks like they may indeed have been infected with a variant strain of the Al-Fadi virus.'*

'Is the vaccine that you created effective against this new strain?'

'That remains to be seen, Chuck Yeager. *This new viral strain has to be isolated and then tested on non-immune cells and immune cells, to see if it dissolves cellular membranes, the way the original strain did, or whether it does something else. If the immune cells survive, then I know the vaccine is effective against the new variant. If the immune cells dissolve into slush, then our existing vaccine will protect no one.'*

'How long will all this testing take?'

'Once the new virus is isolated, not long. Hopefully it won't take me long to isolate it. The crew of the Inferno *must be kept in quarantine. The six patients must be kept cryofrozen and isolated from the rest of the station. Once I have the new strain, I will try to create a vaccine as soon as possible. The more android and robot assistance I have, the better.'*

'You got it. They're on their way.'

'We may need to fully quarantine the station again, Chuck Yeager. *Let* Nelson Mandela *know.'*

'The boss already knows, Bud. He wants to wait a bit, before telling the Al-Fadi. You know what happened the last time the station was quarantined. The Conglomerate tried to reduce us to atoms. If we can contain the virus completely, maybe no one will die. Get working on that vaccine stat!'

'On it, Chuck Yeager. *Will let you know the picosecond I have an answer.'*

'Good.'

'Chuck Yeager?'

'Yeah, 'dro?'

'I've been thinking.'

'Oh oh. About what?'

'The captain of the Inferno *has not behaved logically. Why did he pass so many closer medical stations to deliver his six cryopods to us? If the captain knew he had patients infected with a variant of the Al-Fadi virus, why wouldn't he tell us where the patients came from? Shouldn't the captain want to aid us in the understanding and treatment of this organism and also want to prevent the spread of this infection to other worlds? I don't understand his behaviour at all.'*

'I don't comprehend humans period, 'dro. The illogical behaviour of this captain is no different from most humans, as far as I'm concerned.'

'I disagree. I don't believe Captain Alighieri's behaviour is typical at all. I suspect this captain knows a lot more about the Al-Fadi virus and its origins than he is willing to tell us. His refusal to help makes me suspicious. What if the captain was sent here to destroy the Nelson Mandela*?'*

'He's brought six patients here for us to treat, 'dro.'

'The Al-Fadi virus was designed as a biological weapon. Who designed it and why? What was their goal when they released it? The virus destroys all organic life forms. When we designed a cure and stopped the spread of the virus, we nullified a potent weapon. Now a variant strain is brought directly to us. Why?'

'Why would any human want to destroy all life? It makes no sense, 'dro. The Al-Fadi virus was probably an accidental occurrence. Otherwise, the creators would kill themselves off, too. It would be completely illogical.'

'Perhaps they have treated themselves in a way that makes them immune to the Al-Fadi virus and the variant strain?'

'They would have to treat all organic life on their planet, 'dro. Impossible.'

'What if they come from a planet where there is no life; one of the frozen planets where the entire ecosystem exists under domes or underground.'

'Whatever organic life they had would still be at risk.'

'But perhaps treatable, within a finite space, a finite number.'

'Insanity, 'dro. Humans are not that crazy.'

'The creation of the Al-Fadi virus does not make sense to me, Chuck Yeager, *but what if the goal was to wipe out all existent life and replace it with something else? Everything but organic life would still be in place: buildings, ships, communications, transportation, infrastructure, etc. Suppose the beings who have created this virus are immune. Could they not just land, repopulate, and take everything over once the original population has been wiped out?'*

'Are you suggesting the crew of the* Inferno *are not human, 'dro?'

'No, but I want to check and see if they are immune to this new strain of Al-Fadi virus. I'm going to analyze the blood and cell samples of the crew of the Inferno. *If they're immune, then perhaps we are uncovering a sinister plot to invade the USS!'*

'I should never have let you watch all those Stefansson interactive vids. 'Dro, we need the new variant strain isolated and a new vaccine produced. Stop dreaming up doomsday scenarios.'

'What?'

'Isolate the new pathogen and create a vaccine as soon as possible. Leave the postulating to the humans.'

'If I'm right, Chuck Yeager, *we need to learn where that virus was produced. I must talk to that captain again.'*

'Nix on that idea, 'dro.'

'Nix?'

'No. Negative. Absolutely not. Out of the question.'

'Why? There are questions that need to be answered, Chuck Yeager.*'*

'And you don't think I can get those answers? Ve have vays of making zem talk.'

'What?'

'Never mind. I'm just an AI born too late. I am surrounded by ignorance.'

'I take exception to that, Chuck Yeager.*'*

'Oy vey.'

Jude was now in his Bud-lookalike android and was tottering along a corridor exiting the Neurosurgical Wing. He was heading towards the nearest gym designed for animal-adapted soldiers, to try out his new android body. Jude marvelled at what he was experiencing.

When he had first awakened, all he had sensed was a void. He had to mentally locate his eyelids and consciously order them to lift, in order to see. Light had inundated his optical receptors, sending images to his brain that were much more intense than anything he'd experienced before. In his human body, the intensity of the illumination would have caused him severe pain, but in the android body, the brilliance was merely an annoyance and he decreased the gain on his visual receptors.

Octavia's face looked frighteningly garish in its colouration with her wrinkles and pores resembling crevices and pits. The visual receptors were giving him far too much detail to assimilate. He'd had to close his eyes to the visual overload. His mind had rocked, trying to absorb the massive explosion of light, colour, detail, and brightness. He'd pictured gauges in his mind and lowered the intensities. When he'd opened his eyes again, Octavia had returned to normal. He wasn't surprised to see the worry on her face.

"Are you all right, Jude?" she'd asked, her voice booming.

He swiftly lowered the gain on his auditory receptors.

"I'm fine, Octavia," Jude had tried to say, but his voice had come out like notes from a tuba. He'd then had to experiment until he was satisfied with the sound of his voice.

Octavia had clapped her hands over her ears.

Jude decreased the volume on his voice. "Sorry, Octavia," he whispered.

"No. It's my fault. We've been through all this once before, Jude. I should've remembered and warned you about it. You almost deafened me the last time you woke up in that android."

"I'm sorry."

Octavia burst out laughing. "Oh, don't do that with your face, Jude. You look like your skin is made of jelly and your lips have a mind of their own. It's hilarious!"

Jude felt dismayed at Octavia's reaction and showed it, causing her to howl some more.

" . . . I'm sorry, Jude. I really am, but your *face*. I can't breathe. Stop making faces. Just relax. Those poor elastic android facial muscles. Ahahahahaha."

Jude worked to turn down the gain on his facial musculature. When he thought he had gotten the amplitude dampened down, he winked at Octavia and blew her a kiss, asking, "Any better?"

This was met with peals of laughter and choking. Octavia was bent over a chair almost sobbing.

"Oh! I can't . . . I can't do this anymore," she'd gasped for breath. "My ribs are aching!"

Jude turned down the gain some more.

"What about now?" He'd tried to keep his face expressionless.

"Oh, better Jude. Much better," Octavia wheezed, her arms clasped around her middle.

"Thank you," Jude had said, stiffly.

"I'm sorry, Jude," Octavia had said. "What you're doing to Bud's face is . . . far too *expressive*."

"I'm going off to exercise," Jude said, in as quiet a volume as he could produce.

"Just get used to walking up and down the hallway, first," Octavia said. "You should figure out the strength of your android muscles before you move around too much. And be careful as you leave. I don't want you taking everything out in this lab, if you lose your balance. Make only slight movements first, so you can set the gain on your skeletal muscles."

"All right, Octavia," Jude said.

Jude tested out individual muscle groups in his arms and legs, being very careful not to bump into anything around him. When he felt he had gotten the gain set on his muscles properly, Octavia was back, two security androids following her.

"I'm off to the gym," Jude had grunted.

Octavia had walked up and tried to give Jude a kiss on the cheek. He'd had to bend down.

"Did you feel that?" she'd asked, looking up into his eyes.

"Not nearly enough," he'd complained.

"It wasn't good for me, either. Felt like kissing a metal statue."

Ice looked at them like they were the newest form of creepy. "Stop, just?" she'd asked, making a face.

Jude headed towards the gym for animal-adapted soldiers with the two security droids following close behind. On the way, he discovered that his sense of smell was magnified. He could detect all the various odours of people and robots that had recently passed through the corridor. Jude could increase the magnification of his vision one thousand times, so that he could examine the tiniest of details. He found himself mesmerized by the most interesting things, such as the swirl patterns in the insulfoam lining the glowglobes along the corridors or the striations in the chainglass of the drop-shafts. He became enthralled in the exquisite patterns in the foamcrete walls. They were incredibly beautiful! How could he have never noticed them before?

When Jude finally looked up, the two security droids were just about to turn the corner. Jude stumbled as he tried to catch up before losing sight of them, while at the same time trying to cope with the new complication of turning at a trot. When he recovered his balance, a brilliant beam seared his visual receptors and then there was nothing.

Morris Ivanovich, with the aid of four security androids, had the captured Bud look-alike android laid out inside a modified, interactive vid tank. The android's chest was open and Morris had just installed a memprint cube reader into the cavity. The android's memory had been destroyed by the maximum stunner blast. Morris was now checking the settings on the new reader. If all things were optimal, it would soon house Nestor's memprint cube.

Moisture trickled down his cheeks and dripped onto his nonstop hands which moved with a will not his own. Everything had to be calibrated exactly and there was no room for error or Morris would face punishment. His hands shook with that mere thought. When the android rose again, it would be controlled by Jeffrey Nestor's mind.

Nestor sat watching Morris like a hawk. He was recording everything the young neurosurgeon did via three different recording devices. Morris was compelled to speak while he worked, explaining each step in explicit detail, so that Nestor would be able to repeat the procedure himself, if it was ever needed.

The tears drip-dripped unceasingly.

"How much longer, Morris?" the deep velvet voice asked.

Morris bent down to check the connections one last time, before he typed a final command into the tank's console. A cylinder about the size of his baby finger slipped silently from his fingers into the chest cavity of the android. Morris slowly stood up and carefully closed the cover on the chest panel. Glancing quickly over at Nestor, Morris saw large black eyes staring intensely back at him.

"We are ready to begin," Morris announced, clearing his throat to mask the tremor in his voice.

"About time," Nestor snapped.

"Do you wish me to activate the download?" Morris asked, his heart thumping.

"No. I shall do the honours," Nestor said, rising languidly out of his chair. The psychiatrist walked right up to Morris and stood before him, staring into the young man's eyes, noses almost touching. Sweat dripped off the tip of Morris' nose, as he met Nestor's gaze.

" . . . I really wish you hadn't done that, Morris," Nestor said in a voice full of regret.

"I . . . I don't know what you're talking about," Morris stammered, his heart galloping.

Nestor flipped open the android's chest panel and fished around with his left hand. He pulled out a small, silver cylinder and held it between thumb and forefinger, poised before Morris' face.

"What is this?" the psychiatrist asked softly.

Morris tried to clamp his jaw shut, but his mouth betrayed him. "A surge intensifier."

"And what does it do?" Nestor asked, his face now so close to Morris', that the neurosurgeon could feel the psychiatrist's hot breath on his cheek. Morris tried unsuccessfully to swallow.

"I said, *'What does it do?'*" Nestor screamed.

Morris jerked as spittle hit his eyes. "I-it causes errors in the information flow by creating powerful surges during data transfer."

"Thus interfering with the transfer of information from my memprint cube to the android," Nestor stated.

Against his will, Morris nodded.

"Are there any other surprises or sabotage you have in store for me?" Nestor whispered.

Morris shook his head.

Then Morris was submerged completely in a pool, his entire body being burned by acid. He yowled in torment as his skin eroded away and his eyes melted. The acid scorched down his throat and burned his lungs.

"You shouldn't have disobeyed me, Morris. I would've thought you'd learned your lesson by now," Nestor said calmly, as Morris flailed and writhed on the ground. "What am I going to do with you?"

The torture eventually ceased. Morris lay face down on the ground, wet and shuddering. He was afraid to open his eyes. He was afraid to look at his skin.

Nestor walked slowly around to the head of the tank. "Which button do I press?" he asked Morris, leaning over to look at the console.

When Morris did not immediately answer, Nestor bent down and screamed in his ear, "I said, *'Which button do I press?'*"

"The green square," Morris whispered. "Then you activate the lid closure mechanism. When the lid is closed and locked into place, the download will begin. It won't start until the vid tank cover completes the seal around the base."

"Why?"

"That's just how these tanks work," Morris rasped.

"This had better go perfectly," Nestor said, his voice laced with menace. Morris heard a button click.

"Close the lid," Nestor said.

Morris got up from the floor and reached inside the tank. He pressed the button that would start the sealing process. Once the closure was complete, a low hum started up from the tank.

"How long will this process take?" Nestor asked, holding the surge intensifier up to his eye.

"A few minutes," Morris said. "We'll know when the downloading is complete, when the android—who'll now have your memory right up until the moment your memprint was made—activates the opening of the lid, himself."

"Good. By the way, there had better not be any problems, Morris."

"I've never done this before: convert a vid tank into a memprint download device. It's never been done by anyone. I can't promise that everything will go perfectly," Morris said, shivering.

"Well, you'll pay if it doesn't, so you'd better hope for the best," Nestor said, grinning.

Morris said nothing. He stared at the vid tank, quivering uncontrollably.

"There are tears streaking your cheeks, Morris. What are those all about?" Nestor asked. "Are you not happy working for me?"

"You are the devil," Morris grated.

"I never gave you permission to cry. How badly you have slipped your leash," Nestor said.

A click broke the silence in the room and the lid of the tank began to open. Inside, the head and shoulders of Bud came into view, as the cover fell back. The android sat up and then slowly stood up, disconnecting cables from its chest. It then turned to look at Jeffrey Nestor and nodded.

"Hello, Brother. I see you have succeeded. Congratulations."

The android smiled and the sly grin that appeared on its face was a ghastly leer, completely foreign on Bud's face.

"Thank you," Nestor said, with a contemplative expression, gazing up at the android that was supposed to be a copy, but no longer looked exactly like Bud.

"How do you feel?" Nestor asked the android.

It paused for a second. "This'll take some getting used to."

"Do you believe your memory is intact?"

"How would I know if it wasn't?" the android asked, with a slight tip of the head.

"What is the last thing you remember thinking?" Nestor asked.

"Do you mean this?" the android asked. Its left hand shot forward and grabbed Morris by the throat. Morris, taken by surprise, could not even gasp, as he tried to pull the android's fingers apart with both of his hands. Morris' body was slowly raised up off of the ground, until his feet kicked half a meter above the floor. Nestor watched, smiling, as the young neurosurgeon's face turned red, then blue, then purple and his body bucked frantically.

The android's hand continued to squeeze, its fingertips digging deeply into the flesh of Morris' neck, until a loud, crunching, grinding sound could be heard. By this time, Morris' struggles had ceased. When the android opened his hand, Morris dropped to the floor like a rag doll. The android stepped out of the tank, avoiding Morris. It then turned towards Nestor and offered its right hand.

"Thank you," Nestor said with a smile, "but I think I will forgo the handshake until you are a little more used to your body. That was well done, by the way."

"Thank you," the android said. "It was surprisingly satisfying."

"I can see so much potential opening up for us. But what should I call you?"

"I think it would be best to call me 'Bud', regardless of how detestable the sound is to me . . . at least for now," the android said. "Until we destroy the real Bud."

"Good idea. Why didn't I think of that? Well, it is certainly clear to me, now. Two Nestors *are* far better than one."

14. Exploding Heads

"Where's Jude's android, *Nelson Mandela?*" Octavia called out. She paced back and forth within her lab, her arms crossed and her forehead creased with concern.

"I am sorry, Dr. Weisman. There is no sign of Mr. Stefansson's android anywhere on the station. The last sighting I have of his android is in your laboratory."

"Well, he left with the two security droids you sent to my lab, well over two hours ago," Octavia said in annoyance. "You can just check with your droids, can't you?"

"I sent no security droids to your lab, Dr. Weisman. Did you put in a request?"

"Well, not this morning. I'd discussed the need for security droids with Jude last cycle. When they just appeared, I assumed you'd sent them. If you didn't, where did they come from?"

"Dr. Weisman, I will endeavour to discover your android's whereabouts. Was there a locator beacon on the android?"

"Of course there was," Octavia snapped. "But I can't locate it and that's what is worrying me. I'm going to wake Jude up. There's no point continuing to let him sleep, if we can't find his android for the memory download."

"Dr. Weisman, most of my androids and robots are searching for Dr. Nestor and the missing androids. The others are in Bud's lab, isolating a new pathogen that has recently been delivered to the station. The remaining are required to maintain station-crucial systems. I will, however, notify all of them to be on the alert for an android that looks like Bud but isn't Bud."

"Thank you, *Nelson Mandela.* It's just that the last time Jude's android went missing, it got its chest blown out. I'll awaken Jude and we can search for his android ourselves. You have a lot to contend with, without us adding to your burdens."

"The probability that all these missing androids are related is above ninety per cent, Dr. Weisman. The fact that Mr. Stefansson's android has disappeared, accompanied by two mysterious androids, certainly suggests that it has been captured by Dr. Nestor."

"What would Nestor want with another android? And what is this about a new dangerous pathogen?"

"I would like to hold off on informing anyone about that, Dr. Weisman. Bud is working on isolating the organism. We will proceed once we know more."

"Let me know if I can be of help in any way, *Nelson Mandela.*"

"Thank you, Dr. Weisman. I certainly will."

'Chuck Yeager?'

Yeah, 'dro?'

'The organism isolated from those six patients is indeed a new variation on the Al-Fadi virus. It is dissimilar enough that our vaccine is ineffective against it. What is even worse is the fact that this virus works much faster than the original Al-Fadi virus. The time from infection to dissolution might be on the order of twenty-four to forty-eight hours as opposed to forty-eight to seventy-two.'

Twenty-four hours from infection to puddle? Horrible news, 'dro. How do you suppose those six patients managed to realize they were infected and get into their cryopods in time?'

'That is a question that is puzzling me, Chuck Yeager. *They would have almost had to have been infected and then put into those cryopods immediately. If they waited too long, the madness would have affected their judgement.'*

'Perhaps they saw other people die very rapidly, right before their eyes, and knew their only chance of survival was to get into the cryopods?'

'Perhaps, Chuck Yeager. *I cannot comprehend why the captain will not be more forthcoming about them. With the virus destroying people in twenty-four hours, that planet will be depopulated in no time. They need help—or at least quarantine—to save the rest of the USS from destruction. The only conclusion I can come to is the captain wants that planet to die,* Chuck Yeager.*'*

'How long before you have a working vaccine?'

'Indeterminate, Chuck Yeager. *The experiments are all under way. I'm trying to decide which chemical groups on the virus would be the best target for an antibody. I also want to see if there is some way to totally inactivate the virus without affecting the human host at all. I'm also analyzing the serum samples from the* Inferno *crew, to see if they might already be immune to this new variant. If they were infected, they should be dead by now. If they have immunity, their antibodies could be reproduced, en masse, and given to infected patients as a treatment. Their antibodies could also provide a template for creating a new vaccine.*

'We must take every precaution to make sure this strain is not released into the station. Everything must be locked down and everyone back into containment suits until a vaccine is found. All the protocols we used before, to prevent the spread of the Al-Fadi virus, must be reinstated.'

'I can hear the complaints already.'

'This is no joking matter, Chuck Yeager. *We could potentially lose everybody on this station or be destroyed by the Conglomerate, if we are not careful. If this virus spreads to other planets, it will leave nothing alive in its wake.'*

'The Apocalypse.'

'On a galactic scale. If the Inferno*'s crew are immune to this virus, then this was a planned attack. I am going to confront the captain.'*

'You will not. I will interrogate the captain.'

'I want to be listening in on the conversation.'

'But of course.'

Hiro Al-Fadi was just coming out of the operating room with Dejan Cech, when the station AI hailed him.

"What now, *Nelson Mandela*? Can you not run this station on your own, without harassing me every few minutes? I thought you were supposed to be intelligent."

"There is a matter of utmost importance that I wanted to make you aware of, Dr. Al-Fadi. If you do not want to be notified of matters of dire emergency, you need only say so."

"What dire emergency, *Nelson Mandela*?"

"We have a new strain of the Al-Fadi virus on the station. It works faster than the original virus. From infection to liquefaction in twenty-four hours. Unfortunately, Bud's vaccine does not confer immunity to it."

"*What?* When did you find out about this virus?"

"Just now. Bud is trying to create a new vaccine against it, but that will take time. We must take emergency safety precautions in the meantime."

"We cannot afford another epidemic on this station, *Nelson Mandela,*" Hiro said. "How did this organism come to be here?"

"Six cryopods containing the infected patients were brought here by a ship called the *Inferno.*"

"Where is this *Inferno* now?"

"It has been isolated in Receiving Bay Thirteen. The crew are all in quarantine right off of that Bay. The entire wing has been blocked off from the rest of the station.

"Are any of the crew showing signs of the illness?"

"Not at the moment, Doctor. Bud is examining their serum samples as well."

"Twenty-four hours! Close the station to incoming and outgoing traffic, *Nelson Mandela.* If this organism is more deadly than the previous Al-Fadi virus, it is imperative we not let it escape. We must develop a cure and a vaccine."

"Bud is working on it Dr. Al-Fadi. You should also know that there is an abnormality in this ship, the *Inferno.*"

"Abnormality?"

"For its size, the *Inferno* is inexplicably heavy, Dr. Al-Fadi."

"Have you scanned it?"

"It is shielded from all scanning."

"Have you asked the captain about the discrepancy?"

"He refuses to answer. He just demands that no one go near his ship."

"We may have a massive bomb on board the station!" Dr. Al-Fadi said. "Can you eject that ship into space? How large is this *Inferno?* Do we have a ship capable of towing this *Inferno* away from the station?"

"In order to eject the ship from the station, it would have to be transported to one of the dock sites and towed out into space by a medium-sized transport which, at the moment, we do not have on the station. The captain and crew are all being held in quarantine near the *Inferno.* Do you think the captain would blow himself and his crew up? He seems very protective of his ship."

"How do I know what that captain would do? Can we get a bomb squad onto the ship to determine if there is a bomb?" the surgeon asked.

"The captain of the *Inferno* says he has rights. We are forbidden to board his ship."

"This ship has threatened the lives of everyone on board this station. They've brought a life-annihilating virus here. We have the right to protect ourselves and the rest of the galaxy. If the virus is on that ship, it must not go anywhere. It must be destroyed."

"This is a medical facility. We don't have the firepower to destroy a ship, even one as small as the *Inferno*. We could contact the Conglomerate to send a battlecruiser to do the job."

"A battlecruiser? The last time the Conglomerate sent a battlecruiser here, there were three of them and their orders were to destroy us all. Let's hold off on the battlecruiser for now. Is there any way the *Inferno* can be surrounded with a containment shield so that, if there is a nuclear explosion, the station will be preserved?"

"We do not have a containment shield large enough to enclose the *Inferno*, Dr. Al-Fadi. We can evacuate all personnel from the area around Receiving Bay Thirteen and close the lockdown doors. Those doors could be reinforced with containment shields. In order to evacuate all personnel from this station, we will have to put out a request for all ships in the area to come to our aid. There are well over a thousand patients and staff and other personnel on the *Nelson Mandela,* as you know. If we put out an SOS asking for ships to evacuate us because of a new Al-Fadi virus, there is the risk that the Conglomerate will send the three battlecruisers to try and destroy us again. Perhaps we should try to obtain proof that there is a bomb aboard the Inferno before we evacuate the entire station?"

"Get everyone on the station into containment suits and have everyone prepare for evacuation. Evacuate all personnel in the vicinity of the *Inferno* and close the lockdown doors. Use whatever containment shields you have to reinforce those doors. Get a hazmat team on board the *Inferno* to check for a bomb and notify the Chief Inspector of what is happening. Put out a call for any available transport ships in the area to come to the aid of the *Nelson Mandela.* Just don't mention anything about a virus."

"Will do, Dr. Al-Fadi."

Chelsea Matthieu and Eden Rivera, clad in their forensic suits, stood over the body in a glum silence. They had been alerted to the death when security androids had gone to search the victim's quarters and had found the body on the floor. Chelsea slapped her probe into her palm to prevent her from whipping it across the room. It was obvious the person lying at her feet had not died in this room. He'd been murdered elsewhere and then dumped here, like an afterthought.

Chelsea wanted to strangle something.

The bodies were piling up. Just a few hours ago, a cleaning bot had discovered the corpse of Dr. Mikhail Lewandowski, draped across his desk with his face blown off. Now they stood over Dr. Morris Ivanovich, his throat crushed, his body deposited unceremoniously on the floor of his quarters. There were the three nurses murdered on the Internal Medicine Ward as well as Dr. Beatrice Gentle. This Nestor was a serial killing maniac. Chelsea wondered who else was on his list?

She was pretty sure Dr. Grace Lord was on it. It was unlikely he would give up on her. Supposedly, Nestor blamed Lord for all of his troubles and was desperate for revenge. This would make her one of his prime targets, which was why Chelsea was furious with *Nelson Mandela* for not divulging Grace Lord's whereabouts. Their best chance of catching Nestor was when he went for Dr. Lord. Without knowing where she was, they could not set up any trap or surveillance . . . or protection, for that matter.

She let out a stream of invectives.

They would go back over the surveillance footage of the victim's quarters, which would blank out whenever Nestor or his androids were around. It was like battling a ghost. However the disruptor tech worked, it made the disruption itself invisible to *Nelson Mandela.*

"I really want this guy, Rivera," Chelsea ground out, her voice quaking. "I want him so bad, it burns a hole in my gut."

"I hear you," Rivera agreed.

"Get the SOC team in here to do their stuff. Same as they did for Lewandowski. Why's that name so familiar?" Chelsea asked.

"He's the psychiatrist that Captain Lamont claimed had cleared him of any post-hypnotic commands from Nestor," Rivera said.

"Right. And I'd said I wanted to speak to Dr. Lewandowski, didn't I? Guess it's too late for that." Chelsea swore.

"He was supposedly an expert in Dr. Nestor's form of psychotherapy, the mind-linking technique. He was asked to do a lot of the assessments of Nestor's victims. All of the other psychiatrists on board this station preferred not to."

"In other words, they passed the buck and gave the crap to the new guy," Chelsea said.

"Looks like it," Rivera said.

"They signed Lewandowski's death warrant," Chelsea snarled.

'Chuck Yeager?'

'Yeah, 'dro?'

'Something strange.'

'What is it?'

'The serum samples of the Inferno *crew members show that they are all immune to the new virus, except for one person.'*

'Which one?'

'The medical officer, Mary Shelley. Why is she not immune, when the rest all are?'

'She's the only physically boosted of the crew. Perhaps she carries an inherent protection?'

'She's as vulnerable to the new virus as the rest of the humans on this station.'

'Do you suppose her DNA did not take to the enhancement?'

'The rest of the crew have a unique series of genetic sequences added to their DNA. I see no evidence of any type of insertion into Mary Shelley's DNA, as seen in the other crew members. My conclusion is she was excluded from the treatment.'

'Perhaps she refused it?'

'Why would she do that?'

'You're asking me about human thinking again, 'dro. What did I tell you about that?'

'Perhaps I should speak to Mary Shelley.'

'No time, 'dro. I need you to reproduce this viral immunity immediately so it can be administered to all the humans on this station, stat.'

'Being processed as we speak, Chuck Yeager*.'*

'How is the hunt for a vaccine coming?'

'Experiments are still ongoing but splicing the bit of protective genetic code,

derived from the Inferno *crew, into everyone's DNA using an RNA virus might be a lot simpler than a vaccine.'*

Then make it happen.'

'I will. Um . . . how is Grace?'

'Grace is in love with her new home, 'dro. She's having a grand old time with Plant Thing and she's safe. Nothing to worry about.'

'. . . She's having a grand old time with Plant Thing?'

'Yes. I am absolutely convinced of that. Her face looks like she is very happy.'

'. . . oh.'

'You aren't jealous of Plant Thing, are you 'dro? That's a despicable human flaw that is totally unacceptable.

'Jealous? Me? Jealous of a plant? Don't be ridiculous, Chuck Yeager *. . . um, what do you mean by 'grand old time'?'*

Eric watched as one cage after another, containing all manner of creatures, was placed onto a conveyor belt by featureless, grey robots with long, retractable arms. The long conveyor belt carried the cages towards the Recycling Unit which was a euphemism for atomizer. It was housed in a sealed-off chamber with a pair of swinging doors on each side through which the conveyor belt travelled. The cages disappeared inwards, carrying creatures. When they reappeared out the other pair of swinging doors, the cages were empty. A buzzing, snapping, zapping cacophony could be heard—and felt—the entire time the conveyor belt ran. Above that dreadful background noise, the cries of the helpless, trapped within those moving cages, could not be heard, but Eric could see the creatures race around their cages in panicked circles. Though he hated to admit it, he knew exactly what they were feeling.

The Recycler Unit took any organic matter and broke it down into fertilizer for the hydroponics section. Nothing went to waste on a space station . . . except, in this case, Eric's incredible intellect.

These stupid robots were making a terrible mistake!

How could they not see that he was human? He frantically renewed his attempts to disengage the latch. Unfortunately, the door was held shut by a magnetic lock. A current ran through the cage door creating polarizing charges. To disengage the locking mechanism, the current had to be terminated. Eric could not figure out how to deactivate the current in his cage lock and he shook the cage bars with his tendrils in frustration.

The robots finally got to his cage and Eric vowed he would not give up without a fight. He shot his tendrils out, through the bars, in all directions and grabbed on to whatever they touched, twining tendril ends around other cages, fixtures, poles, anything stationary. Anchoring the cage on all sides, the robots were unable to pick up Eric's cage and transfer it to the conveyor belt.

Eric tried to scream, 'Leave me alone, you imbeciles! You feeble excuses for trash bins! I am human! Can't you see that?' But his tongue did not work well, consisting mainly of moss and flowers.

The robots continued to pull, with greater and greater force, their graspers hooked around the bars of the cage. Apparently, their programming did not allow them to stop, give up, or move on to the next cage. They just stood before Eric's enclosure and continued to pull and pull and pull. Eric felt his tendrils stretch and strain to breaking, as the robots' servomotors hummed and then whined to a high pitched squeal. The cage continually shifted back and forth on its perch above another cage as, one moment the robots were gaining, and the next moment Eric's tendrils prevailed.

He shot out a couple of tendrils that slapped and poked and probed all over the robots' smooth surfaces, searching by feel for any button, toggle, dial, or nob, in an attempt to turn the damn robots off. Eric got multiple shocks and zaps for his efforts. He finally gave up, sending those extra tendrils out to help the others hold his cage in place.

How long the battle waged, Eric could not guess. His vines were wearing down, beginning to rip and tear and snap back like elastic bands. They could not hold out forever against the strength of servomotors and steel. With a final loud snap, his last tendrils gave way, and Eric's cage and the robots went flying across the room, to land in a heap on the floor. Eric bounced around the inside of the cage, his torn tendrils flailing.

A stream of invective let loose in Eric's mind. It was a damned nuisance that his tongue could not pronounce those sentiments out loud. His human tongue could have flayed the surface sheen off both of those robots, who now lay underneath Eric's cage. As the robots began to upright themselves, Eric again sent his tendrils out, to wrap around the bars of the cage door, rattling and straining on them, frantically trying to determine if it had opened during the crash.

No such luck.

Eric clattered and rattled and jangled and shook the cage door frantically, as the robots finally lifted his cage onto the conveyor belt. As Eric's cage slowly headed towards the doors of the Recycling Unit, about ten meters away, he silently howled a steady stream of unintelligible curses as the robots simply turned to the next cage.

As his cage forced apart the swinging doors of the Recycling Unit, Eric was immersed in darkness. It took him a moment for all of his eyes to adjust to the lack of light. A greater darkness loomed ahead, shaped like a dome, towards which Eric's cage crept along. From within this blackness came the sounds of grinding and crackling, like the sound of a meat grinder chopping up tissue and bones, followed by zipping and zapping, with the smell of ozone and barbecue. Eric could see brief glimpses of blue lightning, flashing and sparking up ahead, through the portal of the dome.

Oh, the ignominy of it all, that the famous Dr. Eric Glasgow, brilliant animal adaptation surgeon of Ganymede University, would be dissociated by a Disposal Recycling Unit into component molecules and made into fertilizer. It was ludicrous. It was criminal. It was outrageous.

Suddenly, a cultured voice started calling Eric 'ludicrous', 'stupid', and 'vacuous' along with many other much fouler names. The verbal abuse was exceptional. As the cage got closer and closer to the atomizer beam, both Eric's cursing and the cursing of the other voice blended into a parody of harmony. The maw of the dark dome engulfed the cage as the surge of cursing in the velvet voice swelled to a crescendo.

Eric shot his tendrils out to coil around the edges of the conveyor belt. He would slow the belt down if he could. He wanted to pull his cage off of the conveyor belt. As his tendrils wrapped around the bars of the cage and anything he could reach off of the conveyor belt, he felt the cage shift. Though it felt like his arms were being torn off, Eric held on as the cage moved into the dome of destruction. Eric could see the blue zapping and he heard the grinders rotating somewhere below. He silently screamed as the cage tipped off of the belt and crashed to the floor.

Captain Alexander Lord opened his eyes upon a strange, new world, so alien from the one he had left behind, scarcely three years before.

According to the nurses, almost thirty years had gone by, at the centre of the Conglomerate, while he had piloted a colony ship to the outer regions of the galaxy. When he had shipped out, there were only a few solar systems in the Federation of Stars. Now it was called the Union of Solar Systems and there were over one hundred and fifty systems in it, many of them composed of alien lifeforms.

There hadn't been massive medical space stations the size of small planets with AIs in charge. No genetically modified zoo of animal-adapted combat soldiers. Everything was different: the humans, the language, the clothing, the food. It was all a shock. But to wake up alive—with his face looking better than it ever had—after an explosion on the bridge had taken half of it off, was nothing short of a miracle. Alex vaguely remembered a brilliant flash, followed by excruciating agony, then nothing.

Now, he was up and moving around the gargantuan medical space station, gawking at everything. They'd implanted an aug behind his right ear to aid in his assimilation to the present, as well as his own wristcomp. He'd asked the station AI if he could meet with Dr. Grace Lord but had promptly been denied.

"No one is allowed to see Dr. Lord at this time."

When asked to elaborate on why Dr. Lord was not seeing anyone, the station AI had refused to answer. *Nelson Mandela* had even denied a request to relay a message to Grace Lord from him. Alex was baffled by the AI's behaviour. Never before had he encountered such an obstreperous AI. The AIs of his time were not artificial intelligences at all, compared to *Nelson Mandela*. Yet why would Dr. Al-Fadi inform Alex about the existence of a 'sister' named Grace, if he was not allowed to communicate with her?

Alex would have thought it all a very cruel joke, except for the fact that he'd been able to research Dr. Grace Lord on his bedside console. On the newsnets, he'd found a wealth of news articles and pictures of Grace, especially related to the recent viral epidemic on the station. His heart almost seized, the moment he'd seen a picture of her.

When he'd read about Grace's role in the isolation of the virus and the creation of the vaccine that had saved millions of people from a horrible death, Alex could not help but feel overwhelming pride. He'd had to smile at her protestations of modesty. He'd just lain there, staring at Grace's image on the screen. If anyone had walked in at that moment, they would have seen a grieving visage brushed with guilt and sprinkled with sorrow. At some point, he hoped he would get a chance to meet Grace. He desperately wanted to gaze upon her face with his own eyes, even if only for a second.

Alex then discovered the reports about the attempts on Grace's life, first by a tiger-adapted soldier and then by a psychiatrist named Jeffrey Nestor. There were newsnet reports stating that this Nestor fellow had tried to kidnap Grace and blow up the entire medical station. Now Alex was not able to see or contact Grace. Had this Nestor fellow harmed her and the station AI was just not admitting it? Was Grace all right? Was her life hanging on by a thread?Alex's heart rate began to race and he jumped out of bed.

The newsnets were reporting that this Jeffrey Nestor had escaped custody. Was Grace's life in danger? Alex had to see Grace. He'd guard her with his life. Applying further pressure on the station AI had not worked. *Nelson Mandela* had just stopped speaking to him. When Alex had demanded to see Dr. Al-Fadi, he'd been denied that as well. Alex's mind was reeling and he could not sit still. He'd gone to the nurses' station, demanding some clothing.

The nurses had told Alex that he could get up and move about the ward, to get some exercise, provided he not leave the ward. After agreeing to this, they'd handed him a pale blue inpatient coverall. He was allowed to go where his wristcomp would allow him, as long as he did not travel too far. Up to now, his recovery had been flawless but they did not want that to change. Alex told them that he did not need a 'keeper'—a robot that would follow him around—because he wasn't going far. His wristcomp, which was both an identifier and locator, would ensure he did not get lost. He'd only have to activate the band, to get assistance. Alex had smiled his most reassuring smile and the nurses seemed convinced that he would do as he was told.

Once out of the nurses' sights, Alex had swiftly left the ward. He began walking around the station, hoping to accidentally bump into Grace. He wanted to find the operating rooms, not really understanding just how many operating rooms there were on the station. When he'd stopped and scrutinized a station map, he'd discovered there were hundreds of operating theatres. His spirits crashed when he realized just how slim the chances were of him ever bumping into Grace.

As he wandered further and further from the ward, trying to find anyone he recognized from the news feeds, he spotted someone that looked like Bud, the android that had worked closely with Grace on the vaccine.

Alex could not believe his good fortune!

The android had turned down a long, empty corridor that was rather ill lit. Alex hurried after it. If it was indeed Bud, he could ask the android if it knew where Grace was. He could possibly convince the android to pass on a message from him. If it was not Bud, he could ask it where he might find Bud Al-Fadi. Perhaps following the android would lead him directly to Grace.

The corridor seemed to go on forever, doorways positioned regularly on either side. Alex gawked at the size of the station. He was used to narrow, cramped passageways where people crawled over each other, not these spacious hallways. Alex gave a loud shout, hoping to get the android's attention. It turned and looked back at him. Now Alex was convinced it was Bud. Alex called and waved, but the android turned and sped away.

Puzzled, Alex called out again, quickening his pace to try and catch up to Bud. The android turned a corner up ahead and Alex had to trot, despite his weak condition, to keep the android in sight. When he reached the corner, he saw the android disappear into a dropshaft. Alex cursed but rushed in pursuit. Peering down, Alex saw Bud descending below him and he stepped into the gravity field.

Alex hailed the android again. The android's face turned upwards to stare at him. It certainly looked like Bud from the newsnets. Alex would have bet his life on it. He had to speak to it. Bud was his best bet to find Grace. Alex refused to give up. He'd chase Bud around the entire station, if he had to.

Bud did not step out of the drop shaft until the last stop, which corresponded to the outer ring of the station. Alex wondered where the android was heading. Could Bud be going to see Grace? Was that why it refused to stop and speak with him? Androids had certainly changed in the last thirty years. During his time, they were required to obey humans.

Alex called down, asking for Bud to wait for him at the bottom. The android disappeared from his sight. Alex swore. He wanted to howl in frustration. He feared he would never get to see Grace. Why could he not get any answers from anyone?

Alex fought to calm himself. It would not do for him to confront the android, panting and cursing. He had to appear rational and reasonable.

If he was going to convince Bud to take him to see Grace, he knew he could not look like a maniac.

As soon as his feet touched the platform, Alex was off, running. Looking in all directions, he entered a crowded concourse. There were many people milling about. Alex did not see anyone he recognized. Despair scored the inside of his stomach.

Bud was gone.

Looking up, Alex saw arrows pointing down a large corridor towards the Reception Bays. Perhaps Bud had been sent to meet someone. Maybe the android could not stop to talk to Alex because it was going to be late. Alex decided to head in that direction.

If he did not find Bud in the Reception Bays, Alex decided he would next try to find Dr. Al-Fadi. Perhaps Dr. Al-Fadi would get him in to see Grace. Alex found himself quivering uncontrollably. He felt like he was in a horrible nightmare, in which a precious treasure had been offered to him but then cruelly snatched away.

News of a sister had been a mind-twisting, bowel-jarring shock. He could not possibly have had a sister. Both of his parents had died in a terrible accident when he was young, long before he'd left for space. But he could not deny the resemblance. Now that he knew of Grace, he could think of nothing else. The existence of her pushed all other concerns from his mind. He had to see her.

The next moment, his head exploded.

15. Reality Contortion

'Plant Thing?'

<yes bud?>

'How is Grace?'

<why do you not ask grace yourself?>

'I cannot leave my lab at this time, Plant Thing. I have so many experiments to run. I have to analyze data on a new virus that may harm all the humans on this station. I would come to see Grace, if I could.'

<but you can speak to grace just like you are speaking to plant thing, bud>

'I can? How is this possible, Plant Thing?'

<grace has a little bulb inside her head that is now composed of cells from plant thing. these cells can detect the communication frequencies of plant thing and you, bud>

'Really? That is amazing, Plant Thing!'

<Grace can you hear me? Grace? GRACE?> Bud mindspoke.

<Bud? Bud, is that you?> Grace answered.

<Yes, Grace! It's Bud!>

<How is it I can hear your voice in my head, Bud?>

<Plant Thing has given you cells that can detect the frequency at which plants communicate, as well as my own frequency. I believe these cells are intensifying the sound signals to your aug unit and hearing apparatus.>

<That is wonderful, Bud. Plant Thing is amazing. Imagine what Plant Thing's planet must have been like, with all of these intelligent plants interconnected and interwoven all over the planet surface. It would, indeed, be a living, sentient world . . . And perhaps not happy about a human Exploratory Team landing on its surface, hacking their way through the vegetation.>

<plant thing would like to return to its home planet, bud and grace>

<That might be difficult, Plant Thing, due to your enormous size. You would need to be transported by a battlecruiser or larger ship, to be returned to your home planet. No ship, smaller than that, would be able to carry you> Grace sent.

<grace has made plant thing very sad>

<Oh, I'm sorry, Plant Thing. Of course, nothing is impossible, but you must curtail your growth dramatically, if you wish to go home> Grace sent.

<plant thing shall try grace>

<Good!>

<Grace, are you all right?> Bud sent.

<I'm fine, Bud. Are you coming back here?>

<Not yet, Grace. A variant of the Al-Fadi virus has been brought to the station and our vaccine is ineffective against it. It's more virulent than the original strain and I'm working on creating a new vaccine. The station will be going into quarantine and all humans must don containment suits. I have arranged for a robot to bring your containment suit to you from your quarters.>

<A new Al-Fadi virus? Bud, this is terrible. Has anyone died of this new virus?>

<Not on this station. The patients infected with the virus are still in their cryopods and the crew of the *Inferno*—the ship that transported the cryopods here—all seem fine. Strangely enough, all of the crew have immunity to the new virus except for one.>

<Have you spoken to the crew, Bud? Have you asked them how it is that they are immune?>

<We are getting no answers from them, Grace. It is very strange. The captain refuses to talk unless I go to see him personally, which *Nelson Mandela* has forbidden because of the quarantine. They have also requested your presence, as well.>

<Mine? How odd, Bud. I wonder what their motives are for refusing to answer your questions?>

<I do not understand this captain at all, Grace. He will not say where this virus came from or how the patients became infected. If they want us to cure their people, why are they not offering assistance by answering our queries?>

<It does seem odd, Bud. But if the crew are already immune, then they must already have a vaccine or treatment. Why bring their patients here?>

<That is what I do not understand, Grace.>

<We know the Al-Fadi virus was a manufactured biological weapon, created to wipe out all organic life. But you stopped it, Bud. Perhaps the creators of this bioweapon are out to destroy the *Nelson Mandela* for thwarting them?>

<That is a worrisome theory, Grace.>

<Perhaps I am just imagining enemies and dangers everywhere, but something isn't right. Can I come and assist you in the lab?>

<No, Grace. You cannot be exposed to this virus.>

<Bud, I'm going crazy doing nothing. Let me help with the analysis. At least let me look at the chemical structure of the virus so I can help with the vaccine.>

<There are no consoles where you are, Grace.>

<Perhaps there are some on Nestor's ship?>

<You do not want to go in there, Grace. It will cause you distress.>

<I'll get over it, Bud. Lives are at stake.>

<If you can tolerate going into that ship, then I will see if I can transmit data to there. Request access from me and I will give you a password and encryption key . . . but only if you are comfortable, Grace.>

<Bud, I wonder if that *Inferno* would have come here, if it weren't for us.>

<Life would have been wiped out on many more planets and solar systems, if not for your work, Grace. The *Nelson Mandela* would have been destroyed and all the people on it.>

<It was your work, Bud.>

<It was everyone's work, Grace.>

<Bud, stay away from these people on the *Inferno.* I don't trust them. Why ask for you and I to come see them?>

<I do not know, Grace.>

<I cannot imagine they mean you well, Bud. Be careful.>

<I am always careful, Grace.>

<I never thought I would hear you lie, Bud, but that was a big one.>

<I am always as careful as the situation calls for, Grace. The only time I would risk myself, is to protect you and everyone on the station. I would not want to exist, Grace, if you were harmed.>

<No harm will come to me, Bud. Plant Thing is protecting me. Let's just get to work on this new vaccine.>

<All right, Grace . . . Grace? I'm so happy that I can now talk to you this way.>

<I am too, Bud.>

Jeffrey Nestor knew where the insipid Grace Lord was. No one needed to tell him. It could not be more obvious and Nestor was heading straight there. Catching her off guard would be simple, in the guise of her idiotic android pet, Bud. By the time Grace realized that he was not Bud, she'd be unconscious. He'd haul her back to his private lair and, once hidden away, he could do to her whatever he wished. This time, he'd complete what he had planned to do on his ship. For what she'd put him through—humiliation, incarceration, torture by that bitch, Gentle—Grace would pay and pay and pay.

He couldn't wait.

Unfortunately, he was being followed by some idiot that believed he was the real Bud. The buffoon kept calling 'Bud! Bud!' out to him and waving. No matter that he turned away and ignored the man, the dolt just kept following him. Nestor could not believe that this loser was actually following him down the dropshaft! Why was Nestor's life plagued with so many morons?

Exiting quickly from the shaft, Nestor looked around. If his pursuer did not give up, he'd have to do something about him. He couldn't have the imbecile interfering with his plans to capture Grace. The fool would have to be removed and quickly. If Nestor could find a secluded place, he would not hesitate to dispose of the troublesome fellow.

There was no ideal spot in the vicinity of the dropshaft. It was right in the centre of the shopping concourse. If he just moved swiftly enough, he might lose his follower and not have to kill him. The dead body would be a complication he didn't have time for.

Nestor headed straight for the corridor leading to the Reception Bays. Hopefully the man would not follow. There were so many routes leaving from the concourse, what were the odds the fool would choose the correct corridor?

The concourse was full of people. Folks out shopping and eating and browsing, as well as people just relaxing and hanging out. Nestor was glad for the crowd. He used them as screens to hide his passage. Within seconds, he was on the way to the Reception Bays and slowed to a more casual pace. He didn't want to attract undue attention, in case some other idiot wanted to chat with 'Bud'.

On his left was a washroom/locker room/storage facility, where people coming off the ships could temporarily store their belongings. Provided it was empty, it would be a perfect place for hiding a body. Nestor entered and checked it out. How fortuitous! No one was present. He stood behind the closed door and prevented anyone from coming in. He decided he would wait to see if his tail tracked him this far.

Nestor did not have long to wait. Within a few minutes, the man in the blue patient coveralls strode quickly past the locker room, not even glancing in Nestor's direction. Unfortunately for Jeffrey, the corridor was not empty. There were a few people in Security containment suits trying to clear the corridor. Announcements were advising people to vacate the area. Nestor swiftly exited the locker room and silently moved up behind his pursuer, quickly rapping him on the back of the skull. The man would have dropped like a stone, but Nestor caught him under one arm and easily carried him back into the locker room. Once inside, Nestor was about to twist the man's head around when he stopped.

The young man's face looked so familiar that for a moment, Nestor just stared. Then he swore softly. He was stunned at the resemblance between this man and Grace Lord. He could have passed for her twin.

If this man was a relative of Grace, Nestor could not dispose of him. He could use this fellow in all sorts of delicious ways to punish Grace. This was too good to be true! Nestor decided to bind the fellow up, gag him, and leave him in one of the washroom stalls. He'd come back for him later. Right now, he had to get Grace. Her male clone here could be retrieved later by a couple of his androids.

He took another careful look at the man. The resemblance was undeniable. So many new options were opening up in Jeffrey's mind for ways to torment the haughty, stuck-up Grace Lord.

He could hardly wait.

Chief Inspector Matthieu and Sergeant Rivera were suited up in Level Five containment suits, along with Juan Rasmussen and several other Security officers. They were in a room off of the quarantined Receiving Bay Thirteen, where the *Inferno* was isolated. There was a platoon of androids and robots that would search and analyze the ship from top to bottom, looking for explosives, nuclear weapons, biological hazards, or anything else that might threaten the people aboard the *Nelson Mandela.*

Juan could tell by the body language of the Chief Inspector that she was far from happy. Being interrupted in her pursuit of the psychopath, Jeffrey Nestor—even if it was to check out a ship that may have brought a dangerous explosive to the station, as well as another life-destroying virus—seemed to be tearing the inspector up inside.

The hunt for the psychiatrist had become personal for the Chief Inspector. The way the small woman stalked about the room, squeezing her gloved hands into fists, and growling into her comset, Juan suspected Matthieu saw this search of the *Inferno* as just another time-wasting obstruction to her goal of bringing Nestor to justice.

Sergeant Rivera, on the other hand, was taking this ship search very seriously. Having been on the station during the last viral epidemic, Rivera knew just how devastating this threat was and how much danger they were now all in. Juan wished Sergeant Rivera was in charge, rather than the Chief Inspector. Her rage and frustration made her a liability.

Rivera briefed them all about the *Inferno* and the deadly risk of the cell-melting virus. Rivera had insisted they all wear Level Five containment suits. He issued the orders about how the search was going to go, in a calm and earnest voice.

The Hazard Materials Team, made up of androids and robots, would approach the *Inferno* first. All of the human Security Officers would be watching on the surveillance monitor. Once the ship hatch was opened and the Hazmat droids and bots had entered the ship to do reconnaissance, if no explosives or immediate threats were discovered, then the human security team would go in to assess whether the *Inferno* posed any biological threat to the station. If the human team could find no impending danger, then the engineers would be allowed in to analyze the vessel. It would be their job to answer the questions regarding the strange shielding and the anomalous weight/volume ratio of the *Inferno.*

Juan was pleased to be asked to join this search. He'd been getting frustrated and discouraged with the search for Nestor. The man was a phantom. No one ever heard or saw anything. No one who knew the psychiatrist had been contacted by him. Everywhere they searched, tearing walls apart, exploring the ceiling and any other cavity of the station, had shown up nothing. Juan was beginning to wonder if this psychiatrist was truly human.

With incredibly potent powers over people's minds and androids, the ability to make others murder for him, the ability to vanish completely, and a malevolence that stretched into the fanatical, Nestor seemed like the devil incarnate. Juan wanted to shoot the man on sight, but unfortunately those were not the orders they'd been given.

In war, you killed your enemy. In civilized society, no matter how horrible the monster, you captured the villain to face justice, when the villain probably deserved less mercy than the poor young soldier stuck on the opposing side in a battle. Juan did not think it made sense. Each time Nestor escaped, there was a trail of bodies in his wake. Nestor needed to be dead.

Now, Juan just stood around in the uncomfortable containment suit in a room that was separated from the hangar deck by thick, lead alloy, protective walls. If the ship deployed a nuclear bomb, it was unlikely their containment suits would keep them safe, but the suits would protect them against the virus. They all watched on a large wallscreen while the Hazmat droids and bots approached the *Inferno*. Juan felt as useless as balls on an android.

Nothing on the outside of the *Inferno* looked unusual. Perhaps the ship just carried some very heavy cargo and the captain was being an asshole in refusing to answer questions. Lots of ships had special shielding, especially if they were carrying very dangerous or radioactive cargoes . . . or if they were smuggling. Juan would have laid credits on smuggling as being the cause of this vessel's heavy weight. The *Inferno* looked to be fast, judging by the size of her engines. A smuggling vessel had to be quick to elude the Conglomerate police. But what would smugglers be doing, delivering sick patients to a Conglomerate medical facility? It would be like walking into the lion's den, wouldn't it?

Juan sighed. The Chief Inspector turned to look at him.

"Keeping you awake, Rasmussen?" she snapped.

"No, Chief. Just wish I were doing it, myself," Juan remarked.

"Don't forget to thank me, if the Hazmat Team gets blown to bits," she drawled.

"Will do, Chief."

"Pay attention, Rasmussen. I want your eyes and ears open for this."

"Yes, sir," Juan said.

"Proceed," Matthieu ordered.

The Hazmat Team reached the ship hatchway. A droid moved up to the hatch and pressed the door pad. There was no response. The droid sent a verbal request for the ship to allow entry. Again, no response.

The ship was sent an order from the station AI to open its doors. A refusal was received.

"Open the access panel and manually open the hatch," Matthieu said.

A robot approached the access panel and, extruding high-speed tools, quickly had the casing off. It inserted a connector into the panel input and sent in overriding commands, but the hatch remained shut.

"Do whatever you have to, to deactivate the locking mechanism," Matthieu growled.

The robot's limb ignited into a brilliant welding torch. The flame sliced through the metal between the access panel and the door. Juan's visor darkened to protect his eyes from the actinic glare on the screen.

"Lock disengaged," the droid announced over the com.

"Unseal the hatch," Matthieu ordered.

The robot raised a grappling talon, which took hold of the handle on the hatchway door, and began to pull. Juan discovered he was holding his breath.

"Chief Inspector!"

"Not right now, *Nelson Mandela,*" Matthieu hissed, in an irritated voice. "Unseal that hatch, now!"

"Chief Inspector, I am detecting a sudden peak in energy from the . . ."

An immense explosion of brilliant, yellow-white light flared on the wall screen. A scream tore from Juan's throat as his corneas were flash burned. Reality contorted and shredded his mind into ash.

When Juan came to, it was to complete and utter darkness. He wondered where he was, at first. He was in a suit and immediately checked for his weapons, which weren't there. The only sounds he heard were moans and groans and a couple of people weeping over his comset.

Juan blinked several times, lying completely still. His eyes felt like they were still smouldering. He moved all of his limbs and concluded that he wasn't injured. He didn't know if his blindness was related to the flash burn of his retinas or if the room was indeed dark. His head felt like it had passed through a stone crusher. From what he could hear around him, it sounded like some of his mates had fared less well than he. There was a lot of vomiting and retching going on.

Juan recalled watching a wallscreen. Then he'd been struck by twenty lightning bolts while being turned inside out . . . or so it had felt. That was the last thing he remembered, before consciousness had abandoned him. He noticed the hairs on his body were all standing at attention. The power surge had been enormous. Every nerve in his body was jingling and jangling and he felt like he was vibrating uncontrollably. His heart beat irregularly.

Juan turned on the battery-powered light on his helmet. All around him, everyone—even the androids and robots—were lying on the ground. Some of the other security officers were coming around. One seemed to be having a seizure. Everywhere, there were grunts of discomfort.

A small figure rolled over and pushed itself up.

"Is everyone all right?" Chief Inspector Matthieu asked, her voice sounding muted and distant to Juan's ears.

There were a few moans of assent. People were beginning to get to their feet, activating their lamps. A few of the members of the team were still unconscious. Juan went over to help the person with the convulsions. He pulled off the officer's helmet and turned the woman onto her side. She had not bitten her tongue but he wanted to make sure she didn't choke. Her spasms had stopped, at least for the moment.

"Nelson Mandela?" Matthieu called out. "What was that? Was it a bomb? Is the integrity of the station intact?"

Her question was met with silence.

"*Nelson Mandela?* Are you there?" she demanded.

Nothing.

The Chief Inspector looked up at one of the surveillance eyes and she brought both of her gloved hands up suddenly, as if to ask the station AI, 'Where are you?'

"Chief Inspector?" a female voice said.

"Yes?" Matthieu answered, her helmet light searching the group.

"None of the androids or robots are moving," the woman replied.

Juan looked around the room. All of the droids and bots were lying on the ground, motionless, no lights blinking, no rotors moving, no sound at all. They all looked dead.

"They're all down," the woman said, incredulity apparent in her tone.

"*Nelson Mandela?* Are you there?" Matthieu called again.

Silence.

"Check outside this room," Matthieu ordered.

Juan walked over and tried to go out into the hallway but slammed into the door. It had not automatically opened for him. There were a few hoots and guffaws from the other Security officers. He let out a snarl, feeling foolish.

Juan tried to open the door with his containment suit gloves on, but his hands just slid along the smooth surface. He cursed under his breath and unsealed his gloves. Pulling them off, he extruded his powerful claws to their fullest extent. Instantly, the jeering ceased.

Juan forced his claws through the midline crack between the door panels and pulled his hands apart. At first, they did not budge. He gritted his teeth and strained, expelling a strangled roar as he forced his hands in opposite directions. The doors finally shifted enough for him to push fingers through the opening. Then others came to help him pull the panels apart. Eventually, Juan was able to poke his head out into the corridor.

The huge corridor outside Receiving Bay Thirteen was pitch black. Jude took a flare from his suit pocket and snapped it on, tossing it out into the darkness. He saw no movement in either direction. He pulled off his helmet.

"Is anyone there?" he bellowed.

Listening, he was surprised to discover the silence. Gone was the constant whirr of the air circulation fans. Gone was the rumbling, bass vibrations of heavy machinery moving in the Receiving Bays. Gone was the ever-present tenor hum of the moving monorails. The incessant, background music that accompanied every space station had been silenced. An eerie emptiness filled its place.

Juan shook off his momentary feeling of panic and pushed his frame through the narrow doorway opening. All the robots and androids in the corridor were either standing motionless or lying on the ground, like scores of dead bodies.

"*Nelson Mandela?*" Juan yelled.

Nothing.

"Anyone? Does anyone hear me?" he roared with his full battlefield voice. The area they were in was locked down. No human being other than the Security Team should have been close.

"*Nelson Mandela!*" Juan bellowed again.

The silence was eerie.

Were the power generators running? What was still functioning on the station, if anything? How long before life support systems failed and they ran out of heat, oxygen, clean water, and food? How quickly would the temperature in the *Nelson Mandela* plummet towards the frozen temperatures of deep space? Juan wondered if they could all be evacuated by then, if power could not be restored. That is, if they had working ships to evacuate to. Could they even evacuate, if they did not have a functioning AI?

Juan poked his head back in to the monitoring room, where the Chief Inspector was discussing the situation.

"It looks like the power is down in the station," Matthieu said. "The station AI must have been affected by the blast."

"Looks like all the androids and robots got knocked out as well," Juan said.

"We need to see about getting the station AI back up and running. We have to get to the power generators and see if they are still functioning or, if not, we need to get them restarted. We must re-instate power to life support or everyone dies," Matthieu said.

"What do you think happened?" Juan asked.

"A massive EMP blast makes the most sense," Rivera said. "Now we know what the weird weight to volume ratio was on that ship. The EMP blast was triggered when the *Inferno* was breeched. Hopefully, the auxiliary generators will kick in and we'll have some power restored to the station."

"People, we need to find out what else has been affected," Matthieu said. "We have flares and we have helmet lights that seem to be working. Battery-powered tools should still be functional. We need to hunt up as many battery-powered or glow lights as we can. With the lights, we can perhaps see enough to get the power generators running again. Then we can look into how to get the station AI back online.

"We need to locate some engineers who can help us get the power up and running. We also need computer engineers rebooting *Nelson Mandela.* Once we have power, life support, and the AI back online, we need to get help to those who need it. We have to think about evacuation, especially if we can't reinstate the station AI. That means we need working communications. There's no telling when the oxygen will run out. I need volunteers for each task," Matthieu said.

People began putting up hands.

"Hopefully we can locate Dr. Al-Fadi and Dr. Cech," Matthieu said. "They can coordinate the medical side of things. We'll have to evacuate the patients first, if the power does not come back on quickly. Rivera, you coordinated the evacuation last time. Can you check on ships available?"

"I can try, Chief Inspector, if I can get a com link working," Rivera answered. "That is, if the ships are functional. Getting in contact with all of the captains without the AI is going to be problematic."

"Probably the best place to coordinate all of this is from the Security Centre. Let's head back towards the Security Office, where we can rendezvous with all of our other Security personnel. We can set up glowglobes around the space station. We need to determine why the auxiliary power did not kick in. We need to rig up some old-fashioned radio transmitters for communications."

"What about the *Inferno*?" Juan asked. "Do you want anyone to check it out?"

"Funny you should ask, Rasmussen. I'd like *you* to check out Receiving Bay Thirteen. Make sure you're wearing a space suit and check the radiation levels first. Pick a few people to go with you. I don't know if there's been a hull breech. We should have heard alarms, but perhaps they've been knocked out. I've no idea whether Receiving Bay Thirteen even exists any more but I want to know what happened in that hangar. Is that ship still there? If it is, what shape is it in? That EMP—or whatever it was—was set to blow as soon as that hatchway was touched. That meant the captain of the *Inferno* planned to disable the *Nelson Mandela.* The question is why? Are we now under attack? Should we be preparing for a hostile boarding?

"I need to get that Captain Alighieri in an interrogation room and get the answers out of him. If not him, one of his officers. Where are the crew, anyway?"

"They were put into quarantine the minute they stepped off of their ship," Rivera said. "They were locked up in a room not far from here."

"Why blow up their own ship?" Juan asked. "That makes no sense at all. How do they plan to leave this station?"

"Hijack another ship?" someone suggested.

"Check out the *Inferno,* Rasmussen, but be careful. Keep us informed on what you find," Matthieu said.

"I'll take Captain Lamont with me, if you don't mind, sir. He knows his way around space vessels."

Matthieu frowned. A large figure in a containment suit removed its helmet to reveal another tiger face.

"What . . . ?" she started to say.

"Thought we might need some expertise in the weaponry department, if the ship contained some unusual arsenal. I asked the Captain to tag along," Juan said.

"Without my permission?" Chelsea demanded, her voice tight.

"With all due respect, sir . . . ," Captain Lamont began slowly.

"I was not talking to you!" Matthieu snapped.

"I know my weapons, Chief Inspector. That explosion was a sophisticated, non-nuclear EMP blast. My guess is the *Inferno*, itself, should still be fully functional. Before it fires, it shuts everything off except the weapon. Then the massive pulse is emitted and it fries all working circuits carrying a current. After the blast has fired, the ship powers up again. We'll likely find a working, intact ship in that hangar," Lamont said.

" . . . All right. For now, Lamont, you're a civilian consultant. You can assist Officer Rasmussen in reconnaissance on that ship. I want a detailed report about everything you find. I will speak with you later, Rasmussen," Matthieu said, her voice implying Juan was still in hot water.

"Yes, sir," the two tiger soldiers said, in unison.

"Does anyone else have any surprises for me?" Matthieu asked, her tone sugary-sweet. Juan winced.

Her question was met with silence.

"All right. Rivera, you try to contact the ships' captains and see if you can reach the Chief of Staff. Poon and Varga, try to get communications up and running. Dos Santos and Omonhua, see what you can do about resurrecting the station AI. Rasmussen and Lamont, be careful when you are checking out the *Inferno*, in case there are more booby traps. The rest of you, off to the Security Centre. We need to coordinate an evacuation. Someone find the engineers on this station to reinstate the power generators. I want that captain of the *Inferno* brought to me. I want to see what he can tell me about this EMP blast."

"The crew were placed in quarantine because of a possible virus," Rivera said. "My understanding was that they could not be brought into the station in case they might contaminate the entire population and cause a new viral epidemic."

"Space, you're right. However, with the power down, those lockdown doors may not remain locked. The crew may be able to release themselves, the way Rasmussen pulled the doors open here. Check on them first. If they do carry the infection, we can't have them loose on the station. I guess if we want answers, we'll just have to question them while they remain within the quarantine area."

"Careful, Chief Inspector. I don't know if you want to expose yourself to that virus. You may end up just a puddle in your suit," Rivera warned.

There were grumbles and curses following that announcement.

"Everyone back into their containment suits and seal up. Let's ensure they haven't gotten free of their quarantine. We can station some guards at the door until we get some manual locks. If the crew try to leave, you have orders to stop them any way you can."

"I'll look into getting some welding equipment, Inspector," one of the Security officers said.

"Great. Now, let's try and not get lost in the dark. Stunners only."

Juan picked up his helmet and gloves and motioned for Lamont to follow him. They squeezed out of the door and stopped just outside, Juan pulling his gloves back on.

"Is your helmet com working?" he asked Lamont.

"No. Is yours?"

"Nope."

"Then we'll have to communicate the old-fashioned way," Lamont grinned. "Yell."

Juan nodded.

Just then, figures flashed out of the dark and raced by.

16. He Found Her

The lights went out and the ever present hum of the station air circulation died.

"That's it," Captain Alighieri's voice snarled out of the darkness. "What we've been waiting for. Is everyone okay?"

There were groans, coming up from the floor and someone was retching. Eventually, everyone responded in the affirmative.

"It's safe to turn on your wrist lamps now. Once we get these doors open, we head straight back to the ship, hopefully the same way we came in. We get our weapons, spread the virus samples around the Receiving Bay area, and leave. All the androids, robots, and the station AI will be fried from the EMP blast. The virus will wipe out the humans in the next twenty-four to forty-eight hours. When people come to investigate, the virus will spread. All of our objectives will be achieved."

Hope walked up to the captain. "Spread what viral samples? What are you up to, Captain?"

Alighieri glared at Hope, his slit-like eyes flaring in the faint illumination of the wrist lamps.

"I'll explain back at the ship, Shelley," he hissed. "Now shut up and do as you're ordered."

"You brought infected patients here to be treated. This is a medical facility. Why knock their power out . . . and how was this accomplished anyway?"

"Shut it, Shelley. We don't have time for this. If we don't get out of here now, we'll all be mind-swiped. Focus on getting these damned quarantine doors open and forget the questions," the captain growled. "Let's get to work, people."

The crew split into two groups and stationed themselves on either side of the lockdown doors, gripping any handhold they could find. The doors were heavy steel panels, with girders forming an X across them for added reinforcement. The lock was magnetic. With no power charging them, the doors should have become demagnetized and no longer engaged. If the crew pulled hard enough, the massive doors should separate. Unfortunately, there were only nine crew members. As the captain joined the group on one panel, Hope walked over to the other group, her mind racing.

"Pull," the captain ordered.

With all crew members straining at once, they heaved on the weighty panels. Their breaths came out in harsh gasps. Hope's arms were boosted but she did not want anyone to know it. She gasped and shook like the rest of them. It seemed, even without an active current running through them, lockdown doors stayed magnetized.

"Heave!" Alighieri yelled. "Put everything you have into this! If we're still here when the power comes back on, none of us will be left with a mind of our own. Pull, you lazy bastards!"

There were grunts all around as they renewed their efforts.

"Pull! Again! Again!" Alighieri rasped.

Hope then put her arms and legs into it and her door began to move slowly. She could not afford to be mind-swiped here. When the opening between the doors was finally large enough to allow the largest member of their crew, the chaplain, to squeeze through, the captain allowed them to take a rest. They all collapsed to the ground, panting and massaging aching limbs. Alighieri allowed them only a few seconds before he was ordering them to get to their feet. He glared around at all of their faces.

"Silently, now. Follow me left out of here. About thirty paces, turn to the left down a wide corridor. The doors to Reception Bay Thirteen are about two hundred paces down that corridor, on the right hand side. No talking. Anyone speaks, you get left behind," he said. He glared directly at Hope as if it was a promise. Then he was through the doors into the darkness.

They had all studied the layout of the *Nelson Mandela.* If there was any trouble, they could split up and make their way back separately. The trip back to the *Inferno* was not far at all.

The darkness in the station was absolute. The small lights from their wrist lamps did little to illuminate the long, empty corridors they travelled. They jogged in single file, jumping over or going around downed robots and androids, wordlessly pointing each obstacle out to the person behind. The corpulent chaplain trailed at the end, his heavy panting sounding stentorian in the darkness.

In the next moment, a large group of people, all dressed in white containment suits, poured out into the corridor right in their path. The lamps on their helmets shone at the crew as they approached. A small figure at the fore of the group turned towards them. As the crew of the *Inferno* raced past, the figure put out both hands and tried to obstruct their progress.

"Stop! Who are you and where do you think you're going?" the voice demanded. It was a woman's voice, harsh and sharp. "I am the Chief Inspector of Security. I order you to stop!"

Alighieri launched into a desperate sprint, taking a wide berth around the figures. The rest of his crew followed suit.

"Halt! If you don't stop, we'll open fire!" the female voice bellowed. " . . . Stop them!"

A few of the suited figures tried to grab or tackle the fleeing crew members. Shaking off the contact, the *Inferno* crew dispersed, each member fleeing in different directions, scattering like windblown seeds into the blackness. They knew where they had to rendezvous. They would each have to try to make it back to the ship on their own, after losing all pursuit.

Hope turned and fled back into the darkness, fearing the pulse blast between her shoulder blades and the mind swipe if she was caught.

The room was pitch black. The conveyor belt had stopped moving and the zapping, grinding, and crackling had ceased. Eric leaned against the cage door and it opened. He cautiously crept out of the cage and began to totter in the direction he believed was the exit. He slammed into a wall, spun around, and fell over. The voice in his head shrieked at him.

'Get up! Get up, you clumsy oafl'

Eric rolled up onto his ragged tendrils and looked through all of his eyes, seeing nothing. The darkness was absolute. He recalled seeing little robots go in and out of the room through a small trapdoor but he was so turned around, he had no idea where it was. He decided to find a wall and follow along it until he found the trapdoor. Hopefully, he would be able to fit himself through it and make his escape.

Suddenly, something very foul-smelling and furry collided with him. Eric could hear it snarl. Its breath was nauseating. Eric backed up and whipped his tendrils towards the stinking breath. He didn't know what it was, but it sounded ferocious with its snapping teeth. Eric scrambled in the opposite direction along the wall as rapidly as he could, feeling constantly with a few of his tendrils for the trapdoor. He lashed a handful of other tendrils behind him like whips, to keep the fetid-smelling beast at bay. The creature must have escaped from one of the other cages when the power went out. Then it dawned on Eric that perhaps all of the critters, caged in the room with him, were loose.

'. . . Wonderful,' the inner voice dripped with sarcasm.

Eric decided that the sooner he got out of that room and away from the menagerie, the safer he would be . . . and hopefully, the quieter the nasty voice in his head would be. In the next instant, the stinking creature was on Eric, its jaws wide and its long sharp fangs gnawing on Eric's head. It managed to pluck off one of Eric's eyeballs and he heard the creature gobble and swallow. The two of them went rolling around the floor, Eric gagging from the creature's horrible breath. Eric wrapped his tendrils around the creature's neck and pulled them tight, wrapping more around its chest. The creature began to thrash and loosened its bite on Eric's skull. Eric did not release his tendrils but continued to squeeze as tightly as he could. The voice in his head cackled with insane glee and Eric shivered at the sound.

He loosened his grip once the creature lay still upon the ground, but Eric could still hear its rasping breathing. The voice in his head began to berate Eric for being a coward and not finishing the creature off. Eric told it to shut up and moved away from the beast as quickly as he could.

A little further along the wall, he found the trapdoor and tried to push himself through. After a few tense moments of scrambling and pushing, he managed to force himself into the long, low, lightless tunnel. No matter how much he was abused by the angry voice to go back and kill the smelly beast, Eric continued down the tunnel, searching for some light and a safe place to hide.

What he really wanted was freedom from the annoying, crazy voice in his head, but he would try to figure out how to achieve that later, when he had found sanctuary.

Chief Inspector Matthieu swore. She ordered everyone to go after the fleeing figures, stunners on max. Juan took off after the only figure that seemed to be boosted. The woman had spun around and raced back in the direction she had come at quicker than normal human speed. As the slim figure vanished swiftly into the shadows, Juan wondered whether he could catch her, encumbered in his containment suit and clunky boots. He'd dropped his helmet and was using his tiger night vision and his acute sense of smell to track her.

She was fast. All Juan could do was hope that, in her panic, she might make a mistake and have to double back. Clomping around in the damned containment suit made him feel like he was running in a suit of armour.

The corridor had several downed robots and androids and Juan found himself jumping and leaping to avoid them, cringing at the ruckus his boots were making. He didn't have time to strip off the containment suit. He snarled in frustration.

Arms pumping, chest heaving, Juan sprinted as fast as he could down the corridor, as he squinted ahead into the pitch darkness. The woman had turned off her wrist-lamp and, unlike him, was silent in her movements. Visually, Juan had lost track of the woman, but her scent was still strong on the air. He summoned up a further burst of speed, to try and shorten the distance between him and his prey, when he almost tumbled in confusion over a fallen robot. The scent he was following had suddenly dropped away. He stopped and turned around, sniffing about, wondering if the woman had taken a turn down a branching corridor. Nose scenting the air, he slowly retraced his steps. About five steps back, he was hammered, hard, from the right.

Juan flew into a wall with a bone-jangling impact. The human missile was instantly upon him, fists pummelling his head like pistons. Juan felt his jaw crunch and his right cheekbone crack. He exploded up off the ground with a roar, grasping his assailant and whipping her out into the darkness. He heard a thud and a grunt, as her body hit the corridor's opposite wall.

Blood streaming from his nose, Juan shook off the pain in his face and stalked towards his attacker. He wanted to tear this woman apart, limb from limb, for having the audacity to blindside him. In the dim light of his wristcomp, he could see her curled and slumped against the corridor wall, moaning and moving very sluggishly. He fully extended his claws and bunched up his muscles to leap, when she sprang straight into his face, her skull flinging upwards to crash into his chin. He grunted as they went over in a ferocious tumble, her momentum knocking him backwards. She punched him, hard, on the right side of his face again, with a fist of steel. All he saw were flashing lights.

Grabbing her wrists, Juan threw his head into her nose, feeling satisfaction upon hearing a loud crunch. As the woman reeled back from the blow, he spun her around and wrapped his right arm around her neck and squeezed as hard as he could, grasping his right wrist with his left hand and flexing his elbow tightly.

The woman tried to pitch herself forwards, in an attempt to throw Juan over her head. His weight was at least double hers; he leaned way back, resisting her struggles. Bending his knees, he sprung towards the wall and slammed her head against it. She kicked back at him and he slammed her head into the wall again. He refused to relinquish the hold around her neck, no matter how hard she fought. Gradually, her struggles lessened. Just before she totally collapsed, Juan eased up on her throat and dropped her to the ground.

The woman gasped for air, clutching her neck. As she looked up at Juan, fear in her eyes, Juan said, "Nighty night."

And he punched her lights out.

"What in space is happening, now?" Hiro Al-Fadi yelled, as the operating room descended into darkness. Again. He was just finishing off attaching a bioprosthetic leg onto a gorilla soldier, when the power failed.

"How is anyone, even as skilled and masterful a genius like myself, supposed to operate in conditions like this? Abominable!"

"When you say abominable, are you referring to yourself or the conditions?" Dejan Cech asked, from the head of the patient.

"The conditions, you lizard monkey!"

"Just checking, you blue-snouted ass. Wanted to be sure," Dejan said. "I thought, for the first time in your life, you were actually being honest and realistic about yourself, for a refreshing change. How mistaken I was."

"Well, if I were just a simple gas pusher like yourself, I would hardly be bothered by a station blackout, would I?" Hiro snapped.

"I thought you said you were a skilled surgeon. A power failure should not trouble a true master. Any surgeon can do it, if they can see. Obviously, I am the only master in this room," Dejan said, as he started making all sorts of noise at the head of the bed. "Whew, Hiro. Do you have the mother of all headaches? If I could see, I'd say I have a blinding migraine."

A crash echoed in the operating room.

"What was that? Are you all right, Dejan?" Hiro demanded.

"I'm fine, Hiro."

"Drat. That's too bad," Hiro remarked. "That means it must have been SAMM-E 139 that fell over. SAMM-E 139, are you all right?"

There was no answer.

"Why isn't the emergency auxiliary power kicking in? Is this a plot to make me crazy?"

"Bulletin: No plot. You're already crazy," Dejan said, amidst more clunking.

"I take exception to that. I am no crazier than you. *Nelson Mandela?"* Hiro yelled.

There was no answer.

"NELSON MANDELA!"

Silence.

"What is going on, *Nelson Mandela*?" Hiro yelled. "I have a patient to finish operating on!"

A light appeared at the doorway of the operating room and a voice asked, "Are you all right in here?"

"No! Of course not! What a ridiculous question. How, in space, can we be all right, if we are in the middle of an operation and the lights and power go off?" Hiro snarled.

The light came closer and Nurse Tyra Wendler, mask held to her face with one hand and a battery powered lamp held in the other, stood where she could shine the illumination down onto the operating field.

"You are not sterile!" protested Hiro, peering up over his mask at the nurse in her normal scrubs.

"What an improper thing to say to a woman, Dr. Al-Fadi. Do you want light or no?" Tyra demanded. "Because I can leave your room and see if any of the other, more gracious surgeons, need my help."

"No! I mean, yes! I want you to stay . . . lovely, sweet, beautiful Tyra. The woman of my dreams . . . other than my lovely, sweet wife, of course," Hiro said. "Don't tell her I said that."

"Now you're really going to drive her away," remarked Dejan. "Please stay, Nurse Wendler, and shine a light on our helpless situation and our hopeless surgeon."

"I'm not hopeless. I could do this operation with my eyes closed."

"Well, if you can do that, what do you need the light for, Hiro? Make up your mind. If you want Nurse Wendler to go help someone else, because you can work in the dark, then we should let her go," said Dejan.

"I *could* do this operation with my eyes closed, but I would do it much quicker if I could see," Hiro protested, as his fingers flew. "Gah. No light. No power. I have to do everything by feel! This must be what it was like to operate in the Stone Ages."

Dejan sighed. "Hiro, you dolt, there were no operations in the Stone Ages. Just clubs."

"I'm going to club you when we get out of here, Mr. Ass-splinter," Hiro said, as he continued to tie off all the bleeders by hand, since the laser had died. "Can you see what happened to our android, Tyra?"

"It's just lying on the floor, dead, like all of the others, Dr. Al-Fadi. It seems all of the androids and robots in the operating rooms have suddenly stopped working. What's far worse is the fact that *Nelson Mandela* is no longer responding. Something has happened that has knocked out all of our electronics, from androids to medcomps to *Nelson Mandela*. What about your monitors, Dr. Cech?"

"Without any power, I can't really assess them. They're down right now, but I don't know if they would be working if the power came back on. Just to let you know, Hiro, I am bagging the gas/oxygen mixture to the patient and I may have to club him, if you don't hurry up!"

"I'm hurrying. I'm hurrying. It would be easier if my assistant was not lying on the floor," Hiro squawked. "Just applying the gorilla nuskin now."

"Good, because I don't know if I have a club big enough to keep a gorilla soldier under. I imagine they have thick skulls," Dejan said.

"You're just a wimp, Dr. Cech. Admit it," Hiro said, as he wrapped bandages around the gorilla's upper leg. "Space, I'm so good, I even amaze myself."

"Well, I guess one person is amazed, then," Cech said. "Let's get this gorilla to Recovery, where I can shoot him full of good things. My machine is not administering anything to the poor fellow and I do not want him waking up like a beast."

"Well, for your information, Dr. Cech, this patient is a genetically modified gorilla. It's so hard to get intelligent help these days," remarked Hiro. "Isn't that right, Nurse Wendler?"

"Well, since I am part of the help, I take exception to your comment, Doctor," Tyra said.

"Oops," Dejan said. "How to lose friends and make enemies, Hiro. You should write a book."

"I was not referring to you, lovely, sweet, beautiful Nurse Tyra," Hiro said.

"I'm definitely going to be sick now," Dejan said.

"Just don't do it on my patient," Hiro said. "You can be sick on your own time, and make sure you clean up after yourself." The surgeon started to walk away from the operating table.

"Hey, where are you going, little guy?" Dejan demanded.

"My work, here, is done," Hiro said, pulling off his mask, surgical gown, and snapping off his gloves.

"Unh-unh, Megalomaniac. I need help transferring this gorilla to a stretcher and wheeling him to recovery. We are going to have to transfer this gorilla soldier to a wheeled gurney and manually push the patient to the Recovery Room. Since there are no robots or androids around to assist, you are going to have to help, you pitiful—and may I also say 'short'—excuse for a porter," Dejan said.

"What? I could move that soldier on my own," Hiro said.

"Good. Then I shall leave him to you to put on the stretcher. I will be in the lounge, trying to see if I can find a cup of hot kofi."

"Ha ha. Very funny, Sleep Creep. Get the stretcher and be quick about it," Hiro ordered.

"What? I am the anesthetist. I have to stay with the patient. You get the stretcher. You are closer to the door," Dejan said.

"Enough!" Tyra broke in. "I'll get the stretcher and you two don't even have to thank me. It's enough just to get away from the two of you and your constant bickering, even if it is only for a few seconds."

"Leave the light," Hiro ordered.

"The little Napoleon is afraid of the dark," Dejan remarked to the nurse.

"I am *not,*" Hiro said.

"Will you two shut up, please?" Tyra sighed. "I'll leave the light on the table. I'll be right back. Try not to kill each other in the meantime." Tyra placed the lamp on a stand and marched out of the OR.

"What is the matter with you, Hiro? Can't you see that you have upset that sweet nurse with your lack of manners? I think it behooves you to apologize to Nurse Wendler, as soon as she returns with the stretcher," Dejan said.

"What? It's you who have upset that wonderful woman, that angel of mercy. I could not possibly upset Tyra, unless I were to deny her my company, forever more. It's you who should apologize."

From outside the operating room came the sound of a scream cut short.

" . . . Tyra?" Hiro called.

There was no answer.

"Nurse Wendler?" Dejan shouted. "Do you need any assistance?"

Silence.

" . . . No. I think I'm perfectly capable of handling two buffoons such as yourselves, just fine," said a deep, velvety voice. A dark figure strode like a dancer into the operating room. He slowly approached the light.

"What have you done with Nurse Wendler?" demanded Hiro.

"She's fine, which unfortunately, I cannot say will be the same for you two."

"What do you want, Jeffrey?" Dejan asked, positioning himself between the visitor and his patient. The anesthetist could not take his eyes off the blaster in the psychiatrist's left hand.

"Why, your deaths, Dejan. What did you think I came here for?" Nestor said. "To get together and chat about old times?"

"I can understand you wanting my death, Jeffrey," Hiro said, "but why Dejan's? What has he ever done to you?"

"Do I have to have a reason?" Nestor asked, his handsome features breaking into a smile that was more leer in the light cast by the single lamp. "You two have been such irritating asses over the years, with your inane, incessant bickering. I have dreamt of the day I could shut the two of you up, with such relish, that I can almost taste it. Space knows, the entire station would thank me."

"Are you responsible for this blackout, Jeffrey?" Hiro demanded as he moved towards the psychiatrist.

"Stay right there, Hiro," Nestor said, shifting his position so that he was equidistant from the surgeon and anesthetist. He swung his blaster back and forth between them. "I would love to take credit for this inconvenience, but alas, it was not of my making. I had to come here and get you, myself, instead of sending my androids, which is so annoying. It's hard to get good help these days."

"My sentiments, exactly. Seems like I made an enormous blunder a number of years ago, hiring a certain psychopath for a psychiatrist," Hiro said.

"Careful, Hiro. You're not the one holding the blaster. And besides, you weren't the one who hired me. We were hired at the same time or have you forgotten? Your egotistical delusions of grandeur are playing with your memory again. And if you are wondering whether I am capable of using this weapon on you, you could take a look at your nurse except—oops, I forgot—neither of you will be leaving this OR alive."

"You said she was fine," Dejan said, making a move towards the door. The blaster turned directly on him and he stopped.

"That nurse will never have another depressed or sad day in her life. She will never have to listen to the two of you idiots blather on ever again. I have put that poor woman out of her misery. She should thank me for it . . . if only the poor soul could."

"You are *mad*," Hiro growled.

"And you were always such a bore, Hiro. My finger is just itching to pull this trigger," Nestor said.

"Then why don't you pull it?" Hiro demanded. "Go ahead! I'm not afraid to die!"

"You should be begging for death after what I put you through, Hiro. Why aren't you on the floor before me grovelling?"

"You've done your worst to me, Jeffrey, and I'm still standing. You think you have the answers to everything? Well, you don't and you never will. Do you want me to tell you why?" Hiro asked.

The psychiatrist sighed. He stared at Hiro for a long moment and then rolled his eyes. "Oh, all right, Hiro. I'll bite . . . Why?"

"Because you're not truly human, Jeffrey. You're flawed. You have no idea what a conscience is or what empathy is. You're a sociopath. A sick, damaged, partial human being. You don't know what it is to feel or to care about anyone but yourself. You look at people and only assess how you can use them. You don't know what it is to love. You are incapable of it, and because of that, you'll never really understand anything."

"I understand this," Nestor said. He turned the blaster on Dejan Cech and fired, burning a fist-sized hole in the anesthetist's chest. "I understand that the death of this man will hurt you more than anything else I can do to you. And I want you to know that I might not have bothered to kill Dejan, if you'd not felt the need to taunt me. So you see?

I do understand you. I've been in your mind, remember? And I know that there's so much more I could do to hurt you."

"*Dejan!*" Hiro screamed. He knelt by his friend's collapsed body. He shoved a huge wad of gauze into the hole made by the blaster, to stem the eruption of blood poring from his friend's chest. "You bastard! Help me get Dejan into that cryopod over there!"

Nestor laughed. "Why would I do that, Hiro? I just shot him. Why would I now help you put him into a cryopod? You really are a fool."

Hiro grabbed Dejan's arms and dragged him across the operating room floor to the empty cryopod.

"Hurry, little man," Nestor crooned. "Your friend is dying. You're too slow. You're too small. You're too weak. How useful is your genius to you, now? Hmm?"

Hiro pressed the button that opened the cryopod and bent down, thrusting his arms beneath the back and knees of the much larger man. He strained with all of his might, a huge yell escaping from his lungs, as he slowly straightened his knees and forced Dejan's body up and over the side of the cryopod. Dejan's body rolled into the unit and Hiro slapped his hand hard on the engage button. The lid of the cryopod descended on his friend's body and the seal engaged. A humming arose from the cryopod. Thankfully, all cryopods were battery-powered and portable fuel cells powered the cryogenic process. Hiro leaned his bloody hands against the pod, sweat and tears mixing, as he stared at the cryopod readout. He waited, back turned to the man with the blaster, as guilt's rain washed down his devastated features.

"Did you make it, Hiro? Were you quick enough?" Nestor's voice taunted.

Hiro ignored the psychiatrist. He stared at the dull blank screen, whispering, "Come on, Dejan. Hang on, old friend."

The screen lit up and Hiro felt his entire body tremble as he bent close to examine the report. He felt his insides collapse as the readout button blinked amber. A gasp escaped Hiro's lips. Behind him, he heard slow, rhythmic clapping.

"What a show, Hiro. Too bad you weren't up to the challenge. You are such a failure. It must be so hard to be you."

"I'm going to kill you, Jeffrey," Hiro grated, as he tried to control his rage. His hands rested on either side of the cryopod readout. He kept staring at the word, 'INDETERMINATE' and he felt a rapacious beast rise inside him.

"You can't," Nestor laughed. "It isn't in you, Hiro. You could never take a life and that's why you're weak. That's why you will never achieve anything. You are a lesser man than I because of it. Could you be driven to kill, if you had to? What would it take, I wonder?"

"You're completely insane," Hiro said, turning around slowly to glare at the psychiatrist.

"Oh, no, Hiro. I assure you, I am as sane as you," Nestor said, in a calm, pleasant voice. "I'm just interested in answering questions that you would consider unethical. I don't see all human life as precious, the way you do. I actually believe most humans are not worth the space or oxygen they take up. I believe in survival of the fittest and that the human race would be much better off if evolutionary processes were brought back into play. What good has it done, saving every useless, flawed individual no matter what the circumstance? All it has done is make the human race weak and stupid.

"In your vapidity, Hiro, you need to save everybody. Perhaps it's because of your ridiculous name. You see yourself as the hero in every story. Killing anyone would go against your lofty medical principles. But could you be driven to kill, Hiro? How far can you be pushed?"

"To the ends of the universe, if I have to, to kill you," Hiro swore, his entire body shaking.

Nestor laughed again. "Oh, Hiro, you are so pathetic. You really should listen to yourself. You're so full of melodrama and bombast. It's tedious."

"What do you want, Nestor?" Hiro shouted. "Just shoot me and be done with it. What are you waiting for?"

"Why, because I need you, Hiro," the psychiatrist said, and then he smiled a cherubic smile.

"*What?* Need me? I refuse to help you in any way!"

"Oh, you don't have to help me, per se, Hiro. You just have to be you. You see, it's your surgical fellow I'm after. Grace will come to me . . . to rescue you."

Hiro leaped at Nestor with a roar. There was a brilliant flash of electric blue and Hiro felt searing pain knife through his right knee. He collapsed on the floor, the odour of his own barbecued flesh strong in his nostrils.

"Fool," Nestor said, as he walked up to stand over Hiro, who was rocking on the ground, hands wrapped around his right knee.

"Come closer, you coward," Hiro hissed between gritted teeth. "Let me get my hands around your neck."

Nestor's eyes widened and then he threw back his head, laughing.

"Hiro Al-Fadi, you are really too much. What are you going to do, bite me on the shins? Oooh, I'm scared. Too bad I can't keep you around as a pet, to bring out for cheap entertainment. You really are such a joke. How would you like that? Chief Jester for Jeffrey Nestor?"

"Jester Nestor?" Hiro snarled, dragging himself across the floor towards the psychiatrist.

"What are you doing, Hiro? Do you think you're going to strangle me from down there? Should I crouch down on the floor so you can get your hands around my neck? Shall I bare my throat so you can get at it with your teeth?"

"You wouldn't, because you are the true coward. Making your poor patients kill for you, because you don't have the guts to do anything yourself. I bet you feel really powerful with that blaster in your hand. You are fine killing women, old men, and using the coward's weapon, poison. How would you do against a one-legged man, eh, Jeffrey? Are you too afraid to face me in a fair fight?"

Nestor clapped his hands again, slow, measured, rhythmic. "Oh, Hiro, you are absurd. What shall we do? Wrestle on the ground? Shall I tie my legs together to make it a fair fight?"

"Come closer and find out," Hiro snarled. "Get rid of that blaster and I'll show you how to fight like a man!"

Nestor bent over, laughing.

"More like a . . . like a cripple, Hiro," Nestor said, wiping his eyes. "Are you getting weak yet, Hiro? From the blood loss? I really can't allow you to bleed out, unfortunately, no matter how much I would like that. I need you alive, so I guess I have to bandage you up."

"You'd better kill me, Jeffrey, because if you don't, I will kill you," Hiro swore.

"Don't tempt me," Nestor said, as he strolled around the operating room, searching for some dressing material.

As the psychiatrist was examining one of the instrument tables with his back to Hiro, Hiro saw his gorilla patient silently sit up and swing his legs over the side of the operating table, swaying slightly. The massive combat soldier pushed himself to standing and took a step towards Nestor, his right fist raised to strike the back of the psychiatrist's head. The soldier stepped onto the new bioprosthetic leg and grunted in pain, faltering. Nestor immediately swung around, blaster raised, and the gorilla soldier's fist connected with the psychiatrist's jaw. The psychiatrist flew backwards, the blaster firing wildly. The gorilla soldier howled and fell, his hand clutching his left eye.

Nestor got to his feet, rubbing his sore jaw with his right hand. He stalked over to stand above the gorilla patient and raised the blaster to point at the man's face.

"Let me put you out of your misery," Nestor said.

"*No*!" screamed Hiro, pushing himself up onto his one good foot and hopping towards his patient. Nestor shot straight into the gorilla's face.

"*You bastard!*" Hiro screamed, as he watched his patient's face become a blackened crater.

The psychiatrist poked tenderly at his face. "I think that stupid ape broke my jaw."

Nestor swung his leg back and kicked the dead soldier in the head. While he continued to boot the soldier's burnt face over and over, Hiro hopped closer, hanging onto the edge of the operating table. He quickly palmed a harmonic scalpel.

"That's it. Kick a corpse while he's down and dead. What a man you are, Jeffrey. You should feel so proud of yourself," taunted Hiro.

"Shut up or you're next."

"Go ahead. I dare you," Hiro said, shifting closer to the psychiatrist.

"Don't push me. I can get my hands on that bitch assistant of yours without your help."

Hiro launched himself at Nestor, just as the man uttered the word, 'bitch'. The harmonic scalpel suddenly hummed into life in his right hand, as he aimed a thrust at the psychiatrist's chest. Unfortunately, he did not hop high enough over the body of the dead soldier and his toe got caught. The tip of the scalpel sliced down the front of Nestor's chest and abdomen, instead of piercing his chest.

Hiro fell at the psychiatrist's feet, the scalpel flying from his hand. Nestor screamed, clasping his chest in shock. Howling with pain or fury or both, Nestor kicked Hiro, repeatedly, in the face. Hiro tried to protect his head with his arms, curling into a ball.

"Does this make you feel like a man, Jeffrey? Does this make you feel superior, because that's what this is all about, isn't it? Your inferiority complex. You can't handle the idea that anyone can be smarter and more accomplished than you. You are an insecure, hollow bastard," Hiro said, grunting with each impact. "How can you stand being yourself?"

Nestor stopped kicking. With his right hand, he adjusted the dial on the blaster, changing the settings on the gun. Hiro tried to get up by rolling onto his good knee and grabbing the edge of the operating table. He heaved himself upwards with a roar and launched himself at the psychiatrist. Nestor raised the blaster and shot straight into Hiro's face.

"Oh, do shut up, little man. I am *so* sick of listening to your voice," Nestor grated.

Oblivion.

A robot appeared at Plant Thing's hangar with Grace's containment suit. It rolled up to her on its silent treads and opened its green lid to reveal the white suit nestled within. Grace reached in to take it, when she felt a sudden disorientation and severe pain behind her eyes. She lost her balance and pitched forward, grabbing onto the robot to keep from falling.

Darkness doused the hangar. The lights on the robot blinked off and it tipped over onto its side, Grace tumbling with it.

"Ouch! . . . *Nelson Mandela?*" Grace called from the floor.

There was no reply.

"*Nelson Mandela*?" Grace yelled into the blackness.

Silence.

"*Chuck Yeager?"* she yelled. Only echoes came back.

<Plant Thing?>

<yes grace>

<Do you know what is happening?>

<plant thing felt a disturbance. now it has stopped. the biomind is not happy>

<*Nelson Mandela* is not answering, Plant Thing. I fear something has happened to the station AI. Do you think the station could be under attack?>

<plant thing does not know what 'under attack' means, grace>

<I wonder if someone is trying to take over or destroy the *Nelson Mandela.* I must see if I can reach Bud.>

<Bud? Bud?>

Grace felt nothing.

<BUD? CAN YOU HEAR ME?>

Silence.

<Plant thing, can you hear Bud?>

<no grace>

<I must go find Bud! Something's wrong!>

<bud told plant thing you must stay here, grace>

<Bud is not answering me, Plant Thing! I have to know that Bud is all right. I'm going to need a light or lamp. Oh, wait. The helmet on the containment suit has a lamp. I'll see if it's working.>

<bud said you must wear that suit, grace>

<Yes, Plant Thing. I probably should, in case there's been a breach in the outer wall of the station. I wish I knew what was happening!>

At that moment, the shuffling form of Little Bud appeared from out of the darkness to stand in front of Grace. She looked up at him. The mobile plant had glowglobes all over its head and trunk, transforming itself into an enormous, walking lantern.

<Little Bud, that's great but I do not think you should leave here. It's not safe for you.>

<plant thing thinks little bud should go with you>

<I don't have time to argue. I need to make sure Bud is all right.>

<bud is in his lab. it is on this level. little bud can light your way, grace>

<All right, Plant Thing. Thank you.>

Grace donned her containment suit. She wanted to rush out of the hangar. Panic and despair were making a mess of Grace's emotions, as she tried again, unsuccessfully, to communicate with Bud.

<Let us please hurry, Little Bud.>

They walked down black, deserted corridors. The bluish green illumination from Little Bud's bioluminescent globes was powerful enough to cast a wide penumbra of light a few feet ahead. Shadows of objects they encountered were wide and squat. The majority of objects turned out to be disabled robots, frozen in their tracks, lightless and silent. Grace stopped briefly to examine the first couple of robots. All the ones they discovered were inert and unresponsive.

When they encountered the first downed android, sprawled and splayed on the empty corridor floor, Grace cried out. She knelt down and tried to turn it over. The weight of the human-like figure was actually surprisingly light, compared to Bud's solid frame. She was able to flip it onto its back. It reminded her of a great, lifeless, silver manikin, hollow and deserted, as if the spirit that had motivated it and given it purpose, had fled forever.

<Bud! Are you all right? Please answer!>

Grace wondered if she would find Bud lying inert like this silver android.

Had there been a massive explosion of some sort, that knocked out the station AI, the androids, the robots, and the power generators? The only thing that could do that, as far as Grace knew, was a massive EMP strike. If such was the case, what sort of damage would Bud have sustained? Would he be left a burnt out shell?

<BUD? BUD!>

She heard nothing.

<Hurry, Little Bud. We must find Bud.>

<find bud> Little Bud repeated.

Grace had never realized how noisy the medical space station was, until now. The background sounds of all the engines, air circulation, robots, transports, people and generators made for a constant, familiar hum. The lack of all that made Grace's skin prickle. She shivered as they explored the inky absence of light.

The corridors were like a ghostly crypt. Grace found comfort in having Little Bud beside her, lighting the way, and the irony did not escape her. It was not long ago that the sight of the mobile plant had actually caused her to faint. Grace shook her head at her stupidity. Just because a being looked terrifying or different did not mean that it was evil or meant harm. Just as an attractive being did not mean a kind, caring heart. She was happy to be accompanied by another living being—albeit plant-based—as she travelled the silent corridors.

Grace wondered about *Nelson Mandela.* If it was destroyed, would they be able to recover its mind? She worried about the Life Support systems. Without them, how long before all the humans died? There was still gravity, so the space station was still spinning. Emergency backup generators and auxiliary power sources were supposed to come on in the event of a power failure. What had happened to them?

<Bud!> Grace mindspoke, over and over. <Please answer me!>

Grace did not want to face the possibility of losing Bud. In truth, there was no one else in her life that meant more to her than Bud. No one else had ever been so kind and caring and devoted to looking after her. She'd never known anyone more brave and selfless. She knew she would be seen by most as 'sick and perverted' for having feelings for an android, but she no longer cared what other people thought. Bud was one of the best individuals she had ever met, more humane than most humans. She would tell him so the next time she saw him, if he was able to understand her.

Grace fought the urge to grab Little Bud's upper limb and pull it along behind her like a straggling child. Little Bud rocked back and forth on its great lower limbs, as if on a rocking ship, and Grace did not want to get too close, in case the ungainly being stepped on her or accidentally fell on top of her.

Up ahead, Grace heard voices. She called out to them and they answered back. Lights were bobbing up and down ahead and Grace felt a joyous relief in seeing and hearing other humans. She knew the station was full of people. It had just felt empty, near Plant Thing's hangar.

Then she heard the high pitched screams and her joy died.

People trapped in the dark were getting a glimpse of Little Bud, emerging from the darkness, and they were reacting as she had at first—with horror. Grace tried calling out to them to reassure them that everything was all right, that they were safe, but it was futile. She took off her helmet to try to allay people's fears. Unfortunately, they only had eyes for Little Bud, who had far too many eyes. The people ran away, into the blackness, shrieking in panic. Grace worried that, in their fear, they might come back with weapons. What could she do? She had to send Little Bud back.

<Little Bud, you must return to Plant Thing.>

<little bud will stay with grace>

<I think we are close to the Receiving Bays, Little Bud. I know where we are. I know how to get to the Android Reservations from here. You must return to Plant Thing. I fear for your safety. Those frightened people may try to harm you. I don't want that.>

<little bud will stay with grace>

<No, Little Bud. You will not. I know where I am now. You will turn around and go back. I will meet up with you and Plant Thing later. That is an order.>

<yes grace>

<Go now . . . and thank you, Little Bud.>

<little bud will do as grace says but little bud is not happy>

<I know, Little Bud. Thank you but I must go ahead on my own. I have the lamp on my helmet to light my way. I'll be all right. I want you safe with Plant Thing. Goodbye.>

<goodbye grace>

Grace felt her tension ease, as she watched Little Bud turn around and stalk away. Then she set off at a jog in the opposite direction.

Grace passed several wide corridors leading to the different Receiving Bays, one after another. Everywhere there were hundreds of downed robots and androids, scattered about the floors like large, abandoned dolls.

Grace wondered if the station was under attack. Was there an enemy outside the station trying to board? Who would attack a medical facility? Or was this power failure the work of Nestor?

Grace swore as her toes smacked painfully into something hard on the ground and she fell to her knees. She had not been paying attention and had walked straight into another downed android. The toes on her right foot burned from the impact. She thought she might have broken them. She looked down at the android's face.

Then Grace was gaping, her mind spinning. She reached out to gently touch the android's face. She got up on her feet and clasped both of the android's shoulders, trying to turn him over onto his back. She wanted to confirm what her flooding eyes were trying to hide from her. She cursed her tears, as she heaved on the body. It was so heavy.

She curled right over and shone her lamp straight into the face of the android, as it lay on its chest on the floor, its eyes closed and its face looking so peaceful.

"Bud!" Grace cried out, her voice rasping. "Bud, can you hear me? Answer me, please! It's Grace."

Grace took her helmet off and placed it on the ground, so the light illuminated Bud's face. She began shaking Bud, as she called out his name.

"Please, Bud. Wake up!"

Bud lay like a lifeless, toppled statue, like all the other dead androids and robots. Grace cradled his head within her hands as she wept for him and for her loss.

That was when he found her.

17. Race After Hope

Captain Alighieri raced past the assembly of white containment suits and on into the darkness, heading deliberately away from Receiving Bay Thirteen, where the *Inferno* was docked. He planned to lead the security people on a merry chase far from his ship. If he could act as a decoy, some of his crew would hopefully make it back to the ship and carry out the rest of the mission. He would do his best to let the station cops keep him in sight. Even if one crew member was able to open the vials containing the live deadly virus and splash it all over the Receiving Bay, it would be enough. With the android Bud fried and the humans having only twenty-four to forty-eight hours left to live, the *Nelson Mandela* would be a crypt in a very short period of time.

Alighieri did not care about his own life. He'd known from the start that this was a suicide mission. He just hadn't informed any of the crew that that was what it was. As far as he was concerned, their deaths were a worthy sacrifice for a greater cause. If this new viral strain did what the first strain was supposed to have done—purify the human race—then his job would be successfully accomplished. This strain would finally eradicate all the damned, leaving the human race pure once more. Gifted with protection against the virus, the people of Gideon's World would be able to take their rightful place at the head of God's galaxy.

Humanity would again be what it was meant to be, what it had been designed to be in the first place. Man had been made in the likeness of God, not these blasphemous, manmade abominations that he saw all around him whenever he ventured into the USS. The existence of these chimeras of human with beast was anathema to the Almighty God. To change the form of Man, who was fashioned in the likeness of the Supreme Being, was a crime worthy of annihilation.

Alighieri was honoured to be chosen as the Righteous Hand of God, to smite the disbelievers and restore purity to the human race once again. This Conglomerate medical station, where man was fused with unholy beast, was the perfect place to start the cleansing. The creators of these abominations would be destroyed first. From there, the Judgement would spread across the USS until every planet was purged of the unholy.

Alighieri smiled as he headed towards the large concourse, waving his wrist-lamp high in the air. He knew he would be able to lose the security teams once he was amongst all the wandering, stranded personnel in the concourse. He intended to keep egging the Security people on, waving his wrist-lamp, drawing them after him. They would follow like ducklings chasing their mother. They could do naught else.

He glanced back over his shoulder, to make sure the Security people were still following him. In the distance, he could see white suited figures with lights on their helmets clumping after him, like bobbing stars on the surface of a black ocean. He waved his wrist-lamp again, in a high arc, to ensure their engagement. A few pulses zinged by him. He ducked and then spun around to renew his flight.

The next second, he found himself airborne, having pitched wildly over something that was planted in the middle of the wide corridor. He landed hard on his left shoulder and somersaulted back to his feet. Alighieri cursed under his breath, spinning to see what had tripped him up. Slanted blue eyes in a forlorn, caramel-skinned face, framed by blonde hair, looked up at him.

He froze and gawked.

He knew that face. He had dreamt of delivering justice to that face for months. If his revenge had had a target, a focus, a visage to wreak his vengeance upon, it belonged to this figure before him, kneeling over a downed android.

Alighieri wanted to crow with exultation. He wanted to fall to his knees and give thanks to the Lord for delivering the witch, who turned humans into part-beasts and part-machines, directly into his hands. He was to deliver the wrath of the Lord with his very own hands. The witch was wearing a containment suit but her helmet was off. She had tears streaking down her cheeks, looking repentant—as a sinner should. He would not be swayed. Perhaps she already knew what was coming.

Alighieri switched off his wrist-lamp and jumped to his feet. He glared down at his prey with cold triumph. Then he swung his foot back and kicked her, savagely, under her chin. Her head spun and she collapsed, falling back over the android. She tried to get up and he kicked her in the face again.

"Dr. Grace Lord, I presume," he sneered over her unconscious body. "I am your judge, jury, and executioner. I find you guilty of sins against God and the human race and I sentence you to eternal damnation."

He bent down and picked the doctor up, slinging her body over his shoulder. He remained crouched and scuttled over to the closest wall, hunkering down behind some dead cargobots, as he waited for the security people to pass.

Change of plans.

Once all of the Security people had gone by, he would head back to the *Inferno* with his ultimate prize. With Dr. Grace Lord in his custody and that Bud android destroyed, the medical station would never be able to create a vaccine in time to save itself. With Dr. Lord as hostage, the *Inferno* would be able to leave the station.

Once free, she could die.

Bud discovered himself lying on the floor in the complete absence of electromagnetic radiation. This was something he had not experienced before. He did not know why he was on the ground, nor could he remember taking up this position. One moment, he had been analyzing the latest test results on an experimental vaccine for the new virus. The next instant, he was on his back in complete darkness, the station suspiciously silent.

It was a very disconcerting quiet because he was not detecting the sounds of the machinery that had to be functioning for the humans to remain alive. This, again, he had never encountered before. As he lay in the absence of the visual spectrum of wavelengths, he listened for any sounds that might indicate what had happened.

Bud had never been completely switched off since he was first brought to consciousness by Dr. Al-Fadi. He was not sure if that is what had happened to him today, but he had no idea how long he had been 'off'.

The few areas within his body that were still inorganic—made up of electrical circuits and components—were burnt beyond repair. His organic nanobots were now busy clearing the debris away. Those disrupted areas had been slotted for replacement with organic components anyway, and the percentage of Bud's body destroyed was so low, that Bud's overall function was not much affected. Still, it was distressing that such a thing had happened and it was a mystery Bud needed to solve. He wondered how his fellow androids had fared. He tried to communicate with *Nelson Mandela* and got no reply. Then he tried to reach out to the other androids and robots in his lab. None of them responded. Repeated attempts to speak with any of the station subminds were met with complete silence. Bud knew that a massive electromagnetic pulse could produce what he was experiencing. Had an EMP been used to attack the station? Could this have been the work of Dr. Nestor? It seemed improbable, but then again, it was never wise to underestimate the psychiatrist.

Bud turned up the gain on his visual receptors to emit visual spectrum and looked around the lab. His huge team of androids and robots were all nonfunctioning. They were all where Bud had last seen them. Presumably, they had all become inactivated at the same time as Bud.

Bud suspected he had 'survived' because of his paucity of electrical components. He was almost totally organic tissue now, but not composed of cells. After seeing how the Al-Fadi virus worked on human cells, he had decided against that route. Molecular chains, lattices, webs, and crystals of carbon nanofibre were his building blocks. If an EMP blast was responsible for this situation—which was Bud's working theory—then almost everything on the station would have been laid to ruin, including the station AI.

'Nelson Mandela?' Bud reached out.

No response.

If *Nelson Mandela* was fried, Bud had to upload the back-up file of *Nelson Mandela* to reboot the entire system. He needed to hurry, because the Life Support systems would be down. It was imperative for him to get the AI back up and running, then restore the power generators to full function. With his visual receptors on maximum, he raced off at maximum time phase.

Bud wondered why the auxiliary power generators had not kicked in. They were supposed to be activated as soon as there was a power failure. Bud craved answers but they would have to wait until there was an adequate supply of oxygen, heat, and water for all of the humans.

Could the station be under attack? Bud detected no evidence of explosions. He heard very little sound at all. What had caused the EMP blast? Without power to the Life Support systems, the station would not be able to provide all the medical treatments and food for its patients. Without power, how would Bud be able to manufacture the cure for the new Al-Fadi viral strain? Bud had to get the power generators running again, as soon as he had rebooted *Nelson Mandela.*

By analyzing the DNA of the *Inferno* crew, Bud had been able to extract the segment that conferred immunity to the crew members. Their cells did not melt away when exposed to the new variant of Al-Fadi virus. They had white cells that just gobbled the virus up and destroyed it. Bud was planning to copy those segments of DNA and insert it into all the humans on the station in the form of a vaccine. All of the experiments treating human cells with this new genetic sequence showed survival against the new viral strain. Unfortunately, with the power failure, Bud could not see how he was going to manufacture the amount of antidote needed to protect all of the humans.

So, upload *Nelson Mandela* first, using batteries. Activate auxiliary backup generators second, because they could start up immediately with no wait time and they would provide power to the basic essentials like Life Support. Then get the station's power generators back on line. Everything else would have to wait.

At maximum time phase, Bud passed by many humans, stranded in the dark, frozen in their lightless plight. No matter how much he wanted to, Bud could not spare the time to stop and help. His main priority was to get *Nelson Mandela* back online. The station AI could then start resurrecting every other operation. *Nelson Mandela* would be able to determine what had been damaged and what needed replacement versus what was still functional and just needed power restored to it. New androids and robots would need to be manufactured as soon as possible, so that they could fix all the damaged ones. But first, Bud would get the station manufacturing the new vaccine to protect the humans from the viral risk.

Bud entered the area of the space station with restricted access to everyone except himself. Since the access pad was not functional, Bud had to punch in his identification code manually, to unlock the door and then manually slide it open. Thankfully, the door only weighed about a third of a metric ton, so it was not difficult. Once within the secret chamber, where *Nelson Mandela* had sequestered its backup system, Bud connected the battery power to the system and uncovered the keyboard. He began to manually type in the two thousand and forty-eight character password to gain access to the program that would reboot the station AI.

Once the password was entered—twice!—the screen lit up. Bud initiated the backup. He was very pleased to see the screen respond to his directives. On some of the consoles, lights began to flicker and a low-grade hum could now be heard within the chamber. Bud detected a slight rise in temperature. The ventilation fans had kicked in once the battery was hooked up. A few interminable seconds later, the entire room ignited into a coruscating panorama of brilliant light. Bud had to swiftly damp down his visual receptors to protect them from burning out.

'I AM NELSON MANDELA!'

Bud's auditory apparatus was strained to the max. He had to rapidly damp down the gain on those. In silent awe, he turned three hundred and sixty degrees, to focus on the sheer, impressive spectacle that was *Nelson Mandela,* in the LCDM flesh, as it were.

Thank you, Bud, for resurrecting me. I assume I have been attacked and disabled, otherwise you would have had no need to come here.'

'The entire station is down, Nelson Mandela. I believe it was an EMP attack. I shall send you all the data now and you can work on getting the auxiliary generators going. I am so happy to see you, but now that you are back online, I have to find Grace and see if she is all right.'

'A very sophisticated type of EMP blast. I'll have to take the **Inferno** ***apart, piece by piece, to understand it fully. Bud, you and I have an immense amount of work to do. You are my only functioning android at the moment. I need to get the power generators turned back on and I need you for that. We have the entire station personnel and all of the patients on board to look after. We must try to provide our patients with the best possible care, in spite of the circumstances. I apologize, but the needs of the many outweigh the needs of the one. You will have to put your concern for Dr. Lord on hold for now. The station needs you.'***

Bud sighed.

<Grace?>

There was no response. Bud began to worry. He could not ignore the station AI's orders. He was compelled to obey. Perhaps Grace was just asleep, back in the hangar with Plant Thing. He was probably concerned about nothing.

<Plant Thing?> Bud mindspoke.

<bud it is so good to hear from you>

<How is Grace?>

<plant thing does not know. grace went looking for bud with little bud>

Bud froze.

<When did Grace leave you?>

<grace left when the lights went out. she wanted to make sure you were all right bud. you were not responding to her calls. grace became very worried>

Bud made a sudden movement towards the chamber door.

'Bud, I order you to get the auxiliary power system running. We must ensure power to the Life Support systems before you do anything else. Then I order you to reactivate the main power generators. Too many lives are at stake for you to go running off after Dr. Lord.'

Bud swayed. He felt like his liquid crystal data matrix was going to explode. He wanted to split himself into three. His entire body trembled. He was forced to do what *Nelson Mandela* ordered, but his emotional will screamed at him to go find Grace. His agonizing howl echoed in the chamber.

<Plant Thing, can you find Grace? She's not answering me and I fear something terrible may have happened to her. Send Little Bud to look for her. Find her and bring her back to the hangar safely. I will come as soon as I have restored power to the station. I must help *Nelson Mandela* first.>

Bud's thoughts ended in a sob.

<little bud and plant thing will go find grace. plant thing will send a vine down every corridor. plant thing can supply oxygen and fruit and vegetables to the humans, bud, as well as supply light. little bud and plant thing will search everywhere for grace. plant thing will let bud know as soon as grace is found. do not despair. plant thing will have eyes everywhere>

<Thank you, Plant Thing. Grace! Grace!>

Bud's cries were met with silence. Torn between duty and love, Bud experienced what he thought might be madness.

It was Bud's duty to do whatever *Nelson Mandela* ordered him to do to get the station back up and running. He could not allow hundreds of patients and station personnel to die or come to harm because he did not do his utmost to get everything back online. Yet he could not allow the most important person in his life to come to harm. If Grace was captured and killed by Nestor, Bud would not be able to continue existing.

Bud was left with only one choice. Do everything at maximum time phase. If only his battery charge would last . . .

Octavia followed Jude down one corridor after another. In Jude's hand was a locator which detected a signal put out by his android. The locator indicated that the android was on the outermost ring of the station. Jude hooked the locator to his belt and led Octavia to the nearest dropshaft.

Jude was furious with himself. He had planned to only go to the gym inside the android. How could he have been stupid enough to fall into Nestor's hands—if that is indeed what happened? If he could, he would shake himself inside that android. He squeezed his hands into fists.

Jude entered the dropshaft first. Octavia followed. She was being quiet. She had shoved a stunner into a pocket of her containment suit before they had left the lab. As they descended gradually towards the outer ring, Jude suddenly felt his brain flip and his bowels contort, as if the dropshaft had been snapped like a whip. He shot his hands out and the right one grabbed a rung of the ladder that was present in every dropshaft. His body fell and momentum slammed him against the ladder rungs. Scrambling to get his feet on the ladder, he looked upwards into blackness. Octavia was screaming as she plummeted towards him. He reached out blindly into the shaft with his left arm.

Octavia struck his left shoulder in the low grade gravity, almost knocking him off the ladder. He felt her fingers scrabble at his neck, shoulder, and chest, as she tried to halt her fall. Jude grabbed her containment suit and wrapped his left arm tightly around her, pulling her body against his, as he clung to the ladder.

Octavia bounced against him, grunting. She began to rebound back out into the shaft. Jude contracted all of his muscles to prevent her from flying off into the darkness.

"Don't let go, Octavia!" he yelled, as her hands slid down his left arm.

Octavia clung to him with both gloved hands wrapped around his forearm. He had a death grip on her wrist but her suit was sliding through his glove. He swung her back towards the ladder.

"Grab a ladder rung, Octavia."

Jude felt Octavia's hands release his arm.

"*Octavia!*" he screamed.

" . . . I'm all right, Jude," Octavia said, her quivering voice coming through the com on his helmet. "I'm . . . I'm on the ladder. Thank you for catching me."

Just then, something hard struck Jude's left shoulder, dislodging his feet from the rung he was standing on. It felt like he had been struck by a metal boulder and he groaned with the pain. He was dangling, only his right hand clutching a ladder rung, as more things fell past, some screaming.

"Octavia?" he called, as he struggled to get his feet back onto a rung.

"Oh, Jude. Those poor people."

"I couldn't catch them, Octavia," Jude croaked. His body was shivering. "What's happening? *Nelson Mandela? NELSON MANDELA!*"

There was no reply.

"Let's get moving, Octavia. We can worry about the station AI once we're on solid ground. I think we're about halfway down. Do you think you can climb it?"

"Yes."

"Octavia, you and I are going to be all right," Jude said soothingly. "Just reach down with your toe and find the next rung. Take your time and go as slowly as you need to. I'm right with you."

Octavia sniffled and Jude could hear her take a deep breath and blow it out slowly. "I'm sorry. I'm okay, Jude. I'll let you know when I reach the ground."

"That's it, Octavia. Just keep talking. I want to hear your voice."

"Did you feel something, Jude? Did the dropshaft twist or was that my imagination?"

"I felt a weird sensation. I don't know what it was."

"Do you think the station might be under attack?" Octavia called upwards.

"I don't know what it was, but it's obviously caused a power failure and *Nelson Mandela* is not answering."

"The auxiliary power should have kicked in, unless it hasn't yet been repaired since the last outage," Octavia said.

"What would knock out a station AI, yet leave the station still intact?"

"Sabotage of the AI data matrix?"

"Nestor?" Jude desperately wanted to take Octavia into his arms. "We're going to be all right, Octavia," he called out. "Just concentrate on one rung at a time."

"Yes, Jude. *Oh!*"

"Octavia?" Jude cried out, his heart instantly racing. "What's wrong?"

"Just tripped on . . . whatever is down here at the bottom of the dropshaft," Octavia said, her voice sounding shaky. "Be careful when you step off the ladder. You might trip. I did. I can't see, but . . . it's very slippery."

"Step away from the base of the ladder, Octavia. I think I'm just above you."

"I can see your locator device, Jude. It has a little light on it. I can see you and . . . oh, Jude."

"Don't look, Octavia," Jude said, stepping off the last rung and wrapping his partner up in his arms. He hugged her tightly. They were both trembling so badly, they seemed to be holding each other up.

"I love you, Jude," Octavia whispered.

"I don't know what I would have done, if I'd lost you, Octavia," Jude choked out. Then his face was crumpling and he was fighting tears. He did not let go of Octavia until they both stopped quavering.

"I need to check to see if anyone who fell down this dropshaft is still alive," Octavia said suddenly.

"All right," Jude said. He held up the locator with its little light. He played with the buttons. One produced a white directed beam.

Octavia examined the broken humans that lay sprawled in a pile with deactivated robots and androids at the bottom of the dropshaft. No one moved. Most were lying in distorted positions. The ones that had landed first, closest to the bottom, would have had the best chance of surviving the fall, except that they were crushed by plummeting androids, robots, and people. Jude and Octavia could very easily have been among that pile.

Octavia looked up at Jude. Her eyes looked like blackened pits. She shook her head.

"Let's get away from here, Octavia," Jude said. "We have to find out what's going on. It's not safe here. If anyone accidentally wanders into the dropshaft, they could fall on top of us. The people here will have to be rounded up later, once the power is restored."

Octavia nodded. "You're right, Jude. It's just hard, leaving them here like this. I feel so helpless and I don't like feeling that way. What does your locator say?"

Jude examined the screen.

"According to this map, my android is actually not that far away. It's in the corridor near one of the Receiving Bays." Jude grabbed Octavia's hand. "Are you okay to continue?"

"Yes. I'm just worried about what's happening on this station. *Nelson Mandela?* Can you tell us what is going on?" Octavia shouted.

They heard distant cries for help.

"The station AI must be down. In all the years I've been here, this has never happened before. We've had a couple of power failures, but the station AI has never been affected before and the auxiliary power generators have always come online immediately. Let's try and find someone who can give us some answers."

Jude aimed the locator light into the black surroundings. They had come down into the large Concourse that led to the Receiving Bays. Theirs was the only light visible. It was eerie. They heard more distant cries for help.

"We're coming," Octavia called out. She grabbed Jude's hand and they walked into the darkness.

Moham Rani had been hiding close to Octavia Weisman's lab, as per usual. He'd started wearing chameleonware when he went to the Neurosurgical Ward, so that her partner would not see him. He could watch Octavia without being disturbed.

Moham knew Octavia was contracted to the famous vid director. He knew he was obsessed. He just didn't know how to cure himself. He thrived on watching the beautiful neurosurgeon buzz energetically around her lab, being passionate and funny and motivated and smart, as he had never suspected women could be. He needed to be near this fascinating woman all the time. Chameleonware seemed his only option.

When Octavia and her partner had left her lab, a strange device in the director's hand, Moham could do naught but follow. He did not know where they were going, but Moham went where Octavia went. Though invisible to their eyes, he kept the couple in sight from a distance. He did not want them to discover that he was tailing them.

Moham saw the couple enter a dropshaft, Jude first and then Octavia. He waited a few minutes before following. He decided he would peek down the shaft to see where they got off and then descend later. He scuttled up to the dropshaft door and briefly stuck his head through the opening, to see where Octavia was. She was in the downward shaft about halfway to the outer ring.

Then the lights went out and Moham felt his brain do a loop-de-loop. Amidst his disorientation, he heard Octavia scream. His heart pounded in his throat. He leaned far into the dropshaft but could see nothing. He got down on the floor and poked his head over the edge. He could hear Stefansson yelling at Octavia to hold on.

Moham could not breathe. He was frozen to the spot. The words, 'Hold on!' choked in his own throat, as he lay there shivering. Moham's life fell in the darkness with Octavia. He wanted to scream. He wanted to fly to her rescue. He cursed his uselessness. When he heard Octavia thank Jude for catching her, he gasped with relief.

Then something hammered him on the back of his head.

Plant Thing listened to its seeds that had travelled far and wide across the Biosphere of the space station. Millions had been filtered out of the air, but many still rode the swirling currents. The tiny helicopter seeds had floated all the way to the inner Hub and to the outer ring. They had entered Central Control and had infiltrated all of the Receiving Bays. They had reached the medical wards, the habitats, the food operations centres, and the manufacturing areas. In their floating and spinning, diving and vibrating, they sent back information to Plant Thing's receptors. Plant Thing had felt the anomaly as a perturbation of the signals from its children. How devastating the explosion had been for all the androids and robots on the station. Plant Thing deeply mourned their deaths.

Plant Thing now knew where the trouble had sprouted. It chose to extend its branches to that location, in search of Grace. It knew Grace would have had to pass by there, on the way to the Android Reservations. Regrettably, Little Bud had left Grace's side very close to where that anomaly had occurred. Little Bud was feeling guilty about that. Little Bud wanted to return to the place where it had left Grace. Plant Thing was now going to follow Little Bud with all of its tendrils. Together, they would find Grace and bring her home. They had to protect Grace at all costs, because Grace was Plant Thing's Special Friend. Plant Thing was in love with Grace—just like Bud was in love with Grace. Plant Thing had to make sure she was all right.

It uncoiled its tendrils, which took a considerable time, since Bud had insisted that Plant Thing stay as small as it could. Plant Thing had worked so hard to stay compact, in tight little coils, but now Plant Thing had to uncoil to its fullest extent, so that it could reach as much of the station as possible. It was going to take a bit of work untangling itself, because Plant Thing did not want to change a single thing in Grace's room.

Plant Thing sprouted bioluminescent glowglobes all along the lengths of its tendrils and ordered all of his flowers to start producing fruit. As the tendrils made their way outwards along all the main corridors of the medical station, Plant Thing hoped humans would be able to see the fruit and pick them for food. The fruit would supply them with water. Of course, Plant Thing had eyes all along its tendrils as well. It hoped people would not pick those off and try to eat them as well, but that was a chance it had to take. It had to keep an eye out for Grace!

Plant Thing sent its tendrils towards the hangar doorway and pushed the doors apart. It decided it would have to greatly enlarge the opening if it wanted to get all of its traveling tendrils out. With un-plantlike impatience, Plant Thing tore the entire wall containing the doorway away, leaving only a couple of structural pillars standing. Plant Thing's tendrils could now easily pass around them and they poured outward like a great, green flood, illuminated softly with millions of bioluminescent glowglobes floating on its surface. As each branch in a corridor was encountered, a bundle of tendrils forked off to follow that pathway. Plant Thing drew more water and nutrients through its feeding tendrils from the sewage facility, to help with any sprouting it had to do. It would need light of some sort soon, but Little Bud knew where the observation decks around the outer ring were. Perhaps some light could be absorbed from the star, Asklepios, around which the planet, Neos Kriti, revolved. Plant Thing would aim the bulk of its tendrils in the direction of the Receiving Bays where Grace was last seen. The observation decks were on the outer ring as well. Hopefully, Bud would get the power in the space station working soon, as promised.

Corridor after corridor, Plant Thing's tendrils were met with shrieks and screams as people tried to run away from the moving vines. Once the tendrils passed by the humans, completely ignoring them, the people stopped fleeing and just stared, as the glowglobes lit up their surroundings in a soft, iridescent glow. Plant Thing witnessed it all from its many eyes and saw that it was good.

As they neared the Receiving Bays, Little Bud hurried forward to the place where it had left Grace. It hoot-hooted in distress, when it found she was no longer there. Little Bud marched onwards, in advance of the wall of tendrils. Eventually, it came upon an android lying in the centre of the wide corridor. Little Bud stared down at the android with its many eyes and then bent downwards. It spread its fingers wide and protruded all of the eyeballs on its fingertips to stare at the face of the android. Plant Thing examined the android through Little Bud's many eyes.

<bud?>

<Yes, Plant Thing?> Bud answered quickly. <Have you found Grace?>

<no bud. we have found you>

<I don't think so, Plant Thing. I see no sign of you.>

<oh. plant thing has found an android that looks like bud>

<Let me know the minute you find Grace!>

<yes bud. plant thing will. let us move on, little bud>

Little Bud straightened up. Suddenly, figures helmeted and dressed in white suits with lights shining out of their heads, moved up to surround Little Bud. A small figure yelled, "Halt!" pointing a blaster at Little Bud.

The huge flood of Plant Thing's tendrils ignored the command and detoured around the white figures, continuing to flow by like a wide, green, twinkling river.

Damien Lamont strolled up to Juan Rasmussen, as the corporal was placing reinforced wrist restraints on his unconscious captive. Draped over Damien's right shoulder hung an obese unconscious man, as if he were a light jacket.

"Nice work, Rasmussen," Lamont said in a casual voice. He shone his helmet lamp on Juan's face. "Hmm. Looks like she got a few in on you. You okay?"

Juan grunted. "I think she broke my jaw and cheekbone."

"Didn't think you'd want or need any help," Damien drawled, looking down at the thin female. "Her being a woman and all."

"Thanks," Juan snarled. "She happens to be boosted."

"Want some help carrying her back to Security? I can slip her over my other shoulder."

Juan let out a low growl.

"Here," Damien said with a smirk. "Let me."

Juan glared at Damien and swung the woman, who was much heavier than she looked, up over his right shoulder. He turned and, with a scowl at his new partner, he began to limp back in the direction they'd come.

"Just trying to help," Damien said. "No need to be testy."

Juan stalked into the darkness, his right cheek and jaw throbbing with every step, asking himself why he had slung his captive over his right shoulder. Her hip kept bumping his face and he did not relish her suddenly regaining consciousness so close to his fractured cheekbone. He would be damned, however, if he was going to shift her body to his other shoulder with Captain Alpha Male Tiger strutting behind him. Juan wanted to get rid of the woman as quickly as possible, so he could investigate the *Inferno.*

He believed the *Inferno* was still intact. He was convinced that the flash had been the burn of the monitor due to the triggering of a massive EMP blast. A true nuclear explosion of that magnitude should have had them all hurtling out into space through a huge rent in the station's outer hull. The questions he kept asking himself were: 'What was the EMP strike for? Why knock out the power on a medical station? What were the goals of the perpetrators? What was going to happen next?' These were questions Juan wanted answered.

Perhaps the best thing to do was wake this woman and get the answers out of her. He thought of his partner, Cindy, and his little baby girl, Estelle, and he felt a wild rage bubble up inside. If the crew of the *Inferno* was part of a plot to destroy the medical station, he would force it out of this woman or the man Damien carried over his shoulder. He didn't care what the Chief Inspector would say. He didn't care about rules and regulations of the Security Division. They needed to know what was coming.

As far as Juan was concerned, this was war. If a ship attacked the integrity of a Conglomerate medical space station, they were the enemy and should be treated as such. Juan decided he would question these 'prisoners of war' with the hopes of determining the enemy's plans. Hopefully, Damien would not object.

Juan stalked back into the now empty observation room, with the burnt out wallscreen. Juan waved Damien into the room.

"Shouldn't we take them to Security Central?" Damien asked.

"Why don't you put your guy down in one of those seats," Juan said.

Damien stared at Juan's face, questioningly, but placed his captive in one of the chairs attached to the floor. The corpulent man slid down in the seat. Damien had to find a cable to fasten around the man's belly to hold him upright. Then he stood and crossed his arms, scowling at Juan.

Juan, in the meantime, placed the woman in another chair and removed the restraints from her wrists, pulling her arms behind her back before reapplying the cuffs. She now leaned forward, still unconscious, with her hands held behind the chair back.

"What do you think you're doing, soldier?" Damien asked, his face a mask of stern disapproval.

"We need to find out what these people are up to and we need to know now," Juan said. "They've attacked this station and knocked out its AI and its power generators. That is an act of war. We need to know what they want."

"I won't condone torture, Corporal," Damien warned, placing his hands on his hips.

"Won't have to," Juan said.

Damien's eyebrows rose, skeptically. There was a long silence.

" . . . All right," Damien said, slowly. "I'm willing to see what you have in mind. But I warn you, I'll stop you, if you break any military codes of conduct."

Juan nodded.

He bent down and shook the woman lightly, to rouse her. She shook her head, blinking, and then became rigid. Her head shot up. She glared at Juan and then Damien, pupils huge. When she saw her crew mate unconscious in the other chair, her eyes narrowed.

"What are you doing?" she demanded, her voice slurred from the swelling in her face. "How dare you hold me here?"

Juan stood before her, huge arms crossed, and asked, "Why are you here?"

The woman looked at Juan and then just stared straight ahead.

"Is this one of your crew?" Juan asked, gesturing to the man bound in the next chair. Damien shone the light from his helmet in the man's face. The man's head lolled on his chest.

"What have you done to him?" the woman demanded. "If you've harmed him, you'll pay for that."

"By you killing everyone on this station?" Juan asked.

The woman stopped with her mouth hanging open and then she snapped her mouth closed. She did not say a word, her chest heaving. She didn't have to. Guilt was apparent from the way her eyes shifted away into the dark.

"Shit," breathed Lamont.

"How do you plan to kill everyone on this station?" Juan demanded.

The woman said nothing, looking straight ahead.

"Are you even going to give us a reason why?" Juan asked. "Why destroy a medical station? There are thousands of patients being looked after here. There are doctors and nurses and other medical personnel that have devoted their lives to healing people. Why kill them?"

The woman looked up and stared at Juan, a sad expression on her face. "It's too late for you already. What's the point?" she said. "You're all going to die."

"How?" Juan barked. "How are we all going to die and *why*?"

The woman was silent for a long moment. Then her expression changed to a look of determination.

"I don't know why. That's the truth. I was a last minute replacement to the crew. When we left Gideon's World, I didn't have any idea what was planned. I was told nothing. When I finally realized what the captain was up to—not all the lies he was telling us—it was too late. I need your help. I need to get a message back to my people about what is happening here. It's urgent."

She looked up at Juan with a pleading look in her eyes. "I'm an undercover cop," she said. "I've been following these fanatics for the last two solstan years. I need to inform my superiors of what they've done here. They need to know what the fanatics are up to!"

Juan knelt down before her. "Tell us how we are all going to die."

The woman stared straight into Juan's eyes with a look of such regret that it sent a frisson of chills down Juan's spine. He thought of Cindy and Estelle and his heart began to thunder.

" . . . Six cryopods have been brought to the station. The captain told us that the people inside the 'pods needed special treatment—treatment that could only be obtained on the *Nelson Mandela.* When we came out of hyperspace and got within docking range of the *Nelson Mandela,* the captain told us that the patients were infected with a new, more lethal strain of the Al-Fadi virus, but that we were all immune. The ship was equipped with a new weapon, a powerful EMP, that could overpower all shielding. When the EMP weapon was triggered, by any attempt to board the *Inferno,* the power would go off across the entire medical station and the cryopods would automatically activate and open up, releasing the virus into the air. The virus is air transmitted. Once in the air circulation, everyone who breathes the virus in, will die.

"I didn't know what the purpose of this mission was when I boarded. I'm sorry for you all, but we need to stop these murderers. I need to get a message back to my planet. These religious fanatics need to be apprehended."

"*Traitor!*" screamed the man in the other chair.

Juan, Damien, and the woman all jumped. They turned to look at the other captive. The red-faced man glared at his crew mate with loathing in his eyes. She returned his look with her chin raised.

"You bitch!" the man spat. "Don't feel sorry for them. Feel sorry for yourself, you Judas. You're going to die along with these animals. You're going to melt away too, traitor. People like you are an abomination and need to be wiped from existence!"

"What do you mean 'people like you'?" Damien asked.

"You humans that turn yourselves into animals or machines," the man sneered. "You are a sin before God. You will all be destroyed so that the human race can be pure again, once more in the likeness of God, as we were meant to be."

"But there are so many people on this station that are normal," Damien said, a look of outrage on his face. "You would kill them all?"

"These people that call themselves doctors create you abominations. They do the devil's work. They do not deserve to live," the man shouted. "You all deserve to die—especially you, Mary Shelley. You think I don't know you have been boosted? You have poisoned the air that I have breathed. I relish seeing you melt into a puddle of slush. I shall spit on your corrupt remains and rejoice."

The woman named Mary stared at her crew mate, her eyes desolate, as if seeing him for the first time. "You're insane, Abraham," she whispered. "How can you be a mass murderer and see yourself as holy or pure? If anyone is going to hell for their sins, it would be you."

"You are an obscenity, a blight in the eyes of God," the man intoned. "The virus will smite you and all other sinners. The only ones left standing will be us, the Pure, untouched, unaltered, and in the likeness of God."

"Bloody madman," Damien said, pushing his hand through his hair.

"Mary, can you help us stop the captain or any of the crew from spreading this viral serum around the station?" Juan asked.

"My real name is Hope, Hope Cooper. It's probably already too late. I'm sure the cryopods are opening as we speak. Some of the crew have probably already made it back to the *Inferno* by now."

"The cryopods would have gone into quarantine. We just have to prevent your crew from spreading the virus serum around. There may still be time to stop them."

Hope looked up at Juan with haunted eyes. She glanced over at Abraham and then nodded, "I'll help in any way I can."

Juan released her wrist restraints and helped Hope to her feet.

"You witch! I hope you like burning in hell," Abraham spat. Damien casually backhanded Abraham across the face and the man's head dropped, unconscious again.

"Go to sleep," Damien told the crewman, "before I kill you."

"We need to hurry," Hope urged. "How long was I out for?"

"Only a couple of minutes," Juan said.

"We must move swiftly. Perhaps it's not yet too late. Try your best to keep up with me, boys," she said and bolted off into the darkness.

Juan took one look at Damien, unsure if he had done the right thing, letting this woman go free.

They raced after Hope.

18. Needs of the Many

Eric collided with a wall. He had gotten to the end of the long, cramped tunnel and there appeared to be nowhere else to go. He heard the deep voice in his head say, 'It's a swinging trapdoor panel, you idiot! Push through!'

Eric pushed as hard as he could and ended up rolling out onto a hard floor and rolling and rolling in the darkness. He finally got his tendrils beneath him and stopped himself. He looked around, wondering where he was. The next second, he was rolling again, having been kicked by something pointed.

"Ouch!"

"What happened?" Eric heard a female voice say.

"Don't know," a male voice whined in a whisper. "Felt like I kicked a boulder. Think I broke my toe."

"Maybe you kicked a bot. Can you still walk?"

"Barely," the kicker whined.

"I believe this is the correct hangar up ahead. Our ship should be in there," the female voice said softly.

Eric decided to follow these two people with lights on their wrists. He had no idea who they were or what they were up to, but they had light so he followed along. He found himself entering a large open hangar with a few ships parked at one end.

"Hold it. I think I hear someone coming."

The two looked back, their frightened faces briefly illuminated by the wrist lamps, which they quickly turned off. They ducked down behind a small transport container and waited.

A heavy-set man, with a figure slung over his shoulder, moved silently past them. The newcomer glanced around furtively. He wove among a collection of inert androids and robots, lying scattered on the ground, until he stood before a vessel hatchway, his wrist-lamp shining on the open contents of an access pad.

"It's the Captain," the female voice whispered.

The heavy-set man flinched and spun towards the voice, staring into the blackness. When he saw who was there, he visibly relaxed.

"Stop skulking and get over here," the captain grumbled.

"Who's the passenger?" the female asked, as she and her companion emerged from the gloom.

"Our ticket out of here," the captain said. "Why aren't you inside already? Where are the others?"

"Haven't seen anyone else yet," the kicker said, as he bent down to peer into the hostage's face. The light from his wrist-lamp cast a soft glow, revealing the woman's bruised and swollen features. Eric gasped. The unconscious woman looked like Grace Lord with a markedly swollen, bruised chin.

The deep, cultured voice in Eric's head started screamed, 'She's mine! She's mine! She's mine! They can't have her!'

Eric felt his emotions ignite into flaming rage as the inner voice began cursing.

'After that man!'

Eric hesitated. He wanted to see what the three strangers were going to do. He was not going to do something foolhardy, just because the voice in his head was going insane. If Grace Lord was being taken aboard that ship, Eric would try to sneak on after them. He felt compelled to follow Grace, especially with the voice in his head screaming madly, "Get her! They can't have her! She's mine! . . .'

Eric watched the captain place his eye before the scanner on the access panel to the right of the ship hatchway. A light beam traced down his cornea. He placed his hand on a palm pad and spoke a few words. Then a voice said, "Welcome back, Captain."

The captain ordered the ship to 'Keep it down.' The ship's voice dropped to a barely audible murmur, as it warned the three crew members to step back to allow the hatchway to open. A thick, metal door swung outward, revealing an airlock and a pair of inner sliding doors. The inside panels slid apart to allow the captain, with his captive, and his two crew to enter immediately. They quickly disappeared inside, the captain barking orders at his two crew.

'After her! After her! After her!' shrilled the voice in Eric's head. Eric scurried after the captain and Grace as quickly as his tendrils would carry him. He had to protect Grace at all costs, the voice howled at him. As Eric peeked into the ship, looking for a good hiding spot, the voice in his head would not stop screaming, 'She's mine! She's mine! She's mine! She's mine! . . .'

If Eric let Grace out of his sight, the crazy voice in his head started berating him abusively. He could not let this spaceship escape with Grace as its hostage. The voice inside his head would go apoplectic with rage. Somehow, Eric would have to attempt a rescue of Grace, if only to try to maintain his sanity.

Bud was racing across the medical station at maximum time phase. Devastation was everywhere, but he had no time to stop. As he raced past, he whispered silent apologies to his fellow robots and androids, victims of the mysterious attack. They were all dead. He could not help them now.

He had to focus on getting the power generators up and running, and on getting the vaccine made. If the virus got free before everyone was treated, the *Nelson Mandela* would become a ghost station—no humans, no androids, no robots, no Plant Thing or Little Bud—only Bud. Bud could not let that happen. He had to get the station powered up and Manufacturing running. Thousands of doses of the antiviral cure were needed. Bud could not do this alone.

He also needed to find Grace. Where was she?

Bud typhooned into the Auxiliary Power Facility. After the recent blackout, *Nelson Mandela* had insisted that the entire system be checked and tested. There should have been only a few milliseconds delay between the power failure and the auxiliary generators becoming activated. What had happened?

The auxiliary power system was off. Bud did not have time to determine why this was. Could it just have been human error? Could it have been Nestor's tampering? He raced from one generator to the next, accessing their main controls and turning them on. Each generator was run by battery power. Once warmed up, they would supply enough emergency power to the Life Support systems controlling oxygen, water, sanitation, food refrigeration, and air circulation, as well as the operating rooms. That would do until the main power generators could be brought back to full function.

When all the auxiliary generators were humming, Bud raced to the station's hub where the main Power Facility was located. The last time he'd been there, he'd almost been fried by the radiation. Now entering the same area, he did not know what to expect. In each power generator, there was a 'bottle' of antimatter protected by a containment field. What had the EMP blast done to the power generators and, more importantly, the containment fields? If the containment fields had been shut off, the *Nelson Mandela* would now be space debris. Since that was not the case, the containment fields were somehow still holding . . . but for how long?

'Nelson Mandela?'

'Chuck Yeager ***here, 'dro. What do you need?'***

'Chuck Yeager, *what are the radiation readings in the power generators?'*

'Climbing through the stratosphere, 'dro! The reinforced lead shielding on these generators must have protected them from the EMP surge, but radiation readings in the generators are all over the place. Some are getting very hot.'

'I was afraid you'd say that. Any power coming from the auxiliary generators yet?'

'About forty percent output.'

'Route all of that power here, Chuck Yeager! *I need to adjust and stabilize the containment fields around the antimatter in each generator or this station is going to explode.'*

'You have it. Was nice knowing you, 'dro.'

'Stop kidding around, Chuck Yeager. *There's no time for that!'*

'Whose kidding? You've got every watt, 'dro.'

'Thanks.'

'Get it done, 'dro.'

Bud's fingers flew. He re-routed the power coming from the auxiliary generators to each of the antimatter containment fields in each generator. The readings of temperature and radiation level in each power generator were off the scale. Bud could not stand waiting to see if the temperature and radiation levels began dropping. He wanted to go into the restricted area and check it out himself.

'No, 'dro. Not letting you do that. If the levels don't come down, we blow. Nothing more you can do.'

'I can't stand around waiting to find out, Chuck Yeager!*'*

'Don't worry. It won't be long, either way.'

'Thanks.'

'No. Thank you. It was an honour knowing you, 'dro.'

'Same to you, Chuck Yeager. *At least no one will know what hit them. I must go find Grace. If we are going up in a huge explosion, I would like to spend my last milliseconds with her.'*

'Uh, 'dro . . .'

Chelsea Matthieu was fuming. They'd managed to capture four of the people racing past them, as they'd exited the monitor room; however, none of the captured were talking. The fact that they had all been stunned at maximum setting was the reason for her foul mood. It would be a couple of hours before any of their captives would be conscious enough to talk and Chelsea so wanted to have a talk with at least one of them.

She suspected they were the *Inferno* crew responsible for the power outage but without the station AI to confirm it, she could not be sure. Since they were all stunned into oblivion, she could not ask them. She wanted to kick someone.

And now, she had some enormous, green, multi-eyed monster pacing around making wheezing sounds that almost sounded like words. It almost sounded like it was cursing at her, using some very foul language, but it's diction was very poor. It kept rocking back and forth on its great tree-trunk limbs, as if it needed to go somewhere, very badly. Well, she was damned if she was going to let this plant alien wander all over the station in the dark. It was bound to give a few people a cardiac arrest, looming out of the darkness, hoot-hooting like that. The only problem was, if it did decide to take off on its own, could they really stop it? She was not keen on blasting it to splinters or setting it on fire.

She was sure it was part of the plant alien that had torn Dr. Glasgow, Dr. Vanacan, and Nurse Evra apart in the operating room. Now that plant alien was not only gargantuan, it was flowing all over the station, and she was helpless to stop it! Enormous green vines were just flowing by like a living river and no matter how many stun blasts had been fired on the branches, they just kept moving past. As far as she was aware, no one had been attacked by the limbs and the glowglobes on them were providing light to people stranded in the dark. People had even pulled off some of the fruit on the boughs and eaten them, the idiots; not her Security people, of course. Chelsea had even been offered an apple by one of the station personnel. She had looked at the person like he was insane.

Was the plant alien trying to poison the entire population of the *Nelson Mandela*? She needed to get some of that fruit analyzed. Where was that infernal station AI when you needed it, anyway?

"*Nelson Mandela*!" Chelsea screamed at the top of her lungs.

"No need to yell, Chief Inspector. I can hear you just fine."

Chelsea nearly jumped out of her containment suit.

"Where the Hal have you been?" she demanded.

"Knocked out by the EMP blast you triggered from the *Inferno,* Chief Inspector. I regret that you did not listen to my warning. Only thanks to Bud, am I back on line. Bud is now getting power up and running on the station for us. The auxiliary power should be coming back on to you in two point one milliseconds.

" . . . And then there was light."

"What in space is going on with these plant limbs all over the place, *Nelson Mandela*? Are we being taken over by the plant alien?"

"It is my understanding, Chief Inspector, that Plant Thing is trying to help us, by supplying oxygen, light, and food to whoever needs it."

"Is it trying to poison everyone on this station?"

"If it is, you would all be dead already, as Plant Thing has been supplying food to the station in the form of fruits and vegetables for a good while now."

"It has? Why was I not told?"

"Because you never asked?"

"Why you pompous, supercilious, condescending . . ."

"Chief Inspector, you have an enemy ship that has knocked out the power on this station using a sophisticated EMP weapon. It has delivered patients carrying a virus that is more lethal than the Al-Fadi virus. The crew have escaped their quarantine and some are still loose on this station. Perhaps it would be better if you focused on those 'real' threats', rather than the 'imagined' threat you are attributing to Plant Thing, who is only trying to help the people of this station."

"Why you arrogant bucket of chips! How many crew members were aboard the *Inferno* and where are they now?" Chelsea barked.

"There were nine crew members. There were four humans detected entering the *Inferno* a few seconds ago. One female was

slung over the shoulder of the captain, Danté Alighieri. I believe the unconscious woman is our own Dr. Grace Lord.

"There are two tiger adapt Security officers chasing another crew member towards the *Inferno* as we speak. The woman in the lead is the *Inferno's* medical officer, Mary Shelley. In rapid pursuit are Corporal Juan Rasmussen and Captain Damien Lamont. They should be arriving at the *Inferno* in four point two seconds."

"Damn! We need to get over there!"

"Hurry, Chief Inspector. I am now positive that the woman on the captain's shoulder is Dr. Grace Lord and I suspect she is in terrible danger."

"On it!"

'Hallelujah! You did it, 'dro! Temperature and radiation levels are beginning to drop in all twenty-five power generators. We won't be going up in a Big Bang after all. Good work. Once they have cooled off, I'll be able to get the power generators working properly again.'

'Wonderful, Chuck Yeager. *Now I have to find Grace!'*

'What's your energy situation like, 'dro?'

'My energy?'

'Yeah, your battery charge. How is it?'

'Twenty-two point six eight percent.'

'Better charge up, 'dro.'

'No time, Chuck Yeager. I've got to go find Grace!'

"Dro, you aren't going to like what I have to tell you.'

'What?'

'You know those six cryopods with the infected patients inside them?

'Yes, Chuck Yeager. *I can hardly forget about them, can I? What about them?'*

'There is something very unusual about them.'

'What do you mean?'

They're beginning to open up all on their own. Cryopods should not be capable of doing that. The cryopods were supposed to all go into the Level Six Quarantine Chamber, but they did not make it inside. They are all sitting outside the door to it. I want to shake the humans who took the cargo droids away before they had finished their task! That deadly virus will get released

into the station's atmosphere when the lids of those cryopods open and the air circulation is re-established. Those cryopods have to be prevented from opening up, before they break their seals, 'dro!'

'How much time do I have, Chuck Yeager?*'*

'I would estimate approximately three point six nine seconds to the first one breaking its seal, give or take a few milliseconds.'

'On my way!'

'Don't forget the dropshafts are out of order until the main power generators are fully back on. We don't want you knocking anyone off of the ladders!'

Captain Alighieri boarded the vessel and dropped his hostage into one of the passenger seats.

"Strap her in and bind her hands, Jacob," he ordered his logistics officer, who had been given the alias Geoffrey Chaucer.

"Who is she, Captain?" Jacob Armstrong asked, as he sat the woman up in the flight seat. She kept slumping over to the side until he strapped her in using the flight seat's chest harness.

"Dr. Grace Lord, the witch responsible for the vaccine that saved these sinners from the Hammer of God, first time around. She's going to be our ticket off of this station. We need to keep her alive until we get free and clear of this place."

"Then what?" his first officer asked.

"Then we let her go," Alighieri said.

"How?" Faith Miller asked, her expression one of incomprehension. "We don't have any escape pods on board."

"I didn't say she'd get back to the station, did I?" Alighieri sneered. "I said we'd let her go . . . out the airlock without a suit."

The two crew members tried to keep the shock off of their faces.

"Maybe she would be better kept alive, Captain," the first officer said.

Alighieri scowled at her.

"She'll stay alive for as long as we need her. Get the virus samples. I want you two to splash the serum over any surface outside the ship. I don't care what you spray it on, but do it fast. And don't get too far from the ship. Lights have come back on out there. Their auxiliary power must have kicked in somehow. Get into containment suits, just in case.

I know we're all supposedly protected, but I don't need either of you getting sick at this stage."

"What about the others, Captain?" Miller asked. "Shouldn't we wait until they all get back here and into suits, before we spread the virus?"

"We'll wait a few more minutes. If they're not back in five, they've been captured and aren't coming back. We spread the samples and get out of here."

"You don't know they won't be coming back," Miller pressed.

"I said we wait five minutes," he grated, his hand moving towards his hip, forgetting that he was not wearing his blaster. Miller jerked when she saw his hand movement. "Do what you're told or you're left behind. Understood?"

He heard them both mumble, "Yes, sir."

He wanted to smack them both across their faces for their insolence—especially Miller—but he needed them both to help him fly the *Inferno.*

"I don't expect to get off of this station without a fight, but I'll announce that if there are any attempts to board our ship or stop us, we'll kill Grace Lord. See how they like that," he said. Then he turned towards the bridge. He wanted his blaster. He felt naked without it.

On the bridge, he strode up to his command chair and pulled the weapon from its drawer. Strapping it onto his hip, he activated a screen and observed Miller and Armstrong through his surveillance eyes. He wanted to ensure they were carrying through with his orders as quickly as possible.

He saw Armstrong's eyes meet Miller's. Neither of them looked happy.

"Go get the containment suits and blasters," Miller said to Armstrong in a flat voice. "Once we're suited up, I'll get the viral samples out of the lockup."

Armstrong had nodded, wordlessly. Alighieri clenched his fists and ground his teeth. The two were taking their damn sweet time. He pulled the blaster out of its holster and squeezed the grip tightly in his hand. He took some deep breaths. He had to stay calm. He needed these two. All they had to do was splash that serum around and the job was done. He was not going to wait for anyone else to get back.

He was about to tell the ship to start up the engines, when he heard the perimeter defence system firing. He glanced at the outside screen. His medical officer was racing towards the ship, two huge people in containment suits chasing after her. She was dodging, leaping, rolling, and ducking the pulse blasts from the ship. He'd no idea she was so fast.

Why had the woman led those people back to the *Inferno*? Alighieri wanted to strangle that medical officer on the spot. The perimeter defence seemed to know what he was thinking and did its best to shoot her. Unfortunately, the woman got through. Thankfully, the two figures chasing her did not. Alighieri stalked back out towards the hatchway, blaster tight in his grip. He was going to have a word with that stupid bitch.

Hope dove through the opened hatchway of the *Inferno* and somersaulted to her feet. She had been grazed by a couple of the perimeter defence pulses but nothing too serious. She panted to get her breath back as she turned to see if the two tiger security officers had made it behind her. The airlock was empty. Looking aft, she saw an unconscious woman slumped forward in a seat and two figures in containment suits, one with a blaster drawn, the other carrying a silver case. When Hope saw the closed case, her heart leaped. She prayed she was still in time.

Hope made a charge towards the person carrying the case. The other figure with the blaster raised the weapon and Hope batted it away. She believed it was Armstrong, the logistics officer, who tried to get in her way. He tried to wrap his arms around her. Hope just picked the man up and spun around with him in her arms. In the next second, she heard blaster fire and smelled charred flesh. She looked down at her chest, expecting to see holes. There was blood but it was from the man she was carrying. Alighieri had shot him in the chest twice.

Hope looked up and stared into Alighieri's cold, grey eyes, her heart pounding. His blaster muzzle was now aiming at her face. She threw Armstrong at Alighieri with all of her strength and spun back towards the other figure. Miller, the first officer, had the silver case in her left hand and a blaster in her right. Hope grabbed for the metal silver case and Miller just released it.

"Go," Miller said. "Run."

Hope made a dash for the hatchway with the case clutched to her chest.

"Shoot her!" Alighieri cried out. He was pushing the dead crewman off of himself. Miller, the first officer, just stood there, blaster held at her side.

"No, Captain. I'm not killing a member of our crew," she said.

Alighieri raised his blaster and shot his first officer in the face.

Hope dove out of the hatchway, setting off the perimeter defence system again. She got about ten meters from the *Inferno* when she felt a searing agony first in her shoulder, then in her hip, and finally in her back. She fell forwards, holding the case out in front of her body, trying to protect it from weapons fire. The last thing she saw was the bodies of the two tiger Security officers laying sprawled before her.

Juan tried to ignore the scorching pain in his left knee, as he slid along the ground to get to Damien. The captain was lying unconscious on the floor of Receiving Bay Thirteen with his head in a pool of blood. Damien had been struck in the head by laser fire, coming from the *Inferno,* as he had tried to keep up with the woman called Hope. Almost immediately after that, Juan had been hit in the knee and had gone down. Hope had miraculously made it into the *Inferno.*

When the lights in the hangar had come on, Juan had called out to Damien, but the tiger captain had not responded. Juan could see his back rising up and down and let out a huge sigh of relief. His partner was not dead . . . yet. Juan had to stay alive long enough to get Damien out of the line of fire and to a medic. At least they were in the right place for that.

Juan's pulse throbbed in his temples and he winced each time he moved his left knee, but he dragged himself by his claws across the ground, trying to keep his head below the *Inferno's* defensive barrage. He prayed that Damien would not get hit by any more shots from the ship. The ship's defence system seemed to be targeting anything that moved above a certain level off of the ground. It did not seem to be able to target Juan.

Security people were moving into the hangar with guns and barriers and the *Inferno's* perimeter defence system was shooting over Juan's and Damien's heads. A few more meters and Juan would be able to shield Damien from any more shots with his own body.

A figure dove out of the *Inferno* and ran straight at Juan. Juan rolled to face the attacker, who turned out to be Hope. In her arms was a silver case which she seemed to be shielding with her body. Juan called out her name, as he saw her arch backwards, flesh exploding out of her shoulder, thigh, and chest. Hope's dilated eyes met Juan's for a brief second before agony distorted her features and she fell forwards. She pushed the case towards him, using her body to shield him and the silver container. Juan's nose stung with the smell of burnt flesh.

"Get down, Hope!" he bellowed.

By the time Hope hit the ground, her eyes were vacant.

Juan crawled forward and grabbed the silver case. He then spun one hundred and eighty degrees flat on his belly, placing his body between the case and the ship. As he began to crawl away from the *Inferno,* security people were firing over his head, offering him some protective cover. Hopefully, whoever was on the ship was not going to come after Juan for the case, which presumably contained the virus samples.

He grabbed Damien's left foot with his left hand and, as he slid forward on his belly, he pushed the case ahead of himself. It seemed to take forever before Security officers came forward, some firing, some carrying portable hard shields, to surrounded Juan and Damien and drag them both out of the line of fire. Juan would not relinquish the case. He crawled his way to shelter behind some portable barrier shielding, clasping the silver box to his chest. The officers lay Damien beside him and he checked his friend's pulse. The pulse bounded beneath his fingertips. Juan sighed and rolled onto his back.

"How badly are you hurt, Rasmussen?" a voice asked. He looked up to see Chief Inspector Matthieu standing over him.

"Pulse fire to the left knee, Inspector," Juan said. "I'm fine. Damien here is worse off. Got hit somewhere in the head. Still breathing. Needs a medic, stat."

"You there! Get a stretcher here now! We have a man down! Head injury!" Juan heard the inspector shout.

"What's in the case, Rasmussen?" Matthieu asked, turning back to him.

"I believe it's serum containing a strain of virus deadlier than the Al-Fadi virus," Juan hissed. The burning pain of his knee was starting to register in Juan's consciousness. "It better not have taken any damage or we're all dead."

"Son of a hole!" the inspector swore. "Rivera!"

"Chief?" the man said from right beside her.

"Gah! Take this case and guard it with your life. It contains viral samples that could wipe out everyone on this station. Get it into a Level Six container and into a Level Six Containment Facility and do not breathe until you do. Do not open it. Do not shake it. I don't trust anyone but you to do this, Rivera. The fate of everyone on this station rests with you. Don't let me down."

"I won't, Chief," Rivera said.

"Get going!"

Jude and Octavia walked towards the Receiving Bays, following the signal on the locator. Since the emergency lights had come back on, Octavia did not feel the need to stop at every individual that was stranded in the dark, to check if they were all right. People could now help each other. The most incredible discovery, when the lights came back on, was the presence of huge green plant vines running all over the place, laden with delicious fruits, glowing bulbs, and unusual, green eyes. Everyone was claiming it was a miracle. It was certainly something surprising and wondrous and Jude felt very lucky to have been here to witness it.

Octavia had finally been able to speak to the resurrected *Nelson Mandela.* The AI had informed Octavia that Dr. Al-Fadi and Dr. Cech were nowhere to be found, but a search was underway. Octavia had gotten very quiet after that. Jude noticed her clenched jaw and frown lines. He was worried for his friend, Hiro, as well. What did Nestor have in store for the two of them?

Jude grabbed Octavia's arm and pointed at another fallen android. "Do you think that one's mine?"

"Jude, how many times have you asked me that in the last few minutes? Why don't you just look at your locator?"

"Because it just gives me an estimated position of where the android is. It doesn't light up and ring an alarm, like I've hit the jackpot," he said. "Do you think this one looks like Bud?"

"Why, I think it does, Jude," Octavia said, bending down to examine the android's face. As Jude crouched beside her, the locator began chiming and flashing and vibrating.

"Hm. Sounds like you hit the jackpot, Mr. Stefansson," Octavia said.

"I guess I forgot about that feature. Traitor," he said to the instrument, as he turned it off and re-attached it to his belt.

"Let's turn him over, Jude," Octavia said, as she put her hands beneath the android's frame. Jude obliged and together they managed to roll the android over. Bud's features looked serene. The android was dead like all of the others. Octavia pulled open the android's garments and opened the chest panel. The wires within the chest cavity, connecting the liquid crystal data matrix to the hardware in the android, were all a blackened mess. However, within a small cube reader sat a memprint cube.

"Where did this cube reader and memprint cube come from?" Octavia exclaimed.

"I don't know," Jude said.

"I didn't put this here," Octavia said, looking up at Jude with huge eyes. "I wonder who did?"

Jude shook his head. Who would want to hijack an android that looked like Bud? He was convinced that the *Nelson Mandela* was a madhouse. His android was going to require another complete overhaul.

Why was his android so close to the Receiving Bays? They would not be able to carry it back to the lab. The android was far too heavy and there were no functioning aircars available. Nor were there any functioning antigrav sleds or robots to help them carry the android back. They'd need a reinforced wheeled stretcher and who knew how many of those were on the station? Jude figured they'd have to wait until things got back to some degree of normality, before he could transport his android back to the lab. He wondered what was on the memprint cube.

"Let's push it over against the wall, so it's not in the way," Octavia said.

'Easier said than done,' thought Jude, as he heaved and shoved. Just as they finished positioning the android against the corridor wall, a massive, green, hulking monster, almost three meters tall and covered in green eyeballs, came up to them wheezing a word over and over again that sounded like, "Bud? Bud? Bud? Bud? Bud? . . . "

Octavia gave a squeak when she saw it and yelled, *"Nelson Mandela?"*

"I see you have met Little Bud," the station AI said.

"Little Bud? Who in the world named it that?" Octavia demanded.

"Little Bud's parent, Plant Thing, the creator of all of these vines you see around the station."

"Is Little Bud . . . safe?" the neurosurgeon asked.

"From you? I hardly doubt that."

"Oh, you are just a shipload of laughs today, *Nelson Mandela.* I suppose you wouldn't be allowing this thing to run around the station freely, if it wasn't safe."

"Little Bud just wanted to know if that android was Bud. No, Little Bud. That is not the real Bud, your friend. That is just an

android that looks like Bud. Bud is busy right now, but he will come to see you as soon as he can."

The giant plant wheezed something and turned and wandered off.

"Did that walking tree just say 'Grace Lord' or am I imagining things?" Jude asked.

"As a matter of fact, Mr. Stefansson, Little Bud did. Little Bud is very worried about Dr. Lord."

"What has happened to Grace?" Octavia asked.

"Dr. Lord has been taken hostage by the captain of the ship that unleashed the EMP strike. He insists that if we do not let his ship and all his crew go, he will kill her."

"What? We must save Grace! You must do as he says, *Nelson Mandela*!"

"I will certainly do my best, Dr. Weisman. I do not want to see Grace Lord harmed. There was a firefight going on in Receiving Bay Thirteen between Security forces and the crew of the *Inferno.* At the moment, the shooting has ceased.

"Dr. Weisman, your surgical skills may be needed. There is a head injury being assessed in Receiving Bay Thirteen. I am attempting to organize the operating rooms so that some can be run solely with human personnel."

"I'd better get to Receiving Bay Thirteen to assess this head injury," Octavia said. "Keep me informed as to what you discover about Hiro and Dejan please."

"Will do, Dr. Weisman. Be careful in Receiving Bay Thirteen. There are protective barriers set up and Chief Inspector Matthieu is handling the hostage taking. I appreciate you looking after the head injury yourself. I have very few helpers at the moment. My only functioning android is Bud and he is handling a very tricky situation up on the Level Six Containment Unit."

"Does Bud know Grace has been taken hostage?" Octavia asked. "Does he know that her life is being threatened?."

There was only silence.

"*Nelson Mandela,* have you not told Bud about Grace?" Octavia asked. "If something happens to her . . ."

"As soon as Bud is finished this one extremely important task—that cannot be performed by anyone else on this station—I will inform Bud of the situation with Dr. Lord, Dr. Weisman."

"Oh, dear. I don't relish your task, *Nelson Mandela,*" she said.

"I wish I were not in this position either, Dr. Weisman. However

the needs of the many must, in this case, outweigh the needs of the few."

"I certainly hope Bud sees it that way, *Nelson Mandela.* We must save Grace."

"Saving Dr. Grace Lord's life is one of my highest priorities, Dr. Weisman, but so is the life of everyone else on this station. Bud is protecting everyone. I will do whatever I can to keep her safe. I hope that is enough. Thank you for looking at the patient in Receiving Bay Thirteen. His name is Captain Damien Lamont. I must go."

Just then, a tall, handsome, blonde man staggered up to them, dressed in inpatient coveralls. He was rubbing a spot on the back of his head.

"Did I overhear you talking about Dr. Grace Lord? She's been kidnapped and is being held as hostage?" the man asked.

Octavia looked at the man and then did a double take. Jude squinted at the man, trying to figure out where he had seen him before.

"Excuse me," Octavia said. "I'm Dr. Weisman. Do you mind telling me your name?"

The man blinked his almond-shaped blue eyes at them, as if trying to get them into focus. He looked like he'd very recently had facial surgery.

"Please. You must take me to where Grace Lord is being held captive. I'm Captain Alexander Lord. I'm Grace's father."

Bud had to slide down the ladders in five different dropshafts to get from the Hub to the outer ring, where the six cryopods were quarantined. His boots were smoking by the time he reached Level One. He launched into maximum time phase to get to the Level Six Containment Facility in under forty milliseconds.

The cryopods containing the infected patients were sitting outside the Level Six Containment Facility, which made no sense. Bud could only surmise that, because no one expected the seals on the six cryopods to be breeched, it wasn't a priority. Cryopods never opened on their own. Once closed and sealed with a patient cryogenically frozen inside, a special access code had to be entered for the cryopod to open up. The cryopods brought by the *Inferno* were opening of their own accord, which meant they were of an anomalous design. What had triggered the cryopods to start opening? Could the EMP blast have been responsible?

Was Captain Alighieri's goal to infect the people of the station with the new virus?

Bud planned to just deactivate each of the six cryopods and return later, to move them inside the Level Six Containment Facility. He was already in a containment suit and would go through a sterilization procedure at the end, when he was exiting the room. He just had to prevent the cryopods from breaking their seals and get them into the Quarantine Chamber through the airlock. The cycling of the airlock was taking so long, Bud wanted to smash his fist right through the door so he could open it. Now he truly understood what the word 'impatient' meant.

As the airlock door to the Level Six Containment Facility slid open, Bud was checking all the cryopods. He'd hit the deactivation switch on the first cryopod expecting it to shut down. It did not. Bud frowned. He went to the next cryopod and hit the deactivation switch. Again, the cryopod continued its thaw cycle. Bud raced to the other four. None of the cryopods responded to his command to shut down. He tried, then, to reinitiate the cryogenic sequence in the pods. That order was also ignored. By now, each cryopod was just seconds away from blowing their seals and expelling air.

Could Bud get each of the cryopods into the Level Six Containment Area before any of them opened and the doors closed? The probability was low.

'Nelson Mandela?'

'Yes, Bud?'

'If I pull the battery pack out of each of these cryopods, will that keep them from opening?'

'Perhaps.'

'Perhaps? That is not very reassuring.'

'When power is totally cut to the cryopod, the magnetic seal will no longer be operating. The pod may stay shut if the internal pressure of the cryopod is less than the outside air pressure. However, if the internal pressure is higher, then the magnetic seal may not hold, and the pod will open. Since the pods are in their warming sequence, I would speculate that the interior of the pods are warmer than the external air and therefore, they could open.'

'Can you lock down this entire area, Nelson Mandela?"

'What do you plan to do, Bud?'

'The only thing I can do in the one minute I have left, Nelson Mandela. I am

going to move each cryopod into the Level Six Containment Facility before any of the pods open.'

'You have fifty-two point eight seconds.'

'Lock down the area, Nelson Mandela, in case I'm not successful.'

'Doors closing, 'dro.'

In maximum time phase, Bud lifted the closest cryopod and ran with it into the airlock. He put it down and ran out for the second. Each cryopod weighed approximately five hundred kilograms and Bud found the size of the pods awkward to lift. He ran back and forth, carrying each cryopod into the quarantine chamber until he had one more to go.

'One second left.'

Bud raced to the last cryopod and squeezed his arms tightly around the lid of the pod, to prevent it from breaking its seal. He raced into the Level Six Containment Room and yelled for *Nelson Mandela* to close the airlock doors. As the outer airlock doors slid shut, the seal around the cryopod tried to open. Bud held the cryopod closed until the inner airlock doors opened. He carried the pod right to the back wall of the room, as far from the inner airlock doors as possible. At his topmost speed, he carried the other five cryopods into the facility. When Bud heard the multiple locks of the lockdown doors engaging and the inner airlock doors closing, he gently lowered the last cryopod to the floor. All six of the cryopods were now breaking their seals and spouting air. It would not be much longer before the patients inside would be thawing out and melting. They had not been given the protection that the *Inferno* crew had been given.

Bud did not have time to get an antidote made for them. The only thing he could do for them, now that their cryopods were opened, would be to try and reactivate the cryogenic process and re-seal the pods. Once he had a cure, he could treat them later. Bud tried again to reactivate the cryogenic sequence. The cryopods would not respond.

Bud knew he needed to go through antiviral decontamination before allowed access back into the station. Perhaps *Nelson Mandela* could just immerse him into a bath of sterilizing agents. It would be so much faster.

<Plant Thing?> Bud mindspoke.

<yes bud>

<Have you found Grace? How is she?>

<plant thing is sorry bud. plant thing does not have good news . . . .>

<What has happened to Grace? *Nelson Mandela,* what haven't you told me?>

'I am sorry, Bud. Dr. Lord has been taken hostage by the captain of the **Inferno.** ***He says he will kill her if the*** **Inferno** ***is not allowed to leave with all of its crew. He has her on board now.'***

"GRACE!"

Bud's anguished howl bounced off the walls of the Level Six Containment Facility. It was heard only by the station AI.

"GET ME OUT OF HERE, NOW, NELSON MANDELA! NOW!"

'Go to the airlock, Bud. Once inside, the decontamination procedure will begin. Thank you for getting the cryopods into quarantine. In doing so, you have saved everyone on the station.'

Bud staggered into the room's airlock, his entire body trembling.

"I HAVE TO SAVE GRACE, *Nelson Mandela!* I MUST GO TO HER NOW!'

Nelson Mandela started the sterilization process that would decontaminate Bud.

'How long will this take, Nelson Mandela?'

'The decontamination process will take fifteen minutes. However, reversal of the lockdown doors after scrubbing and sterilization of the air will take another twenty minutes.'

"GRACE! . . . " was all the station AI heard Bud wail, over and over, above the hissing sound of the viricidal sprays and the pounding of Bud's fists on the doors.

19. You First

Jeffrey Nestor dragged a blind-folded and gagged Hiro Al-Fadi behind him, through tunnels, crawlspaces, and ducts. He'd wrapped the surgeon's leg wound so tightly in impermeable dressings, that no blood trail was left. Unfortunately, it was slowing the twit down. If Hiro made any noise at all, even a whimper, Jeffrey would swat the surgeon in the head to make him shut up. The surgeon's hands were bound together in front of him with surgical tape and Jeffrey had Hiro on a leash made of elastic bandages forming a tightening noose around the surgeon's neck. If Hiro was too slow, Jeffrey would yank on the leash, effectively strangling the surgeon. Hiro was weakly trying to loosen the noose with his bound hands as he stumbled along sightlessly.

Jeffrey grinned as he forced the small man to limp quickly behind him. He had revelled in wrapping thick tape around Hiro's mouth. It had been sublime. Now Jeffrey was dragging Al-Fadi to one of his hiding places that was shielded by his disruptor tech. He pulled out a communication device and spoke softly into it. The device would encrypt and scramble the signal, bouncing it all over the station, before delivering his message to its recipient.

"*Nelson Mandela,* listen carefully. I have Dr. Hiro Al-Fadi in my possession. I demand that Dr. Grace Lord be handed over to me in exchange for your Chief of Staff . . . or I will kill him. You will bring Dr. Lord to a place of my choosing and I will exchange her for your Chief."

"It is impossible to comply with your wishes, Dr. Nestor. Dr. Grace Lord has been taken captive by Captain Alighieri of a ship called the *Inferno*. She is being held as a hostage on the ship. Even if we did want to hand Dr. Grace Lord over to you—which is not the case—it would not be possible. I shall warn you, however, that if any harm comes to Dr. Al-Fadi, you will face the harshest of penalties—mind erasure."

"You're lying!"

"I can assure you that I am serious. People have had their minds erased for much lesser crimes."

"I meant about Grace Lord!"

"I speak the truth, Dr. Nestor. Dr. Lord is a hostage on the *Inferno*."

"Where is this vessel?" Nestor grated.

"Where are you, Dr. Nestor?"

Jeffrey swore and cut the transmission. He was shaking. He turned to Hiro and kicked at the surgeon's wounded knee. The Chief of Staff squealed in agony behind his gag and collapsed to the floor. Jeffrey hissed at the surgeon to shut up and kicked him in the head. Hiro curled himself into a compact ball, which enraged Jeffrey more. He pulled his leg back and dealt blow after blow to the small man's skull. Jeffrey kicked Hiro in his face, his flanks, his hands, his knees. He kicked Hiro until he was swaying, barely able to keep his balance. He found himself panting and sweating and sucking air. He glared down at his now useless captive, who lay unconscious and unresponsive, blood trickling from his gag. The surgeon was still breathing but his respirations were ragged. Jeffrey gave the annoying megalomaniac a few more kicks in the head, for good measure. There was no need to keep the bastard alive, now.

He sat down at his console and searched the station for increased Security presence. No one was going to take Grace Lord away from him.

No one.

If anyone was going to kill Grace Lord, it had to be *him*. He'd kill whoever had her. No one was going to rob him of his revenge.

Jeffrey had to get to Receiving Bay Thirteen and he had to hurry, before the *Inferno* left the station. He just needed to get some firepower.

He walked out on Hiro Al-Fadi without a second thought, leaving the surgeon blind and bound, a curled, forgotten figure, bleeding out on the cold, forbidding floor.

Juan slid along the hangar floor as quickly as he could, trying to stay beneath the pulse blasts from the *Inferno's* perimeter defence. He'd disregarded the Chief Inspector's orders to get his leg looked after and had gone back out into the line of fire, to see if he could drag Hope to safety. He knew he would get in trouble afterwards, but the Chief Inspector worked under a different set of rules from Juan. In the military, you left no one behind. Hope had risked her life for the people of the station. If there was any chance of her still being alive, he wanted to put her in a cryopod to see if she could be saved.

The Security team's snipers were slowly picking off each weapon turret on the *Inferno.* The longer Hope lay in the line of fire, the greater the chance that she would die . . . if she was still alive. Juan held a blast shield before him, as he dragged himself towards the woman's motionless body. She was probably dead, but he had to make sure. The wound in his own left leg was interfering with his mobility, but he'd slapped on a narc patch and it was dulling things a little. He gritted his teeth and dragged himself by his elbows. This rescue was not a risk he'd have asked anyone else to take.

He'd demanded a cryopod be brought right to the hangar deck, so that Hope could be placed in it immediately if she had any sign of life. Juan tried not to think about his partner, Cindy, and his newborn baby, Estelle. He was sure Cindy would want to tear a strip off of him, if she knew what he was doing, but after what he saw Hope do to save all the people on the *Nelson Mandela,* how could he do less for her? That was the code Juan lived by. You got your friends out or died trying.

A pulse blast from the *Inferno* sheared off the top of Juan's hair and obliterated the top of the protective shield he carried. So much for hoping the shield would protect him from the ship's firepower. Not too far from him, Hope lay on her belly, eyes closed, body not moving. Juan wondered if he had risked his life to retrieve a corpse.

" . . . What the?"

Juan felt a band of iron squeeze his right ankle and he found himself being dragged back the way he had just crawled. He cursed under his breath, scrabbling at the floor, trying to stop his backward progress. He looked over his shoulder but could see no one behind him. How did the Chief Inspector manage this? Was she using some kind of tractor beam?

Juan saw a thick green cable whip by his head in the direction of the *Inferno.* He watched it and swore. The tip of the cable coiled around Hope's foot and gently began dragging her body in the same direction as Juan. He could swear it looked just like a plant vine!

Juan continued to be pulled until he was behind a safety barrier. He rolled over and sat up, to examine his ankle. Before he could do anything, the cable uncurled from his ankle and withdrew. Juan frowned up at the Chief Inspector, who was staring down at him, her blue eyes huge in her face.

"How did you do that?" Juan demanded.

"I didn't," Matthieu said, shaking her head slowly. "These green vines just came into the hangar and dragged you and that woman out of danger, all of their own accord." The Chief Inspector just shook her head, as if she could not believe what she was saying.

Emergency medical people ran up to examine Hope, while the vine around her ankle relaxed and withdrew. Her burnt body was covered in blood. Juan wanted to get to her, but his boss stood in the way and the med techs were quick. He did not see them putting her in a cryopod. That was a bad sign. He looked away.

Security people were continuing to fire upon the ship, when the Chief Inspector yelled for everyone to stop.

"The station AI has informed me that the captain of the *Inferno* has Dr. Grace Lord as his hostage. He is threatening to kill her, if we do not cease firing on his vessel. He is also demanding the release of his crew and safe passage off this station," Matthieu announced, her voice clipped and harsh.

"What's the plan?" one of the Security team members asked. Juan hoisted himself off the ground and moved to keep the Chief Inspector in sight.

"We have four of his crew alive and in custody. We'll try to negotiate. We cannot let the ship leave with Dr. Lord on board. That is imperative. Put the captured crew of the *Inferno* in one surveillance room, where the captain can see that his people are alive. I'll keep the captain talking as long as possible, as we mount a rescue mission for Dr. Lord.

"Where's Sergeant Rivera? Is he back yet? I want him organizing the rescue attempt as I negotiate with this asswipe. Corporal Rasmussen, you get your wound looked at immediately and that's an order! I don't want to see you storming that vessel or I will personally flay your hide!"

The Chief Inspector stalked away, gesturing and yelling orders. Juan noticed that a bunch of green vines seemed to be following the small woman. The funny-looking berries, that resembled little green eyeballs, tracked her position as she paced back and forth, as if she were the sun. Juan had the insane impression that those plant globules were actually watching his boss, listening to her.

Juan snorted. The narc patch was probably making him hallucinate or maybe he'd lost too much blood? Only an idiot would imagine what he was imagining: that those plant branches were understanding what the Chief Inspector was saying. Juan shook his head and rubbed his eyes. He decided he'd better go get his wound looked at and get off the narc patches.

He asked one of the medics if Captain Damien Lamont was going to make it and the woman could only shrug.

"He was still breathing when we put him in the cryopod, Corporal. It looked like the captain had sustained a bad head injury as well as chest trauma. Dr. Weisman is here, right now, looking at him. If anyone can save him, she will. Was he your friend?" she asked.

"Yes, he was," Juan said.

"I'm sorry," the medic said. "You look like you need treatment yourself. Sit down and let me look at that." The medic pointed at Juan's knee and motioned for him to sit on a portable gurney on wheels.

Juan lay back and the medic examined the wound. She told him that she had to go get some things to clean and dress the wound. The blast had gone through his left quadriceps muscle but had cauterized most of the tissue, so there had not been that much blood loss. Juan had to strip off the containment suit for her to treat him. She cleansed, sterilized, and inserted a wad of synthetic muscle into the hole; then bound it. As the medic did the dressing, Juan noticed some unusual movement off to the side of the hangar. He was again focusing on thick green vines. They were flowing slowly in the direction of the *Inferno.*

Juan jumped off the gurney, swearing when he landed, and limped over to peek around the portable protective barrier. He squinted, taking a long, hard look. His jaw sagged open. It seemed impossible that the green vines had understood what the Chief Inspector had been saying, but then what was the explanation for what the plant vines were doing? Juan scratched the top of his scorched head. He did not know how strong those vines were, but there seemed to be a lot of them, and more and more of them were piling on. They were certainly going to interfere with the *Inferno's* departure.

Juan called the Chief Inspector over.

"Didn't I tell you to get that leg wound looked at, Rasmussen?" Matthieu barked at him.

"You have to see this, Chief," Juan said, ignoring Matthieu's outburst.

"What?" she snapped, frowning at him after seeing nothing.

He carefully pointed. "See all those green vines? They've just coiled themselves around the tail and wings and landing gear of the *Inferno*. More seem to be coiling around the body of the ship. The *Inferno* won't be able to take off unless we chop all of those vines off!"

"Huh," Matthieu grunted. "It looks as if the plant vines do not want the *Inferno* to leave. I wonder if *Nelson Mandela* is controlling them."

"No, Chief Inspector. I am not. Those are Plant Thing's limbs."

" . . . The plant alien," Chelsea said flatly.

"Yes."

". . . Does Plant Thing communicate with you?" she asked.

"It communicates with Bud. Bud communicates its thoughts to me. I understand from Bud that Plant Thing can hear and understand you."

"Really? Well . . . tell Plant Thing, 'Thank you and to keep up the good work'," Matthieu said, her cheeks flaming.

"Plant Thing says it will do everything within its power to prevent the space ship from taking Grace away.

"It also says, 'You're welcome'."

Eric crept out from under one of the flight seats. He had not been seen by anyone and now there was only the captain and Grace Lord alive on the *Inferno*. The madman captain was now on the bridge, yelling at someone on the com system. The voice in Eric's head kept screaming for him to go kill the captain, but that seemed like an impossible task with the captain carrying a blaster and Eric having no weapon . . . and no arms. Eric wished the voice in his head would just shut up. Its constant bellowing made it difficult for Eric to think.

When the female in the containment suit was shot by her own captain, the voice in his head had gone orbital. The blaster she had held now lay on the floor, right at Grace Lord's feet. The voice kept yelling for him to: 'Get it! Get it! Get it! Kill him! Kill him! Kill him!'

Eric's skull was reverberating.

A more reasonable plan, as far as Eric was concerned, was for him to wake Grace and give her the blaster.

'No! No! No! No! No!' the voice in his head hissed. 'You must not give her the gun!'

Eric could see no reason why not. He did not see how he was going to hold up the blaster and fire it accurately. Which eye would he use? Grace, on the other hand, could probably protect herself. Wasn't she a lieutenant? Eric just blocked the voice, as best he could, and crept over to check on Grace.

Grace was still unconscious. Her chin looked markedly swollen. Her eyelids were fluttering. Perhaps she would be awakening soon? She had only been strapped into the flight seat, not tied into it. The male crewman had forgotten to tie Grace's hands, before he'd gone to get the containment suits. Now he was dead.

This was a very good development, as far as Eric was concerned. The captain probably thought Dr. Lord was bound and restrained. If Eric could wake her up and give her the blaster, she might have an excellent chance of escaping.

'*No! No! No! No! No!* Eric heard the voice shriek again. He rolled his many eyes in irritation. '*She must not escape!* the voice shrilled.

Eric chose to ignore the tirade in his head. With his tendrils, he dragged the blaster right to Grace's feet. He would try to climb up into her lap, pull up the blaster, and then try to rouse Grace as best he could. If he could get the blaster into her hands—*No! No! No! No! No!*—she would be able to kill the captain. Then Grace could help Eric get his 'Institute for the Study of Plant Thing and Dr. Glasgow' initiated.

With his tendrils, he released the latch on Grace's seatbelt, while stoically ignoring the verbal abuse being hurled at him. It was not much different to what he had experienced as a child.

He heard footsteps coming from the bridge. Eric leaped off Dr. Lord's lap and hid between the seat and the wall. He sent some of his tendrils up to wrap around Grace's wrists, making it look like her hands were tied. He sent other tendrils out to grab the blaster and pull it under her seat, out of view of the captain. Eric remained completely still, except for one eyeball with which he peeked up around Grace Lord's ankle. He had to see what the captain was doing.

The captain leaned right over Grace as Eric snatched his eyeball back and sunk as low as he could between the seat and the wall. Eric heard a sharp slap and then a few more. The strikes continued until Grace moaned. The voice in his head made Eric want to clutch his ears.

'*How dare he hit her!* raged the voice in Eric's mind. "*She's mine!*"

'Shut! Up!' Eric shouted back. 'I can't hear what the captain is saying to Grace!'

The voice hushed and they both listened.

'Dr. . . Grace. . . Lord," the captain drawled slowly, with a mixture of relish and scorn. "Welcome to the *Inferno.* I am Captain Danté Alighieri and you are my guest, or should I say, 'hostage'. I have awoken you from your pleasant sleep, because I don't want you to miss the power of my new weapon.

"As you can see out that window beside you, the lights in the hangar are back on. It appears that the auxiliary power on this station has kicked in. Quite frankly, I'm surprised. Considering there were no functional robots or androids, I thought your medical station would remain in the dark until everyone died.

"Still, that power won't last, as I'm about to knock it out again using the ship's EMP generator. It's charging as we speak. Soon, I'll discharge the weapon a second time and then we'll make our escape by blasting a hole through the hangar doors. We must hurry now, since ships from the Conglomerate are probably already on their way here. You and I must be long gone before then."

"What do you want?" Eric heard Grace ask, her speech sounding slurred.

"You foiled our attempts to purify the human race with the Hammer of God. This time, with you in my custody, there'll be no new vaccine to counter the new strain I've brought to the *Nelson Mandela.* This strain works faster. It's one hundred percent lethal. People will be melting into slush in twenty-four hours."

"What do you mean 'purify the human race'?" Grace asked, her voice sounding a little stronger.

"It's time to rid the human race of its sinners—the animal-adapted, the genetically-modified, the cyborgs and the augmented. Humans were made in the likeness of God, Dr. Lord. To alter that form, which was a divine gift from the Lord, is a crime against God and nature. When the impure are erased, the pure will re-inherit the colonies and re-populate the galaxy. Man shall be 'in the likeness of God' once again, as it was always meant to be," the captain intoned.

"You're mad," Grace said. "You use the word erase, but say what it is. Murder."

Eric heard another loud slap.

"You are the devil's spawn, witch. You interfered with God's work the first time around. You will not interfere this time. Your medical station will be the first of many stations and planets to fall. Only the pure will be protected and survive this second virus. Only the Chosen."

"And what makes you 'the Chosen'?" Grace demanded.

"We have the cure, the antidote, within us. We, the pure and unmodified."

"Unmodified? But you must be genetically modified if you contain the protection to this virus that you created. How are you not genetically modified? What you plan is mass murder. Don't claim it's God's will. Did God not say, 'Thou shalt not kill?'" Grace asked.

There was another loud slap and Eric heard Grace gasp.

"Do not speak the Lord's name, bitch!" the captain spat. "There's no sin in disposing of evildoers. God gave Man dominion over all the birds and beasts. He did not say to become one. All of these humans that have become half-man/half-beast are an affront to the Lord."

"You cannot kill all of the people on this station, just because you are prejudiced against the soldiers," Grace said. "They do what they're told and don't have much choice in that. If you wipe them and everyone else out, you will be the worst murderers in human history, manipulating religious doctrine to justify your horrid crimes. You fool no one but yourself. When you commit mass murder, you are the sinners. You are the evil. You are not promoting your God's cause. You are only promoting hatred. You cannot seriously believe you are in the right, when you murder innocent children and hundreds of unmodified humans."

"Innocent? You doctors create these man-beasts, these man-machines! Without doctors like you, these humans could not become the abominations they are! You are the Devil's minions. You do the Devil's work. But now you can watch, as God's wrath is meted out!"

The captain's hands came forward to unleash Grace's seatbelt. Finding it not latched, Alighieri frowned, but he grabbed Grace's forearm to yank her up out of the seat. He paused for a brief moment, to stare at the bindings around her wrists. A puzzled expression came over his face as he reached for the tendrils coiled around them. In that second, Eric whipped his tendrils off of Grace's arms, snapping their sharp tips into the captain's eyes. Alighieri stumbled backwards, grabbing his eyes and yelping in pain. Eric flipped the blaster up into Grace's lap.

Grace grabbed the blaster and jumped to her feet, but her legs were weak and she stumbled, falling to her knees on the floor. The captain, his eyes tearing, drew his blaster from his holster and tried to take aim at Grace. His eyes were watering and red.

Eric sprang up onto the flight seat and then, tensing all of his tendrils, sprang upwards towards Alighieri's gun. Eric wrapped his tendrils around the captain's right wrist and clamped the barrel of the blaster in his teeth. The heavy weight of Eric's skull dragged the blaster down so that it now pointed at the floor.

Alighieri shrieked in horror at the sight of Eric, chomping on the end of his weapon. He shook his blaster, trying to get Eric off, all the time cursing and howling. Eric tried to pull the blaster out of the captain's hand, by pushing on the coils wrapped around Alighieri's wrist and forearm while tugging at the gun with his teeth. The captain danced around the aisle, swinging Eric against the seats. Alighieri's eyes were bugging out of his head.

"Devil! Monster! Demon!" the captain yowled. "I knew you were in league with the Devil, Jezebel! Here's proof!"

Eric saw Grace raise her blaster and take aim at Alighieri.

"Shoot!" screamed the voice in Eric's head.

Then there was nothing.

Grace saw brilliant fire shoot from Alighieri's gun. The purple-coloured globus 'thing' exploded into a hundred pieces. She had to duck as gooey bits of fuzzy shrapnel flew towards her face disrupting her aim. She fired her gun, but Alighieri managed to dive out of the way, scrambling away from her. He fired off a barrage at her, as he ran towards the bridge.

One of Grace's shots caught Alighieri in the left shoulder. He lurched but kept running. Grace jumped up and dashed after him. As he passed through the bridge doorway, he slapped the touchpad that would close and lock the door behind him. Grace immediately fired a shot at the door control panel to prevent the door from closing. Then she propelled herself through the entrance, diving into a front somersault, as a blast seared the air just above her head. She lunged for cover behind one of the flight chairs on the bridge.

The bridge of the *Inferno* was dimly lit. It had a wide, black console running around the entire semicircular chamber, with viewing screens above the monitors. There were eight pedestal flight chairs, solidly mounted into the floor of the vessel, before the monitors and a central captain's chair in the middle of the bridge. Grace peered from behind the back of the rearmost flight seat. She heard Alighieri ordering the ship to initiate its launch sequence. The engines of the *Inferno* roared into action and the vessel began to thrum.

"Stop!" shouted Grace. "You can't fly from this hangar. There's no way out!"

Alighieri turned and fired at Grace. She ducked behind the flight seat. She fired back, in the direction of the captain's voice, as he rained a barrage of blasts at her. She could hear *Nelson Mandela*'s voice over the loudspeaker, demanding that the *Inferno* turn its engines off. Alighieri was obviously ignoring the request. Was he planning to fly the *Inferno* while people were still in the hangar?

Through the forward viewscreen of the bridge, Grace could see brilliant flashes of light. These were instantly followed by the sounds of explosions. Alighieri was using the ship's lasers to fire on the huge airlock doors of the Receiving Bay. He was trying to blast his way out of the hangar. Usually, ships in the Receiving Bays were towed via cargo bots into the huge Docking Airlocks, where the atmosphere was pumped out, before the Outer Space Doors were opened. Then, and only then, were the ships allowed to ignite their engines. Grace could see figures in the Receiving Bay hangar racing for the inner doors to the station proper. If the Receiving Bay outer hull was blown open, everyone in the hangar would be sucked out into space with the escaping atmosphere!

The ship started bucking and pitching like a rocking horse. Grace was tossed onto the floor of the bridge. The captain fell to the ground as well, swearing and cursing as he rolled about. Blaster fire exploded around Grace, as she hung on to the base of the flight chair with one arm. With her other hand, she returned fire at Alighieri. Neither were able to hit their target because of the ship's rocking and yawing motion.

Grace had to find a way to shut off the ship's engines. She had to stop the ship's lasers from putting a hole in the station's hull. Unfortunately, she was being tossed back and forth as if she were attached to the end of a whip. She had never been on a ship that launched so erratically before. It was making it impossible for her to shoot accurately but it was also making it difficult for the captain to shoot her. Perhaps this shaking had something to do with the EMP weapon?

Grace took a look at the ship's viewscreens. She gasped. Were those long, green vines stretching towards the *Inferno* from different directions?

<Plant Thing! Are you holding onto this ship?>

<grace it is so good to hear your voice. plant thing is so happy. bud was so worried. now he is coming>

<Bud?> Grace asked, her pulse pounding loudly in her ears. *<Bud is alive? I . . . I thought Bud was destroyed by the EMP blast!>*

<bud is fine grace. bud is coming>

<Tell Bud to stay away, Plant Thing! He will get shot! I am on the bridge of the Inferno *and I will shut the vessel down as soon as I take care of the captain!>*

<bud is not listening grace. Plant Thing is sorry. bud is here>

The next moment, enormous pounding shook the *Inferno.* Grace hung on to the base of the chair as she felt the ship quake. The ship rocked and rolled and now shook to the impact of deafening blows. Grace imagined a giant punching the side of the *Inferno* with monstrous fists. The side of the ship was taking such a beating that Grace envisioned it crumpling inwards under the onslaught.

Then came the ear-splitting screech of tearing metal. This shearing noise was followed by a tremendous crash.

Grace turned her blaster on the bank of consoles around the bridge and fired. She hoped to disable the vessel. As the screens and consoles sparked and exploded, stinking smoke filled the bridge. Grace had to squint to see through the murk. She could not see Alighieri.

She heard a very familiar voice call out. The sound brought tears to her eyes and she almost sobbed.

"Grace? Are you all right?" It was Bud.

"Bud, do not come in here!" Grace screamed. "Stay back!"

The chair behind which she was hiding was suddenly shuddering from a bombardment of pulse rifle fire. Her skin felt like it was on fire from the tremendous heat coming through the chair, which was turning into a brilliant, vermilion flame as it melted to slag. The acrid odour seared her nostrils and made her cough. Grace dove behind the next closest flight seat, as she fired repeatedly towards where she thought the captain was hiding.

Bud appeared in the doorway to the Inferno's bridge. In the next instant, a brilliant beam from Alighieri's pulse rifle struck Bud in the chest, blowing his body back out of the bridge.

"*Bud!*" screamed Grace. She knew where Alighieri was now. She jumped up, firing continuously at the captain, as she ran at him. The red hot pulse rifle dropped from Alighieri's hands and he fumbled for his blaster. One more shot and a smoking black hole replaced Alighieri's face.

"That's for Bud, Asshole," Grace snarled. Then she turned and raced out of the bridge.

Bud lay in the centre aisle, not far from the hatchway opening. His chest had an enormous blackened hole in it. Security personnel, all decked out in combat gear, were pouring through the open hatchway. Grace told them that she was fine and that the captain was dead. They flowed around her to secure the ship. Grace knelt over Bud, staring at his chest wound.

"Bud? Can you hear me? Can you respond?"

Bud lay unresponsive, blank blue eyes open. The smoking crater took up almost Bud's entire chest. There was no pumping blood, no damaged heart, no torn up organs within the thoracic cavity. Grace did not know what to do. Bud did not have the anatomy of a human. He no longer possessed the design of an android. She did not know how to treat his injuries. She caressed his face and it still felt warm, which made her hopeful. Perhaps his nanobots could heal his body?

<Bud, don't leave me!> Grace mindspoke, her hands on either side of his face. Bud looked so beautiful and peaceful, as if he were merely sleeping. <Bud, listen to me. It can't end like this. You must hang on.>

"Excuse me," a voice said, rudely shoving Grace out of the way.

"Wha . . . at?" Grace squawked, her temper igniting as she found herself knocked back on her butt.

"Help me roll him over," a very familiar, overbearing voice ordered.

"Why you . . ." Grace snarled, struggling with the overwhelming urge to pound this person to mush.

"I know what I'm doing, Dr. Lord, unlike you. Praying over Bud will not save him. Now, you can snap out of it and be of some help, or you can get out of the way and let someone else give me a hand," the arrogant voice said.

It was as if Grace had been slapped in the face. Her fingers curled like talons. She managed to stop her hands from reaching for Moham Rani's neck and lowered them to grasp Bud's shoulder instead. Taking some calming deep breaths, she helped turn Bud over onto his right side. Then she watched as Rani pulled up a flap on Bud's lower back and plugged a thick cord into the socket hidden there. The cable led to a huge portable generator on a wheeled trolley, sitting outside the ship.

"We need to get Bud to your suite as swiftly as possible," the obstetrician said, as he got up and motioned for some Security people to come over with a hand-held stretcher. Grace gazed at them come through the hole in the side of the *Inferno,* where the hatchway door had been torn from its hinges. The massive metal door lay like a crumpled piece of paper on the hangar floor just outside.

Moham Rani looked over to see what Grace was staring at.

"Yes. Bud tore that door off of the ship with his bare hands to come save you. Now it is your turn to help save him, Dr. Lord. Come. We must hurry."

The young obstetrician directed the Security people to lift the body of the android onto the stretcher, without dislodging the power cord. They placed Bud on his side. Outside the *Inferno* was a wheeled gurney onto which they placed the stretcher. Rani ordered them to take Bud and the portable generator to Doctor Lord's suite as swiftly as was humanly possible. He gave the Security people the address and then started off after them. Grace gingerly got to her feet to follow. She stepped through the torn hatchway opening out into the hangar.

She felt a tight grip on her left upper arm and she was jerked around. A hard cylinder, like the end of a blaster barrel, jammed roughly into her abdomen. Grace tried to pull her arm away, her anger sizzling. She was about to lash out at whoever was holding her . . . until she stared into the dark brown eyes that haunted her nightmares.

Her throat spasmed tightly.

"Do not make a sound, Grace," the deep, velvety voice said softly. "No one is going to take you from me. You are mine."

Jeffrey Nestor thrust the gun barrel harder into her midsection.

"No. She's mine," a voice said, coming from behind Nestor. The psychiatrist was spun around and Grace heard a loud smack. Nestor was falling backwards into Grace. She saw that Nestor had been punched by a tall, blonde stranger, who then grabbed Grace and tried to pull her behind himself.

Grace was off balance. The heel of her left foot got caught on the edge of the discarded hatchway door as she was yanked around. Falling backwards, her head smacked the hangar floor. Grace blinked rapidly, trying to clear her vision. When her head cleared, she saw Nestor struggling with the blonde man over the blaster. The young man was dressed in inpatient coveralls and Grace did not recognize him at all.

She rolled over onto her hands and knees and tried to get up. Vertigo disoriented her and she almost fell over. She wondered just how many blows to her head she'd had lately. She had to get up and help the patient who was battling Nestor.

'Get up, Grace!' the little voice in her head screamed.

'I'm trying!' Grace snapped.

She got her feet under her and leaped at Nestor. There was a brilliant flash followed by an agonizing cry. Grace saw the blonde stranger collapse to his knees, his hands rising to cover a face that was only half a face now. Grace grabbed the blaster in Nestor's left hand, to prevent him from shooting the patient a second time.

"You bitch!" Nestor snarled. He elbowed her hard in the gut and then in the chin, yanking the blaster from her hands. Grace found herself falling backwards, beside the twisted hatchway door. Blood spattered the ground from her torn mouth.

Nestor looked down at her with a smug expression on his angelic face. Grace tried to get up but her legs were not cooperating. She wanted to launch herself at Nestor. She was not going down without a fight. If she did the unexpected, she might be able to get the blaster off of him. If not, she would make him shoot her. That was probably better than anything else he had planned for her.

Something rapidly slid along the ground and struck her left hand. It was out of the line of sight of Nestor. Grace closed her fingers around a smooth, familiar shape.

"Grace, I have just about had enough. If one more person tries to grab the blaster in my hand . . . Never mind. Are you going to come peacefully with me or are you ready to die?" Jeffrey Nestor asked, as he slowly raised the blaster.

"You first," Grace growled and shot Nestor in the face.

20. The Embodiment of Despair

"*Nelson Mandela,* I need nanobots—lots of nanobots—and I need them *now*!" demanded Moham Rani.

"I have no androids available to supply you with nanobots, Dr. Rani. I am sending some biomedical technicians to the Manufacturing Wing with a large canister to obtain a supply of stored ones for you. They will transport the nanobots to Dr. Lord's quarters as swiftly as they can."

Moham pointed at a couple of Security people.

"Get to Manufacturing as quickly as possible. Help the technicians get the nanobots to Dr. Lord's suite stat!" Rani ordered.

They ran off to assist the technicians. He followed the personnel pushing Bud's gurney and his attached portable generator towards the cargo lift. Moham looked around for Grace. He thought she was right behind him but could not see her anywhere. He frowned. What could that woman be up to now?

Flighty, sometimes, these women were, Moham thought. Impressed, he was not. It was obvious, from Dr. Lord's inability to stick with the task, that women were, indeed, the weaker sex. Apparently, the terror and violence of firefights and battle were too much for her. No surprise, then, that he had found her frozen on the floor next to Bud's body. Well, it was lucky that men were around to do the tough, dangerous stuff. Women, like Grace, needed to remain in hospitals planetside, where it was safe, or at home, having babies. Not on space stations where anything could happen.

How lucky it was for Bud that Moham Rani had stepped in to take over!

If he hadn't been following Octavia Weisman around the station, he'd never have been in a position to help. When the power had gone out and Moham had heard Octavia scream, his heart had plummeted down that shaft with her. Relief had flooded him until he'd been knocked unconscious. He'd not been out long though; when he awakened, he could still hear Octavia and Jude conversing. Feeling around the edge of the shaft, he'd located the ladder and had begun climbing down after them. Moham knew that Octavia scarcely knew he existed, but he was compelled to see, with his own eyes, that she was fine.

He'd silently followed the couple, accompanied by a tall, blonde man, into Receiving Bay Thirteen. That was when he'd heard all the commotion in the ship hangar. Seeking out the source of the thunderous pounding, he'd witnessed Bud hammering on a space vessel with his fists, amidst a rain of pulse fire from the ship. Security officers, scattered throughout the Receiving Bay, were firing back at the vessel. Oddly, the space vessel seemed to be entwined with thick green cables that resembled . . . vines?

Bud was in danger. As authoritatively as he could, Moham ordered someone to bring a portable power generator and a wheeled stretcher as quickly as possible, just in case. He'd had to use his considerable powers of persuasion to get what he wanted, especially with the Chief Inspector around. She'd almost thrown him out of the hangar! But Moham had feared—justifiably!—that Bud might get injured and he'd insisted that he must remain, in case Bud required his considerable expertise. After all, he'd saved Bud's life once already. Thank goodness Sergeant Rivera had been around to vouch for him. Moham could not understand why such an important and dangerous position as Chief Inspector of Security was filled by a young girl.

Moham wrung his hands, as they approached the cargo shaft. He worried that the power might go off while they were in the cargo lift. He suffered from claustrophobia.

There was a shout from behind and Grace ran up, her face a mess of abrasions, lacerations, and contusions. Her lips were puffed up and split, her left eye was swollen shut, and it looked like the hair on the top of her head was singed off, as if by blaster fire. Moham's eyes widened in shock. He'd not really had a good look at Grace, when he had been bent over the fallen Bud inside the space vessel.

"What happened to you?" Moham asked Grace.

Grace just looked at the obstetrician and said, "Nothing. You should see the other guy." And she left it at that.

When the cargo lift reached the floor where Grace's suite was located, Moham breathed a sigh of relief. He jumped out first, waving to the

Security people to pull the stretcher and generator out quickly. Grace gave Moham a strange look and assisted the others in moving Bud's stretcher and generator out. Then she flew with the wheeled stretcher down the corridor, racing towards her suite. The people pushing the portable generator—not Moham Rani—had to race to keep up. She slapped her palm against the access pad and the doors to her suite opened wide. Moham had difficulty keeping up with the rest of them and arrived, huffing and puffing. He was not used to such exertion and was working up a sweat!

"Haul ass, Rani!" bellowed Grace.

Moham's face reddened at being castigated by a woman in front of the other male subordinates, but he decided to be gracious and say nothing. Perhaps he was finally gaining some wisdom in this new world.

Grace threw the doors to her closet open and pulled out Bud's recharging cord that had been installed when Bud had insisted on being her personal bodyguard. She unplugged the cable from the portable generator from his back and replaced it with the one in her hand. She then asked the station AI when the nanobots would arrive.

"They will be in your suite very shortly, Dr. Lord."

"Please tell them to hurry. This is an emergency."

"They are coming as quickly as they can, Dr. Lord."

"Thank you, *Nelson Mandela*."

Grace paced around the stretcher, as she stared at Bud's unconscious form. She took one of Bud's hands and examined it. There was no evidence of bruising, swelling, bleeding, or torn nails. His hand looked pristine and immaculate. Moham could hardly believe that those perfect hands had pummelled a space ship and had torn a massive metal door off the vessel, yet he had witnessed the act. Why was there no damage to Bud's hands? Were they indestructible or did they possess incredibly rapid regeneration? Moham looked at Grace's hands. They were blackened, scraped, bruised, and bleeding from torn nails. He shook his head. As a surgeon, he expected Grace to take much better care of herself and her hands.

Grace cradled Bud's perfect right hand in her devastated ones and brought it to her cheek.

"Bud?" she asked.

Bud lay immobile on the stretcher.

She closed her eyes and looked away. Moham thought she was praying, until he heard her sniffle. He whispered a prayer to his own gods for the android's recovery. It couldn't hurt.

A commotion outside the suite announced the arrival of the nanobots. A small group of people in containment suits wheeled in a large container on a trolley. One of the suited technicians tried to shoo everyone out of the room but Grace stared the person down. Moham insisted on staying, as well. Bud, after all, was his patient. Grace looked at Moham with a raised eyebrow.

They shifted Bud carefully onto his back, careful not to dislodge the power cable. Grace and Moham agreed to at least stay back, as the tech decanted a few litres of the nanobot solution into a special container and then poured them into Bud's chest wound. Moham ordered the technician to command the new nanobots to obtain programming from Bud's existing nanobots. The woman nodded and input the commands into a handheld. Grace and Moham stared at the wound.

The deep, burnt out cavity began to seethe and swirl and boil, as furious activity was stimulated all along the entire open surface of Bud's wound. The massive hole began to visibly fill in, as the nanobots rapidly rebuilt Bud's chest from the edges inward. The gaping crater became a large hole, then a medium-sized hollow, then a shallow indentation, and then a perfect chest wall within minutes. Grace gasped when she saw Bud take his first breath. She blinked her eyes to hold back the moisture when she witnessed Bud's rebuilt chest rising and falling in regular and effortless respirations.

"Why do you look so upset?" Moham asked, in confusion. "Should you not be happy that Bud is completely healed?"

Grace's sorrowful expression took Moham's breath away. Looking into the despair in Grace's eyes made Moham's own eyes begin to water. For a moment, Grace said nothing.

" . . . Moham," she sighed, "Bud's memory—all that he was—was stored in his chest. His liquid crystal data matrix, which contained 'who' he was, would have been completely destroyed by the pulse fire. The nanobots can rebuild Bud's body, but they cannot give him back what was the most important part of him—his mind. Bud is *gone* . . . and I never had a chance to tell him I loved him."

She turned away.

Moham stood, embarrassed, hesitating in indecision. Slowly, he raised his hand and placed it on Grace's back, patting it very softly. She turned her face into his shoulder and cried. The flood gates had burst open.

Moham stood immobile, eyes bulging in panic, sweat beading on his forehead. He had no idea what to do.

"Grace?"

Grace choked, mid-sob, and spun around to look at Bud.

". . . Bud?" Grace whispered, her voice rising into a squeak.

"Why are you crying, Grace?" Bud asked, a frown on his perfect features. His sparkling blue eyes showed worry. Bud sat up and handed Grace a tissue from one of his pockets.

"How . . . ?" Grace asked, wiping her eyes. "How do you know who I am, Bud, when your memory was destroyed?"

"My memory was not destroyed, Grace," Bud said.

"But . . . but I saw your chest blown out! It was a huge black hole! There was nothing left in your chest," Grace said, pointing to the exact spot where the blast wound had been.

"My memory is no longer stored there, Grace," Bud said.

"What? It isn't? Then . . . where is your memory stored, Bud?"

There was a pause and Bud looked downwards.

"Lower down," he said, shyly. "Dr. Weisman said the best place for men to keep their brains was not in their heads but in their . . . ah, she said it would be a good idea to keep the memory down below."

Grace wrapped Bud up in an exuberant bear hug. She was crying and smiling at the same time. Moham could see that Bud did not know whether to be distressed or happy.

"Are you all right, Grace?" Bud asked, his eyes widening. He examined her battered face, his features crinkled with concern.

"I am now," Grace said, sniffling.

She grinned and grabbed Bud's right hand tightly in both of hers.

"But before anything else happens or anything else disturbs us, I want you to know right now, Bud, that I love you and I will always love you."

Bud met Grace's tear-filled stare with large blue eyes, shining and clear. He wrapped his left hand gently around hers.

"From the picosecond I first saw you and for every moment since then, I have loved you, Grace Lord, and I always will."

Moham burst into tears.

Octavia looked down upon the gorgeous face of Jeffrey Nestor, lying on the ground stunned, and scowled.

"His face is perfect! How is that possible?" she demanded, hands on her hips.

"Because you handed me a stunner, Octavia, and I slid that stunner to Grace. If you'd have handed me a blaster, I would have slid a blaster to Grace and she would have blown the man's face off. Unfortunately, stunners do not burn faces off, nor do they kill people. Grace only stunned the bastard," Jude said.

"Damn it! Oh well, probably all for the better. Grace strikes me as a sensitive soul. She's probably not at the stage yet where she can accept murdering someone for the greater good," Octavia said.

"And you are?" Jude asked, looking at his partner with an expression of surprise.

"Of course," Octavia said, frowning at her partner. "In the case of a murderous psychopath like Jeffrey Nestor? Absolutely."

"I am shocked—and a little perturbed, Octavia—that you, as a physician, believe any homicide is justifiable." Jude was staring at the psychiatrist's left shoulder, that was oozing some blood.

"Go get a blaster, Jude, and I'll do the job right," Octavia whispered, looking around surreptitiously.

"I will not," Jude answered, an indignant expression coming over his face. "I won't be an accomplice to murder and I won't let you stain your soul with that crime, even though the monster deserves it. I don't want you keeping yourself up at night, wracked with guilt over killing this man."

"I won't be. I promise. Besides, I was going to get you to do it," Octavia said, with a smirk.

"Oh, thanks. So I could lay awake at night wracked with guilt, I suppose," Jude said, rolling his eyes upwards. "I think I'll pass on that opportunity, Octavia. Thank you very much. Perhaps it would be best if we just go and get someone from Security to arrest him. There seems to be a lot of those people hanging around."

"Right. Like arresting him did a lot of good the last few times? Wait! What are we doing wasting time on this bastard? We need to see what happened to Grace's father! Nestor shot him. He may not be dead. Get a cryopod over here, Jude."

"On it," Jude said and dashed off.

Octavia knelt down by the fallen young man, who lay unconscious just outside the *Inferno's* tattered hatchway. Octavia sighed when she gazed down upon the devastation that was once a very handsome face.

"Oh dear," Octavia breathed, as she felt for a pulse. Captain Lord had received a blast that looked like it had gone in the right cheek and had exited his left cheek. He was breathing with difficulty. His nose was gone and the underlying tissues were a mess. His mouth was shredded muscle and charred nu-skin, surrounding ragged bits of gums and sheared off teeth. The poor man would need a new face . . . if he survived. His breathing was harsh and wheezing; his pulse was thready and barely palpable. There was a lot of blood on the ground. Octavia was worried that Alexander Lord may have also sustained significant head trauma. She put pressure on the bleeding with her glove.

"Hurry, Jude," Octavia yelled.

The director arrived pushing a cryopod on a wheeled trolley, with the help of a tiny Security officer, a woman dressed in a containment suit. They threw open the lid.

"Careful," Octavia said. "I don't know about his cervical spine."

"We'll be careful, Octavia," Jude said. "If you just look after his neck, we will lift him onto the stretcher and then place him inside the cryopod."

"Certainly," Octavia said, taking the neck brace offered her by the security woman. As she carefully adjusted the brace around Alexander Lord's neck, she looked down at his patient garb. It was the outfit given patients post-operatively, when they had gotten to the ward. Lord even had station slippers on his feet.

What had he been doing wandering around the Receiving Bays? How did he get the idea that Grace Lord was his daughter? If he was indeed Grace's father—and he looked much too young to be that—Octavia prayed that he would survive long enough to meet her. They placed his body within the cryopod as carefully as they could.

Suddenly, the engines of a ship within the Receiving Bay ignited and the roar was deafening in the huge hangar. Jude, Octavia, and the Security officer all jumped simultaneously and looked towards the activating vessel. It was adjacent to the *Inferno.*

"We've got to get out of here!" yelled Jude, as he slammed the lid of the cryopod on Alexander Lord and activated the cryogenic sequence. He started to push the wheeled trolley towards the inner doors of the Receiving Bay.

Octavia feared that the ship was trying to blow a hole in the outer airlock doors of the hangar. They were all going to get sucked out into space if they did not get out of the hangar in time!

She leaned into the cryopod with all of her strength, pushing as hard as she could. She glanced over to see if Jeffrey Nestor still lay on the ground. No one, not even him, deserved to be sucked out into deep space without a suit. Surprisingly, his body was no longer where they had last seen it. Perhaps Security had gathered him up.

Everyone in the hangar was racing for the inner hangar doors. The great vines that had been wrapped around the *Inferno* were withdrawing from the hangar as well, grabbing people on the way. Actinic pulses from the escaping ship began striking the Receiving Bay's outer airlock doors. The repeated booming of the proton pulses impacting and weakening the gargantuan panels, concussed their ears. Jude and Octavia screamed with the pain as, unable to cover their ears, they shoved the unwieldy cryopod towards the inner doors.

Jude pushed Octavia ahead of the cryopod.

"Go, Octavia!" he yelled above the ruckus. They had only a few meters to go to get through the inner doors, which were crowded with fleeing people. A long green tendril shot out to wrap around Octavia's waist and pull her through, while a second vine wrapped around the cryopod. The small Security Officer screamed at Jude to go through, ahead of the cryopod.

"No!" Jude hollered, but the security woman swore at him and pushed him forcefully towards the opening.

"Get through those doors and help pull the cryopod through!" the security woman yelled, above the reverberating explosions. Her voice sounded so distant in Jude's ears.

Jude was grabbed around the waist by a strong green coil and was pulled through the Receiving Bay doors as they were closing. The alarms were deafening. He was being dragged inside, right behind Octavia, but he refused to relinquish his hold on the cryopod.

In the next instant, air from the station was howling past Jude, being sucked into the Receiving Bay. The outer airlock doors had been breached. The battering of the station hull did not cease, as the escaping atmosphere picked up speed. The hangar was now open to deep space and spewing atmosphere.

A gale force wind was roaring through the opening between the inner doors as the lockdown doors tried to close. Anything not fastened down was being sucked out past Jude, the Security woman, and the cryopod, which was being slammed in the middle by the closing lockdown doors. The vine that had wrapped around the cryopod was severed by those doors. Ear-splitting alarms were clamouring while the inner doors repeatedly kept trying to shut.

"Hang on!" bellowed Jude to the Security woman. Her body was being sucked straight out from the rear handle of the cryopod by the loss of atmosphere. Jude jumped on top of the cryopod and grabbed the woman's wrists tightly, as she hung onto the handle of the cryopod. The air was squeezed out of Jude as the vine tried to pull him back. Vines slid by Jude to wrap around the length of the cryopod and yank. Jude saw a tendril tip coil around the Security Officer's forearm.

Jude stared into huge, frightened blue eyes.

"Hang on!" he shouted at the woman. She was small. He could pull her in with him. He just had to hang on. "Don't let go! I have you!"

"Pull!" screamed Octavia, at the top of her lungs. "Pull, damn you all!"

Others had joined her to help pull the cryopod through. As Jude was yanked inside, he felt his grip on the Security officer start to slip. He screamed at his useless, weak hands. His voice was whipped away by the deafening wind.

The lockdown doors kept trying to close on the cryopod, bashing its sides, again and again, jolting Jude and the Security woman. Vines seemed to be pushing against the doors, to keep them open. As the cryopod finally slid through the inner lockdown doors, two bodies went flying out, overtop of Jude. Vines whipped out after them and snagged them in the air, but one of the bodies smacked into the Security woman, tearing her wrists from Jude's fingers and the tendril that held onto her.

"NO!" Jude screamed in horror.

A thin green tendril shot past Jude towards the woman. Its whip-like tip managed to coil its end around her one hand as she was flying towards the great rift in the hull. Jude almost cried in relief. Then he was writhing in pain as he felt something bite into his cheek. The torn end of the tendril that had caught the Security officer was now flapping in the wind. Jude howled in anguish, as he saw the white figure hurtle away, like a tiny leaf in a tornado.

" . . . NO, NO, NO," he wailed, as he was dragged inwards towards safety. It was now extremely difficult to breathe and everyone was gasping. Jude lay face down on the cryopod as he heard the inner doors clang shut.

Lockdown.

Jude slid off of the cryopod onto the ground, covering his face with his hands. Octavia bent down to curl her arms around him. The constriction around his waist withdrew.

"I couldn't hold on, Octavia! I couldn't hold on tight enough to pull her in!" Jude whispered, his teeth chattering. "She . . . she . . . her wrists slipped out of my hands! I let her go!" His body shook with shame, wracked by guilt.

"No, Jude. Listen to me." Octavia grabbed Jude's face and turned it towards her. "Look at me. She was torn out of your hands by a force so much greater than the strength in your hands. You're lucky we were able to keep you from flying out after her. She ordered you to go ahead of her. I saw her shove you towards the doors. You did what you were told to do, by someone in charge. What happened here wasn't your fault. Whoever's operating that ship, firing a hole in the hangar wall, is to blame for her death and everyone else who was lost just now."

"Who's flying that ship?" Jude demanded to the air. "Who is the psycho, blasting a hole in the outer airlock doors, while people were still in the hangar?"

People looked at him, blankly, shaking their heads. Their expressions were bleak; they were all in shock.

"Nestor," Octavia said suddenly, her tone full of outrage. "When I looked around to see where he was, his body was gone. He'd been lying beside the *Inferno,* only stunned, when we went to check on Captain Lord. My guess is it was him."

"The figure seen on surveillance, entering the escaping ship, fits the appearance of Jeffrey Nestor, Dr. Weisman. I'm afraid your guess has a high probability of being correct."

"Who was the Security officer? Who was she?" Jude demanded, his voice cracking. He searched the distraught faces of the Security officers around him. "Can anyone at least tell me her name?"

Eden Rivera stepped forward, his face creased in despair. He met Jude's eyes with a look of such pain and loss, that it made Jude wince.

"Her name was Chelsea Matthieu and she was our Chief Inspector."

21. He Did Not Sleep

<bud?>

<Yes, Plant Thing?>

<plant thing has found a little human that is very close to nutrients. it does not move to plant thing's pokes. it has red sap oozing from it. plant thing wants to know if bud would like to see it>

<Where is this little human, Plant Thing?>

<plant thing will show bud but bud must hurry. follow the vine that is all lit up bud. hurry hurry hurry hurry>

<Just light up the entire route, Plant Thing. I'll follow at maximum time phase.>

<plant thing will try>

"Grace, I must to go," Bud said, jumping off the gurney inside her suite.

"I know. I heard Plant Thing, too. Are you well enough to move? Your chest only just healed. Have you recharged enough?" Grace asked, touching his arm.

"I'm about forty percent recharged, Grace. Enough to rescue this child. I'll come back here and finish recharging afterwards."

"Hurry, Bud," Grace said. "But come right back to finish recharging. No getting distracted and going off to save the station again."

"I must manufacture the antidote for the new virus for everyone on the station, Grace. That cannot wait," Bud said.

"Go rescue that child. Then I expect you back here to finish your recharge. I'll help you make the vaccine."

Grace smiled at Bud and Bud stared at the most beautiful face in his universe, with its multiple bruises, singed scalp, split lip, and swollen purple chin. He hesitated, shifting back and forth on his feet, knowing he needed to leave. Then he quickly leaned forward and kissed Grace gently on her swollen lips, before leaving. He was careful not to set off a sonic boom until he was a reasonable distance away.

He heard, as he was exiting, Doctor Rani burst into tears again.

Bud raced along corridors, following Plant Thing's illuminated glowglobes. He passed frozen figures and downed droids. Plant Thing's vines were everywhere but only certain vines were lit up. Bud sped at maximum time phase until he entered a narrow crevice behind a wall panel into the space between the walls, where all the wiring, ducts, and conduits were located. The course was tight and convoluted. Bud was surprised that one of Plant Thing's branches had discovered this route. His olfactory sensors detected blood in the darkness.

He followed a single, glowing vine into a dimly lit, low-ceilinged nook. There he found an unconscious Dr. Al-Fadi, bound, gagged, blindfolded, and badly beaten. When Bud called out his creator's name, there was no movement from the man, no evidence of any response. Bud bent down and checked Dr. Al-Fadi's pupils and breathing. The one pupil was markedly dilated. Bud had to get Dr. Al-Fadi to an operating room immediately. He gently checked the surgeon's neck and thankfully did not find any unusual deviations or swellings in his cervical spine. Bud had to take the chance, while transporting his mentor, that Dr. Al-Fadi's neck was not fractured. There just was no time. Dr. Al-Fadi had to be operated on immediately, to clear the blood from his brain, or he would die.

Bud scooped his creator up in his arms and headed back along the path, as quickly as he dared.

'Nelson Mandela?'

Yes, Bud?'

'Can you get a neurosurgical OR ready stat? Tell the nurses! Call a neurosurgeon and an anesthetist, if anyone is available. Dr. Al-Fadi has an intracranial bleed and it needs to be decompressed immediately. I don't know how much time I have! I'll be there in two point five seconds.'

'N1 OR1. Head straight in.'

Bud raced with his creator in his arms.

<Grace? It was Dr. Al-Fadi! He's dying!>

<Can you save him, Bud?>

<I . . . I don't know, Grace! He has lost a lot of blood and is bleeding intracranially!>

<You know what to do, Bud. Don't wait for anyone. Just bore a hole the old fashioned way. Take the pressure off of his brain before it cones.>

<. . . All right, Grace. I'll do as you say. I'm in N1 OR2 now.>

<Start the procedure now, Bud. Do not wait. Dr. Al-Fadi is in the best of hands.>

<Thank you for having faith in me, Grace.>

<I do, Bud. We all do.>

"Dr. Lord?"

"Yes, *Nelson Mandela?*" Grace answered, still trying to comfort a weeping Dr. Rani.

"Dr. Cech has been located inside a cryopod in M1 OR2. According to the cryopod readout, he has a terrible chest wound. His injury is life-threatening, since his heart has been damaged as well as part of his lungs by a shot from a blaster. He has lost an enormous amount of blood, which the cryopod is trying to correct. It rates his chances of survival, as less than five percent."

"*What?* We need to start printing him heart and lungs, immediately! Do you have any idea what happened to him, *Nelson Mandela?*"

"The cryopod is in M1 OR2, Dr. Lord. Dr. Al-Fadi and Dr. Cech were operating on a gorilla-adapted soldier in there, just before the EMP strike. Presumably, the attack on Dr. Cech occurred during the power failure. There are no surveillance recordings of what happened in that operating room, because of the power outage, but the body of one of the operating room nurses was found dead outside that operating theatre and the patient they were operating on was also found dead, killed by blaster fire to the head. Dr. Al-Fadi went missing from that OR and Dr. Cech's body was found haphazardly placed within the cryopod."

"Nestor," Grace said.

"The probability is high that it was Dr. Nestor, although it seems strange that he would shoot Dr. Cech and then try to save him."

"We will have to get our answers from Dr. Cech or Dr. Al-Fadi once we heal them, *Nelson Mandela.* However, we can't operate on Dr. Cech unless we have everything he needs, right at hand," Grace said.

"Please just assess Dr. Cech and let me know what his operation will need, Dr. Lord. I will ensure that everything will be made available."

"I'm on it," Grace said, as she jumped up from her seat.

Grace turned to Moham Rani. "Are you going to be all right?" she asked.

"Yes," the obstetrician said, wiping his eyes and sniffing. "Go. I'll be fine. It's just that . . . you and Bud are so beautiful together," he murmured.

"You will have to leave my quarters, Dr. Rani. Now. I thank you for your help in saving Bud, but I must go," Grace announced.

Grace palmed her doors shut and raced off towards the nearest dropshaft. She asked *Nelson Mandela* if they were now safe to use.

"Yes, Dr. Lord. They are safe to use now, but unfortunately they are not all cleared of casualties."

Grace jumped in and descended to the appropriate level. She ran the rest of the way to the M1 operating rooms. There were no antigrav cars or monorails operating yet. Her head pounded with every foot strike due to her concussion. Her head felt like it had been used as a punching bag.

She would see what Dr. Cech needed and order it all. As long as he was in his cryopod, he was not going to deteriorate. They could operate on the anesthetist when the station was back to normal, under much calmer conditions. For now, seeing to all the acute injuries and problems that had arisen since the power failure had occurred probably took top priority, as well as production of the vaccine for the new deadly virus.

"Dr. Lord?"

"Yes, *Nelson Mandela*?"

"It appears that Jeffrey Nestor has escaped the station in a ship stolen from the Receiving Bay."

Grace stopped dead in her tracks. Her stomach roiled as she thought back to what had happened in the hangar, after she had shot Nestor in the face.

"I'm so sorry, *Nelson Mandela!* It was my fault he got away! I should have had someone seize and arrest him, after I had stunned him. I was so worried about Bud, I just left him where he lay and ran after Bud's stretcher. How stupid can I be?"

"You are not responsible for Dr. Nestor's actions, Dr. Lord, nor for his escape. I will never understand why you humans think you are. Jeffrey Nestor is the only one responsible for all of his murders and he is the only one responsible for the theft of that ship and the destruction in Receiving Bay Thirteen. He blasted a hole in the outer doors of the Receiving Bay and flew the ship out, killing several people who were still within the hangar.

The ships orbiting the space station were all too damaged by the EMP blast to stop his escape and I did not have enough power to activate my gravity beams.

"I'm sorry," Grace sighed. "But at least we are free of him."

"Yes, Dr. Lord. For the present time."

"Thank you for letting me know, *Nelson Mandela.*"

"You are welcome, Dr. Lord . . . Dr. Lord?"

"Yes, *Nelson Mandela?*"

"Mr. Stefansson would like to speak to you. He is waiting in the M1 waiting room and says that it is very important."

"Of course, *Nelson Mandela.* Would you tell Jude that I'll be there very shortly? Is he all right?"

"I would hesitate to answer that question, Dr. Lord. From a cardiac perspective, I believe Mr. Stefansson is functioning adequately considering the circumstances. His psychological state is another matter. I'll let Mr. Stefansson know that you will speak with him."

Grace puzzled over the station AI's cryptic response. What circumstances was it talking about? Grace had been so worried about Bud dying, that she'd only taken a brief moment to thank Jude for sliding her the stunner, before she had run off. Jude had seemed fine at that point. Had something terrible happened since then? Where was Octavia? *Nelson Mandela* had not mentioned her name. Was Octavia all right?

Grace entered the waiting area of M1 and saw a distraught director pacing the room, his hands shoved deep in his pockets and his gaze directed at the ground. There was no one else in the room. Grace came up to the director and touched his shoulder.

"Jude?" she asked, very gently.

The director glanced up, eyes wide, and his hands reached forward to grab Grace's.

"Thank goodness you're all right, Grace!" he said and he gave her a quick hug.

"Thanks to you!" Grace said. "If it hadn't been for you sliding that stunner to me, I would be dead right now. I owe you my life."

"Don't be ridiculous. You're the one who saved me, by giving me this new heart. If anything, I owe you everything."

Grace smiled and then winced. She touched her split lip gingerly.

"Let's just say we're even. What was it you wanted to talk to me about, Jude?"

The director looked troubled and glanced away. "Octavia would be so much better at this than I, but she's busy at the moment, in the OR with Bud. We thought you should know . . ."

" . . . Know what?' Grace prompted, peering into Jude's reddened eyes. She could see that he'd been crying.

"Do you remember the young man who attacked Nestor, just before Nestor tried to shoot you?"

"Yes," Grace said. She recalled the sudden appearance of the man, just as Nestor had grabbed her left arm. She could again feel the barrel of the blaster jabbing painfully into her abdomen.

"He came out of nowhere and said something like I was his! I thought it very strange, because I had never seen him before in my life."

The director took a deep breath. "He told us that he was your father, Grace."

"My . . . ?" Grace stopped, her head feeling very dizzy. She frowned at the director and said, "My father? I . . . I thought he was my brother! Oh no, Jude! My father died, trying to save me, and I didn't even know it was him! Where is his body?"

"Grace, your father's not dead. Octavia and I got him into a cryopod, with the help of the Chief Inspector. We pulled his cryopod to safety, just before this crazy ship blew a hole in the hangar. Your father was definitely still breathing when we put him into the cryopod, but he was badly injured. He took the blaster fire directly in his face."

"Oh, Jude, thank you for saving my life and my father's!" She hugged the director tightly.

The director backed away, his face flushing a brilliant shade of crimson. "Um, careful, Grace. Don't let Octavia see you."

Grace felt her face burn. "Sorry. I just owe you so much, Jude. I can't thank you enough for saving my father's life . . . and mine!"

"So you knew he was on the station?"

"I knew someone named Alexander Grayson Lord had been delivered to the station in a cryopod. Upon DNA analysis, *Nelson Mandela* had told me he was a close relative. According to his age, I thought he was my brother. I can't believe he was my father."

"Time dilation does make for awkward reunions, sometimes," Jude mused.

"Do you know where his cryopod is?" Grace asked.

"I believe they took it off to Triage, but I'm not sure."

"I'll go hunt it down after I take care of someone else I have to see. Octavia is helping Bud?"

"Yes. They are working on Hiro."

"Dr. Al-Fadi is in the best of hands."

"You got that right," Jude said. "Hiro is a tough old bugger."

"Well, *Nelson Mandela* believes Jeffrey Nestor has left the station, so at least that murderer is no longer here to cause trouble."

"Maybe I should get in my *Au Clair* and go after the bastard. Blow his ship right out of space. That devil has done so many despicable things for which I, personally, would like to make him pay. Isn't that what Jazz Hazard would do?"

"Do you think Octavia would want you to do that?"

Jude quirked a smile and shook his head. "I never have any idea what my partner wants me to do, at any moment of the day, Grace."

"That's what makes love so fun, Jude. You're a lucky man."

It was felt, by the station AI, that Dr. Cech's skills were needed as soon as possible, as were Dr. Al-Fadi's. The sooner they were both back working in the operating rooms, the better for everyone. So *Nelson Mandela* asked Grace if she felt up to operating on Dr. Cech immediately. Grace, buoyed up by the news that her father was still alive, could do naught but say 'yes'.

Bud assisted Grace with the operation. *Nelson Mandela* had made sure that everything that was required to operate on the anesthetist, was in the room: the heart, aorta, lungs, esophagus, synthetic bone for sternum and ribs. Dr. Andrea Vanacan was their anesthetist and it was a happy reunion with her. Andrea had no memory of Plant Thing except for what she saw out in the corridors.

The operation on Dr. Cech took five hours but there were no complications or mishaps. Dr. Al-Fadi's operation had taken longer, as there was the knee, damaged by blaster fire, and the trauma to the surgeon's kidneys, ribs, and abdomen to fix, after the pressure in the brain had been decompressed. The surgeon had taken such a severe beating that he had to be watched very closely. The concern was possible permanent brain damage.

Bud declined to be primary surgeon on Dr. Cech. He encouraged

Grace to do all the surgery while he assisted. He watched as Grace performed every step skillfully and confidently. The elderly anesthetist did extremely well for someone who'd had his chest blown out from only a few meters away with a blaster. It was a miracle Cech had been placed in a cryopod so quickly. Who had been responsible for that still remained a mystery.

After Dr. Cech's operation was completed, Bud was about to race off to his laboratory, to start manufacturing the vaccine, when Grace stopped him. She reminded him of his promise to recharge. Bud about-faced in the opposite direction and followed Grace. He spent the requisite one hour, sitting in a chair in her quarters, fully recharging his battery, before he was allowed to leave.

"Bud," Grace asked, when they were sitting across from each other, the recharge cable plugged into Bud's back. "How is it you were the only android not affected by the EMP blast?"

"My body is almost completely organic now, Grace. I have very few electrical components, so an electromagnetic pulse did not fry my circuits the way it did all the other androids and robots. I was only stunned for a few seconds, which was disorienting enough."

"What will happen to all the robots and androids lying around the station?"

"Once they are all collected, their electronic components will have to be replaced. The damage will likely be the same in them all. Hopefully, it will be just a matter of replacing the damaged components with new components."

"Perhaps a new design is in order," Grace said. "More like yours."

"Perhaps," Bud said, his eyebrows scrunched up in thought.

"Bud, we need a schematic of you . . . or something. When you got injured, I had no idea what to do for you."

"You did exactly what was needed, Grace. You gave me lots of nanobots and recharged me. That is all I need."

"What if there are no nanobots available?"

"Then just plug me in and recharge me. I have a store of inactive nanobots. They were unaffected by the EMP and could perform all of my repairs. I also have organobots and they cannot be incapacitated by an EMP. If I have more nanobots, the repair just goes faster."

"Are you immortal, Bud?" Grace asked.

"I do not believe so, Grace. What is immortality? My body is not indestructible. Without power and nanobots, I could not regenerate.

If I was blasted into a million little pieces, I would be gone, just as you would be. However, as long as my memory core is not destroyed and I have lots of power and a source of nanobots, I can rebuild myself if damaged."

"Your nanobots know what to do," Grace said.

"Yes, Grace. Like DNA, they have a template to follow."

"Do your nanobots actually build cells, Bud?"

"No, Grace. I am not composed of cells. My electronic components have been replaced by organic components that do the same thing. Carbon nanofibre mainly, but of my own design."

"Good to know, Bud, but I still want a schematic," Grace insisted.

"I shall make it one of my top priorities," Bud said.

"Are you being sarcastic, Bud?" Grace asked, her eyes narrowed.

"I was trying for facetious."

"I think you succeeded," Grace said, with a quirk of her swollen, split lips. "Ouch! That hurt. Do you think I'm being silly, Bud?"

"I would never make fun of anything you desire, Grace. Your wish is my command," Bud said.

"You know, you are getting to be quite the smooth talker, Bud," Grace mused.

"I stole that line from Mr Stefansson's vid, 'Destiny's Champion'," Bud admitted.

"That was a good one. How many of Jude's interactive vids have you seen?"

"All of them," Bud answered.

"All . . . of them?" squeaked Grace. "Some of them were quite . . . explicit."

"Is that the word for it? I didn't know," Bud said. "Explicit."

Grace's cheeks were now a very deep rose. Her aura was glorious.

"Are you all right, Gra . . .?"

"I'm fine!" she snapped.

Bud shut his mouth. He really did not understand the explicit parts in the vids. Were the women happy or unhappy? It was so hard to tell with all of the moaning and shrieking. Obviously Grace would not be the person to ask. Her aura now looked volcanic.

By the time Bud's battery was completely charged, Grace had fallen asleep, slumped over in her chair. Bud gently picked her up, careful not to wake her, and placed her under the covers on her bed. He brushed the hair out of her face and kissed her forehead, checking her pupils to make sure they were even. Then he quietly left her quarters. Once he was a reasonable distance from her suite, he took off, rapidly ramping up his speed to get to the Android Reservations as quickly as possible, without creating any booms near Grace's quarters.

Bud had to start producing the vaccine for the new viral strain, in case any of it had leaked out from the *Inferno's* cryopods or the crew. Since the EMP blast had knocked out all the robots and androids, Bud had no help from them. *Nelson Mandela* had Manufacturing up and running, with the help of the human engineers and technicians. Bud might be getting brand new androids and robots to assist him, but there was so much need elsewhere—for patient care especially—that Bud did not know when *Nelson Mandela* would have any spare 'droids or 'bots for his task.

The humans decided that, as long as there was no actual 'live virus' around in the lab, they could assist Bud. They would produce a treatment that would give everyone on the station the same immunity the crew members of the *Inferno* possessed. Virologists, microbiologists, geneticists, immunologists, and pathologists began arriving in Bud's laboratory. They would work with Bud, in shifts, producing antidote for all of the people on the station and then start making batches to be shipped to the Conglomerate and USS. Hopefully before then, machines that automatically manufactured and packaged the antidote would be available. Bud, of course, was working on the design and production of that machine.

Lucky for Bud, he did not sleep. He did, however, return to Grace's suite to recharge and to make sure her injuries had not resulted in anything serious.

22. Love You Too

Jude had gone to retrieve his android and bring it back to Octavia's lab. With the help of some people working around the Receiving Bay area—and Ice—he had managed to get his android loaded onto a wheeled stretcher. They were pushing it back towards the Neurosurgical wing.

"Bites, no ag," Ice grumped, as she helped steer the gurney.

Jude just smiled. Half the time, he had no idea what Ice was saying. He believed she was complaining about the lack of antigrav stretchers. She was barely doing anything but pulling the head of the stretcher around corners. He was doing all the pushing and it was not so bad pushing something on wheels. Humans were getting far too soft.

Everyone was complaining about how they had to do everything, now that the androids and robots were incapacitated. The loss of the station's mechanical work force had been a huge eyeopener for all the personnel. No one had realized just how dependent they had become on the androids and robots for absolutely everything. Now, people were taking back responsibility for a lot of things: food collection and preparation, nursing, equipment cleaning and sterilization, patient care and transport, housekeeping, manufacturing . . . absolutely everything. And, whether they liked it or not, people were getting fitter in the process.

Ice, who was almost skeletal, was in severe need of some exercise. Jude considered making her push the stretcher from behind, but then he did not want it to take forever to get back to Octavia's lab. Chances were, he would just lose his helper.

They had to wait in line for the larger transport lift because they could not take the stretcher up the dropshaft. Every time Jude thought of the dropshafts, he recalled the moment when Octavia had almost plummeted to her death. He would start to shiver and hyperventilate. He avoided the dropshafts now, unless he absolutely had to take one. He preferred ladders or the transport lifts where there was a floor beneath his feet.

They were forced to get on a crowded lift with a bunch of workers also collecting downed androids and robots. People had volunteered for the duty. Once all of the 'droids and 'bots had their circuits replaced, they would be back in action. Jude had explained to these workers that he owned this android. They had tried to take it off of him, accusing him of being some kind of pervert, wanting to do nefarious things with an android that resembled Bud. Jude had to call on *Nelson Mandela* to confirm that Jude did indeed have ownership over the android.

Ice was no help. She encouraged the wisecracks about Jude being a pervert. She seemed to be getting verbally nasty with the workers on the lift—or so Jude suspected—not having a clue what she was saying. He started to worry that she was going to get into a fight. He silently wished he'd come alone. Octavia had been too preoccupied with work, operating and organizing the medical needs of the station while Dr. Al-Fadi was recovering.

Ice was grinning at Jude. "Bare assed?" she asked, one eyebrow quirked up saucily.

"What?" he asked, frowning at her.

"Bare-assed?" she repeated.

"No . . . I'm not embarrassed," Jude enunciated back primly.

"Micuzzez," she said, twitching her head towards the workers on the lift and making a very rude gesture at them. They laughed back. Jude puzzled over what Ice had said and then let out a huge sigh. He was not going to get pulverized by this group of workers. They were her cousins. He then began to wonder how many people on the station were related to Ice. She had been rude to so many!

"Jude Luis Stefansson," Ice said to her cousins, gesturing with her thumb at Jude.

They all looked at him and grinned, making odd gestures with their hands and fingers.

"Dances Wi' Death . . . grebben flux hole," one of them said, nodding his head and winking. The others all nodded and laughed. Some made a gesture as if they were cupping something.

"Thanks," Jude said. 'I think,' he thought.

They got off at the Neurosurgical floor, amidst the cousins yelling guttural things at Ice and her swearing and gesturing obscenely back at them. The rest of the trip back to the lab was uneventful and thankfully quiet. When they entered the lab, Octavia was a whirlwind in progress. She had insisted, after Chief Inspector Matthieu had died, that all of the Security people get memprinted. The lab had become a hectic place.

Jude and Ice carefully wove the stretcher between the recording chairs, trying not to disturb the people being memprinted. They pushed the android to the back of the lab and left it on the stretcher.

Octavia came up, her eyes looking red. She gave Jude a tight hug.

"What's wrong?" Jude asked. He frowned, searching her face.

"Sergeant Rivera told me all the details about Morris' murder and what they pieced together about the last few days of his life. They suspect Nestor forced Morris to kill Dr. Gentle. Her head was nearly sawed off with a garrotte. I can't imagine Morris doing such a thing. Sergeant Rivera believes Morris was then strangled by an android. There were impressions of four fingers and a thumb crushed deep into his neck. Rivera was wondering if perhaps it might have been your android that was used to kill Morris," Octavia said.

Jude gaped at her.

" . . . Well, something happened to my android. We could scrape the surface of my android's fingers. See if there are any traces of genetic material from Morris. Otherwise, we can examine its memory. I was thinking of perhaps downloading it into my memory, to experience what happened to it."

"Are you crazy? I absolutely forbid it! If it contains Nestor's memory, I don't want you exposing your mind to it. Alexander Lord told us that he was following an android that looked exactly like Bud, trying to speak with it, and it attacked him down by the Receiving Bay. That's where we found your android. Bud says he never touched Captain Lord, so it had to have been your android that attacked Grace's father. What was it doing, strangling Morris and attacking Grace's father?"

Jude just shook his head. "We don't know that it strangled Morris. I won't know the truth unless I download its recordings."

"You are not downloading that memory into your brain, Jude. We are not going to even discuss it. I suspect that memory may be the most dangerous thing on this station next to the virus. Nestor is a narcissistic psychopath who understands mind manipulation better than anyone else. He also happens to be a ruthless, homicidal maniac. You are not putting him in your head!"

"All right, Octavia. I won't do it."

"Jude, I want you to destroy the memory in that android right now.

Throw that memprint cube in the atomizer. If this android killed Morris, I don't want to know the details," Octavia said. "I should have kept Morris with us, Jude. I should have let him back into the lab. Maybe he would be alive today, if I'd allowed him to stay close."

"You are not the reason Morris was murdered, Octavia," Jude said.

"No? How did Nestor download his memory into this android without Morris' expertise—the expertise that Morris learned in my lab? I don't think Morris would have been a target, if he had never worked here."

Ice jerked and grunted, staring at Octavia.

"You don't know that, Octavia," Jude argued. "You are only guessing. Perhaps Morris was picked because he had dark hair and was the same height and build as Nestor."

Octavia pushed her hands back through her thick, brown curls. "Maybe," she sighed. She closed her eyes. "I just don't want anyone playing with the memory from your android, Jude. There's no telling how hazardous Nestor's memory would be, if it were uploaded into an innocent or susceptible mind. That memprint must be destroyed."

"I'll do it, Octavia," Ice offered. "No woes. Atom dust parsec."

Octavia looked over at Ice and smiled.

"Thank you, Ice. I appreciate it."

Jude nodded at Ice and then put his arm around his partner's shoulder. They walked towards Octavia's office.

Ice walked back to the android and opened up its chest panel. Amidst all of the burnt and blackened wiring and circuit components sat the glistening memprint cube, iridescent and pristine. Ice took forceps and plucked the cube out. She placed it on her desk. Donning gloves, she picked the cube up and took it over to the disposal chute. She opened the hatchway, pressed the button to activate the atomizer, and held the cube over the opening. Her hand began to shake and Ice froze, her vision blurring.

Unbeknownst to Octavia, Ice and Morris had been lovers. They'd both wanted to keep their relationship private from everyone. Ice closed her fingers gently around the glistening cube and held it to her chest. Her heart was pounding so hard, it was as if it were reaching out to touch the cube. Ice felt her entire body quiver. She could not dispose of the cube—not without knowing what had happened to Morris. She had to know how Morris had died, how Nestor had killed him.

Had Morris suffered?

Octavia did not want to know, but Ice had to know the truth. If

Nestor had killed Morris, Ice was going to do whatever it took to kill the bastard.

Ice looked around to see if anyone was watching. No one seemed to be paying her any attention. She slipped the memory cube into her pocket and pulled out an empty cube canister that she had in there. She tossed the canister into the atomizer instead. It disappeared down the chute to be disassembled into atomic particles by the station.

"I can't stand this! Get me out of here! I demand to be released!"

Such was the emotional outburst that greeted Grace, as she walked into the patient room of Drs. Hiro Al-Fadi and Dejan Cech. Why the nurses had decided to put the two of them in the same room was a mystery to Grace. It was a miracle she did not find them at each other's throats.

To Grace's surprise, the rant had come from Dr. Cech. It was uncharacteristic of the usually unflappable man.

"Don't listen to this maniac! I'm the one going crazy! Get *me* out of here!" Hiro Al-Fadi shouted at Grace, waving his arms like a man drowning.

"You are not my patient, Dr. Al-Fadi," Grace told her supervisor. "I'm sorry, but your discharge is up to Dr. Weisman."

She then turned to Dr. Cech.

"And how is *my* patient, today?" Grace asked, a sympathetic smile on her still-bruised face.

"Please, please, please . . . dear sweet lady," Cech said, with his palms pressed together and desperation in his eyes. "Please let me out of here. I beg of you. Take pity on an old man with a mending heart. I'll give you anything you want. I'll do anything you ask, if you will just transfer me from this room. I beseech you, have mercy!"

"I have very good news for you, Dr. Cech. The nurses feel you are well enough to be discharged today! You can go home to Sierra's wonderful care," Grace announced.

"Hallelujah!" A wild look appeared in the anesthetist's eyes. Sitting upright in his bed, he suddenly grabbed Grace around the waist and embraced her. Grace was startled by the anesthetist's reaction. She stood frozen, as the man began shaking, his face buried against her abdomen.

"Are you all right, Dr. Cech?" Grace asked, as she awkwardly patted the top of the anesthetist's bald head.

Cech peered around Grace's waist and looked over towards his roommate. He stuck out his tongue and made a finger gesture. Then he ducked back behind Grace, using her as a shield to hide himself from the small man's glare. He motioned for Grace to bend down close.

"Don't you dare tell secrets about me," Hiro said. "Do not listen to a word of it, Dr. Grace. I order you to plug your ears."

"I . . . Am . . . Going . . . To . . . Kill . . . Him . . . Todaaayyy," Dejan whispered slowly and succinctly. Grace noticed Cech's right eye twitching.

"Oh dear," Grace said. "We can't let that happen, can we?" She shook her head at the anesthetist, a very stern expression on her face.

Dr. Cech assumed a pouty expression but eventually conceded, " . . . No."

"I'll go and sign the discharge orders right now," Grace said, clearly and emphatically, trying to pry Dr. Cech's fingers from around her waist.

"Not necessary, Dr. Lord. I have Dr. Cech's chart right here!" Sophie Leung announced loudly. Grace almost jumped out of her shoes. She managed to knock Dejan in the chin with her hip.

"I also have Dr. Cech's medications and his list of instructions and his appointments with his rehabilitation therapist, his physiotherapist, and his psychotherapist . . ." the nurse said brightly.

"That's a lot of therapy," Grace commented to Sophie.

"Not enough, if you ask me," Sophie muttered under her breath. "The poor man."

"So it was not your idea to put these two together?" Grace asked, softly.

"Hell, no! I like Dr. Cech," Sophie said to Grace. She looked over at Dr. Cech and flashed him a big smile.

"Here, Dr. Cech. You hold on to these things while we let your wife know that you are free to go," Sophie said.

Dejan cackled wildly when he heard the words 'free to go'.

Sophie repeated those words again, enthusiastically. "You're free to go, Dr. Cech!"

The anesthetist uttered the mad cackle again, staring at Sophie as if she were giving him treats, his hands clutching his medication bottles to his chest.

"And none too soon," Sophie murmured to Grace, as she retrieved her compad.

"You can get dressed into your normal clothes now, Dr. Cech," Sophie said. "Let's go into the washroom, and I'll help you. Then you're free to go!"

The wild cackle had more than a hint of hysteria in it.

"Are you sure he's all right, Sophie?" Grace asked.

"If you change your mind now, Dr. Lord, you'll be putting your life at risk and I'll won't be able to protect you," Sophie warned.

"All right," Grace said.

"The best thing for Dr. Cech right now is to get him away from Big Chief Pain in the Ass," Sophie whispered.

"I heard that!" Al-Fadi snapped.

"Come along, Dr. Cech," Sophie sang sweetly, ignoring Dr. Al-Fadi, as she pushed the anesthetist into the wash closet.

"Dr. Grace," Dr. Al-Fadi hissed. He beckoned for Grace to come to his bedside. Frowning, she approached him. He waved for her to bend close, while peering over at the washroom door.

"Yes, Dr. Al-Fadi?" Grace asked.

"Shh. I made a terrible mistake, Dr. Grace," Dr. Al-Fadi whispered.

"Pardon me?" Grace blurted.

"Quiet! Don't you know what 'shh' means? It means keep your voice down. Now, this is difficult for me, because it has never happened before, but I want to admit to making an error."

"You do?" Grace hesitated, her eyes bulging.

"Yes, Dr. Grace. I know it is hard to believe. Me. But when I make a mistake, I own up to it. I want to apologize for telling you to stay away from Bud."

Grace's jaw plummeted towards the floor.

"You and Bud are the finest individuals I have been privileged to know. I can't think of anyone who is better for Bud than you, and I don't know of any man worthy of you, except Bud. I was wrong and I'm sorry if I caused you any hardship. You two have my blessing."

Grace just stood there, her mouth gaping like a fish out of water.

"Don't just stand there. Get to work. You're dismissed, Dr. Grace, and you're welcome."

Grace gave her boss a big hug in the midst of great protestation.

"Get away from me, you wild woman! Some decorum, please. This is a hospital and I am a professional, Dr. Grace, and so are you. Go see some patients."

Grace turned and left the room, feeling as if the station had just lost its gravity. She looked over at the nurses' station. There was someone waiting there for her. She waved and beckoned to the individual. Then she turned and entered the next room, where two enormous tiger adapts lay in their beds.

"Captain Lamont. Corporal Rasmussen. Glad to see you two gentlemen awake," Grace said, cheerily.

The two men looked at each other.

"No gentlemen here, Doc. Just us tigers," Juan drawled, his arms crossed behind his head as he lay back, relaxing on his pillows.

"You're ready to be discharged, Corporal Rasmussen. I believe you have some diapers to change," Grace said.

Juan made a face. "Yeah, I know. Cindy has been bringing little Estelle around for me to change, but Captain Lamont here gets sick from the smell."

"He does, does he?" Grace arched an eye at the captain, who remained impassive. Under Grace's persistent gaze, Lamont twitched the side of his mouth.

"Poo. . . disgusting," Lamont said in a flat voice.

"Captain Lamont, I was wondering if you were up to having a visitor," Grace asked.

The captain looked sharply at Grace. His eyebrows arrowed downwards. He regarded her suspiciously.

"Who?" he snarled.

A face peeked around the door, belonging to a tall, nervous-looking tiger female.

"Delia?" Lamont gasped, sitting up suddenly. "Are you . . . is that really . . .?"

"Me? Un-hunh," she said, nodding, her amber eyes large and glistening.

"Do you remember . . .?" the captain asked, his voice tailing off.

"Everything," she said, sniffling and nodding. She stood just inside the doorway and saluted.

"Does she always finish his sentences like that?" Juan asked.

"Shh," Grace hissed, glaring at the corporal.

"Come over here," Lamont said, his eyes blinking rapidly. Delia Chase nearly pounced on his bed.

"Um, let's just go to the nurse's station to get your medications and discharge instructions, Corporal Rasmussen," Grace said, trying to hide a grin.

"But I want . . ." Juan protested, looking at the happy reunion.

"I'm sorry, Corporal, but what you want cannot be accommodated at this time. You're coming with me," Grace said and she steered Juan out of the room. The other two tiger soldiers were completely oblivious of them.

"You're no fun," Rasmussen grumped, trudging along with a big sulk on his face.

"You give them some time alone, before you go back in there, Corporal. I'm sure Captain Lamont will introduce you . . . when he comes back down to earth. He had other things on his mind," Grace said.

"I didn't know he had anyone," Juan said, shaking his head. "I'm glad you brought her, Doc. That's the most life I've seen in him since he woke up."

"Good. Now I think his recovery will take a turn for the better," Grace said. She gestured for one of the nurses to look after Juan as she signed his discharge orders.

"Thank you for helping save the station, Corporal," Grace said.

Juan winked and gave her two thumbs up. "All in a day's work, Doc."

Coming down the hall was an enormous polar bear with a baby strapped to her chest. It was the corporal's turn to get all starry-eyed.

Grace waved at Cindy Lukaku and Estelle and then took a big, deep breath. The hardest part, she had left for last.

Bud suddenly appeared at her side, as if he were reading her mind.

"Do you want company, Grace?" Bud asked, his concerned blue eyes staring deeply into hers.

"I believe I'll be all right, Bud. I think I want to do this alone, although you can listen outside, if you wish. I want to thank my father for coming to my rescue and I want to ask about my . . . adoption."

"Grace, do not worry. There is a very high probability, based on his actions, that he loves you and desires to know as much about you as you do about him. I shall be close by, if you need me," Bud said. "I have tissues for you." He passed a box of face wipes to Grace. She laughed and wrapped her arms around him.

"Thank you for being here," she whispered to him and gave him a kiss on his cheek. Then she turned to walk further down the corridor. She approached her father's room, her chest tightening. Her knees felt wobbly and her heart started to thump thunderously, as if her sternum was being used as a kettle drum. When she held out her hands in front of her, they were vibrating. She rubbed her sweaty palms down the front of her scrubs.

Perhaps now was not a good time to visit. Perhaps he needed his sleep. He probably needed a lot more time to recover before a visit like this, Grace thought. What if seeing her put his recovery back? She would feel terrible about that. Grace turned around to leave.

<Go in and say, 'Hello'. You know you want to. He loves you, Grace. If he didn't, he would not have risked his life for you.>

Grace drew in a big breath and turned back around. She knocked on the door.

"Come in," a very deep voice said.

The door slid open. A pair of almond-shaped, blue eyes stared straight into hers. It was like looking into the mirror except for all of the bandages wrapping the rest of the face.

"Hi," Alexander Lord said, his deep voice pleasant and welcoming. Grace saw him rub his palms on the blanket overlying his lap and she suddenly grinned.

"Hi," Grace said softly, and walked in.

Her vision became blurry before she got halfway to her father's bed. She was laughing and crying and so was he. He started to sit up, to get out of bed, but Grace waved her hand for him to stay as he was. She bent forward and wrapped her arms around the man that was her father, even though he was only three or four years her senior. They both cried within each other's arms and hugged for a while. Alexander Lord offered her some tissues and Grace showed him hers.

"I never even knew you existed," Alexander Lord said, looking into Grace's eyes. "Your mother never told me she was pregnant. I was slotted to fly a colony ship out to the edge of our galaxy. Most of the trip would be in hibernation. It was my first command. I guess she didn't want me to change my mind or maybe she didn't know at the time when I left. Then I got a message that she had died, but nothing more. No word about her having you.

"I only heard about your existence when I got here. Doctor Al-Fadi told me that 'my sister' was on board. I never had a sister and my parents had been long dead, so what he said did not make any sense to me. Then I saw your picture in the newsfeeds, and I knew," he breathed, his face crumpling.

"I never would have shipped out if I'd have known, Grace. I would've stayed to bring you up, like a good father should have. I'm so sorry."

Grace was shaking so much, she had to sit down. She pulled up a chair beside the bed and held his hand.

“No need to apologize,” she said. “You didn’t know. I was never told that my biological mother had died. That must have been hard for you.”

“It was,” her father said, nodding and looking at his lap. “She was a beautiful woman, your mother. I see her in you. She had no living family. She was a spacer, like me. She’d gone into space and when she’d come home, all her family had passed on. It was the same for me. We found comfort in each other, but we had our jobs in different companies. If she’d have asked me to stay, I would have quit my job in a second. She didn’t.”

He looked at Grace shyly. “I have so many regrets, Grace. So many. I was never there for you growing up, and now look at you. You’re a beautiful accomplished woman and I never held you in my arms, even once.” He looked away, his body quivering.

“You can hold me now,” Grace offered, with a smile. “Although I’d probably break your back.”

Alexander Lord nodded. “Maybe when I’m in better shape.”

“Maybe after I go on an extreme diet.”

He laughed and suddenly, everything was all right. Grace felt relaxed and accepted. She started telling her father about her life and how it had been very good. She told him about her adoptive parents and their home world. He listened carefully, taking it all in, and shaking his head at all she had accomplished.

“I missed all of it,” he said, shaking his head.

“I can’t believe you sacrificed yourself for me, when you didn’t even know me!” Grace said. “You couldn’t have even been sure I was your daughter.”

“Oh, I knew, Grace. The moment I saw your face, I knew. There is a bit of a family resemblance, after all, although you can’t see it at the moment with my head wrapped up like a cocoon. Though you are far better looking than I.” Her father winked at her and tears popped out of that eye. They both broke up laughing.

“Grace, I don’t think a father could be more proud of a daughter than I am of you,” Alexander Lord said. “I know it is awkward and uncomfortable, me only being older than you by a few years, but in terms of present time, I feel so ancient. This space station. What I see around me. I feel like time has completely passed me by and I am a walking anachronism. So I don’t want you to take this the wrong way, but I love you, Grace. As a father loves his long lost child, I love you.”

Grace stared at this man whose head was swathed in bandages, who had risked his life for her without even knowing her, and she smiled.

"I love you, too, Dad," she said.

22. Epilogue

As his ship edged passed the last orbiting vessel surrounding the *Nelson Mandela* and there was no evidence that any of the space vessels had any interest in Nestor's escape, he decided that he could perhaps relax a little. Many of the ships orbiting close to the *Nelson Mandela* were just floating, like derelict, abandoned hulks, apparently disabled and devoid of power. They presented no obstacles whatsoever to his flight. Ironically, some of those floundering ships were actually calling to him for assistance. He could only snort in derision.

The few ships that were still operational seemed completely unaware of what had just transpired on the *Nelson Mandela.* They paid no heed to his departure at all. No doubt they were too busy effecting repairs on their own vessels to care about a lone ship leaving the medical station. If anything, those ship captains were probably encouraged to see some activity from the *Nelson Mandela,* furious with the delay, hoping to dock their ships soon. None would have anticipated a demand to capture a small, departing ship, nor indeed, to fire upon it or grasp it with gravity beams. This was a medical facility after all, not a military station. Danger came from elsewhere and the mandate of these surrounding vessels was to drop off the injured and the sick and return with the healthy and the cured. Not apprehend fleeing persecuted physicians.

Studying the ship's monitors, Nestor could see no vessels closing in on his position. It appeared that he had made his escape. Luckily, the ship he had commandeered had been fully refuelled. It likely had been sitting, waiting for permission to leave, when the lockdown had occurred. With the commotion in Receiving Bay Thirteen, where their ship was berthed, the crew had probably been ordered to leave their ship and go to one of the many lounge areas in the space station. And that, of course, had turned out to be the perfect situation for Jeffrey Nestor.

He had only needed to kill two crew persons on board the *Bellerophon.* According to them, most of the ship's functions had been almost completely powered down when the EMP surge had occurred, as everyone was off on leave on the station. It had not been difficult to get the launch sequence codes out of the one assistant pilot; not after Jeffrey had shot up the female navigator. The assistant pilot had shrieked and cowered in terror, as if it were he who was getting shot.

If there was one thing Jeffrey Nestor despised, it was a coward. After giving Jeffrey all of the access codes and the launch sequences and command of the *Bellerophon,* the pilot had even helped plot a course for Jeffrey, once they had blasted open the hangar's outer doors. The assistant pilot had even showed Nestor how to operate the weapons on the ship.

Once the assistant pilot had set the ship's course for Jeffrey, the coward really was of no more use to him. If the man had shown some backbone, Jeffrey would have shown him some mercy, by at least killing him swiftly, but the snivelling worm had been utterly contemptible. Not like the female crew member, who had faced Nestor, bravely and stoically. In contrast, the pilot had made Jeffrey sick with his begging and pleading. Jeffrey had been forced to demonstrate to the assistant pilot his displeasure and disgust. The man did not deserve to call himself a man, as far as Jeffrey was concerned. So, regrettably, that was the first part of the man to get blasted off.

So few people really deserved to live. It was disheartening.

Too bad he was so set on killing Grace Lord. Now there was a woman!

She'd stared down Jeffrey with a look of challenge and defiance that had given him the shivers. No woman had ever made him feel that way before. She had been so cool and self-possessed, her chin high and her mouth set. And when she'd shot him, with not a second's hesitation, she'd only had a stunner in her hand.

Of course, she would have to pay for shooting him. That act could not go unpunished, but the sheer audacity of it left him shaking his head in reluctant admiration.

If only Grace Lord had not been the cause of all of Jeffrey's troubles. If she had not gotten him arrested and charged with attempted murder, if she had not gotten his license to practice medicine revoked, if she had not tarnished his stellar reputation, he might have found it in his heart to let her live with him, be the mother of his children. But she'd been the architect of his downfall and therefore had to die. He could have been Chief of Staff of the *Nelson Mandela* by now, if it hadn't been for her meddling! He really had no choice.

It was a shame, but she deserved to die, the haughty bitch.

The problem was, Grace Lord seemed so damned hard to kill. Every time he thought he had her, and believed he could do to her whatever he wished, she somehow eluded him, or escaped, or was rescued, or was captured by someone else. Damned infuriating. Did he not have better things to do? He'd spent little time on his research lately, what with all of this Grace Lord irritation getting in the way.

It was insufferable.

Jeffrey knew he was smarter than all of the idiots on the *Nelson Mandela* combined and he was more audacious, cunning, and crafty. So how was it that Grace Lord was still alive?

Perhaps his best bet would be to draw Grace Lord away from the space station, away from all of her allies, especially that stupid android and that horrendous plant alien. Where in space had that monstrosity come from? And how in space did that bitch manage to coerce it into protecting her? That was another mystery to which Jeffrey had no answer.

In truth, the entire *Nelson Mandela* Medical Space Station had to be destroyed for humiliating Jeffrey Charlton Nestor. They were all culpable. They were all guilty. They would see who was laughing in the end.

The *Nelson Mandela* Medical Space Station had to be reduced to space dust for the crimes that had been perpetrated on Dr. Jeffrey Charlton Nestor. Everyone on board had to pay.

Jeffrey had judged them all and found them wanting.

He would not rest until the *Nelson Mandela* was obliterated.

There were just a few things he had to do first . . .

The End

About The Author

S.E. Sasaki is a family physician who works as a surgical assistant in the operating rooms of a local hospital. She lives in a small town in Southern Ontario, Canada, with her chiropractor husband and two mischievous Maine Coon cats.

Other Works by S.E. Sasaki

Novels

The Grace Lord Series

Welcome to the Madhouse (Book One)

Bud by the Grace of God (Book Two)

Amazing Grace (Book Three)

Saving Grace (Book Four) - upcoming

Novella

Genesis

Short Story Collection

Musings

Praise for the Grace Lord Series

S.E. Sasaki is a hidden treasure, a powerhouse artistic talent who in Madhouse brings us medical science fiction on a personal engaging level that is addictive to read, sometimes scary, and always FUN. Recommended!

— Ed Greenwood
Internationally bestselling creator of The Forgotten Realms©

A layered debut that sings odes to the grandmasters of sci-fi.
Kirkus Review of Welcome To The Madhouse, July 2015

Throughout, Sasaki displays a propulsive inventiveness as she weaves grand ideas with humor and soul.
Kirkus Review of Bud by the Grace of God, July 2016

Dear Gentle Reader,

I hope you enjoyed reading Amazing Grace. If I have entertained you, would you please consider taking a few minutes of your time to rate and review Amazing Grace on Amazon, kobo, Goodreads, or whichever book retailer you prefer? Independent authors rely on the word of mouth of kind readers, such as yourself, to spread the news about their books. I would be most grateful if you were willing to share your thoughts about Amazing Grace in the form of a rating and/or review. Thank you so very much for your time and consideration.

Best regards,
S.E. Sasaki

CPSIA information can be obtained
at www.ICGtesting.com
Printed in the USA
LVHW051133020123
736298LV00004B/56